MW00772743

10

TO JIM & MARY FRANCES..

WHO KNOW PLENTY OF
WEIRD SOUTHERN STORIES
OF THEIR OWN!

Andy Duncan

Beluthahatchie
and Other Stories

Andy Duncan

With a Foreword by Michael Bishop
and an Afterword by John Kessel

Golden Gryphon Press • 2000

Foreword, copyright © 2000, by Michael Bishop.
"Beluthahatchie," first published in *Asimov's*, March, 1997.
"Saved," first published in *Dying for It*, HarperPrism, 1997.
"Grand Guignol," first published *Weird Tales*, Winter, 1999.
"The Executioners' Guild," first published in *Asimov's*, August, 1999.
"The Premature Burials," first published in *Gothic.Net*, September, 1998.
"Fenneman's Mouth," copyright © 2000, by Andy Duncan.
"Lincoln in Frogmore," copyright © 2000, by Andy Duncan.
"The Map to the Homes of the Stars," first published in *Dying for It*, HarperPrism, 1997.
"From Alfano's Reliquary," first published in *Weird Tales*, Fall, 1999.
"Liza and the Crazy Water Man," first published in *Starlight I*, Tor, 1996.
"Fortitude," first published in *Realms of Fantasy*, June, 1999.
Afterword, copyright © 2000, by John Kessel.
Author Notes, copyright © 2000, by Andy Duncan.

Copyright © 2000 in the individual stories belongs to Andy Duncan

LIBRARY OF CONGRESS CATALOGING-IN-PUBLICATION DATA

Duncan, Andy, 1964–
Beluthahatchie and other stories / Andy Duncan — 1st ed.
p. cm.
Contents: Beluthahatchie — Saved — Grand Guignol — The executioners' guild — The premature burials — Fenneman's mouth — Lincoln in Frogmore — The map to the homes of the stars — From Alfano's reliquary — Liza and the crazy water man — Fortitude.
ISBN 0-9655901-1-9 (hardcover : alk. paper)
I. Fantasy fiction, American. I. Title.
PS3554.U463395B45 2000
813'.54—dc21 00-028802

All rights reserved, which includes the right to reproduce this book, or portions thereof, in any form whatsoever except as provided by the U.S. Copyright Law. For information address Golden Gryphon Press, 3002 Perkins Road, Urbana, IL 61802.
First Edition.

Contents

Acknowledgment

Thanks to: my friends and family, especially Sydney; my classmates and teachers at the University of South Carolina, Clarion West, North Carolina State University, and the University of Alabama; my writers' group in Raleigh, N.C.; the North Carolina Writers' Network; the attendees of the 1997 and 1999 Sycamore Hill Writers' Conferences; my creative-writing students; the late Jim Turner; Shawna McCarthy; Michael Bishop; John Kessel; everyone mentioned in the story notes at the back of the book; and all my editors, especially Gary Turner at Golden Gryphon Press, the type they supposedly don't make anymore but do.

Andy Duncan
Tuscaloosa, Alabama
February 2000

A Manufacturing Note

Three thousand copies of this book have been printed by the Maple-Vail Book Manufacturing Group, Binghamton, NY, for Golden Gryphon Press, Urbana, IL. The typeset is Elante, printed on 55# Sebago. The binding cloth is Arrestox B. Typesetting by The Composing Room, Inc., Kimberly, WI.

For Sydney

Foreword

The Once and Future Andy Duncan

AT MY STEP-GRANDFATHER CODY PHILYAW'S funeral in Harrisburg, Arkansas, in 1990, a man long known to our family gripped my hands and said to my first cousin and me, "You boys come to see us, now. We'll treat you so many different ways, you'll have to like a couple of 'em."

The eleven strong stories in Andy Duncan's remarkable first collection have beaucoups in common with that kind of down-home hospitality—they'll shake you up good. They'll draw out so many different feelings, with such a generous auctorial spirit and such a mastery of setting and character, that you'll like not just a couple of 'em but the whole authentic lot.

Flip past this introduction and see for yourself. Read the title story, "Beluthahatchie," or "Liza and the Crazy Water Man," or "Lincoln in Frogmore," or "Fortitude," or the stunning "The Executioners' Guild," in my opinion the best fantasy novella of 1999. (Indeed, it compares favorably to any long story of 1999, from any publication.) Read the stories.

You'll find yourself in the hands of a writer of wit, grace, and empathy—a stylist with a powerful story sense, a budding narrative magician, a bespectacled reincarnation of the Bard of Stratford-on-Avon. Whoa. Maybe I stretch a bit here, but I have no doubt that *Beluthahatchie and Other Stories* marks the arrival of a talented new hand in the too often nutrient-depleted fields of "imaginative literature." In fact, I can liken Andy Duncan's happy advent to the coming of his own fictional Robert Johnson to the droughty barrens of Hell-abutting Beluthahatchie. My analogy won't make complete sense until you read the title story, but the stories, appropriately, offer you the best point of departure for a journey into Andy Duncan's mind and methods.

I've known Andy for a while now, but *believe* that we first met in 1995 at a Conference for the Fantastic in the Arts in Fort Lauderdale. One evening, we packed into a friend's cramped car with four other people and drove to a waterfront restaurant, where, as Andy recalls, "the only affordable thing on the menu was an appetizer basket of fried alligator tail." We riffed good-humoredly on our out-of-placeness and got back to the hotel late for an event now forgotten. Subsequently, Andy and I have bumped shoulders on several panels and indulged our taste for country vegetables at less pretentious eateries in Birmingham, Atlanta, and Tuscaloosa.

Moreover, Andy attended a pair of Slipstreaming-in-the-Arts conferences at LaGrange College in LaGrange, Georgia, where I've taught a creative writing course every winter since 1997. In March, 1999, we linked up again at the World Horror Convention in Atlanta. Later that spring, Andy and his fiancee Sydney Sowers (now his wife) invited me to speak to a summer science-fiction seminar at the University of Alabama in Tuscaloosa, where both Andy and Sydney teach, and where Andy has just earned an M.F.A. in fiction writing—to my mind, an achievement somewhat akin to Meryl Streep's taking a degree in advanced acting.

My wife Jeri and I drove over for the seminar, but not before reading aloud to each other from "The Executioners' Guild" in the August issue of *Asimov's Science Fiction* magazine. This novella dramatizes life in a backwater Mississippi town in the 1940s as lovingly—and as pitilessly—as any story by William Faulkner or Eudora Welty. We read with mounting admiration and suspense. As the tale progressed, our respect for Andy's talent grew. We had known that he could write, but the subtle inventiveness of this simultaneously dark and funny story stunned and delighted us. Hey, I thought, this fella has it in him to piggyback SF, fantasy, and horror fiction into the next century almost by himself.

Crazily, I reached this conclusion on the basis of only two stories, "Beluthahatchie," Andy's first sale (and second story to see print), and "The Executioners' Guild," a *tour de force* and a total revelation. I *thought* I had read other pieces of Andy's, when, in fact, I had merely heard him read story excerpts at cons or internalized reviews of his work; and yet I already knew that he deserved a collection. I also knew that when his collection appeared, it would inspire young imitators and revitalize writers already at work in the field.

How could I boldly assume these things? Because Andy's work has inspired me to look at my own writing afresh. He writes to high standards, respecting his readers' intelligence and paying tribute in the coin of first-rate stories to a host of exemplary forebears. He includes among his heroes and influences Lewis Carroll, Mark Twain, Arthur Conan Doyle, P. G. Wodehouse, and James Thurber. Add to that eminent roll call the names Theodore Geisel (Dr. Seuss), Roald Dahl, Ray Bradbury, Walt Kelly (of *Pogo* fame), John Bellairs, and the creators of such pop-culture icons as *Batman, Spider-Man,* the *Fantastic Four,* and *Howard the Duck*. Moreover, Andy loves and respects old movies, folk and pre-Beatles country music, the peculiar power of urban legends, and both the allure and the kick of research, not only as a way to smuggle true grit into his fiction but as a path to knowledge about our mysterious workaday world.

Andy's love of getting things right, of nailing down the quirky fact and breathing life into it, reminds me of a writer of my own generation, Howard Waldrop, for Waldrop's attention to historical detail and fondness for the odd incident have clear parallels in Andy's work. When I asked Andy his opinion of the author of "The Ugly Chickens" and "Night of the Cooters," he replied, "I have difficulty writing about sacred subjects such as Howard Waldrop."

Maybe so. But he has no trouble writing about people alive in other times, in places far from his native American South, as I found when I received from Gary Turner at Golden Gryphon Press the complete manuscript of *Beluthahatchie and Other Stories* and sat down to read the nine tales I had *not* read. In these stories I met the mute functionary of a medieval pope; a former slave witnessing to the night that Honest Abe preached a sermon in the swamp; the strange people orbiting about a horror-theater company in Paris at the turn of the (previous) century; a silent-film actress who escapes the sinking *Titanic*; a tonic salesman and a backwoods nightingale in Charlotte, North Carolina, in 1936; an American military legend rendered more famous by actor George C. Scott than by any biographer; and more. The variety of settings, the diversity of characters, and Andy's expert narrative control blew me away (as I had figured they would), and I gloated.

I also relaxed.

Betting on any writer on the basis of one or two stories is a galoot's gamble. But Andy's ability to spelunk the psyches of people utterly unlike late-20th- or early-21st-century Americans proved a reliable predictor of his overall talent, and the other nine stories simply piled on the evidence. As one who values the revelation of alien mindsets (human or otherwise), I asked Andy how he gained insight into a medieval papal attendant, a pair of 19th-century lovers, and an ex-slave responding to questions from a Federal Writers' Project interviewer in 1936? What did he do to make them so credible? How did he do it?

"I'm pleased to hear you say this," he said, "as that degree of empathy, on the part of writer and reader, for all these long-gone people, is something I strive for. I'm afraid I'm not much good at answering the *how,* though, other than saying I tend to spring on any factual detail that moves me, for whatever reason. The *why* probably springs from growing up by far the youngest member of an extended family in the South, and thus feeling the past co-existent with the present all my life. When I finally hit Faulkner's famous line—'The past is never dead. It's not even past.'—it was the perfect expression of something I knew to be true all along."

Andy went on to credit his parents with nourishing in him a love of history: "My parents were considerably older than the parents of my classmates. For everyone else in the classroom, the Depression and World War Two, for example, were remote events that existed only in books. For me, though, they were vitally real, immediate events, because my parents and their siblings talked about them *all the time.* So I concluded that all the other stuff in the history books must have a similar immediacy."

Andy Duncan, the man, has obvious charms: a ready smile, a friendly demeanor, and a mellifluous Southern accent. He laughs infectiously, finds almost everything interesting (in some cases, profoundly so), and genuinely *likes* people, surely as a result of growing up in that big South Carolinian family. Born September 21, 1964, in Columbia, he spent many of his first fifteen years aspiring to draw cartoons or create comic books. He remembers churning out "reams" of such work, all of it long since vanished into the metaphoric landfills of his youth.

In high school he developed a parodic streak, abetted by his deep familiarity with such signature American humorists as

Robert Benchley, S. J. Perelman, and the younger, edgier Woody Allen. When a teacher asked Andy's class to read homegrown 19th-century novelist William Gilmore Simms's *The Yemassee*, he wrote a send-up of it in installments called *The Pekingese*. It so conspicuously amused his classmates that the teacher felt obliged to confiscate it. Andy feared bullwhipping or defenestration, but instead his teacher, an early fan, asked for a copy, and he began to suspect that "my fiction writing alone, without illustrations, might have merit."

But even writers have to eat. To put green beans and fried okra on the table, Andy majored in journalism at the University of South Carolina, in Aiken and Columbia, then worked for seven years at the *Greensboro News & Record* as reporter and editor. Reporting must have honed his eye for the significant detail, just as editing, along with reading, surely gave him a feel for the graceful and fitting sentence. As a result, the writing in these stories displays an economy and an eloquence rare in the work of tyros—because Andy does not quality as a beginner in any traditional sense. He has worked hard to reach this point, and diction and style preoccupy him as fully as do idea and plot.

"I obsess about diction and style," he admits. "In writing a story such as 'Lincoln in Frogmore,' I compile my own glossaries, dozens of pages long, of rich and strange words, determined to make the language as colorful as possible. . . . I read every sentence, paragraph, page, aloud a dozen times, convinced that what *sounds* good *is* good."

Listen to these stories. Read them aloud. Andy conceals his effort. The labor he exerts from love of craft doesn't grunt and whicker on the page unless the scene in question calls for such sound effects. When you get to "The Executioners' Guild," find and read aloud the executioners' credo. Andy wrote it in "five minutes flat." Then, afraid that it had created itself too easily, he spoke it aloud. Because it set his nape hair a-tingle, he left the credo in. Hooray. This ringing "I Believe" pronouncement not only *sounds* good, it also provides important insights into the characters of both Mr. Ellis and Jimmy Simpson, for they live by its words, tenaciously.

"Mr. Ellis prefers the old-fashioned rope to dispatch persons sentenced to death," I say, "while Jimmy hauls an electric chair around in a truck. And yet you allow us to identify with both men."

Andy replies that when reading history, he actually feels that "all these people are my next-door neighbors, that I share their problems, that it's in my interest to know something about them. That empathy carries over, inevitably, into fiction, but for me it's less a writing technique than a personality trait, one that's hard to separate out and view dispassionately."

Given that he views historical figures as his contemporaries "in some metaphorical but deeply meaningful and truthful way," what excites him about fantasy, SF, horror, and all the other woods and pastures of "imaginative literature?"

"I always have read and loved the stuff," Andy declares, "in addition to all the other stuff I've read and loved, so it never occurred to me *not* to write it. . . . I never felt any stigma connected to the field as a reader, so initially I didn't feel any as a writer either. Rather, my concern was breaking *into* the field as opposed to breaking *out* of it."

At the age of twenty-seven, his long-suppressed urge to create fiction reasserted itself irresistibly, and he quit his job at the *News & Record.* He enrolled in a graduate fiction-writing program at North Carolina State University in Raleigh, where he studied under respected writer, critic, and teacher, John Kessel. Then, to facilitate breaking *into* the field, he attended the Clarion West writers' workshop in the summer of 1994. Not terribly long thereafter, as he recounts elsewhere in this book, he succeeded in placing stories in the anthology *Starlight 1* and in *Asimov's.* He hasn't stopped writing, or selling, since.

Meanwhile, Andy continues to study and teach, activities that inevitably complement each other and enrich his work. Does he regard teaching as a calling?

"I do . . . and I wish that teachers who *don't* feel called would quit and do something else. The most gratifying aspect about working for a university is constant contact with really smart, interesting, inspirational young people, whom I try to inspire in turn, so that I can help ensure another generation of writers and readers." Like many other teachers, he finds the end of the semester, grade-assigning time, the least enjoyable part of university employment.

At this stage in his career, Andy has two solo stories, not yet published, that still please him, "The Pottawatomie Giant," featuring Harry Houdini and the Great White Hope, and "The Chief Designer," a "novella-length secret history of the Soviet space program," which may or may not achieve print in 2001, in an anthology from Avon. He admits that he has given up on maybe a dozen other stories, but adds, "No lurking treasures there, I assure you."

What currently occupies him creatively?

Even given his academic work, Andy has at least four projects going. These include a novel, *Redemption Songs*; a screenplay based on "Liza and the Crazy Water Man" (I'd *love* to see that movie); the adaptation of some Manly Wade Wellman stories into a one-act play; and a short story starring three dissimilar but fascinating characters: agent, editor, and collector Forrest J. Ackerman, the late horror-movie actor George Zucco, and a young writer by the name of . . . Andy Duncan.

Andy has also written poetry, reviews, criticism, literary essays, and a wry memoir about the perils of writing SF in the Deep South. (He had to defend himself, on religious grounds, at an eye doctor's.) These pieces have appeared in the *SFRA Review*, the *New York Review of Science Fiction, North Carolina Literary Review, Tangent, Tangent Online*, the British journal *Foundation*, and *Nova Express*, as well as in conference program books. At an ICFA in the late 1990s, Andy gave a well-researched and -argued paper on the short fiction of Tom Godwin, whose story "The Cold Equations" has sparked controversy ever since its appearance in *Astounding* in 1954. One day, Andy tells me in an aside, he hopes to gather his essays into a small-press volume, rather as James Blish did as William Atheling, Jr., and as John Clute has done as his inimitable self.

In the fall of 1996, Andy Duncan met Sydney Sowers, academic and poet, at a reading of "Beluthahatchie." "She approached me in the hubbub afterward to introduce herself," Andy says, "and to bend my ear about Manly Wade Wellman, Fred Chappell, Red Sonja, the Nelson Bond Society, and her *Flash Gordon* videos, which subsequently played the role in our relationship that etchings served for previous generations." They married early in 2000, and the creativity of the one demonstratively sparks that of the other. Andy declines to try to quantify Sydney's impact on his teaching, writing, and life, but notes that it has benefited them all, as anyone who cares to look may easily see.

Exactly what, then, does he have in mind for himself?

"My literary ambitions are vast and overweening," Andy tells me, "and you would be embarrassed for me if I were to share them in detail." (Not so. But maybe it takes one goal-oriented writer to understand and empathize with another.) "Suffice to say," he adds, "that I want to be a universally lauded Renaissance man of letters, with publications and acclaim in every conceivable form and genre, and every award to boot. That's pretty embarrassing right there, isn't it?"

Actually, I find it heartening because Andy Duncan has the talent and the dedication to deliver on the promise of these extraordinary stories. And what more can we as readers ask of good young writers than that they work to fulfill the pledge implicit in their talents?

I applaud Andy's ambition. Clearly, he'll treat those of us already firmly in his fictive camp so many different ways that we'll *have* to like a couple of 'em. And I feel sure we'll like almost all of them—just as you, if you'll move on to the stories, will find such reward in them that you'll stand perpetual watch for any fresh appearance of the Andy Duncan byline.

Happy, and unsettling, reading, my friends.

—Michael Bishop
Pine Mountain, Georgia
February 2000

Beluthahatchie

and Other Stories

Beluthahatchie

EVERYBODY ELSE GOT OFF THE TRAIN AT HELL, but I figured, it's a free country. So I commenced to make myself a mite more comfortable. I put my feet up and leaned back against the window, laid my guitar across my chest and settled in with my hat tipped down over my eyes, almost. I didn't know what the next stop was but I knew I'd like it better than Hell.

Whoo! I never saw such a mess. All that crowd of people jammed together on the Hell platform so tight you could faint standing up. One old battle-hammed woman hollering for Jesus, most everybody else just mumbling and crying and hugging their bags and leaning into each other and waiting to be told where to go. And hot? Man, I ain't just beating my gums there. Not as hot as the Delta, but hot enough to keep old John on the train. No, sir, I told myself, no room out there for me.

Fat old conductor man pushed on down the aisle kinda slow, waiting on me to move. I decided I'd wait on that, too.

"Hey, nigger boy." He slapped my foot with a rolled-up newspaper. Felt like the Atlanta paper. "This ain't no sleeping car."

"Git up off me, man. I ain't done nothing."

"Listen at you. Who you think you are, boy? Think you run the railroad? You don't look nothing like Mr. George Pullman." The conductor tried to put his foot up on the seat and lean on his knee, but he gave up with a grunt.

I ran one finger along my guitar strings, not hard enough to make a sound but just hard enough to feel them. "I ain't got a ticket, neither," I bit off, "but it was your railroad's pleasure to bring me this far, and it's my pleasure to ride on a little further, and I don't see what cause you got to be so astorperious about it, Mr. Fat Ass."

He started puffing and blowing. "What? What?" He was tea-kettle hot. You'd think I'd done something. "What did you call me, boy?" He whipped out a strap, and I saw how it was, and I was ready.

"Let him alone."

Another conductor was standing outside the window across the aisle, stooping over to look in. He must have been right tall and right big too, filling up the window like that. Cut off most of the light. I couldn't make out his face, but I got the notion that pieces of it was sliding around, like there wan't quite a face ready to look at yet. "The Boss will pick him up at the next stop. Let him be."

"The Boss?" Fat Ass was getting whiter all the time.

"The Boss said it would please him to greet this nigger personally."

Fat Ass wan't studying about me anymore. He slunk off, looking back big-eyed at the man outside the window. I let go my razor and let my hand creep up out of my sock, slow and easy, making like I was just shifting cause my leg was asleep.

The man outside hollered: "Board! All aboard! Next stop, Beluthahatchie!"

That old mama still a-going. "Jesus! Save us, Jesus!"

"All aboard for Beluthahatchie!"

"Jesus!"

We started rolling out.

"All aboard!"

"Sweet Je—" And her voice cut off just like that, like the squawk of a hen Meemaw would snatch for Sunday dinner. Wan't my business. I looked out the window as the scenery picked up speed. Wan't nothing to see, just fields and ditches and sway-backed mules and people stooping and picking, stooping and picking, and by and by a porch with old folks sitting on shuck-bottomed chairs looking out at all the years that ever was, and I thought I'd seen enough of all that to last me a while. Wan't any of my business at all.

* * *

When I woke up I was lying on a porch bench at another station, and hanging on one chain was a blown-down sign that said Beluthahatchie. The sign wan't swinging cause there wan't no breath of air. Not a soul else in sight neither. The tracks ran off into the fields on both ends as far as I could see, but they was all weeded up like no train been through since the Surrender. The windows over my head was boarded up like the bank back home. The planks along the porch han't been swept in years by nothing but the wind, and the dust was in whirly patterns all around.

Still lying down, I reached slowly beneath the bench, groping the air, till I heard, more than felt, my fingers pluck a note or two from the strings of my guitar. I grabbed it by the neck and sat up, pulling the guitar into my lap and hugging it, and I felt some better.

Pigeons in the eaves was a-fluttering and a-hooting all mournful-like, but I couldn't see 'em. I reckon they was pigeons. Meemaw used to say that pigeons sometimes was the souls of dead folks let out of Hell. I didn't think those folks back in Hell was flying noplace, but I did feel something was wrong, bad wrong, powerful wrong. I had the same crawly feeling as before I took that fatal swig—when Jar Head Sam, that harp-playing bastard, passed me a poisoned bottle at a Mississippi jook joint and I woke up on that one-way train.

Then a big old hound dog ambled around the corner of the station on my left, and another big old hound dog ambled around the corner of the station on my right. Each one was nearbouts as big as a calf and so fat it could hardly go, swanking along with its belly on the planks and its nose down. When the dogs snuffled up to the bench where I was sitting, their legs gave out and they flopped down, yawned, grunted, and went fast to sleep like they'd been poleaxed. I could see the fleas hopping across their big butts. I started laughing.

"Lord, the hellhounds done caught up to me now! I surely must have led them a chase, I surely must. Look how wore out they are!" I hollered and cried, I was laughing so hard. One of them broke wind real long, and that set me off again. "Here come the brimstone! Here come the sulfur! Whoo! Done took my breath. Oh, Lordy." I wiped my eyes.

Then I heard two way-off sounds, one maybe a youngun dragging a stick along a fence, and the other maybe a car motor.

"Well, shit," I said.

Away off down the tracks, I saw a little spot of glare vibrating along in the sun. The flappity racket got louder and louder. Some fool was driving his car along on the tracks, a bumpety-bump, a bumpety-bump. It was a Hudson Terraplane, right sporty, exactly like what Peola June used to percolate around town in, and the chrome on the fender and hood was shining like a conk-buster's hair.

The hound dogs was sitting up now, watching the car. They was stiff and still on each side of my bench, like deacons sitting up with the dead.

When the car got nigh the platform it lurched up out of the cut, gravel spitting, gears grinding, and shut off in the yard at the end of the porch where I was sitting. Sheets of dust sailed away. The hot engine ticked. Then the driver's door opened, and out slid the devil. I knew him well. Time I saw him slip down off the seat and hitch up his pants, I knew.

He was a sunburnt, bandy-legged, pussel-gutted li'l peckerwood. He wore braces and khaki pants and a dirty white undershirt and a big derby hat that had white hair flying out all around it like it was attached to the brim, like if he'd tip his hat to the ladies, his hair would come off too.

He had a bright-red possum face, with beady, dumb black eyes and a long sharp nose, and no chin at all hardly and a big goozlum in his neck that jumped up and down like he couldn't swallow his spit fast enough. He slammed the car door and scratched himself a little, up one arm and then the other, then up one leg till he got to where he liked it. He hunkered down and spit in the dust and looked all unconcerned, like maybe he was waiting on a tornado to come along and blow some victuals his way, and he didn't take any more notice of me than the hound dogs had.

I wan't used to being treated such. "You keep driving on the tracks thataway, hoss," I called, "and that Terraplane gone be butt-sprung for sure."

He didn't even look my way. After a long while, he stood up and leaned on a fender and lifted one leg and looked at the bottom of his muddy clodhopper, then put it down and lifted the other and looked at it too. Then he hitched his pants again and headed across the yard toward me. He favored his right leg a little and hardly picked up his feet at all when he walked. He left ruts in the yard like a plow. When he reached the steps, he didn't so much climb 'em as stand his bantyweight self on each one and look proud, like each step was all his'n now, and then go on to claim the next one too. Once on the porch, he sat down with his shoulders against a post, took off his hat and fanned himself. His hair had a better hold on his head than I thought, what there was of it. Then he pulled out a stick and a pocketknife and commenced to whittle. But he did all these things so deliberate and thoughtful that it was almost the same as him talking, so I kept quiet and waited for the words to catch up.

"It will be a strange and disgraceful day unto this world," he finally said, "when I ask a gut-bucket nigger guitar player for advice on auto-MO-bile mechanics, or for anything else except a tune now and again." He had eyes like he'd been shot twice in the face. "And furthermore, I am the Lord of Darkness and the Father of Lies, and if I want to drive my 1936 Hudson Terraplane, with its six-cylinder seventy-horsepower engine, out into the middle of some loblolly and shoot out its tires and rip up its seats and piss down its radiator hole, why, I will do it and do it again seven more times afore breakfast, and the voice that will stop me will not be yourn. You hearing me, John?"

"Ain't my business," I said. Like always, I was waiting to see how it was.

"That's right, John, it ain't your business," the devil said. "Nothing I do is any of your business, John, but everything you do is mine. I was there the night you took that fatal drink, John. I saw you fold when your gut bent double on you, and I saw the shine of your blood coming up. I saw that whore you and Jar Head was squabbling over doing business at your funeral. It was a sorry-ass death of a sorry-ass man, John, and I had a big old time with it."

The hound dogs had laid back down, so I stretched out and rested my feet on one of them. It rolled its eyes up at me like its feelings was hurt.

"I'd like to see old Jar Head one more time," I said. "If he'll be along directly, I'll wait here and meet his train."

"Jar Head's plumb out of your reach now, John," the devil said, still whittling. "I'd like to show you around your new home this afternoon. Come take a tour with me."

"I had to drive fifteen miles to get to that jook joint in the first place," I said, "and then come I don't know how far on the train to Hell and past it. I've done enough traveling for one day."

"Come with me, John."

"I thank you, but I'll just stay here."

"It would please me no end if you made my rounds with me, John." The stick he was whittling started moving in his hand. He had to grip it a little to hang on, but he just kept smiling. The stick started to bleed along the cuts, welling up black red as the blade skinned it. "I want to show off your new home place. You'd like that, wouldn't you, John?" The blood curled down his arm like a snake.

I stood up and shook my head real slow and disgusted, like I was bored by his conjuring, but I made sure to hold my guitar between us as I walked past him. I walked to the porch steps with my back to the devil, and I was headed down them two at a time when he hollered out behind, "John! Where do you think you're going?"

I said real loud, not looking back: "I done enough nothing for one day. I'm taking me a tour. If your ass has slipped between the planks and got stuck, I'll fetch a couple of mules to pull you free."

I heard him cuss and come scrambling after me with that leg a-dragging, sounding just like a scarecrow out on a stroll. I was holding my guitar closer to me all the time.

I wan't real surprised that he let those two hound dogs ride up on the front seat of the Terraplane like they was Mrs. Roosevelt, while I had to walk in the road alongside, practically in the ditch. The devil drove real slow, talking to me out the window the whole time.

"Whyn't you make me get off the train at Hell, with the rest of those sorry people?"

"Hell's about full," he said. "When I first opened for business out here, John, Hell wan't no more'n a wide spot in the road. It took a long time to get any size on it. When you stole that dime from your poor old Meemaw to buy a French post card and she caught you and flailed you across the yard, even way back then, Hell wan't no bigger'n Baltimore. But it's about near more'n I can handle now, I tell you. Now I'm filling up towns all over these parts. Ginny Gall. Diddy-Wah-Diddy. West Hell—I'd run out of ideas when I named West Hell, John."

A horsefly had got into my face and just hung there. The sun was fierce, and my clothes was sticking to me. My razor slid hot along my ankle. I kept favoring my guitar, trying to keep it out of the dust as best I could.

"Beluthahatchie, well, I'll be frank with you, John, Beluthahatchie ain't much of a place. I won't say it don't have possibilities, but right now it's mostly just that railroad station, and a crossroads, and fields. One long, hot, dirty field after another." He waved out the window at the scenery and grinned. He had yellow needly teeth. "You know your way around a field, I reckon, don't you, John?"

"I know enough to stay out of 'em."

His laugh was like a man cutting tin. "I swear you are a caution, John. It's a wonder you died so young."

We passed a right lot of folks, all of them working in the sun. Pulling tobacco. Picking cotton. Hoeing beans. Old folks scratching in gardens. Even younguns carrying buckets of water with two hands, slopping nearly all of it on the ground afore they'd gone three steps. All the people looked like they had just enough to eat to fill out the sad expression on their faces, and they all watched the devil as he drove slowly past. All those folks stared at me hard, too, and at the guitar like it was a third arm waving at 'em. I turned once to swat that blessed horsefly and saw a group of field hands standing in a knot, looking my way and pointing.

"Where all the white folks at?" I asked.

"They all up in heaven," the devil said. "You think they let niggers into heaven?" We looked at each other a long time. Then the devil laughed again. "You ain't buying that one for a minute, are you, John?"

I was thinking about Meemaw. I knew she was in heaven, if anyone was. When I was a youngun I figured she musta practically built the place, and had been paying off on it all along. But I didn't say nothing.

"No, John, it ain't that simple," the devil said. "Beluthahatchie's different for everybody, just like Hell. But you'll be seeing plenty of white folks. Overseers. Train conductors. Sheriff's deputies. If you get uppity, why, you'll see whole crowds of white folks. Just like home, John. Everything's the same. Why should it be any different?"

"Cause you're the devil," I said. "You could make things a heap worse."

"Now, could I really, John? Could I really?"

In the next field, a big man with hands like gallon jugs and a pink splash across his face was struggling all alone with a spindly mule and a plow made out of slats. "Get on, sir," he was telling the mule. "Get on with you." He didn't even look around when the devil come chugging up alongside.

The devil gummed two fingers and whistled. "Ezekiel. Ezekiel! Come on over here, boy."

Ezekiel let go the plow and stumbled over the furrows, stepping high and clumsy in the thick dusty earth, trying to catch up to the Terraplane and not mess up the rows too bad. The devil han't slowed down any—in fact, I believe he had speeded up some. Left to his own doin's, the mule headed across the rows, the plow jerking along sideways behind him.

"Yessir?" Ezekiel looked at me sorta curious like, and nodded his head so slight I wondered if he'd done it at all. "What you need with me, boss?"

"I wanted you to meet your new neighbor. This here's John, and you ain't gone believe this, but he used to be a big man in the jook joints in the Delta. Writing songs and playing that dimestore git fiddle."

Ezekiel looked at me and said, "Yessir, I know John's songs." And I could tell he meant more than hearing them.

"Yes, John mighta been famous and saved enough whore money to buy him a decent instrument if he hadn't up and got hisself killed. Yes, John used to be one high-rolling nigger, but you ain't so high now, are you John?"

I stared at the li'l peckerwood and spit out: "High enough to see where I'm going, Ole Massa."

I heard Ezekiel suck in his breath. The devil looked away from me real casual and back to Ezekiel, like we was chatting on a veranda someplace.

"Well, Ezekiel, this has been a nice long break for you, but I reckon you ought to get on back to work now. Looks like your mule's done got loose." He cackled and speeded up the car. Ezekiel and I both walked a few more steps and stopped. We watched the back of the Terraplane getting smaller, and then I turned to watch his face from the side. I han't seen that look on any of my people since Mississippi.

I said, "Man, why do you all take this shit?"

He wiped his forehead with his wrist and adjusted his hat. "Why do you?" he asked. "Why do you, John?" He was looking at me strange, and when he said my name it was like a one-word sentence all its own.

I shrugged. "I'm just seeing how things are. It's my first day."

"Your first day will be the same as all the others, then. That sure is the story with me. How come you called him Ole Massa just now?"

"Don't know. Just to get a rise out of him, I reckon."

Away off down the road, the Terraplane had stopped, engine still running, and the little cracker was yelling. "John! You best catch up, John. You wouldn't want me to leave you wandering in the dark, now would you?"

I started walking, not in any gracious hurry though, and Ezekiel paced me. "I asked cause it put me in mind of the old stories. You remember those stories, don't you? About Ole Massa and his slave by name of John? And how they played tricks on each other all the time?"

"Meemaw used to tell such when I was a youngun. What about it?"

He was trotting to keep up with me now, but I wan't even looking his way. "And there's older stories than that, even. Stories about High John the Conqueror. The one who could—"

"Get on back to your mule," I said. "I think the sun has done touched you."

"—the one who could set his people free," Ezekiel said, grabbing my shoulder and swinging me around. He stared into my face like a man looking for something he's dropped and has got to find.

"John!" the devil cried.

We stood there in the sun, me and Ezekiel, and then something went out of his eyes, and he let go and walked back across the ditch and trudged after the mule without a word.

I caught up to the Terraplane just in time for it to roll off again. I saw how it was, all right.

A ways up the road, a couple of younguns was fishing off the right side of a plank bridge, and the devil announced he would stop to see had they caught anything, and if they had, to take it for his supper. He slid out of the Terraplane, with it still running, and the dogs fell out after him, a-hoping for a snack, I reckon. When the devil got hunkered down good over there with the younguns, facing the swift-running branch, I sidled up the driver's side of the car, eased my guitar into the back seat, eased myself into the front seat, yanked the thing into gear and drove off. As I went past I saw three round O's—a youngun and the devil and a youngun again.

It was a pure pleasure to sit down, and the breeze coming through the windows felt good too. I commenced to get even more of a breeze going, on that long, straightaway road. I just could hear the devil holler back behind:

"John! Get your handkerchief-headed, free-school Negro ass back here with my auto-MO-bile! Johhhhnnn!"

"Here I come, old hoss," I said, and I jerked the wheel and slewed that car around and barreled off back toward the bridge.

The younguns and the dogs was ahead of the devil in figuring things out. The younguns scrambled up a tree as quick as squirrels, and the dogs went loping into a ditch, but the devil was all preoccupied, doing a salty jump and cussing me for a dadblasted blagstagging liver-lipped stormbuzzard, jigging around right there in the middle of the bridge, and he was still cussing when I drove full tilt onto that bridge and he did not cuss any less when he jumped clean out from under his hat and he may even have stepped it up some when he went over the side. I heard a kerplunk like a big rock chunked into a pond, just as I swerved to bust the hat with a front tire and then I was off the bridge and racing back the way we'd come, and that hat mashed in the road behind me like a possum.

I knew something simply awful was going to happen, but man! I slapped the dashboard and kissed my hand and slicked it back across my hair and said aloud, "Lightly, slightly, and politely." And I meant that thing. But my next move was to whip that razor out of my sock, flip it open and lay it on the seat beside me, just in case.

I came up the road fast, and from way off I saw Ezekiel and the mule planted in the middle of his field like rocks. As they got bigger I saw both their heads had been turned my way the whole time, like they'd started looking before I even came over the hill. When I got level with them I stopped, engine running, and leaned on the horn until Ezekiel roused himself and walked over. The mule followed behind, like a yard dog, without being cussed or hauled or whipped. I must have been a sight. Ezekiel shook his head the whole way. "Oh, John," he said. "Oh, my goodness. Oh, John."

"Jump in, brother," I said. "Let Ole Massa plow this field his own damn self."

Ezekiel rubbed his hands along the chrome on the side of the car, swiping up and down and up and down. I was scared he'd burn himself. "Oh, John." He kept shaking his head. "John tricks Ole Massa again. High John the Conqueror rides the Terraplane to glory."

"Quit that, now. You worry me."

"John, those songs you wrote been keeping us going down here. Did you know that?"

"I 'preciate it."

"But lemme ask you, John. Lemme ask you something before you ride off. How come you wrote all those songs about hellhounds and the devil and such? How come you was so sure you'd be coming down here when you died?"

I fidgeted and looked in the mirror at the road behind. "Man, I don't know. Couldn't imagine nothing else. Not for me, anyway."

Ezekiel laughed once, loud, boom, like a shotgun going off.

"Don't be doing that, man. I about jumped out of my britches. Come on and let's go."

He shook his head again. "Maybe you knew you was needed down here, John. Maybe you knew we was singing, and telling stories, and waiting." He stepped back into the dirt. "This is your ride, John. But I'll make sure everybody knows what you done. I'll tell 'em that things has changed in Beluthahatchie."

He looked off down the road. "You'd best get on. Shoot—maybe you can find some jook joint and have some fun afore he catches up to you."

"Maybe so, brother, maybe so."

I han't gone two miles afore I got that bad old crawly feeling. I looked over to the passengers' side of the car and saw it was all spattered with blood, the leather and the carpet and the chrome on the door, and both those mangy hound dogs was sprawled across the front seat wallowing in it, both licking my razor like it was something good, and that's where the blood was coming from, welling up from the blade with each pass of their tongues. Time I caught sight of the dogs, they both lifted their heads and went to howling. It wan't no howl like any dog should howl. It was more like a couple of panthers in the night.

"Hush up, you dogs!" I yelled. "Hush up, I say!"

One of the dogs kept on howling, but the other looked me in the eyes and gulped air, his jowls flapping, like he was fixing to bark, but instead of barking said:

"Hush yourself, nigger."

When I looked back at the road, there wan't no road, just a big thicket of bushes and trees a-coming at me. Then came a whole lot of screeching and scraping and banging, with me holding onto the wheel just to keep from flying out of the seat, and then the car went sideways and I heard an awful bang and a crack and then I didn't know anything else. I just opened my eyes later, I don't know how much later, and found me and my guitar lying on the shore of the Lake of the Dead.

I had heard tell of that dreadful place, but I never had expected to see it for myself. Preacher Dodds whispered to us younguns once or twice about it, and said you have to work awful hard and be awful mean to get there, and once you get there, there ain't no coming back. "Don't seek it, my children, don't seek it," he'd say.

As far as I could see, all along the edges of the water, was bones and carcasses and lumps that used to be animals—mules and horses and cows and coons and even little dried-up birds scattered like hickory chips, and some things lying away off that might have been animals and might not have been, oh Lord, I didn't go to look. A couple of buzzards was strolling the edge of the water, not acting hungry nor vicious but just on a tour, I reckon. The sun was setting, but the water didn't cast no shine at all. It had a dim and scummy look, so flat and still that you'd be tempted to try to walk across it, if any human could bear seeing what lay on the other side. "Don't seek it, my children, don't seek it." I han't sought it, but now the devil had sent me there, and all I knew to do was hold my guitar close to me and watch those buzzards a-picking and a-pecking and wait for it to get dark. And Lord, what would this place be like in the dark?

But the guitar did feel good up against me thataway, like it had stored up all the songs I ever wrote or sung to comfort me in a hard time. I thought about those field hands a-pointing my way, and about Ezekiel sweating along behind his mule, and the way he grabbed aholt of my shoulder and swung me around. And I remembered the new song I had been fooling with all day in my head while I was following that li'l peckerwood in the Terraplane.

"Well, boys," I told the buzzards, "if the devil's got some powers I reckon I got some, too. I didn't expect to be playing no blues after I was dead. But I guess that's all there is to play now. 'Sides, I've played worse places."

I started humming and strumming, and then just to warm up I played "Rambling on My Mind" cause it was, and "Sweet Home Chicago" cause I figured I wouldn't see that town no more, and "Terraplane Blues" on account of that damn car. Then I sang the song I had just made up that day.

I'm down in Beluthahatchie, baby,
Way out where the trains don't run
Yes, I'm down in Beluthahatchie, baby,
Way out where the trains don't run
Who's gonna take you strolling now
Since your man he is dead and gone

My body's all laid out mama
But my soul can't get no rest
My body's all laid out mama
But my soul can't get no rest
Cause you'll be sportin with another man
Lookin for some old Mr. Second Best

Plain folks got to walk the line
But the Devil he can up and ride
Folks like us we walk the line
But the Devil he can up and ride
And I won't never have blues enough
Ooh, to keep that Devil satisfied.

When I was done it was black dark and the crickets was zinging and everything was changed.

"You can sure get around this country," I said, "just a-sitting on your ass."

I was in a cane-back chair on the porch of a little wooden house, with bugs smacking into an oil lamp over my head. Just an old cropper place, sitting in the middle of a cotton field, but it had been spruced up some. Somebody had swept the yard clean, from what I could see of it, and on a post above the dipper was a couple of yellow flowers in a nailed-up Chase & Sanborn can.

When I looked back down at the yard, though, it wan't clean anymore. There was words written in the dirt, big and scrawly like from someone dragging his foot.

DON'T GET A BIG HEAD JOHN
I'LL BE BACK

Sitting on my name was those two fat old hound dogs. "Get on with your damn stinking talking selves," I yelled, and I shied a rock at them. It didn't go near as far as I expected, just sorta plopped down into the dirt, but the hounds yawned and got up, snuffling each other, and waddled off into the dark.

I stood up and stretched and mumbled. But something was still shifting in the yard, just past where the light was. Didn't sound like no dogs, though.

"Who that? Who that who got business with a wore out dead man?"

Then they come up toward the porch a little closer where I could see. It was a whole mess of colored folks, men in overalls and women in aprons, granny women in bonnets pecking the ground with walking sticks, younguns with their bellies pookin out and no pants on, an old man with Coke-bottle glasses and his eyes swimming in your face nearly, and every last one of them grinning like they was touched. Why, Preacher Dodds woulda passed the plate and called it a revival. They massed up against the edge of the porch, crowding closer in and bumping up against each other, and reaching their arms out and taking aholt of me, my lapels, my shoulders, my hands, my guitar, my face, the little ones aholt of my pants legs—not hauling on me or messing with me, just touching me feather light here and there like Meemaw used to touch her favorite quilt after she'd already folded it to put away. They was talking, too, mumbling and whispering and saying, "Here he is. We heard he was coming and here he is. God bless you friend, God bless you brother, God bless you son." Some of the womenfolks was crying, and there was Ezekiel, blowing his nose on a rag.

"Y'all got the wrong man," I said, directly, but they was already heading back across the yard, which was all churned up now, no words to read and no pattern neither. They was looking back at me and smiling and touching, holding hands and leaning into each other, till they was all gone and it was just me and the crickets and the cotton.

Wan't nowhere else to go, so I opened the screen door and went on in the house. There was a bed all turned down with a feather pillow, and in the middle of the checkered oilcloth on the table was a crock of molasses, a jar of buttermilk, and a plate covered with a rag. The buttermilk was cool like it had been chilling in the well, with water beaded up on the sides of the jar. Under the rag was three hoecakes and a slab of bacon.

When I was done with my supper, I latched the front door, lay down on the bed and was just about dead to the world when I heard something else out in the yard—swish, swish, swish. Out the window I saw, in the edge of the porch light, one old granny woman with a shuck broom, smoothing out the yard where the folks had been. She was sweeping it as clean as for company on a Sunday. She looked up from under her bonnet and showed me what teeth she had and waved from the wrist like a youngun, and then she backed on out of the light, swish swish swish, rubbing out her tracks as she went.

Saved

SHE WILL NOT GO BELOW. SHE WILL WATCH. SHE will see all of it, all. She hugs the rail as the *Carpathia* steams into a harbor, a city, gone mad.

Thousands of people. Millions. Every bridge, pier and jetty, every visible street and rooftop, aswarm and howling. Every light ablaze in every building. Stars gone, night banished. Along the shoreline, great popping powder bursts and blinding flashes, as the ship's image is burned into the plates of three dozen front pages. It is like a bombardment. The drifting magnesium clouds sear her nostrils, score her throat. She refuses to cough. The cameras remind her of Noel, a vile and ratlike thought she jabs shrieking from her mind. A great plume of water, spouted by a fireboat, arcs across the glaring skyline: Why? The din is unendurable. The sirens wail. The liner's foghorn continuously blares, as swarms of smaller craft steam back and forth across the bow, jostle one another alongside, are nearly swamped in the big ship's wake. Ferries, yachts, tugboats, dinghies, barges, each one low in the water, leaden with people. "For God's sake, get clear," roars the officer with the mutton chops. He leans over the rail, two feet away, slashes the air with his cap. "You damned chowderheads," he bellows, "get back, get back I say, you'll wreck us yet, damn you to a man!" The veins stand out on his forehead; the cords of his neck bulge. Right below her, a tug scrapes a ferryboat, and the passengers jamming the decks of each craft are jolted to their knees. The shouting men and women atop the wheelhouse somehow hold on, keep waving their crude signs. The cheap paper furls at half-staff; the placards droop. SEEK CLAIRE ADAMS OF PHILADELPHIA. NEWS OF STEVENSON FAMILY—CHICAGO. WHERE MR COLLINGS AND SON AGE 6. "He's a tall man!" wails a woman clawing at one end of a banner that says BILL IM HERE BILL. "You can't miss him! You must have seen him! He's a very tall man!" This is the end; she can bear no more. Clapping her hands over her ears, screwing shut her eyes, Miss Dorothy Gibson, who has stood silent vigil at the rail of the *Carpathia* for hours, her silence remarked on by dozens of people, finally now begins to scream, scream what she thinks is a string of words—a man's name, over and over—but really is just a scream. She collapses, screaming, onto the mutton-chop man, who grapples to check her slide to the cold gleaming slime of the deck, and who interrupts his roaring to whisper, as urgently as a lover: "Christ almighty, woman, not you, too." Still she screams. And the ship has yet to dock.

Darkness. Piano (merry). Lights up.

Skirts billowing in the silent breeze, a little girl waves to the people back home, her hand flailing as if tied only loosely to her forearm. With her other hand she pushes up her sailor's cap, but instantly it slips down again, leaving her one-eyed and shy. Around her neck is a child's-size life preserver bearing the ship's name.

Cut to:

Three distant people stand at the base of a great funnel six times their height. Steam billows from the flat summit of the funnel. The people wave their tiny arms. The one in the middle is shorter. A family, perhaps? Gulls wheel overhead, register as bobbing flecks, imperfections in the film.

Cut to:

A beaming, slick-haired man in white flannel pants and an undershirt shows off his biceps to an admiring crowd. The man bends forward at the waist, places his palms flat on the deck, kicks his feet into the air, straightens his legs, stands on his hands. The onlookers make clapping motions as he lifts one hand, teeters, recovers. Behind, a lighthouse glides past.

Cut to:

The waving child again. For some reason she turns and runs, not looking back. A white-jacketed man holding aloft a tray of drinks springs out of her path. Dowagers in deck chairs point and laugh;

one can imagine them saying, Look at the little missy, Isn't she the cute one. The child grows smaller and smaller as she runs the length of the ship, passes the glaring distant spot where sunlight and deck merge, outruns the limitations of the camera, and vanishes forever.

* * *

Dorothy Gibson and Noel Malachard first met after dinner on the fourth night of the voyage, at a long littered table in the first-class lounge, when a dozen drunken strangers, inflamed by ragtime and seized by a simultaneous primal urge, deserted them, rushed as one chortling, giggling mass for the dance floor, chairs tipping and drinks spilling and hems ripping, men and women arm in arm nearly trampling one another in their lust to perform the fox trot, the horse trot, the chicken scratch, the kangaroo dip, the turkey trot, the bunny hug. They left only three people behind in the ruins, blinking at each other in surprise, like neighbors revealed when an intervening building comes down.

Noel raised his glass and winked at the couple at the far end of the table. "Thank God," he said. "I thought they would never leave."

"Better join us down here, I suppose," said the man with the waxed mustache. "Safety in numbers, what? Don't want to make the table uneven, do we? Heh."

He was a hearty British businessman whose name, though lost to history, was one to be reckoned with on two continents whenever talk turned to shoebrushes, as he invariably made sure it did. A self-made millionaire who would leave his widow an enviable estate, he had attached himself to Dorothy several hours before. Throughout the evening he had struggled against vanishingly small odds, and so his appearance in this story at all is a testament to the tenacity of his hopes.

After brief introductions all around, and more drinks all around, and a brief comparison of travel notes, the conversation took its inevitable plunge, and after holding forth for a couple of minutes on the infinite subtleties of pig's bristles, the man with the waxed mustache politely asked:

"What business did you say you were in, Mister Malachard?"

"*Monsieur* Malachard," murmured Dorothy, bookended by admirers. She cast a languid look from left to right, from dreary past to promising future.

"Nothing so important as shoebrushes, I am afraid," Noel said. "No, I am in the motion picture business."

"Oh, really?" Dorothy trilled.

"I am a camera operator—a cameraman?—for *Pathe Journal.* The weekly newsreel."

"Oh, really?"

"Hum. Fancy that. Newsreels, eh? Must make good money, I daresay, to be sailing first class and all."

"Alas, it is the Pathe brothers who make the good money, and it is they who pay my expenses. You see, I am on assignment."

"Oh, *really?*"

"Yes, I am to film the entire voyage. The crew, the passengers, the ship. 'As much film as your cabin can hold,' my supervisors said. 'We will edit it later.' So all day today I carried my camera about the ship, and how my neck and shoulders ache! By night I am a man of leisure on my first Atlantic crossing, but by day I work harder than the captain, harder than the man in the furnace room. Well, perhaps not as hard as that. But I am boring the beautiful lady with my troubles."

"Oh, no, no, no not at all. Claude?"

"Yes, Miss Gibson?"

"Would you be a dear and run down to my cabin and ask Mother to give you some aspirin for poor Monsieur Malachard's backache?"

"Why, nothing would give me more pleasure, Miss Gibson, but . . . perhaps the pharmacy would be somewhat quicker?"

"The pharmacy? Yes, the pharmacy. How clever of you to think of it. Claude, would you please go to the pharmacy and get me a whole new bottle of aspirin, because Mother and I are almost out and she is prone to headaches in the night and we wouldn't want her to suffer unduly, would we?"

"Of course not. All right, then. I'm off to the pharmacy. Be back in two shakes—"

"And would you be a lamb while you're gone and go by my cabin too and get my silver hatpin, the one that's shaped like a swan? Mother can find it for you. I think I must have left it on the dressing-table, or perhaps the writing-desk, and without it, I just know that the moment I step outside, my hat will blow straight to Newfoundland, and how could I ever look Monsieur Malachard in the eyes again?"

"Right. Very well, Miss Gibson. The aspirin *and* the hatpin."

"You're an angel, Claude, an absolute angel."

"Uh, Miss Gibson . . . Your cabin number would be. . . ?"

"Oh, I have no head for numbers, Claude, one of the stewards can tell you which one. I get so terribly turned around on this big ship. Do *you* ever have that problem, Monsieur Malachard, blundering into other people's rooms?"

"Miss Gibson. *Mister* Malachard."

"Goodbye, Claude. Now, where were we, Monsieur—?"

"Please. Noel."

"Noel, of course. Noel. We were having a fascinating conversation, Noel, but I'm not sure we'll be able to find our way back to where we left off. It'll be like retracing our path in the sea. We'll have to start all over again, as if we were utter strangers, isn't that sad?"

"The sad stories are the most beautiful. So your story, Miss Gibson, must be a very sad one indeed."

"Not yet, Noel, but do please give me time, I'm working on it. Correct me if I'm wrong but I believe you were telling me about the newsreel business."

"It is not very interesting. Parades and speeches, and sometimes a fire."

"How vivid. I can almost feel it. *Pathe Journal*—the words sound lovely, quite aside from their meaning, of course."

"Yes, but in your country it is called, let me see, *Pathe Gazette.*"

"How funny you are. Say it again."

"*Pathe Gazette.*"

"How funny. I never really heard those T's before. And you bare your teeth when you say it. It's delicious."

"Shall I say it a third time?"

"Perhaps later. Tell me more."

"I would prefer to hear about you. What has your voyage been like thus far, Miss Gibson? And remember: You can hide nothing from a cameraman."

"Oh, Noel, that's not true. No one is more easily fooled than a cameraman."

"You speak from experience?"

"I certainly do. I'm a professional fooler. I'm an actress."

"No."

"Yes. A motion-picture actress. On contract with the Eclair Moving Picture Company of Fort Lee, New Jersey. In fact, it's part of a French company. Not as big as Pathe, but every bit as French."

"Then we have much in common."

"There is that potential, Noel. Perhaps you've seen some of my pictures."

"Perhaps so."

"*A Woman and Her Past. The Woman Inside. The Bowery Princess?*"

"I do not think so."

"*The Merry Makers? Small Town Sally? A Modern Helen?*"

"You must forgive me. I am sure the titles are different in my country."

"Oh, *everything's* different in your country, I'm sure. I had *wanted* to get over to Paris and do some shopping but Mother said the exchange rate wasn't good and I found some of the most lovely things at Selfridge's and just kept going back and back and back and—*A Modern Rapunzel?* No? How about *A Daughter of the West?* I got killed in that one. Indians. Actually they were Italians with feathers, stevedores I think, hired for the day. Terribly noisy. Not even *The Heart of a Woman?*"

"When I am in New York I will see them all."

"Oh, don't bother, they aren't very good, none of them. I mean, they're hardly Pathe. But sometimes I myself am quite good despite them, quite good indeed. Do you believe me?"

"Of course."

"You're just saying you believe me, but you're sweet to say it, you really are."

"I do believe you. To disbelieve you, why, it would be to disbelieve life itself."

"Are you *sure* this is your first crossing? You're most awfully good at it."

"I am getting better all the time."

"Well, don't get too good too quick, it's only Saturday. Now where were we?"

"*The Heart of a Woman.*"

"Yes, well, in *that* one, there's a scene where I get to do this look—this particular sort of look that I do."

"I would like very much to see that look."

"Hell, Noel, I just did it. Where were you?"

"Oh, I am terribly sorry. Without my camera I am a blind man, a horse's tail. Again, please."

"All right. There. Do you see?"

"I see, yes."

"I purse my lips just a little, and tilt my head like so, and tilt my shoulders in counterpoint, and I raise one eyebrow the tiniest fraction—not a full lift, mind you, like *this*, then I would look like mad Doctor Crippen, wouldn't I? And not halfway, like this, either, but just the subtlest . . . push . . . upward, see? Just a hint, but in a close-up on a theatre screen, why that's practically a foot. Think about it. Do you know I raise and lower my eyebrows thirty times every morning before the mirror? You'd be surprised how few moving picture actresses have good eyebrow control."

"I am sure I would be."

"But it's hard to find a director who wants close-ups at all, who wants anything but snarling and fainting and gyrations like the Wild Man of Borneo. There's a director over at Biograph who's awfully good, but then we'd all like to work for Biograph, wouldn't we?"

"Or Pathe."

"Or Pathe. Yes, you've done quite well, haven't you? Working at a major picture company, and you so young."

"A major company, but a minor job. I am just a workman, like the man who paints the forests for the fake carriage to ride through."

"I think you're exaggerating, Noel," she said, sliding her hand up his thigh. "I think you have more authority at the studio than you claim."

They looked at each other with absolute recognition of their precarious duet, their breathless perfect balance between thought and act, real and possible. Beneath them and above them and around them the great ship shivered, a teardrop on the surface of the sea.

Moving slowly, and using the extraordinarily sure and gentle touch of a craftsman, he lifted her hand, and returned it to her.

"I cannot lie to you, Miss Gibson," he said. "I have no authority at the studio whatsoever."

She smiled a small, lopsided smile and sighed through her nose, three audible hisses in a rhythm like laughter. She drew a deep breath and said, "All right, Noel. I believe you. Damn it. You're no more powerful than I am." She touched him even higher on his thigh, gripped him and held him this time, and leaned forward and murmured: "But even in a bad picture I'm good enough to bring tears to the eyes of some drummer in Dubuque, and make him forget that he's broke and tired and sitting in a dark narrow sweltering room staring at a sheet on the wall. Everything he thinks and feels, it's up on screen where he can see it, it's pouring out of me. That's my job. I'm good at it. And even in your lowly job you're good enough to do . . . what, Noel? What makes you good at what you do?"

He drew a breath, closed his eyes for a few seconds, opened them and said: "I will tell you. I have never told anyone, but . . . I will tell you."

"Do," she said.

"For Pathe, I go to fairs, markets, races. I go to the seaside. I ask people, may I film you with my camera? Everyone says no, get someone else, people don't want to look at me, I am not interesting, I am dull, I am ugly, I am not fit for a moving picture, go away. But I do not go away, and I can talk many people into it. And in front of my camera these people are like people transformed. Before, they merely swam, or danced, or argued, or loved; now, they act as if the world were cheering them on, as if this moving picture will forever set the model of how others should swim, or dance, or argue—"

"Or make love."

"—or make love. Yes. And when I see the picture later, I cannot breathe, for joy. They are alive, these moving pictures. They contain life. They *are* life. Such a thing was never captured before, never in the history of the world. Yet I, with my camera, I have captured it. I have captured life. And I feel that life. I feel it as part of me."

"And you are good at this."

"Madame, I am very good at this. I am better at this than anybody."

"And you said you were powerless. My goodness. My goodness me. Look, children, look, my dears, beware, beware, here comes Professor Malachard, the stooped and hooded figure who captures people in his camera and carries them away to his laboratory, where he makes them pale and flat and oh so big and forces them to do the same delightful things over and over. And over. Why, I'm a little frightened of the powerless, helpless, pitiful Professor Malachard."

"Are you so very frightened then?"

"No. Of some things, yes. Not of this. What frightens you?"

"May I show you?"

"Please do."

"It is outside."

"Good."

"Your hat, I fear, will blow to Newfoundland."

"My hatpin is in my bag."

"The silver swan?"

"Yes."

"Not long ago, it was in your cabin."

"I summoned it. I summon you."

* * *

They strolled onto the promenade into a steady but pleasant salt-flavored breeze, typical of the perfect weather since Southampton. They walked aft along the rail, away from the babble of the lounge and toward the glow and murmur of the glass-roofed smoking room but with no real destination, sliding their hands down the unbroken stretch of gleaming brass that separated them from the stars and the great darkness beneath. A hand held in one place too long on that vibrating rail would tingle and go numb, as if frozen. There was practically no moon left, only the ship's lights and, here and there in the distance, patches of floating plants that made their own feeble shimmer, more noticeable from the corner of the eye than when looked at directly. The ship, heedless, mindless, ploughed through these delicate colonies, its keel tearing them apart and its wake tumbling them together again, so that seventy feet below the rail, the foam rushing alongside was flecked with bits of fire. But to look straight down was too dizzying; better to look out at the black promise of nothingness, and to huddle, more closely together than warranted by such a warm night, in the shadow of a great upended lifeboat permanently perched on the brink. The breeze caressed, consoled, tugged gently at clothing, was sweet, was salt.

"You were going to show me," she said, "what frightens you."

"This."

"The night?"

"The ocean. Look. There, and there. Look."

"Mmm. Drowning, you mean?"

"You embarrass me. No, no, not drowning. Please. My uncle in Nantes drowned in a bathtub. I once read of a woman who drowned in her own spit. No, drowning is a commonplace, not worth worrying about. But this—look. Even alive, we are nothing, compared to this."

"It's beautiful."

"The frightening is always beautiful."

"You're getting these things out of a book, aren't you? Time-honored French aphorisms for the tourist trade. Balzac, I bet."

"I suppose I talk like an old man."

"No. No. Do you know, you're frighteningly beautiful, Professor Malachard, you are. Look at you. Why, you're practically a fifth ocean yourself."

Faces brushed together, testing contours, textures, smoothness and scent. Lips first sought cheeks, chin, neck, anything but the other's lips; but then, once mated, they fused. Tongues danced, awkward, vigorous, determined. More fervor, then less, then more. Soft wordless cries and handfuls of hair and the sudden awareness of clothing, layers and layers of it, too much to be tolerated but concealing nothing. Slower, slower. Eyes closed, breathing in each other's breaths, they traced the boundaries of the fabric with their fingers; she his collar, and his shirt buttons, and the pleats of his trousers, he her shoulders, her neck, and the small of her back.

She pushed away, laughing. "You have the advantage, sir. I should have dressed more warmly." She pulled him to her again, and fumbled with his clothing, tugged, ripped. A button dropped, bounced, and went over the side, unnoticed.

Darkness. Piano (very fast). Lights up.

Dancers jam the floor in front of the bandstand, each a frenzy of motion. Pearls swing, dresses shimmer, feathers sway. People throw their heads back and laugh. A woman in the foreground makes a great show of swooning and is dragged away by her partner, legs stiff, feet splayed out. One shoe is left behind.

Cut to:

A man and a woman embrace at the rail.

Cut to:

A man in a bib rips apart a lobster.

Cut to:

Two fencers duel on the grand staircase.

Cut to:

Confetti cascades from the ceiling onto the dancers' heads, pours off their shoulders.

Cut to:

The promenade, deserted, at dawn.

She cried out, and he held her.

"I am here. I am here. What is wrong?"

She twisted, burrowed, drew him closer. Their reflections writhed in the paneling. The cord of the bedside lamp shivered, proof of the engines.

"Nothing. Nothing. I'm just stupid, that's all." Her voice was muffled against his chest. "I woke up and thought I was in my own cabin but someone had reversed it while I slept, turned everything backward. It's the same cabin, really, isn't it, just on the other side of the mirror. Of the ship. It's as good as being in my own bed, just entirely different. Don't listen to me. I'm asleep."

"Don't worry, I am too. Here, let me move my arm—there. That's nicer. I like my backward cabin. Everything is polished, everything shines. The bed is not so large, but who knew? Eh? Who knew? You should have heard me, persuading my supervisor that to really film the voyage, I had to have a first-class cabin. Why, if I had not spoken up, Pathe happily would have engaged me a closet beside the boiler room, and then how would I ever have met the famous Miss Dorothy Gibson, the toast of two continents? How would I have seen that special look that she does so well?"

"You're a villain, a cruel and heartless villain to tease me so, and you will pay for it one day, I'm sure you will. But . . . Noel. You might have met me just fine, even in steerage. I'll tell you a secret now."

"You are not Miss Dorothy Gibson at all? Let me guess. You are none other than . . . Sarah Bernhardt!"

"You're awful. No, Mother and I weren't booked for first class at all. We decided we could splurge and afford second class, because we didn't want to settle for one of the lesser ships, and miss our only chance to be part of—well, part of *history*, but we knew it was the off-season and so the first-class cabins were unlikely to be *entirely* filled, and so the first place I went when we got on board was the Purser's Office, and I asked so nicely, and the man there, well, he was very understanding . . . most understanding indeed . . . and so he moved us up a notch. Or two."

"What did he want in return?"

"He wanted quite a lot, actually. But what he *got* was money."

"You are just as persuasive as I am."

"Of course. Isn't that obvious? I mean, here we are."

"Here we are."

"Noel. Do you think that I shall be famous one day?"

"I am sure you will be."

She sat up, rolled away from him, ripped the sheet from his body, wadded the cloth, threw it into the dumbwaiter. The bed was too small to get far. He clasped her ankle, and she jerked. "No, goddamn it," she said. "Tell me the truth. Tell me."

"I don't know."

"It's possible, isn't it? It might happen. Something. Anything." She sobbed once, twice, but no tears came. "Shit, I'm choking," she said. "Tell me it's possible, but only if you mean it. Tell me."

"It is possible. It is not likely. But it could happen."

"And it might not."

"It might not."

"Oh, God." She snatched the passenger list off the bedside table, opened it. "That's all right," she said. "That's all right. We aren't even listed. Printed ahead of time, I'm sure. Weeks. That's all right." She threw the list aside, leaned over him, touched his face. "Don't. Don't cry, Noel. Please stop. I wouldn't mind. Really I wouldn't."

"I know."

"What about you?"

He smiled. "There are no famous cameramen."

"You fool," she said, squirming across the bed and straddling him. "What do you want? Tell me."

"This."

She rubbed herself against him. "You have that. What else?"

"This again."

"Ah, ha. You have that, too."

"This always."

"No," she said. "No, you can't have that." Leaning on her elbows, her forearms cradling his head, she lay atop him, kissed him, their faces wet. "I'm not one of your camera people," she said, reaching down and guiding him in. "I'm not quite as alive as all that. Not yet. Oh, Noel. Oh, Noel. Not yet."

* * *

Harry keeps squeezing the horn. "Come on, people, come on, let us through, please, let us through."

In the back seat Dorothy closes her eyes and clutches the ceiling strap and twists it around and around, binds her hand up tight. She cannot look at the crowds anymore, she cannot, but with her eyes shut she has to think about something.

"It was dreadful, Mr. Raver, simply dreadful." Mother clicks her compact open and shut. "All we wanted to do was stand on dry land again, but they wouldn't let us off the ship, just herded us from room to room, asking us questions. Oh! I am quite talked out. . . ."

The auto. Dorothy will think about this auto. Harry is very proud of it. A Renault, he said. A 35-horsepower Renault. He plans to use it for advertising. He plans to have a sign painter write on each side, Driven to Entertain: Eclair Moving Picture Company, Fort Lee, New Jersey. He will park it in front of theaters showing Eclair pictures. Even Dorothy Gibson pictures. Yes, that is a good thing to think about. All the upcoming Dorothy Gibson pictures. Harry has big plans. He told Dorothy weeks ago, before she and Mother went to England. The car will glide up to the curb, Harry says, and Dorothy Gibson will step out, and a big crowd of reporters and photographers will be there, and people waiting in line will cheer and applaud. Dorothy had never heard of such a thing. Why should there be a big fuss, she asked, about a theatre changing its movie? Trust me, Harry said, you'll see, come over here, kid, come here and sit with old Harry, yeah, just think of it, kid, you can hear the applause now, can't you? Sure you can. Sure you can.

Everyone left on deck applauded as the lifeboat swung over the side. They leaned on the rail with their drinks in their hands and smiled and waved down at Dorothy and one of them, a woman with too many pearls, called to her, sorry you're leaving the party so soon, dearie. Beside her at the rail a man with buck teeth lifted his glass. In the glass was a jagged chunk of ice. It steamed with cold. It's iceberg ice, he said, the very coldest, the very best, the captain just had it delivered. His friends shrieked in merriment as Dorothy craned her neck to keep them in view and watch them grow smaller, and the officer above shouted, first boat away, and then Dorothy was knocked off her seat by the jolt as Lifeboat Number Seven dropped into the sea.

The man who claimed to be a Frenchman had more blankets than anyone else in the lifeboat. No, no, he shouted, do not take my blankets, please, I am a sick man, I am consumptive, I will die if I am chilled, no, stop, as the officers struggled with him, yanked at the blankets, played tug of war. Shut up, will you, there are two blankets for everybody, the boat's not half full, shut up, you filthy frog, shut up. The Frenchman clawed and bit and wept.

Dorothy and Mother were at the other end of the boat. They shared one big blanket. Mother huddled beneath it and prayed. Her words were muffled. The blanket was thick and coarse. It was not well made. Dorothy's face was frozen and hurting, but she kept her head clear of the blanket. She could not stop watching the waves. Every few seconds the stars went away. That meant a wave.

People screamed in the night outside the lifeboat. Sometimes only one voice, sometimes many. One instant very near as if right over Dorothy's shoulder, the next instant faint and far away. Help me, help me, someone please, I'm in the water, it's cold, it's so very cold. The officers scrambled from side to side, saying, for God's sake, the poor devils, where are they? Do you see them? We must help them. We must. Dorothy reached out from beneath the blanket and waved, little clutchings of the air, here I am, don't worry about me, I'm here. When she moved her raw and salted fingers they cracked and bled. My face, she thought, my face. No one looked at her. Dorothy watched the waves. Her feet were frozen. She lifted her feet onto the bench, out of the foul icy sloshing in the bottom of the boat. Eventually the screams stopped. She did not hear the last one. But there were no more screams.

Much later, Dorothy stood at the rail of the *Carpathia* and watched the other lifeboats straggle alongside. The people in each stared up at her in silence. They had the faces of the dead. They made no move to come aboard. The *Carpathia*'s crew had to clamber down and get them, winch them up and carry them aboard like cargo. Noel was on none of the boats. But would she have recognized him anyway? His lined cheeks, his sunken eyes, his gaping mouth?

Dorothy opens her eyes. The crowds press against the auto on both sides. Blank faces stare in. Mouths open, close. Palms press against the windows, leave ghost palms that fade, reappear, fade again, as the auto creeps past the streetlamps.

"Dorothy, you still awake?" Harry asks. "You still with us, kid? Listen, I know it'll take you a while to recover from all this. Three, four days, whatever you need, listen, you take it. And then, the best thing you can do, take my word for this, is get right back to work again. Hah? Hah? Am I right? Because you're an artist, kid, a real artist, with real talent, and even terrible, terrible tragedies like this one can be turned into art. Really. If you're not too tired right now, honey, take a look at what's in that envelope back there. The one on the seat next to you. Just take a look."

Dorothy untangles her hand from the strap. It's numb and is crisscrossed with welts. She rubs it. She picks up the envelope and holds it in her lap. It's a long wide envelope with the Eclair insignia and address printed on it. She unties the clasp, slides out the stiff sheet of paper.

"It's an eye-catcher, huh, kid? Look how you can see each little porthole light, all the way back. I mean, that's art."

In the middle of the poster, superimposed over the background illustration, is a photograph of Dorothy herself. The photograph is in a circular frame, like a portrait in a locket. It is one of the costumed publicity photographs for *A Woman and Her Past*. Surrounding the photograph, covering most of the poster, is a striking black-and-white illustration of a seemingly endless ocean liner, steaming toward the viewer, its stern impossibly remote in the distance. The liner is ramming a cliff of ice. The prow is buried in the ice, and great ice boulders rain onto the deck.

"Who better to play a survivor," Harry was telling Mother, "than one of the real survivors? I mean, the thing is a guaranteed sensation. But we have to work fast. Right, Dorothy? You see why we have to work fast, right? All these crowds, they won't be as interested three months from now. You see what I mean, kid?"

Dorothy is sliding her fingertips across the smooth surface of the poster. The design is mostly black. The black of the ship, the black of the sky, the black of the sea. Only the ice is white. Dorothy opens her mouth to speak, coughs, clears her throat. Perhaps she has lost her voice. "We didn't hit this way," Dorothy rasps.

"Huh? What?"

"We didn't ram the iceberg. We scraped it as we passed. On the side. Most people didn't even feel it. That's why no one cared at first. They thought they were safe. They thought they were OK."

Harry sounds hurt. "And how were we to know that, I ask you? Besides, it's dramatic license. Don't worry about it. What we need, kid, is a story. Now here's what I've been thinking. . . ."

While he talks, while Mother looks at her in silence, Dorothy looks at the poster. All she has left is in this car, and on this poster. That's all. It has to be enough. The poster is taut between her hands. Noel, Noel, if you were here, Noel, then we'd show the bastard a real story. Wouldn't we? The poster tears a little in her grip.

I'll have to tell somebody, she thinks, biting the inside of her cheek. I'll have to tell somebody, or I'll go mad. But not yet.

At one point she had been the only passenger awake, or conscious, on the lifeboat. Just her and the crew. The sea was deafening, a thousand locomotives. The wind pressed her forehead, her cheeks, her lips, smoothed back her hair. Dorothy could see the waves but she couldn't feel them, not exactly. Dorothy felt the boat moving, yes, but not up and down. She felt only a mad rush forward, as if she were tumbling down the rapids and over the falls and then another falls and then another, out of control, hurtling on, on, on, a chip of wood in the torrent. The feeling had not been unpleasant. She would never admit that to her mother, of course, and certainly not to Harry; but Noel knew, she was sure he knew; and one day, when she could weep again, she would weep with shame for that.

* * *

Tuesday, May 14
Eight O'Clock Sharp
SAVED from the TITANIC
Eclair's World Sensation
MISS DOROTHY GIBSON, a survivor of the sea's
greatest disaster, tells the story of the
shipwreck, supported by an all-star cast, in
the film marvel of the age.
ART POSTERS, PHOTOS and HERALDS are ready
Tuesday, May 14 at 8—Tuesday, May 14 at 8
ECLAIR FILM CO.
Fort Lee, New Jersey
Sales Company, Sole Agents

Not too bad, Dorothy decided, stepping backward across the sidewalk and squinting at the poster. Mother wore spectacles at nineteen; Dorothy would hold out until twenty-nine, at least. Yes, still perfectly legible, even at the edge of the curb. She tilted her head as far as she could to the left, then to the right. She wished she could screw her head all the way around, like an owl. But however she contorted herself, the poster still was a striking design. Harry was right; the crumbling ice was better than real.

Three strolling couples, their attention arrested, stopped between her and the poster.

"My God. Do you suppose they have film of it?"

"Surely not. It's possible, I suppose."

"I hope they don't just show that damn christening again. That's all I've seen in the theaters for weeks, and I'm heartily sick of it."

"Couldn't get *me* aboard one of those things."

"She's lovely, isn't she? Poor little thing. How terrible it must have been for her."

"All it does is slide down the ramp into the water, over and over again. I mean, the bloody thing wasn't even finished. Why is that worth seeing, I ask you?"

"I wonder who rescued her? Some gallant officer, I'm sure."

"We all should be so lucky."

"We must come back, after dinner."

"Of course, my dear."

"If it's the damn christening again I shall demand my money back."

"Please do that, Gerald."

"Gerald, why don't *you* take a cruise one day? A nice slow one."

"Couldn't get *me* aboard one of those things."

"No one's making you, dear."

"Perhaps he was the first officer. Perhaps now he will receive a ship of his own, and they will be married on the bridge."

"We are expected at six, my friends, let's not be late."

"We'll come back, then."

"Yes, we'll come back."

Come back, Dorothy thought, come back. She stepped over the curb, lost her balance, almost fell backward; she flailed her arms and caught the lamppost. One of those beastly motorcars blared at her. Steady, girl. Steady. Time to get upstairs, get yourself put together. Time to look like a heroine.

The side door hung crooked on its hinges; the stairwell was narrow and dark and dank. Why was it colder inside than out? We'll make sure not to bring the journalists back here, she decided. She gripped the banister and peered up into the murk as she climbed. Her rustling, clinking bags of clothing and supplies bumped her thigh. The *Dramatic Mirror* was coming, Harry said. That was a good sign, surely. Also *Moving Picture News*. Perhaps even the *World* and the *Sun* and the *Evening Post*. Well, they might come. They might. Anything could happen. This wasn't a theatre, it was an icebox. A very *dark* icebox. Dorothy shivered and hurried. She clattered upstairs, chanting: the world and the sun and the evening post and the world and the sun and the evening—

"Harry?"

As her head crested the top landing, had the door to her "dressing room" just swung shut?

"Harry?"

She fumbled for the key Harry had given her. "It's a couple of rooms," Harry had said. "A wash-basin, a mirror, a bed, some tables. He does business there sometimes. You own a business, you need a few rooms like that, you know?" She knew. She had told Harry, quite firmly, that she would meet him downstairs at seven-thirty. Maybe he couldn't wait. Or maybe—Dorothy stopped, key poised—maybe it was the theater manager. Maybe that was part of the deal. But no, Harry had said it was the *manager* who owed *Eclair* money, not the other way around. Slightly relieved, she unlocked the door, pushed it inward a few inches. "Harry?" she called. Damn, it *was* like an icebox in there

. . . frigid air just pouring onto the landing. Oh, well, she thought, Biograph it ain't. She cried out when the doorknob twisted in her hand; she jumped back as the door swung inward, revealing a dark, cold room.

"Who's there?" she called.

He peered around the door. "Beware the cameraman," Noel said.

"My God," Dorothy said. She dropped her bags. They made a satisfying crash and then, sighing, collapsed on themselves. A lipstick tube rolled across the landing and down the stairs in skips and taps. "My God. My God."

"May I presume," Noel asked, "that in my absence, you have become famous?"

Without looking away from him, she knelt, seized her bags, stood up again, regained her balance. She realized it had looked like some sort of stiff curtsy. "Damn you," she said. She flung her bags, one by one, into his face, starting with the softest one, and he hid behind upraised arms, knocking the bags asunder. When she was done, clothes and jewelry littered the floor. A silken sleeve draped his foot; he tried to gently kick it aside, got entangled, then knelt and began feeding it back into the bag, his long delicate fingers rolling the fabric like a spool of film. She fell on him, knocked him backward. It might have begun as a faint but she recovered quickly, clambered atop him, wrestled with him, both of them grunting and laughing. She sat on him. With her knees she pinned his shoulders to the floor.

"Murder! Murder!" he cried, eyes rolling. "Where are the police, I ask you? In Paris this would never happen."

"In Paris this would happen all the *time,*" Dorothy said, yanking his hair for emphasis. She ran her hands over his cold face. "You are a bastard, Noel, a beautiful bastard, a magnificent bastard, but a beastly beastly bastard all the same."

"It is true," he said.

"And you're *freezing,*" she said. "You're like ice. Why didn't you turn on the pipes?"

"Without you, I was cold," he said, running his hands up her thighs. "I am much warmer now."

She slapped him, a furious *crack* that numbed her hand. She clamped that hand over her mouth, fingers spread, denting her cheeks, and gasped with laughter. Noel blinked, wiggled his jaw comically, and laughed, too. "Oh, God, Noel, that was harder than I meant. But I *did* mean it, you shit. You missing *shit.* They misspelled your name terribly, you know. Serves you right. You weren't there to set them straight."

"Where? On the poster outside?" His dimple, my God, his dimple. "I saw your name, but somehow mine was left off."

"On the *casualty* list, you shit. Don't you read the papers? Even the *French* papers? The list of the people who—the people who—" She clamped his head in her hands, squeezing, clutching. She bent double and rubbed her face against his, her eyes closed. Her face slid across his cold forehead, his cold cheeks, his warm lips. "Noel," she whispered. "Noel."

She stayed on top. They didn't remove their clothes. They didn't even close the door. His feet stuck out onto the landing, in plain sight, but no one interrupted them. No one could have.

Afterward, lying atop him, motionless and spent, but yet so deliciously full of him, she realized the room was colder than ever. She began to shiver. She couldn't help it. He held her, stroked her face. Her teeth chattered.

"I couldn't find you," she said.

"Shh," he said. "Shh."

"I was afraid to leave Mother, and afraid the lifeboat would launch without us, and the crew members were dashing around so, they weren't able to look for you, either—"

"I was below, talking to the emigrants. In Third Class."

"Oh, God."

"I wanted to film them. Such large families. So excited. So talkative. Two brothers from Belfast entertained me after everyone else was asleep. Shipbuilding stories. They were very proud. 'Three million rivets!' they said. They pounded the wall with their fists. 'Three million rivets, and all of them by hand, by God!' Then the stewards went down the corridor banging on doors."

"Mother and I had been playing late bridge with two silly men. The stewards closed the saloon around us, threatened to turn out the lights. You should have heard the whining. 'See here, my good man. See here.' Such dreary men. We were still on the deck when the alarm came. Noel, why were we apart Sunday night? Why did we think that was a good idea?"

"I don't know."

"It's never a good idea. My bridge game was awful."

"I was not too interested in rivets, either."

"What time is it?" she asked. "I have to be downstairs. *We* have to be downstairs. Oh, Noel, you'll get to see one of my pictures, isn't that exciting? And I don't even get killed in this one."

"I look forward to it."

"And the fellow who plays Ensign Jack, listen, Noel, I hardly know him, his breath is awful, I hated kissing him, he can't act, his hands are like great big hams. He looks good on screen, that's all. He won't last." She kissed him, fiercely, anxious for any trace of warmth. She pulled back with a smack. "He won't last," she said. "Wait till you see the shipwreck scene."

"Is it the film marvel of the age?"

She laughed. "Well, let's see," she said, ticking off on her fingers. "The iceberg is plywood. And the North Atlantic is a swimming pool. And the ship is about as long as—well, you know." She held her hands a familiar distance apart. "But since you asked: *I* am quite good in it, Noel, *I* am quite good indeed."

"I think you will be surprised," he said. "Because the audience will see it for the first time, *you* will see it for the first time. It may be more realistic than you think." He sat up, gazed down at her, stroked her cheek with a touch of ice. "I hope you are not frightened by what you see," he murmured.

She closed her eyes. "Of course not," she whispered.

"Remember, they are images, only images. They cannot harm you."

"Nothing frightens me," she whispered, "anymore."

"I would never harm you," he said. "I am here only to help you."

She opened her eyes. "Whatever are you talking about, Noel? Whatever is the matter?"

He turned and began raking her things together. "You will be late," he said. "That is the matter. Come, Madame, I will be your dresser for the evening. I undress Madame, I dress her as well. So! Up up up."

He took her hand and tugged at her. She felt a sudden exultant chill.

"You're leaving," she said.

His face was grim in the darkened room.

"You can't stay," she said.

His hand was positively clammy.

"It's hard for you to stay," she said. "It's hard for you even to be here now. In fact, it's impossible. Isn't it, Noel? Isn't it?"

He held her hand and said nothing.

"Oh, Noel," she said. "Oh, my poor dear Noel. I'm so sorry they misspelled your name."

* * *

The long, narrow room was packed. Harry wanted her down front beside him, but she refused. She was too nervous. Also, she was waiting on Noel. She wasn't sure that Noel could . . . well, she didn't know how Noel would fare in a crowd. She stood in the back, against the wall, near the exit: in case, she told herself grimly, I have to head for the lifeboats again. The floor was sticky, and the wall plucked at her dress when she brushed against it. She was glad the lights were out. Where *was* he, anyway? The piano player was already banging dramatically away.

The journalists nearly had smothered her when she came in. No unexpected questions, thank God. Yes, in the picture I wear the very clothes I wore in the lifeboat. The black pumps are ruined, I'm afraid. No, Mother declined to appear in the picture. Miss Agnes Stuart observed Mother at some length, however, and she delivers a fine and sensitive performance. In fact, the two women have become fast friends. (Harry nodded enthusiastically at this impromptu absurdity.) Yes, if called upon, I will tell Senator Smith's committee all of what little I know about the disaster. No, I never had the pleasure of meeting the Astors.

Damn you, Noel, she thought as the first titles appeared on the screen. You'll miss the whole damn thing. But then she shivered suddenly and uncontrollably, and she knew Noel was beside her in the dark. "Thank you," she whispered, reaching for him. His sleeve was damp.

"I am sorry," he said. "It is difficult."

"I know," she said. "It always is."

The picture wasn't much, she knew, but considering everything, it wasn't bad. "Scenes on land are cheaper," Harry had said. And so *Saved from the Titanic* began on land, with the handsome and muscular Ensign Jack, who

CANNOT BEAR BEING SEPARATED FROM HIS BETROTHED, HIS BELOVED DOROTHY.

Impatient for his fiancee to return from her trans-Atlantic cruise, he visits his friend Bill, a wireless operator.

"I MUST TELL HER I LOVE HER—I MUST!"

Bill dutifully prepares to relay this message, but the two chums are interrupted by an emergency transmission.

"IT'S A C.Q.D., JACK! SOME SHIP IS IN BIG TROUBLE OUT THERE!"

Bill listens to the instruments, eyes wide with horror.

"JACK, IT'S DOROTHY'S SHIP—THE TITANIC!"

Jack reels, gnashes his teeth, and tears his hair. So, back home, do Dorothy's stooped and aged parents, when Jack brings the awful news. A long vigil ensues, until a telegram arrives: Dorothy is safe! Home again, Dorothy agrees to tell her loved ones the story of her ordeal.

Here the flashback, and the real interest of the picture, began. There was footage of the great ship's christening (which prompted a snort of derision from someone in the audience), then footage of the miniature ship bobbing across the swimming pool as chunks of ice floated past, then shots of Dorothy and her fellow actors falling about on the deck as

A TERRIBLE CRASH

ensued. The onscreen Dorothy reeled at the sight of the massive plywood iceberg looming overhead. A retired old stage actor, a cousin of Harry's by marriage but very good despite it, lifted a megaphone.

"ABANDON SHIP!"

So far, so good, Dorothy thought. She watched herself on the screen as she settled into the lifeboat and gravely saluted the gallant officers on deck. She embraced and comforted the curly-headed moppet beside her as the lifeboat dropped out of sight.

That was about it for the shipwreck scene, Dorothy knew, and she started to let out her breath. But then she seized Noel's hand as the shipwreck scene . . . continued.

The room was utterly quiet. Only the clatter of the projector could be heard. Harry's voice in the front, though only a murmur, was clearly audible: "What the. . . ?"

Noel's lips were cold against Dorothy's ear. "Do not be afraid," he said. "The new scenes will add a great deal, I think."

A crowded lifeboat is swung over the side as dozens of men left on deck claw at it. They fight each other and fight the crew members trying to hold them back. One officer crouches atop the winch, shouting at the mob and waving a revolver. He fires into the air. Several of those on deck jump for it; one manages to grab hold of the edge of the boat and kick his legs for a few seconds before dropping. As the lifeboat is lowered, another man swings his leg over the rail and clutches at it. The officer shoots him, and he falls.

"You filmed this," Dorothy whispered. "You set up your camera, and filmed the sinking."

"I had a couple of hours," Noel said. "I had plenty of film. What else could I do?"

Two portly men in tweed jackets scramble up the deserted, tilting deck of the ship, hand in hand. As they pass, the companionway doors are flung open, and hundreds of people surge onto the deck from below, engulfing the two stragglers. The men wear dark knee-length coats and caps, and many are bearded; the women wear scarves tied beneath their chins; the children are shapeless bundles of warm clothing. The families mill about in circles on the deck, beneath the empty sockets where the lifeboats were stowed.

"I'm tired," Noel said. His voice was faint, as if he were speaking into her ear from the far end of a pipe.

"Thank you for the pictures, Professor Malachard." She didn't know whether she had voiced the statement or merely thought it.

Thank you for ours, came the answering thought. Then her hand was empty, and she realized that if she turned her head Noel would be gone. So she didn't turn her head.

A man sits alone on the grand staircase, hands dangling between his knees, head bowed. He has the beginnings of a bald spot. Below him, the ocean is flowing up the stairs. It moves slowly but perceptibly, lapping at each stair, then overrunning it. The reflected water shimmers in the glass of the framed maps and charts along the walls. Above, the chandelier hangs at an odd angle. After a few seconds, it twitches sideways, goes even farther out of true, as if pulled by a magnet in the ceiling. The ocean laps at another stair. The man looks up, faces the camera. It is a look no one in the audience will forget.

Dorothy could not breathe. Saying anything would have been beyond her, even goodbye. She wrapped her arms around herself and held on tight, trying to stop the shaking.

Finally, the new footage ended, and the tired old hokum Harry had slapped together resumed. Chairs squeaked and clothes rustled as the audience relaxed.

The queasy giddiness of the past few hours was gone. Dorothy was alone, utterly alone. What would she do? What would become of her? In minutes the lights would come on, and all these strangers would press around her, wheedling and pleading and plucking at her clothes. Harry would be the most insistent; what would she tell him? How could she explain? She wanted to run from the room, run upstairs, slam the door, lie where he had lain, hug her knees and rock back and forth and wish herself into the place where he was, no matter how dark and cold that place might be.

That's not what I wanted, she heard Noel say. That's not why I came back.

She forced herself to open her eyes, to relax her fists, to stand up straight. No, it was *their* picture now, hers and Noel's, and she would not run away from it. She would do whatever she had to do.

She pursed her lips. She tilted her head just so. She tilted her shoulders in counterpoint. She raised one eyebrow just the tiniest fraction. Then she waited, frozen, at the back of the theater for the lights to come up, and for everyone to turn and applaud. On this picture and the next one and the next, she would keep doing all those things she did so well, and the years would pass, and she would see all of it, all, and one day she would see Noel again, and then life would resume. But until then, moving pictures would have to do.

* * *

Dorothy leans against the rail and laughs silently, the ribbon of her hat almost horizontal in the wind. Noel trots to join her. Facing forward, he mouths an instruction, twirls his finger: Keep going, keep going. He puts his arm around Dorothy. She sticks out her tongue, laughs again. The wind lifts Noel's hat, and he clamps his free hand over it. Dorothy grabs it with both hands, mashes it down over his ears. He struggles, pulls her hands free, and kisses her. She wraps her arms around him, slowly lifts one foot behind like the lovers in Vogue. *After a pause, he lifts one foot behind, too. They maintain this awkward two-legged embrace as the sky and the deck around them become peppered with flecks and streaks in the film. For this is an old, old picture, one that cannot last. Now the picture is shot through with twitching threads of age. Soon a great swirling boil of white will blossom in one corner and engulf the frame. Even the piano player has begun to falter, slow down, muff a few notes. The audience knows what will happen to this picture, to this ship, to these lovers, to this sky, to this sea—to this piano and the man who plays it. The lovers know it, too, always knew it, and yet, there they are. Just look at them. There they are.*

Grand Guignol

Max

CHARLES IS MY FRIEND, MY BROTHER, MY RIGHT arm, my most valued assistant, my comrade in glory and trial since before the Armistice, and to say anything against him is almost more than I can bear—but today he brought me a sack of eyeballs of which, before God, not one was usable. Stress? Love? Syphilis? Who can say? I am saddened beyond speculation.

The instant I hefted the sack, I knew. A director senses these things. Yet to appease Charles, I dutifully held each eyeball, rolled it in my fingers, inspected it, flung it to the floor. Not one bounced—not one! Smack, smack, smack, like so many eggs. They surrounded my desk, gazing up at my shame.

The climax of A *Crime in the Madhouse* is so sublime, and to cut corners would be ruinous! The crones cackle . . . the victim shrieks and writhes, her arms pinned . . . the knitting needles flash . . . first one eyeball, then the other, is ripped free . . . they fall to the stage and bounce, roll, toward the edge, toward the front row. Ah! what a spectacle with which to launch our 1925 season! But if the eyeballs just plop, plop, like clots of pate from a drunkard's cracker—Is this what our patrons demand, deserve? Is this theatre? All this I pointed out to Charles, to no avail.

"Max, be reasonable. You send me for eyeballs, I bring you eyeballs. I bring you three score eyeballs at a good price, from the taxidermist in the rue Duperer. If we keep them on ice, we have enough to last for weeks, we have one less thing to worry about. Do you know, Max, how badly we need one less thing to worry about?"

"I have only *one* thing to worry about, Charles, and that is my *art*. I pay you a salary greater than the premier pays Marshal Petain to worry about everything *except* my art, and how do you repay me?"

"Max—"

"You kick me, you spit upon me!"

"Max—"

"You smear me with offal!"

"Max, you are a melodrama with no audience and a cast of one!"

Finally, of course, we embraced, we wept, we kissed like brothers, the stagehands outside the door applauded, and Charles did as he should have done before: He set out for the slaughterers in the Bois de Bologne. I have high hopes. For *The Garden of Torture* and *The Castle of Slow Death,* they provided commendable eyeballs, outstanding in every respect. Also, once, a truly remarkable liver.

But I still feel all is not well with Charles. Perhaps I will consult Dr. Binet when he calls this afternoon with the latest progress report on the sanity of our resident genius. How I wish he could persuade Andre to return to the theatre, to come in out of the damp! I am weary of transacting business with my star playwright in a cemetery. Pages blow away before we have revised them, surly mourners rout us from tomb to tomb, and Andre is so easily distracted by the play of light on marble, by the wink of a cherub. In my hour of need, all my comrades go mad! Did Aeschylus suffer so?

Andre

I am at home in this city of the dead. I stand on the hilltop and see all around me the spires, the turrets, the battlements of these silent narrow houses, grouped by gravel paths into thickets of gray. I press my palms against their cool gates and peer through the frosted glass at the flowers huddled into slender vases, at the precarious shrines stacked within. No balconied block on the Isle de St. Louis is more noble than these apartments of bronze and stone.

One tomb reminds me of Max's theatre. It is surrounded by a stone deck like a stage, and its angels are large and ridiculous. I sit here and eat my lunch, a cheese quiche and a lemon pastry bought from a cart propelled by a woman in crepe. I alternate bites of citrus and onion and wonder how rehearsals are going, and then I berate myself for wondering. Max will squat upon the stage and deposit his usual pile of miracles, and the patrons will stumble away fulfilled.

Dr. Binet is right to tell me to stay away from that fetid little theatre in the rue Chaptal. He is acting as my amanuensis, delivering to Max the pages of my next play as they are completed. It is an adaptation of de Maupassant's "The Maker of Monsters," which will tax the company's skill with stage deformities. But they may make of it what they will; I no longer care. The true production is the one I envision alone, here in the center of Pere Lachaise. I have no actors to stable, no turnstiles to crank, no boulevardiers to appease. When I am done writing, the play is over.

Charles

While she is onstage, being strangled to death, I am in her dressing room, laying down a bouquet.

Or attempting to. Where to leave it? Like all the dressing rooms, this is little more than a closet, a vertical stall. The vanity is a jumble of overturned bottles, opened jars, and wadded handkerchiefs, every surface tacky with lipstick, rouge and greasepaint. The two chairs are swaddled with layers of evil-smelling costumes, sleeves and bloomers all entwined. The lamp is wearing, at a flirtatious angle, a wig clotted with gore.

Finally I open the shallow drawer of the vanity, insert the clump of stems, and close the drawer so that the blooms jut out horizontally, sagging like broken fingers. It will have to do. I dare not be seen. Max would flay me alive, as in the climax of *The Horrible Experiment.* "Fraternizing with the enemy!" he would trumpet. Max suspects all actors of ongoing subversion, of plotting to overthrow their divinely appointed producer-director and launch another Commune. He suspects even the company's brightest light, its Bernhardt—Sonia Morel, glorious Sonia, beautiful Sonia, whose closet this is, who has been killed on our stage more than 10,000 times. I keep the books, and I know.

Binet

I did not know at first that Andre de Lorde was a playwright. At the time, I knew little of theatre, though I found it prudent several times a season to go on display in my box at the Opera. Andre was a patient of my embarrassingly earnest colleague Dr. Metenier, who would have had a prominent career had he not squandered so much of his time on patients. Metenier called the case the most absolute death fixation in his experience and, in despair, sent Andre to me.

In our first consultation, I saw that Andre would never be cured. He enjoyed the process of analysis too much. He perched on the edge of his chair like an excited child, eyes wide behind his spectacles, and gazed raptly at me as if I were the only visible object in the room. Later I saw this expression on the faces of actors standing in the dark awaiting their cue. He showed a rude lack of interest in the framed certificates and testimonials all around, however prominent and well-lighted. I waited, with steepled fingers, until the silence became unprofitable. Then I sighed and took up my pen.

"Let us suppose, Monsieur de Lorde, that you have a free afternoon in Paris. It is a lovely spring day. What would you do to pass the time? Where would you go?"

"Oh, any of several places, Doctor. Let's see. Well, recently I have been spending much of my spare time in the Place de la Nation."

"Could you be more specific? Do you shop, stroll, do you feed the birds?"

"I walk about, and I think about the guillotines."

"Pardon?"

"The guillotines. That plaza was the site of most of the executions during the Terror."

"Yes, but the Terror was a long time ago."

"I know, Doctor, but—well, while I'm walking, I try to imagine what it must have been like. Oh, I have seen executions in our modern day. I have accompanied my friend Max, who once worked for the police commissioner. But today only vile criminals are executed, and the atmosphere is so . . . sterile. Like the removal of a gangrenous limb in an operating room. Do you follow?"

"I'm not sure, Monsieur de Lorde."

"You may call me Andre."

I simulated gratitude. "Andre. Thank you. Please continue. The atmosphere, you say, is sterile?"

"Not so much sterile, I suppose, as . . . drab. The bureaucrats in their dusty grey suits, the mumbling priest, the journalists smoking and doodling rude pictures in their notebooks. Everyone, even the condemned man, looks bored, going through the motions, ready for everything to be over. There's not even as much blood as one would expect. The very arteries seem . . . inhibited."

"And this differs from the Terror?"

"Oh, yes! As the name implies. The prisoners went screaming to the stocks, and a thousand throats cheered each spurt of crimson. The Old Regime was a Hydra, and its coils spasmed for months after the first head had been severed. Each execution was a separate pageant, unlike any before or since."

"What an imagination! You envision all this, walking there with your hat and cane, with the newsboys yelling and the traffic roaring past?"

Andre smiled and shrugged. "Yes, it is silly, but I confess it. Call me a sentimentalist."

"Do you call yourself a sentimentalist?"

"No. Do you know what I read just this week, Doctor? I read that puppeteers waited beside the guillotines to drag the corpses across the plaza to small stages made of pushed-together cheese crates. There they performed impromptu satiric plays, working the bodies like life-sized puppets." He sprang to his feet and stuck out both elbows, letting his forearms dangle, and did a loping dance about my office. His head flopped about as if his neck had, indeed, been severed. " 'Here is the merry Marquis, dancing at the ball!' Oh, how the crowd laughed."

I clapped slowly, forcefully, holding my arms aloft as if I were at the Opera. "You are most vivid and convincing, Andre. You should go on the stage."

His face fell, and he sat down heavily. "Acting? Pfagh! I am no *actor*." His tone reeked of contempt.

"Forgive me. I meant no offense. What is your profession, Andre?"

"I am a *playwright*." He leaned forward, fixing me with a Jacobean stare. "And I am looking, Dr. Binet, for a collaborator."

Thus it began. I provided Andre with case studies of the wretches I have treated in the lunatic asylums of France, and he turned their madness into melodrama. And so the brilliant Dr.

Michael Binet, director of the Psychological-Physiological Laboratory of the Sorbonne, became a technical adviser to a back-alley theatre in Montmartre, the Grand Guignol.

Andre de Lorde, a fevered scribbler, saw his name in lights, while I saw my name on the back of the program, listed in small type with the milliners who designed the hats and the slaughterers who filled the buckets with grue.

I allowed my resentment to grow, swell, fester.

And now, thanks to Andre's unfortunate turn for the worse, I may at last claim a share of the credit I have so long deserved.

Sonia

I could be at the Theatre Antoine, the Odeon, the Gymnase, the Vaudeville, the Ambigu, even the Comedie Francaise. Why not? I could be playing Portia, Roxanne, Antigone. But no, I am throttled nightly by a bellowing, beery lout on a stage smaller than Max's bed.

"You witch! You strumpet! You will never leave me again!"

"Paul! What are you doing with that wire? Keep away from me! Keep away!"

"You left our baby to die, you slut!"

"Paul, no! No!—Aieeeeeeyeeeeeee!"

"Die! Die!"

"Augggghhhhgugghhhhhh!"

"That blood is coming out very nicely, very nicely indeed." Max's voice in the dark is as bodiless and satisfied as God's. Near the back row, his cigarette glows.

"Eugenie used a bit more glycerin in the mix tonight, Max. Wait till you see how well it clots."

"Thank you, Camille, I look forward to it. Sonia, my dear, could you thrash your downstage leg a bit more? The front row will demand refunds en masse if they don't feel endangered. That's better. Your grimace, Octave, is much improved. You have studied the gargoyles as I suggested, yes? Yes. Can we hear that scrap of dialogue again? Let's return to—where should we resume, Camille?"

"Um, 'You left our baby to die, you slut'?"

"Yes! From there, please, Octave."

"You left our baby to die, you—Augggghhhhgugghhhhhh!"

"Octave. That's Sonia's line."

Octave crumpled, hands jammed into his groin.

"And you'll get another one just like it," I shouted, "if you ever again try to grope me onstage, you bastard!" I slung the prop wire into the wings, beribboning the curtains with blood. Octave whimpered.

"Sonia, my dear, our company is small and our resources limited. I must urge you not to kill any of your fellow performers until the season is over."

"Max, my dear, you are a miserable piece of shit!" I strode into the wings, shouldering aside poor little Eugenie, who cowered behind her cauldron of blood. I entered my dressing room, slammed the door, and righted the vanity mirror. I made fists and bounced on the balls of my feet. I bared my teeth like an ape, screwed shut my eyes, strained all my muscles, and hummed my rage.

Why do I stay? Max believes for love of art; the company believes for love of Max. Love! I love neither as much as I would love a role that did not require me to be strangled or boiled or gutted like a fish twice each evening plus matinees.

Most of all I would love a dressing room in which I could actually pace, large enough for me to admit more than one admirer at a time. One night King Carol of Rumania and his mistress, Mademoiselle Lupesco, came backstage to offer their compliments on my performance in *The Merchant of Corpses.* Deposed monarchs require even larger retinues than active ones—their fiefdoms are rented suites and the lackeys who fill them—and so three rows of the theatre emptied to follow His Majesty and the mademoiselle into the dim and grimy corridors. I was forced to receive them in the passageway! Mademoiselle Lupesco could not precede the king into any room, and the king could not enter a woman's dressing chamber without a chaperone—as if I had space and air enough for a tryst! If His Majesty could maneuver that expertly, he would not be in exile. Even intimacy is too ambitious in this snuffbox.

I have given up on Max. At the theatre, his response is always the same. "What more will you demand of me?" he moans. He flings his hands outward, palms up, as if to receive the nails. "Are you not already renowned? Do you know what the newspapers call you? The High Priestess of the Temple of Horror!" As if this is a compliment. Away from the theatre, at his flat or at mine, Max has a different stock response, one more enjoyably physical, but it leaves my situation equally unresolved.

Here are more flowers. From Charles, no doubt. Poor Charles.

He thinks his infatuation is so well hidden. He is as flamboyant, in his quiet way, as Max: He wants the drama of being a secret admirer. I am tempted to encourage him a little, but at this point in my life I need something more tangible than mute longing. Perhaps, indeed, something more than Max. I have told no one my vow: If I don't get a good notice from a serious reviewer this season, I will quit the company—and Max as well, ululate though he will.

In the meantime, I am at least learning new aspects of my craft. Eugenie is teaching me some of her more elaborate makeup tricks. The child really is talented. If I ever get to play Cordelia, I can also act as technical adviser to whoever gouges out Gloucester's eyeballs. "More bounce! More bounce!"

I will not become hysterical.

Eugenie

Some nights Charles and I are the only ones left in the building, and he is kind enough to walk me home. I always finish my work first; Max leaves him quite a list. I push open the thick oak doors to the theatre proper—I have to lean with my whole body to budge them—and I sit in the middle, toward the back, where Max sits during rehearsals. I sit in the dark and wait for the outlines of the stage, the seats, the beams in the ceiling to appear, to resolve themselves into outlines of black and grey.

It is a curious thing. When I am not in my apartment, I have difficulty remembering what it looks like, even where it is. I keep the address pinned to the inside of my sleeve, on a folded scrap of butcher's paper, just in case. But I can always summon every pulley, every lamp, every alcove in this theatre. I don't need light to study their details. I asked Max once whether I simply could move my few belongings into the theatre, into the garret above the balcony, but he made popping noises and fluttered his hands and said it would not be proper. Surely he knows that I virtually live here already. I certainly live nowhere else.

If I were able to sit here in the dark long enough, if there were enough hours in the night, I'm sure I eventually would be able to see not only the broad strokes of my surroundings, but the most minute flourishes carved into the farthest corner of the ceiling. It is all a matter of concentration, and at the same time of relaxing so that the images come to you, rather than straining yourself to meet them halfway.

One night, as the theatre formed around me, one swatch of darkness became the shape of a man, and I recognized the spectacles of Monsieur de Lorde. He was sitting in the next row, facing the stage.

"They say no place on Earth is quite as dark as a darkened theatre," he said. "This frightens many people, Eugenie. Not you?"

"No, monsieur." I could not recall his addressing me before.

"That's good. Because at this time of night, in a darkened theatre, one can hear the most remarkable things, if one is open to hearing them. Did you know, Eugenie, that this building was once a convent?"

"Yes, monsieur. Charles—I mean, Monsieur Goudron—told me it had been gutted during the Terror. This hall used to be the chapel, and that's why angels are carved into the ceiling."

"Monsieur Goudron—I mean, Charles—is quite correct. I would share with you another part of that history, Eugenie, but I fear it would mean your following me upstairs, into the balcony. Upon my honor," he added, raising his hand, "I mean you no harm, and I will maintain my distance."

I was sure he could feel the warmth of my embarrassment even if he could not see its color. "Oh, I do not doubt you, Monsieur! I will follow you."

We climbed the narrow stairs, which spiral up a chimney-like brick shaft. The darkness of the balcony was, if anything, more absolute than that below. Monsieur de Lorde sat, and so did I, at a proper distance of several feet. For many minutes we said nothing, only sat and looked at the oblong space above the stage. I believe that before I actually heard the murmuring, I felt it in my neck and arms, which prickled as if charged with electricity. The burbling was as faint as a trickle of water within the walls during a rainstorm, but there was no rain this night. The sounds had the tone and timbre of human speech, but the words, if words they were, were inaudible. I thought of Charles's mumblings as he tallied figures in Max's ledger.

"What is that sound, Monsieur?"

"This was their convent, and they are still here, still praying for us all." Monsieur de Lorde's voice was hushed. "Even during the uproar of performances, while this balcony is jammed with patrons, I can sit in this spot and hear the sisters. The terror continues, and so do the prayers."

Far from being frightened, I felt oddly consoled, as one feels when hearing a distant train. I was smiling when the lights came on. Charles was standing at the switch-box just inside the doorway below.

"There you are, Eugenie! Hello, Andre. My, you are a fine pair. Claiming your seats early for this weekend's show?" He laughed and swept a shock of hair out of his face. "Keep sitting up there in the dark like that," he said, "and you'll both be seeing things."

The murmuring had become so muted that my breathing drowned it out, but it continued, soft and frolicsome inside my ears.

Max

I marvel that I can go on. Dr. Binet tells me that poor Andre no longer is well enough to see any of his friends, that he wanders the cemetery like a spectre, hardly eating, and—worst of all!—unable to write. Binet has been kind enough to pass me drafts of a play he himself is writing, *The Maker of Monsters*. Everyone is a playwright. Soon the concierges and streetcar drivers will be handing me scripts as well. Why does no one aspire to be a director? Because they watch me, study the terrible example that is my life, and they learn. Oh, the struggle!

Octave has left the company. He said terrible things—bloodcurdling things!—about Sonia. I could not bear it. Only three days before we open, we have no one to play Paul le Hirec, the insane sculptor who strangles his cruel and faithless wife in *The Dead Child*. Would that I were a dramaturge of ancient Greece, able to recast a play with a shuffling of masks! Would that I were in any other theatre, in any other age, than in this Sisyphean ordeal that occupies me now. Will the very slopes of Montmartre yawn wide to swallow us on opening night? I would not be surprised. The gods are against my endeavor. In the perfection of my art, I have angered the gods.

On the other hand, Charles could play the role. Excellent. It is decided. I will hand him the script today, and Sonia will rehearse with him tonight—all night, if necessary! Perhaps at her flat, where they will have some privacy. Charles will make the usual excuses, but I will not be swayed.

Charles

I woke sweating, naked and disoriented in a close and sultry bedchamber, sheets tangled about my legs. I sat up, startled, felt my stomach lurch, and lay down again, breathing deeply with my eyes closed. The sheets I lay upon were soothing, damp and cool, and I focused on the thin intersection of flesh and fabric, enjoying the contours of my body. I returned to the borderland between waking and sleeping, and wraiths of the evening before coiled around me. My body remembered before my mind how my night had been spent: a soreness in my upper arms and shoulder blades, an unusual coarseness in the play of my tongue along my palate, a detached numbness in my twitching penis. Eventually the room reshaped itself around the absent figure of Sonia, and then I remembered all, and smiled. I sat up, slowly this time, waited a few seconds for my dizziness to pass, and padded unclothed to the doorway, where I looked across the sunny common room of a top-floor flat. At the far wall stood Sonia, with her back to me, bent over a countertop, intent on some project that she blocked with her body. She wore an abundant purple gown as generous as the matted sheets I had left behind; its drape revealed one bare shoulder. Her russet hair, streaked with grey, roamed long and loose; if I walked up behind and clasped her, her hair would enfold me down to my thighs. I moved softly across the room, my memory of the bedroom hours narrowing and intensifying this daytime moment, and just as I reached for her, she turned and smiled and held up her right forearm, to show that where her hand had been was a jagged, bleeding stump, flesh tattered, bone splintered and shining in the morning light. I screamed and lunged backward, falling, bruising my lower back as I hit the windowsill. I twisted and leaned out over the boulevard, my arms numb as I shuddered and heaved. Then her arms were around me, and her hands—both hands!—were caressing my forehead, my cheeks, my chin, and Sonia was saying: "It's makeup, that's all it is, one of Eugenie's tricks, she's been teaching me, I'm sorry, I'm so sorry, what was I thinking, I'm fine, Sonia's fine . . . " I slowly hauled myself into the room, leaving damp handprints in the grime of the windowsill, and sank to the floor, sobbing into her shoulder, my erection wedged between us like a lever.

Andre

Eugenie came to see me today. She found me leaning against Oscar Wilde's tomb, making notes toward an article on "Fear in Literature." The sunlight becomes her. I could not recall ever seeing her before outside the walls of the Grand Guignol. I was amazed but delighted to see her small, pale head cresting the hill, a breeze lifting what hair she has left. Why do young women crop their tresses so? I pocketed my notes on Poe and Baudelaire, stood, removed my hat and bowed from the waist not once, but twice. "Good afternoon, Mademoiselle," I said. "I trust you are well?"

The enthusiasm of my greeting flustered her and disconcerted me. Before I could make amends, she thrust at me a package wrapped in brown paper.

"I hope you will not think me forward, Monsieur de Lorde, but please accept this gift from your friends in the rue Chaptal."

I could think of nothing to say, so I bowed again, took the package and gestured her onto a bench. I gently shook the package as I sat beside her.

"I am surprised that Max has time for such gestures, in the final week of dress rehearsals." I slit the adhesive with a fingernail and began unfolding the paper.

"Monsieur, I must confess, Max knows nothing of this. I was building some props, and this one—well, this one turned out so fine that I felt I should present it to someone." I smoothed out the paper, revealing an ornate dagger of Chinese design.

"It is lovely," I said. "Fake, I hope?"

"Oh, yes, Monsieur, and with the usual spring blade." She slid the dagger gently from my lap, raised it above her head and, with surprising force, drove it to the hilt into her forearm. Then she lifted it slowly, allowing the dull and retractable blade to slip back out of the hilt that had concealed it. The illusion was flawless, as always.

"Wonderful," I said as she gravely handed back the weapon.

"The dagger is not loaded, Monsieur; I did not want to risk fouling your clothes. But here in the hilt is the reservoir that holds the blood—as much as a pint."

"Such craftsmanship. Dr. Binet will be impressed, as well. I will show it to him when he next visits."

"Oh, Monsieur, I beg you, don't tell Dr. Binet I was here! He will be at our opening Friday night, and he will be so angry."

"Hm? Angry? Whatever are you talking about, child?"

"Dr. Binet said that none of us were to contact you under any circumstances. He said your—your treatment required complete isolation. 'A break with his theatrical past,' he called it."

"How extraordinary!" I stood and walked a few deliberate paces on the gravel, like a lone duelist. "What, then, has Binet been doing with the manuscript of our latest collaboration? The adaptation of the de Maupassant story, about the awful woman who turns her babies into monsters? Is it locked away in a lab at the Sorbonne? Has he not been passing the pages to Max as they are completed?"

Eugenie frowned. "Collaboration, Monsieur? Dr. Binet has brought Max such a manuscript, yes, but he says it is his own work. He says your illness prevents you from writing. Oh, I have said too much!" she said, standing. "I have upset you, Monsieur. You are all a-quiver, like the doctor at the climax of *The Kiss of Blood.* Please forgive me. I have spoken out of turn."

"Not at all, Eugenie, not at all!" I mopped my face with my handkerchief and took deep breaths, calming myself so as not to frighten the girl. "I thank you so much for the gift, Eugenie, and for visiting me today. I wonder, could I ask you to bring me one thing more?"

"Of course, Monsieur."

I held the dagger before me. "Might I have some blood with which to load this?"

Sonia

Opening night. My God, what next? Max and I were preparing ourselves in our usual superstitious way, perhaps indiscreetly, behind some balsa-wood trees backstage. I looked up, and there was Charles, pale and staring. I was going to have a conversation with him anyway—after what happened at my flat the other night—Oh! the folly! What was I thinking?—but I didn't want him to find out like this. And now, five minutes before the curtain, Charles is pacing and mumbling and rolling his eyes, ignoring all my entreaties and explanations. A frightening display. The stagehands think he is merely preparing for his role, but I wonder whether he will make it through the performance.

I wonder whether I will.

Georges Choisy, On Theatre

A DARING NEW REALISM AT THE GRAND GUIGNOL
(The World, final edition, 21/9/25)

In recent months, much of the dramatic press in this most dramatic of cities has been devoted to new trends toward realism on our stages. We have seen a decided shift in dialogue this season, for example, from witty bourgeois repartee to rough, often crude, street argot, sometimes with electrifying results. No recent evening of realistic theatre, however, has so impressed this reviewer as tonight's season premiere at a most unlikely location: that venerable Temple of Horror, the Theatre of the Grand Guignol.

All the more remarkably, this overwhelming impression was made in the final minutes of the night's entertainment. Producer-director Max Mitchinn, with the daring of a master showman, began the evening in routine and traditional fashion: a series of short playlets of horror and broad comedy, including *A Crime in the Madhouse,* a new ghastliness from the clotted pen of Andre de Lorde. This included a particularly repellent eye-gouging in which the liberated orbs actually bounced into the front row, causing much commotion. So far, nothing to disconcert or surprise the dedicated "Guignolers," who roared and retched with their customary verve.

The climax of the evening, however, was something else entirely. Messieurs Mitchinn and de Lorde have newly shod a warhorse of their repertoire, *The Dead Child,* the story of a grief-maddened sculptor and his faithless wife. The new production eliminates all the violence but intensifies by many orders of magnitude the emotional power.

After a cataclysmic speech denouncing the perfidy of Woman, the sculptor collapses, howling in wordless grief and rage. Dazed, the wife slowly reaches out to him, holds him, and then her own tears come. The sight of the devastated couple, the raving sculptor and his penitent wife, sobbing together in the center of the stage, holding each other with taut desperation as if encircling arms could possibly join the shards of their sundered lives, is a sight this reviewer will never forget. Nor, I suspect, will the majority of tonight's audience. The silence was as profound as that of a tomb. Never had the patrons seen such naked emotion laid bare in the theatre. The tatty backdrops, the prompter's box, the elbows rubbing my own to right and left, all dropped away like canvas scenery, and for a few anguished seconds I forgot my situation, and believed I was beholding a heartbreak as real and as wrenching as any I have experienced myself. At the curtain the applause was thunderous. The actors themselves seemed dazed as they emerged for a bow with the rest of the company.

As the sculptor, Charles Goudron made a stunning Paris debut. As the wife, Guignol veteran Sonia Morel, who so often sparkles in otherwise dull vehicles, proved herself worthy of comparison even to the great Bernhardt. One glows at the thought of the life force that Mademoiselle Morel would bring to the role of Antigone!

But the evening's revels were not ended. The lights came up, the patrons stood and rummaged for their belongings, and then the final, ultimate act of realistic drama took place, in the very aisles of the theatre itself, without the reassuring distance of a stage! Two shouting men began grappling with one another in the middle of the seats. When one of the men drew a dagger, I was at first frightened and tempted to summon the police. Then I was thrilled beyond words to recognize the assailant as none other than Monsieur de Lorde himself, and to realize that this must be a wonderfully satiric climax staged in the midst of the patrons.

This brief playlet ended comically. In true Guignol fashion, de Lorde shouted, "Die, Binet! Die!" and shoved his dagger into the chest of his gibbering partner, spraying a geyser of stage blood. After staring at the protruding hilt that quivered in the bubbling wound, the victim—wonderful reversal of expectations!—seemed to recover instantaneously. He fairly galloped up the aisle, yelling as he went, "Madman! Insane! Help! Help!" I am told the performance continued through the foyer, out the front door, and onto the pavement outside, until the gifted actor—whose name, I regret, was unavailable at press time—had vanished into the promenading crowds of the rue Chaptal . . .

Max

Our new season is a triumph. Sonia is radiant, and she and I test repeatedly the capacities of her dressing room. Charles is a matinee idol, standing in the stage door and signing autographs for crowds of adoring young women; a new gaiety fills the blind alley where patrons once stumbled only to vomit. Happily, this tradition continues as well—eleven last night, by Camille's count, a record. When the weather is bad, Andre and Eugenie spend an afternoon in the cemetery, stalking hand in hand among the tombs, visiting all their favorite dead. He and I, meanwhile, are at each other's throats on the staging of *The Maker of Monsters,* though Eugenie assures us that the plural of the title is not a problem, for she can produce hunchbacked urchins at will. It is like old times.

Late at night, Andre and Eugenie and Sonia and I sit in the balcony, rest from our labours, and bask in the murmur of the nuns. We toast the stage with cocktails of bicarbonate, and we see in the darkness a capering future, awash with drama and blood.

The Executioners' Guild

WHEN THE STRANGER WALKED INTO BLACKburn's that Friday morning, there were no other customers in the store, unless you counted Stumpy Turlis, which Mrs. Blackburn, a woman of standards, certainly did not. The stranger's entrance set the cowbell above the door to jangling, but Mrs. Blackburn did not look up. She figured the bell was just the youngest Cooper child skipping, or, more accurately, stomping outside with her fistful of already-sodden licorice. The child's penny, suspiciously shiny, still lay on the counter where she had, on tiptoe, placed it. Before putting it in the register, Mrs. Blackburn would give it a chance to dry. In the meantime, she had returned to the task at hand, the slicing of a fresh wheel of cheese, always a delicate operation, and one that couldn't wait until noontime when the sandwich crowd came in, jamming up to the counter and talking at once and wanting everything right *then* and not even having the decency to wash the horse sweat and axle grease and chicken feed off their hands before they unwrapped the wax paper and bit into the cheese-and-baloney sandwiches that would not get made, Mrs. Blackburn felt, if she had to waste her whole morning waiting hand and foot on every white-trash ragamuffin in town. Do I look like some old nigger mammy, she sometimes asked Mr. Blackburn in the quiet of the evening, I am not being hateful but I genuinely want to know, because if that is what I am, the lowliest servant of every ditch-born lint-picker in the county, I suppose I should claim my rightful place, and collect my meager belongings, and leave this bed that my very presence defiles, and sleep in the stable with the other dumb beasts of God's dominion, and having said this, Mrs. Blackburn would dab her eyes with the corner of an apron, and enjoy what, from Mr. Blackburn, passed for reassurance. All that clomp, clomp, clomp, Mrs. Blackburn thought (biting her lip as the wax skin welled up on either side of her sharpest knife), you'd think the child was trying to dig postholes in the floor, and it *just* now polished to a fare-thee-well, and that only after nagging at Mr. Blackburn for a solid month, and thus preoccupied she allowed Stumpy Turlis to be the first person in Andalusia, Mississippi, actually to speak to the stranger, a humiliation that would gall her to her grave.

"Morning," said Stumpy Turlis.

"Good morning," said the stranger, and Mrs. Blackburn looked up, startled.

"I'm not in your way, am I?" asked Stumpy Turlis.

"Not at all."

"Cause if I am I'll move. I don't want to be no trouble. I can find me some other place to lie."

"You're fine. No trouble at all. Please stay where you are."

Stumpy Turlis, as usual, was lying full-length on the hardware counter, hat on his chest, arms outflung and hanging down on either side. His right hand held a cigarette; his left hand, though it was behind the counter and temporarily out of sight, certainly held a Coca-Cola in some stage of emptiness. On the crown of his hat was a crumpled paper packet commemorating the headache powder he had taken when he came in.

Standing over Stumpy, his back to the grocery counter and to Mrs. Blackburn, was a tall, white-haired, broad-shouldered man in a derby hat, striped gray trousers, and a black knee-length coat. In his right hand was a gray suitcase. Some drummer with a line of brushes, Mrs. Blackburn decided, or liniment, or iron pills. Well, let him talk to that old fool Turlis, and waste *his* time for a change. I must be deaf sure enough, Mrs. Blackburn thought, as she added a fresh cheese slice to the growing pile on the cutting board, he's a big man and I didn't even hear him walking. That a *winter* coat? When she swept the porch at nine o'clock, the Royal Crown thermometer already said eighty-six degrees.

"I'm just lying here waiting on my Goody's to kick in," said Stumpy Turlis. "You get headaches much, mister?"

"I can't say that I do."

"Be glad, then. I get 'em something awful. Last for a week. You know why?"

"No, I don't."

"Septum. That's what they told me down in Meridian, I got a septum, a deviated nasal septum. You know what that is?"

"I'm afraid not."

"Causes headaches, that's what it is. Just like someone clipped you tween the eyes with the end of a board, only worse. You ever been clipped tween the eyes by a board, mister?"

"Not that I can recall."

"Pray to God you never do. It's bad, real bad, but it ain't as bad as a deviated nasal septum, no Jesus. You're a lucky man all around, that's all I got to say *about* it."

Mrs. Blackburn wondered where the stranger was from; he talked too well, as if he had learned English from a book. She kept expecting him to turn around or walk off or at least shift from side to side, but no, he just stood there, frozen, with head slightly bowed, like an old friend mourning the prone body of Stumpy Turlis. She peeled from the knife a little stringy gibble of cheese and ate it, being careful not to touch her fingers with her mouth. The cheese was soft and mild on her tongue. As she stared at the drummer's back, she felt the cool breath of the nearest rotary fan as it swept its idle gaze across her, as it ruffled her hair and leafed through the Meridian papers in their stack beside the register.

Stumpy Turlis asked, "You want to buy something, mister?"

"No, I only—"

"Cause I don't work here. I can't sell you nothing. You want something, you got to—" Here his voice became low and conspiratorial. "You got to ask *her*."

Still he didn't turn around. The fan lost interest and moved on, leaving the sweat on her neck to proceed about its business, and in the sudden reminder of heat Mrs. Blackburn found her voice and said, loudly, "May I *help* you?" As she said it, she set down her knife and wiped her hands on the inside of her apron.

The drummer turned, nodded, and tipped his hat. "Good morning, madam. No, I'm just browsing, thank you very much." He might have been sixty or he might have been eighty, it was hard to tell, with those heavy black eyeglasses and that puffed-up jowly face. But from across the store, Mrs. Blackburn could tell that his eyes, magnified through Coke-bottle lenses, were perhaps the saddest eyes she ever had seen.

Though she hadn't intended to—since, after all, she could

show a drummer the door without moving a step—Mrs. Blackburn found herself bustling toward the hardware counter. As always, she went the long way, around the U formed by the grocery and the dry-goods counters, along the depression that her in-laws and their parents had worn in the floor in the 19th century. Mrs. Blackburn disdained any shorter path across the store.

"We don't need anything more to sell, Lord knows," Mrs. Blackburn said as she passed the tablecloths and aprons. She realized she was still wiping her hands as she walked, and flung the corner of her apron down. "Enough trouble these days selling what we have, I don't care what Mr. Roosevelt says about the forties being better, the forties ain't got to Andalusia yet."

"I have nothing to sell," the stranger said with a slight smile, setting down his suitcase and spreading his hands. He turned briefly to Stumpy Turlis, as if for confirmation. "I'm only passing the time. I came in to look around, where it's cool."

"There's cooler places than this," Mrs. Blackburn said, fetching up behind the hardware counter and folding her arms. But her heart wasn't in it. The old man looked not only sad but tired, and in that ridiculous winter outfit, too. Strange he didn't seem to be sweating. They regarded each other across the counter. Lying between them was Stumpy Turlis, who eyed Mrs. Blackburn and pulled his nearly empty Coca-Cola bottle back across his chest, out of her reach.

"I ain't in the way, am I?" Stumpy Turlis quavered. "If I am, I can move. I don't want to be no trouble."

"Hush up," Mrs. Blackburn hissed, slapping her palm onto the counter near his head. "What brings you to town, mister?"

She knew this was rude, and half expected no answer at all, but her curiosity was piqued, and besides, she felt she had to wrest the moment back from Stumpy Turlis *somehow*. Whose store was this, anyway? Well, her husband's, but weren't husbands and wives the same person under God's law?

Without seeming in the least disturbed, the stranger said: "To meet a man. A colleague. He's not from here, either," and he pronounced it *eye*-ther, "but we have some business to discuss, and this seemed a . . . convenient place." He smiled at her and at Stumpy Turlis, clasped his hands across his belly, then added, "It's a lovely town. The forests are much more hilly than I had expected. Mountainous, practically. Do you get much snow?"

"Not since I been here," Stumpy Turlis volunteered, "and I been living here since ought-four. Working the sawmill. That's where I done busted my head with the plank." After a pause, he clarified: "At the sawmill. You ever get hit in the head with a plank, mister? Oh," he said, beneath Mrs. Blackburn's thunderhead gaze. "Oh, I guess I done asked you that, ain't I?"

"Think nothing of it," the stranger said, and did an extraordinary thing: He reached out and patted Stumpy Turlis on the shoulder. "You've nearly finished your Coke, I see. Shall I buy you another?" Mrs. Blackburn stared at the stranger in wonderment. "I presume there's an icebox, a cooler? Ah, here it is. It's a rare thing," he said, lifting the lid and plunging one hand among the cubes, "to be welcomed with a friendly word in an unfamiliar town. Most rare." With a cascading avalanche sound, he pulled forth a fresh Coca-Cola, slick and shiny and dripping, one bit of ice sliding down into the waist of the bottle. "Here you are. Madam? Care for a drink? No? All right, then." He pulled out another and ignored the bottle opener on the wall to pop the cap against the edge of the countertop, catching it in his other hand as it flipped and pocketing it so quickly Mrs. Blackburn almost missed where it went. Without sitting up, Stumpy Turlis, with the grace of years of practice, reached up and slightly behind his head for the bottle opener, popped the cap, then swooped the neck to his lips without spilling a drop, gulping just as the foam surged forth. Both he and the stranger made satisfied drinking sounds. Disgusting, Mrs. Blackburn thought. The stranger pulled from his pocket a handful of coins, which he studied.

"That'll do," Mrs. Blackburn said, snatching a dime. The affable old man in the suit was setting her nerves on edge, and she wanted him gone.

But he just smiled his sad-eyed smile and said, "Thank you."

Stumpy Turlis, meanwhile, was grinning rottenly, evidently feeling he had made a friend for life. He crossed one foot over the other and jiggled it. "Hey, you're all right, mister," he said. "Y'know, I think my headache may be some better, now that you mention it. Not all gone," he added, glancing at Mrs. Blackburn, "not yet, but it's getting there. I'm obliged to you, mister."

The Sunbeam clock showed no more time for this foolishness, yet Mrs. Blackburn was unwilling to leave the stranger alone in the hardware section—alone because Stumpy Turlis, of course, didn't count. "You *sure* you don't want to look at anything?" she asked.

"Well," said the stranger. "Now that you mention it." He pointed over her head, at the wall behind. "Might I examine a length of that rope?"

Was his finger trembling?

"All righty," Mrs. Blackburn said, feigning jauntiness. She turned to the individual twenty-foot coils of rope, dozens of them hanging in ranks from ancient nails. In the back of the store were longer lengths, of course, and one immense wheel from which any length could be cut, but the short ropes suited most people these days, when so many had decided they were too good to keep horses and mules anymore. She reached up, lifted down a coil, and turned to set it on the counter, but the stranger beat her to it, lifting the rope out of her grasp, bearing it the length of Stumpy Turlis, and setting it down on the counter near the soles of Stumpy's boots. He pulled free a few feet, flexed it experimentally, then tied a knot in it so swiftly that Mrs. Blackburn blinked—this was inch-thick, store-bought rope, hadn't even thought about being broken in, and while Mrs. Blackburn's daddy had taught her a good deal about knot-tying, she didn't recognize the one the stranger just made, nor the one he was setting about making now.

"A good rope," the stranger said, mostly to himself. "Not the best, but a good one, nevertheless."

Something about his twisting, dancing fingers and the rope slithering between them made Mrs. Blackburn remember that night when she was little, when she had followed her daddy and several other men into the woods, wondering where they were going with all that rope. Fighting her way back to the present, back to the store and the stranger and the heat and the fans shaking their heads all around, and the newspapers fluttering in the artificial breeze, she remembered the headlines she'd been looking at all morning, the headlines that had made her expect an even bigger lunch crowd than usual, and just as her throat was seizing up she managed to say, in a voice barely above a whisper:

"Withium."

Mr. Blackburn, who was unused to hearing his first name, immediately bestirred himself in the back room he called an office. His grandfather's chair shrieked as he rolled it backward. Mrs. Blackburn heard the curtain whip aside, and then she heard her husband lumber forth, the jingle of coins as he hitched up his pants. He was beside her, his breath audible, his tobacco-tinged sweat awful but welcome. The Blackburns looked at each other, and then at the stranger, who pulled the rope taut and relaxed it again, then taut, then relaxed, then taut again.

"Mister," Mr. Blackburn said. "Hey, mister."

The stranger looked up, blinked, as if peering through a fog. Whatever Mrs. Blackburn had expected, it wasn't the bland, placid expression the stranger had worn all along. "Yes?" he asked. He looked at each of them. "I'm sorry. Is anything wrong?"

"Not yet, no," Mr. Blackburn said. "Listen, mister. We don't want any trouble this weekend, okay? I mean, we know people will be coming from all over, to meet their friends and be sociable, and see what they can see, but as for—well, as for the job itself, that's a job for the county, and the sheriff, and the man what's been hired by the county. Understand?"

The stranger's face darkened. His shoulders seemed to broaden. The rope slipped from his hands. Several feet rustled to the floorboards, but then it slowed and stopped, most of it still coiled atop the counter.

Mr. Blackburn went on: "Now, there's some as think that's a good idea, and some as don't. But I'm on the County Council myself, and I'll tell you, I think it's for the good. But whether we like it or not, it's going to happen at the courthouse, and the townsfolk aren't going to have any part of it, except a few witnesses, and folks from out of town—well, they *sure* pop ain't gonna have anything to do with it. Like I said, it's a job for the sheriff." He nodded in agreement with himself and hitched his pants again. "So I don't think you'll be needing no rope today, mister. You understand me?"

The stranger said nothing. His lips trembled. Mrs. Blackburn was horrified to entertain the suspicion that the old man might cry. Instead, he turned and walked slowly, ponderously, over to his suitcase—he really *is* a big man, she thought, we'd be in real trouble if he—then lifted it and walked to the door, stopped as he pulled it inward, setting off the cowbell, and looked back at the three of them. He said, with great formality and dignity: "I am no murderer. Nor am I an amateur. Good morning." He closed the door behind him, clumped across the porch, and was gone. The little blonde girl holding the buttered slice of Sunbeam said the time was 11:05.

* * *

The sheriff smelled the food before he heard Miss Esther coming up the stairs, mumbling non-stop to God and her ancestors. He was waiting on the landing when the flowers on her straw hat bobbed into view.

"Hey, Miss Esther. Lemme help you with that."

"Thank you kindly, Sheriff."

She was the tiniest, most dried-up-looking little colored woman you would ever hope to meet, and, as she liked to put it, only God knew how old she was. So the sheriff was surprised when he took the basket from her hands.

"My Lord, Miss Esther. What all you got in this thing? You pack the stove you cooked it on?" He held the door for her as she cackled.

"That's my biggest frying pan," she said. "I wanted to fry up a mess of chicken—"

"Oh, my goodness," the sheriff said, lifting the wicker lid. Hooper and Nat gathered round, making wordless appreciative noises.

"—and I remembered I'd done left my big serving bowl down at the A.M.E. We had revival last week. So I just decided to tote it over in the pan. Poured off the grease, now."

"I like the grease myself," Nat said, already munching on a chicken leg. "I sops my biscuits in it." The sheriff nodded at Hooper, who began transferring food from Miss Esther's heavy pans and crockery into tin plates from the jailhouse cupboard.

"Sheriff, if you wouldn't mind . . ."

"Don't worry, Miss Esther. We'll take it on down to him. You don't have to go near."

Miss Esther's voice dropped. She peered over her spectacles and clutched the front of her dress. "I ain't *never* been talked to like that man did, Sheriff."

"I hope you ain't, Miss Esther. It was awful."

"Not even by the trash what lives in the hollow, and *certainly* not by a colored man."

"There was no excuse for it, Miss Esther. Don't get yourself all worked up, now. You don't have to go near that one anymore."

Miss Esther glanced toward the barred door that led to the cells, closed her eyes, and shuddered. "I had been praying for the man," she said, "praying for his repentance, for he like all of us is one of God's creatures." Her voice was breaking. "But Sheriff, I done told the other ladies they gone have to do my share of his praying from now on."

Nat was already on his second chicken leg, and watching Miss Esther like she was some windup toy set moving for his amusement. The sheriff tried to steer her toward the stairs. Lord, these old gals could turn up the melodrama when they wanted to. Just like his own mama—though she'd faint dead away to hear him compare her to a colored woman.

"Now, don't you worry, Miss Esther. I'll have Hooper bring the basket back to you. We thank you again." The others dutifully repeated their thanks, Nat's somewhat muffled by chicken.

On the landing, Miss Esther turned, suddenly dry-eyed, and asked in a low voice: "That truck coming today?"

"Yes, ma'am. Anytime now."

"Good," she said. "Can't come soon enough for that one." She whispered, "He ain't nothing but a *nigger*," and then covered her mouth with her hands.

The sheriff fought a grin. "We thank you again for the dinner," he said. "We thank you kindly."

Miss Esther was paid once a month out of the jail budget, and recently had renegotiated her terms with the council, but she and the sheriff never discussed such unpleasant topics.

"I'm pleased to do it, Sheriff," she said, creeping down the stairs, flowers bobbing. "Does my heart good to know y'all are eating well. Lord, these steps, there's more of 'em ever *time* I come in the door, but Jesus walks where Queenesther walks, yes He does, and Queenesther's feet are His feet, and Queenesther's hands are His hands . . ." She disappeared. The sheriff went back inside and picked up his club, wincing as he did so—he wasn't Sheriff Langley, after all.

"Let's go, Hooper. Nat, keep your ears open. And you *might* save some chicken for the rest of us," he added.

Nat's face fell, and he chewed more slowly. In a small voice, he said: "Ain't had but two legs."

"That's all most chickens got," the sheriff said, unlocking and trundling aside the corridor door. Hooper, carrying the dinner, walked ahead, past three empty cells on the left, three empty cells on the right. Once again the sheriff thanked God the place was otherwise empty. Even the town drunks had lain low the past few weeks; when the heat wave rolled in, the whole town settled down like a dog under a stove. At the end of the corridor was a small grilled outside window, a supply closet on the right, a final, larger cell on the left. The men stopped before this cell. The sheriff studied its inhabitant before moving to unlock the door.

As always, the wiry colored man with the high, bulging forehead sat on the bunk with his back to the corner and his knees up, sock feet on the mattress, looking out the window at the sky and the visible corner of the Masonic Hall. His arms were folded across his stomach, and his hands dangled. There was no sign of energy, until he slowly turned his head and looked at the men with bright, staring eyes.

"Set still, Childress," the sheriff said, shoving back the door just wide enough for Hooper to get in, set the food on the spindly-legged table, and get out. The prisoner didn't move. Skin prickling, the sheriff rolled the door closed, locked it, tugged on it, and turned to go.

"Mr. Simpson got here yet?" Childress asked. He had a voice like a bird chirping.

"This afternoon," the sheriff said, still looking toward the far end of the corridor.

"Cause I got something to tell the man."

"You'll have your chance," the sheriff said. It was what he always said. Childress had been asking for two weeks.

Then Childress asked: "Where's the bitch at?"

The sheriff looked at Childress, whose face was expressionless save for his dancing eyes. He still hadn't moved. If anything, his shoulders had slumped, and he looked even more languid, as if all his energy were going into his words and his eyes.

"The old bitch," Childress explained. "I been all worked up to look at her ass a little bit. Check her out. Old ain't gold but it ain't loose change neither. Reckon she'd slip me some if y'all looked the other way? I ain't got nowhere else to put it, I might's well put some of it in there—"

"You shut your mouth," the sheriff said, his hand tight on his club.

"Don't get all het up now," Childress said. "I won't be putting it in till y'all be taking it out. I magine it's mighty roomy in there, but it ain't roomy enough for both of us."

Hooper muttered a curse. Without looking, the sheriff grabbed his arm.

"Take it easy," the sheriff said.

"I don't mind being at the tail end of the train," Childress went on. "I know where the niggers get to ride. Just so I gets me a little piece of the caboose. Ha-haaaa." It wasn't a laugh so much as a whine, and his face twitched when he emitted it, as if it was involuntary.

"Childress," the sheriff said, "you might as well stop trying to get a rise out of us. We ain't gonna do anything stupid. You ain't dealing with Cooter Langley, you know. You're gonna sit right there until your time comes." As the sheriff talked, Childress looked back out the window, moving his lips silently, as if mouthing the words. "And it's gonna be done by the book, you got me? The old days are gone, Childress."

"Bright, white, quite new day," the prisoner murmured. "I feels less like a nigger all the time."

"By the book," the sheriff repeated. He took a deep breath. Because he had been raised Methodist, he added: "Time like this, a man ought to be thinking about meeting his God."

Childress burst out laughing and turned back to the sheriff, grinning. "Listen at this God shit," he said. "You all the God a nigger needs in this here town. You gone be waiting for me on the other side, too?"

"Jesus," the sheriff said, yanking Hooper's elbow. "Let's go."

"Maybe you gone climb up on that chair and ride out of town with me? That be some kinda ride, all right."

"Let's *go*, I said."

Now facing the window again, Childress spoke in a dreamy voice, as if reciting something half-forgotten: "Fuck your white ass, fuck your white laws, and fuck your white God."

Shoving Hooper down the hall, the sheriff fumbled through his keys. As he slammed and locked the corridor door behind him, Nat handed him a plate. "Here you go, Sheriff," Nat said.

The sheriff looked at the chicken, rice, turnips, and biscuits, and felt a surge of nausea. "You can have mine," he muttered, and strode out of the office. Air, he thought as he stomped downstairs, got to get some air. In the lobby, heels clicking on the newly inlaid tile, he walked to the fountain, splashed his face with warm, rusty water, and felt a little easier. He wondered, as he often did, whether the water in the coloreds' fountain was any better. He doubted it. Less than a day, he kept telling himself. Less than a day to go.

* * *

The truck rolled into town at noon, not from the direction of Meridian, like most Andalusia traffic, but from the north, and so it caught by surprise the dozens of people who were in the courthouse square solely to look for the truck. Most of the crowd, neighbors and strangers alike, had gravitated by silent consent to the southern side of the courthouse. It not only offered a clear view down Tyburn Street, which eventually became the Meridian highway, but was shady thanks to the Confederate oaks. Here groups of men and women, but mostly men, sat on benches or the marble steps or perched amid tree roots or just walked slowly back and forth, fanned themselves and mopped their faces with handkerchiefs and looked down Tyburn toward the ice plant and talked to each other in low tones. There were also many children about, a surprising number, because they normally could find cooler places to play, and dinner should have been waiting at home. But there they were, gangs of them, boys and girls alike ran and shrieked and played tag among the lampposts and raised such a ruckus that the shopkeepers would have complained if it had been a normal business day, but of course it wasn't. The shopkeepers themselves stood in their doorways, on alert, afraid they'd miss something. Most of the adults were secretly thankful for all the whooping hollering children in the square, because the adults were all a damn sight more hushmouthed than usual, and even people who normally hailed each other across the street today just nodded in silence and glanced away, and without the children the square would have suffered a quiet that was unthinkable.

The square was unusual in one more respect: There were no Negroes in sight. The ones who worked in the businesses that fronted the square either stayed inside, finding things to do in the back rooms, or had called in sick. The maids and cooks of the town's few well-off inhabitants, who normally would have come to the square to do the day's shopping, were instead having their groceries delivered, or making do. Old Paul, who shined shoes beneath the largest oak every day, was nowhere to be seen. If any of the white people noticed his absence, or the absence of the other Negroes, no one mentioned it.

The first to see the truck was the youngest Woodham boy, Joshua. He was heading home despite the jeers of his friends because he knew his mama would snatch a knot in him if he didn't have his elbows on the oilcloth to say the blessing by 12:05. As he cut across the north lawn of the courthouse, Joshua saw a pretty new red-white-and-blue sign in his path, with a bald eagle on it. It said: "Keep off the grass." Joshua studied it, decided it was Federal doins, and kept walking. His route took him past the Confederate memorial, which was taller even than Joshua's daddy, but not so big around that Joshua couldn't hope to be able to reach around it one day and join hands with himself on the other side. He stopped and flattened himself against the pillar and made the attempt for the umpteenth time, not because he really thought his arms had gotten longer in the past half-hour, but because the marble was cool and musty against his face, and up close and sideways the letters of the dead men's names looked like a secret code that only Joshua could read. He was standing there against the marble when he heard what sounded like a sawmill truck laboring up a grade. He stepped away from the monument and walked around it, dragging his fingertips across it until the marble slipped away, and there was the truck, shifting gears with a shriek as it rumbled down Rose Avenue toward the square. People were coming out of the stores along Rose to look at it.

Joshua was interested to see that the truck didn't have a skull and crossbones on the side, like Eddie Dunn said it would, and it didn't have skeletons tied across the hood with their mouths open, like the Derrick twins said it would. He hadn't but half believed those stories in the first place. Joshua knew this was the right truck, though, because it had the seal of the state of Mississippi on the door, because a billowing green tarpaulin covered up everything on the flatbed, and because the driver stopped at the corner, stuck his head out the window and hollered to Joshua, "If this ain't Andalusia I don't know where the hell I am."

"It's Andalusia sure enough," Joshua hollered back. "Far as I know," he added. Joshua had learned from the grown-ups in his family to qualify nearly every assertion he made.

"*Out*-standing," the driver said. He looked to left, then right, then left again, though all the automobiles in sight were parked, and then he turned into the square, hauling on the steering wheel with both hands. The hood vibrated like a tin roof in a hailstorm, and the engine was full of cats. Still wrestling the wheel, the driver eased the truck alongside the curb, hauled up on the brake, and choked the thing down. Joshua watched as he flung open the creaking door and stepped out. He was tall, though not as tall as Joshua's daddy, and thin, but there were muscles beneath his rolled-up shirtsleeves, and scars, too, one down one arm like a railroad track, and another, thinner one right across his jaw past the corner of his mouth, so that he looked to be smiling. Then Joshua realized the man *was* smiling. "How you doing today, partner?" the man asked Joshua, hands on his hips and stretching.

Purdie Newall, who had let Joshua kiss her just last week and might again, had said the truck would be driven by a man in a long black robe with fangs. This was the only truck story that Joshua had hoped was true. But to be polite, he answered, just as his daddy would: "Doing all right, I reckon. How you?"

Some of the people from Rose Street were walking across, and others were beginning to come around the side of the courthouse.

"Bout stove up from driving," the man said. "You ain't old enough to drive, I guess."

"No, sir."

"Well, don't you ever start. They ain't much that's worth driving to, and that's the truth."

Grown-ups began, silently, to gather around, and Joshua felt that his chance to talk to the driver wouldn't last long. Joshua tried to prolong it by thinking of grown-up things to say.

"Damn truck bout knocks my teeth out," the driver continued, grinning to reveal two or three gaps. By now a dozen or more people stood there, but the driver acted as if it was still just Joshua. "And I don't know who drew that map, but I'm glad they got the work, because they must a been blind and feeble and on relief. And they ain't no road signs for nigh on thirty miles. Not even a sign that says Andalusia on it. For all I knew this town coulda been named Rotary, or Burma-Shave, or Get Right with God."

"Don't nobody come into town thataway," Joshua said.

"I don't blame 'em," the man said. "I hope there's someplace to eat on the other side of this courthouse. Otherwise I'll just have to cry. Come help me tie down this tarp, partner. It's been flapping for a solid hour."

Suddenly remembering his dinner and then just as suddenly forgetting it again, Joshua trotted with the driver to the back of the truck, where several no-count-looking men whispered among themselves. They backed away from the driver, who still acted as if he and Joshua were alone. Joshua clambered onto the tailgate and sat, bare feet dangling, while the driver fumbled with the knots.

"Never was no good at tying things," the driver said. "I guess you ain't either. I see your shoes done fell off."

"Didn't put on no shoes today."

"How come?"

Joshua felt a stab of pity for the man. "It's *summertime*," he said.

"Oh," the driver said. "No wonder it's so hot. I sorta lose track sometimes. All right, I guess that'll hold her." Joshua jumped down and stood beside the driver, both of them looking up at the vast green bulk on the flatbed. A rare breeze stirred up, and the tarp bulged slightly outward in one place, as if weakly pushed from inside.

Looking up at the truck with his back to the crowd, able to hear the footsteps and the faltering, dying voices as more people joined the group and were silenced, Joshua felt the way he sometimes felt at church, on the front row with the rest of the children. He felt the silence of everyone behind him pushing the back of his head, goading him to break the silence, to jump up and say something.

"What you got in there, mister?" Joshua asked.

"Electric chair," the man replied.

Whenever Joshua or anyone else said something ugly, his Grandma Nellie would suck in her breath like she was trying to pull the words right out of the air and hide them. When the driver said, "Electric chair," all the grown-ups around them made a Grandma Nellie sound.

Joshua knew that most grown-ups driving around the countryside with an electric chair in the back would not admit it to a youngun. Joshua decided to see what else the man would admit to. "What for?" he asked.

"Kill people with it," the man replied. Another Grandma Nellie sound from the crowd.

Joshua liked this man more and more all the time. "What you do that for?" he asked, though he knew the answer to that one, too.

Looking down at Joshua, the driver suddenly seemed a lot older, and the first facial scar Joshua had noticed, he now realized, was far from the only one. The driver looked as sad as Joshua's daddy had looked when they'd buried Aunt Sophie. The driver reached down and rubbed the top of Joshua's head, which Joshua had always hated though he decided this time he could stand it. "Someone's got to," the driver said. "It's the law."

"Can I sit in it?" Joshua asked, and everybody standing around busted out laughing, like it was the funniest thing they'd ever heard. They all got to talking to each other, repeating what Joshua had said and whooping and carrying on, and Joshua felt his cheeks burn and wished they all would shut up and go away, grown-ups thought younguns were so funny. But the driver didn't laugh; if anything, he looked even sadder. Still ignoring the others, he squatted to look Joshua in the face and said, "I can't let you do that, friend. You ain't mean enough to sit in that chair."

Joshua was determined not to cry, but when he spoke he was disgusted to hear a tiny little snubbing kid's voice. "I bet *you* sit in it when you want."

Now the driver did laugh, but it wasn't a smart-aleck laugh, and Joshua grinned back, feeling better. The driver said: "I'll tell you a secret, partner. I'll tell you something I ain't never told anyone."

A large hairy-knuckled hand took hold of the driver's shoulder, not roughly but firmly, and Joshua looked up, and up. The sheriff was so tall and big, with his huge head and his eyes set way back beneath his eyebrows, that some of Joshua's friends thought he was scary, but to Joshua he looked like the picture of John C. Calhoun in his history book, in the chapter about the War of Northern Aggression. And how could anyone who looked like John C. Calhoun be bad?

"Jimmy Simpson?" the sheriff said. His voice rumbled like feed in the chute at the mill.

"Yes, sir, that's me," the driver said, standing up. He didn't look scared, either, just respectful. Joshua scowled. He'd never find out the secret now. He focused all the hatred he had felt for the crowd on the sheriff alone, but the sheriff didn't notice.

"I'm Sheriff Davis." The men shook hands.

"Pleased to meet you, sir."

"Welcome to Andalusia. I think you'll be right comfortable here. Got a room ready for you at Miss Pearse's, and she sets a mighty good table."

"I thank you."

"Now, let's go on in and talk about getting you set up here. Then we'll head to the cafe and get us something to eat, on the county. My deputies will watch your truck, and all."

"That sounds good, Sheriff."

Determined to pretend he wasn't being ignored, Joshua stuck as close as he could to the driver's heels as the two men moved through the crowd. He'd never seen this many people in the square before. He saw a lot of farmer's shoes, with dusted-over dried-up mud, and worse, lining every crack and crease in the leather, but he saw a lot of fancier shoes, too, and a lot of women in heels. As they went up the walk toward the courthouse steps, the sheriff talked to the now-noisy crowd the whole time, low and gentle, the way Joshua's daddy talked to the cows. "Come on, people. Let us through. Go on about your business. Go on back to the store, Bill. There ain't nothing here to see. No, I'm afraid not, Mrs. Burchett. All that's tomorrow. You won't miss nothing by going on home. That's a mighty cute one you got there. What's he, three months old, now? My, my. Yes, ma'am, just go on home. That's the best thing. Move along, folks. Please move along. Mr. Simpson?"

The driver had stopped at the foot of the steps to look around. Joshua, thrilled, tugged at the man's jeans. He looked down and grinned. "Hang on a second, Sheriff," he said. He squatted, looked Joshua in the face, took him by the shoulders, and whispered: "Don't tell nobody."

"I won't."

"Sometimes, when I'm driving around the country all by myself—"

"Uh-huh."

"—and I come to some lonely pretty place, where the road runs longside a river or a mountain valley—"

"Yeah?"

"—I stop the truck, and get out, and roll up the tarp, and climb in, and I sit in that big old chair and eat my sandwiches."

Joshua thought this was about the most worthless secret he'd ever heard, but to be polite he smiled.

"It sits pretty good," the driver said, "and from up high like that you can see a long, long way." The driver squeezed Joshua's arms, nodded at him, then stood. "All right, Sheriff, let's go."

As a deputy opened the door, the sheriff asked, "That your assistant?" The driver said something Joshua couldn't hear, and the men both laughed as they went inside. A big pair of khaki-covered legs moved in front of Joshua, and he looked up to see a gum-chewing deputy looking down at him, arms folded.

"You better not go in there, partner," the deputy said. It was the same thing the driver had called him. Grown-ups were all alike. As Joshua turned to go, the deputy said, "Hey, ain't you Jack Woodham's baby boy? Yeah, that's right. How old are you getting to be? You're a cute little feller."

Joshua looked up at the deputy with the most contempt he had ever mustered for an adult, then looked back down and said, to his own great surprise, "Shit," drawing it out just like his daddy did. He turned and walked back through the thicket of legs to a clear patch of lawn, where his friends descended.

"Hey, you were talking to him, weren't you?"

"What'd you talk about?"

"What'd he say?"

"Is he going to let us see the chair?"

"What'd you talk about?"

"I'll tell you later," Joshua said, not breaking stride. He'd make up something good, but he didn't feel like it just now. He was hungry. "I got to go home," he added, and sped up as the others fell away, making aw-shucks sounds. He called back, "Tell Purdie he's missing a few fangs." Behind him they all chattered about this new information. As Joshua passed the Confederate monument, he kicked it.

"Anything I can do?" asked a strange voice, a voice that didn't sound like anyone Joshua had grown up with. Sounded like Orson

Welles on the radio. He looked around. Standing alone on the lawn, with a suitcase beside him, was a tall old man with glasses, wearing a long black coat. Had he been there before? Joshua must have walked right through him, practically. He had his hands folded in front of him like a deacon. "You look upset," the old man said. "Is something wrong?"

At least he didn't talk like he was talking to a baby. "Naw," Joshua said. "The truck just ain't what I expected, is all."

The old man smiled. "Nor I," he said, gazing toward the crowd.

Joshua looked at him more closely and asked, "Ain't you hot in that coat, mister?"

The old man glanced at him, looking just as sad as the driver. "Actually, I'm a bit chilly," he said, looking back toward the crowd. "Aren't you?"

Disgusted, Joshua turned and headed on home. Grown-ups were all crazy. Must be nearbouts 12:30 by now. His mama was gonna whale him for sure. He hoped there was still some crackling bread, and ham hocks, and molasses. Sits in the chair whenever *he* wants to. Shit. "Shit," Joshua said aloud, drawing out the syllables for effect, and repeated it all the way home.

* * *

This man Simpson could put away the food. As the sheriff toyed with a stale cup of coffee and a piece of apple pie—which Doris *would* put a square of cheese on, no matter how many times the sheriff left it hardening amid the crumbs on his plate—his companion ate two cheeseburgers and a pile of French fries, and these were Doris's fries, thick as railroad ties and nearbouts as heavy.

"You want any more tea, hon?" asked Doris, chin in hands, elbows on counter. The sheriff's coffee had long since gone cold from his and Doris's joint neglect, but she hadn't let Simpson's tea get more than an inch below the rim of the glass in the past half-hour. Granted, the cafe wasn't exactly busy in mid-afternoon, but still, this was a bit shameless even for Doris, known countywide as a fast worker.

"No, thank you, ma'am," Simpson said, mopping the last of his ketchup with his last French fry. Won't be no need to wash the damn plate, the sheriff thought. "It all sure was good, though."

"I'm glad you liked it," Doris said. "Like to keep folks coming back, when I can. How long did you say you'd be in town?"

The sheriff cleared his throat, finally earning Doris's languid attention, and said, "Uh, Doris, Deputy Stewart's been out there in the hot a good while." He nodded toward the cafe's front window, through which Stewart's arm was visible, draped across the back of a bench. "How bout seeing if he wants some tea, and maybe a piece of pie."

Doris looked at the sheriff with her mouth pulled sideways, not fooled, but not quite discouraged either. "Whatever you say, Sheriff," she said, straightening up. To Simpson, she said, "You don't let this tough guy here take *all* your time, now." She squeezed his arm as she sashayed away.

"No, ma'am," Simpson said, turning and watching her go. He looked back at the sheriff and grinned. "Lord have mercy."

The sheriff grunted. He glanced at his notebook, at the few details that he had written down, underlined, and circled. He lifted his pencil. Now he would put check marks beside them. "So, five o'clock is gonna work fine, then?"

"Five A.M., yes sir."

"And the basement is best, you think."

"That's right. Nearbouts soundproof, easy to secure, plenty of hookups. And the truck's right there, so unloading will be some easier. The swinging doors are plenty wide. Need some help toting the thing inside, though."

"You'll get it. You want it in tonight, right?"

"Yes, sir, about midnight would be plenty of time. Don't want to do it when everybody's out and about. The prisoner won't see us, will he?"

"His window don't point that way."

"That's good. No need to worry him any more than he already is."

"Agreed," said the sheriff, wondering again what he ought to tell Simpson about Childress's attitude. He knew his caution was ridiculous; the man who pulled the switch didn't need to be protected from the man who sat in the chair. But Simpson had impressed him. The sheriff could tell when someone's calm was feigned, as his own was just now; Jimmy Simpson's was the genuine article. You'd think he was in town for a Masonic meeting. Bizarre though the feeling was, the sheriff wished he could deliver into Simpson's hands someone more worthy of him. Oh, well, maybe next time. "And I'll double-check with the witnesses," the sheriff continued. "Make sure they know what's expected of 'em, and are willing to do it."

"How many?"

"Three's the law in this county," the sheriff said, proudly; it was one of the newer laws. "Plus a doctor, plus me, plus the deputies, just in case. We don't expect no trouble. Most folks think it's gonna be high noon, or midnight, or some such nonsense. But the deputies will be there to give you a hand, if you need it."

"Shouldn't," Simpson said. "You not gonna eat that pie?"

"Take it." The sheriff shoved the saucer across the table.

"Thank you. No, I ain't needed an assistant yet." He smiled, ducked his head, and for a second his scars seemed to vanish, leaving his face almost boyish. "Frankly, Sheriff, just between you and me, it looks impressive, but it ain't that complicated a machine. Why, in ten minutes I could teach you how to work it yourself."

The sheriff laughed, maybe too loudly. "I believe I'll leave it to you, thank you."

"Fair enough," Simpson said, still grinning. "I guess I'll talk myself out of a job one of these days. But I ain't complaining. I'm glad for the work, and I know there's a lot of others who'd be glad for it, too."

The sheriff bore down hard as he made one more check. "If we're lucky it'll all be over, and the truck loaded again, by the time the town gets stirring good."

"Taking down's always easier than setting up," Simpson said. "Hard work afterward's on your end."

"Tell me about it," the sheriff said. As Simpson made appreciative pie noises, the sheriff re-read his list:

ambulance (remind Mr. Craddock)
funeral home (bring $$$)
autopsy forms (ask Hooper)
FAMILY???
med-school truck 10 A.M.
bread milk shaving cream Goody's

"The cash gonna be any problem?" Simpson asked.

"No, sir," the sheriff said. "I'll have it for you when the job's done."

"*Out*-standing," Simpson said. "Cash, you know, is just easier, on the road and all."

"I understand."

"From here they got me going to Corinth and then way the hell down in Pascagoula, for God's sake. That's some planning, let me tell you. That's some coordination. What sort of roads they think we got in Mississippi?"

The sheriff watched Doris chatting up Deputy Stewart outside. She was doing that thing where she pretended her back hurt, so that she kept stretching backward, hands on hips, pelvis stuck out in the deputy's face, nearly. Her back ought to hurt. Tapping the table with the pencil, the sheriff tried to make his voice as flat as possible, rid it of any hint of insinuation. "You need an advance? For tonight, I mean."

"Naw," Simpson said, dropping shiny fork onto shiny saucer with a clatter and reaching for the toothpick shaker. On his ring finger was a gold band with a little empty rectangle inscribed on it. "Too busy. Got to get the paperwork ready, check the equipment, get it unloaded, get it set up, check the connections. Might have a couple hours' sleep, maybe, but then got to be up again by four, checking everything again."

"Thought you said it wasn't complicated."

"It ain't, really," Simpson said, with a shrug. "But you don't want it to go wrong, all the same."

The sheriff laid down his pencil, sat back with a sigh, flashed the palms of his hands before slapping the table, and asked, "What else can I do for you?"

"Well, Sheriff, I'm curious." Simpson rested one foot on the seat and leaned back into the corner. "I'd appreciate your telling me a few things about him, if you don't mind."

"Bout who?"

"My client." Simpson laughed. "Well, I guess that ain't the right word, is it? *You're* my client, you and the county. But that's the word we—the word I use in my head. The prisoner, I mean."

"Oh, him." The sheriff drummed the tabletop. "Well, he's a bad one. That's all I know to say. Didn't you get a report?"

Simpson pulled from his shirt pocket a dirty, ragged paper square. It looked folded and unfolded many times. "All I got was the usual notice from down at Parchman." He squinted at the typescript as he read aloud. "'Dear Sir: This is to inform you that one execution is scheduled for Friday night or Saturday morning, June twenty-third or twenty-fourth, nineteen hundred and forty-one, at Andalusia, Mississippi, under the supervision of Sheriff Edwin Davis, exact time to be arranged by you and the sheriff, in the case of the murderer William Childress, and we shall expect you and the mobile equipment to be present no later than noon of the previous day. Kindly acknowledge by wire the receipt of this notice. Very truly yours,' yaddy yaddy." Folding the paper again, Simpson squinted at the sheriff. "The state don't figure I need to know any more than that, but I get curious. I figure I ought to know the facts of the case, if I'm gonna be there for the end of it."

The sheriff nodded. "Makes sense to me. Well, like I say, he's a bad one. Strange thing is, he didn't use to be. Long as I've known him, he was the humblest colored man you ever saw. Butter wouldn't melt in his mouth. It was yes sir and yes ma'am and morning and evening to you and head bowed and stepping off the sidewalk and tipping his hat when even the white younguns came by." He laughed, suddenly remembering. "Hell, I used to hire him now and again to clear off brush in my back field, things like that. Never no trouble to anybody."

"No run-ins with the law?"

"Oh, hell yes, I mean he was a colored man after all, no wife and no kids to rein him in, neither. Some drinking and some gambling and a few fights, but nothing much. Nothing to get all hepped up about." Warming to his story, and to the drama of a new audience, the sheriff leaned across the table, lowered his voice. "Then one of his poker buddies, some of that white trash down around Millville way, got to messing around with some yaller woman that Childress was messing with too, and when Childress found out, why he went over to Mr. George's place, where the coloreds get their hair cut, and walked in and snatched up a razor and walked out without a howdy or a by-your-leave or a go-to-hell neither, and by the time we caught up to him he'd done laid that old boy open like a hog, and was sitting on the porch waiting on the yaller woman to come home, so he could do the same for her. He was looking up at the clouds, lounging against the post all limp and dreamy-like, and didn't give us no fight at all. Just shuffled along with us to the patrol car, and that boy's blood running down off his overalls into the dust the whole way." He realized he had a half-smile on his face, as if he had told a punchline he was proud of. He cleared his throat, tried to look somber, and felt ashamed.

Without expression, Simpson asked: "Is that what bothers you so about him? What he done?"

So it was that obvious. The sheriff sighed and relaxed his shoulders. In the fingers of one hand he had been rolling a tiny torn-off bit of paper napkin; he tossed it onto the tablecloth. "Oh, hell no," he said. "I mean, it was bad, but no different from a dozen other bad things I've seen. No, what's bad is what happened to him after."

"After the killing."

"After the trial," the sheriff said. "I mean, after the verdict. He was quiet and peaceful all the way through. Wouldn't say a word. But then, when he found out it was . . . what it was, well, sir, Willie Childress stood up in that courtroom and began telling the judge and all the rest of us exactly what he thought, and kept on doing it while we were dragging him away, and such language you never heard, Lord have mercy. Every time he opens his mouth, something awful falls out. The poor old colored woman who does for us at the jail, she went running off in tears the other day. I can't hardly stand to look at the man anymore."

Now it was Simpson's turn to lean forward. "What sorts of things does he say?"

"Uh-uh. I ain't gonna repeat them. I'm a Christian man. You'll find out soon enough, I'm afraid."

Simpson nodded, then sipped at his tea. The sip led to a second sip, then to a long, sustained gulp. Then he held up the glass, tipped it from side to side, and watched the ice clink. "I don't know, Sheriff," he said. "I ain't had this job long, but I ain't seen a mean one yet that stayed mean the whole way. You know? Seeing what's there for them, well, it pretty much knocks all the mean slam out."

"I hope you're right," the sheriff said. He was suddenly bone-tired, and wished he had some fresh coffee. "Not just for his sake, for everybody's. It just ain't right, the way he's acting. Don't he know where he is? Don't he know what's gonna happen to him? I never heard of such."

Simpson rested the damp tea glass against his cheek. "Listen, Sheriff. I'm gonna ask you something you may think is strange."

The sheriff shrugged. "Well, you got a strange job—no offense. I'm listening."

"I'd like to meet him. This afternoon, if it's possible."

"What for?"

"It's hard to explain." Simpson set his glass down, picked it up, set it down. He looked at the back wall over the sheriff's head, where, the sheriff knew, a calendar cowgirl in a short skirt perched on a split-rail fence, blowing imaginary smoke from the barrel of her gun. Simpson didn't seem to register the calendar. "Think about my position, Sheriff. This is your town. You know everybody that comes through your jail. You may not like them, but you know them. Even the bad ones, even the ones you send to their reward, it's like . . . well, it's sorta like a community thing, a family thing." He squinted at the sheriff again. "Makes it feel more right, somehow. You follow me?"

"I reckon."

"Well, now here I come, driving my rig into town, not knowing nobody or nothing, and I'm the one supposed to be doing the honors on a complete stranger. Now, I know the state decided this is the best way to handle executions, and all, since no one wanted to do hangings any more, and no one could agree on a permanent site for the chair—"

The sheriff held up a finger. "*And* since we sheriffs wanted to keep control over executions in our own counties. Don't forget that."

"I understand that, yes sir—but since we're doing it this way, well, one thing that makes me feel more right about it, is if I get to meet with the client, I mean the prisoner, introduce myself, shake his hand, tell him I'll be doing the best job I know how, ask him if there's anything I can do for him. Let him know I'm there to help him, not to hurt him. You see?"

"What you're there for," the sheriff finally said, "is to kill him."

"Well, yes, but not in a mean way. I mean, I like to keep it all as open and above-board as possible. Not anything mysterious or sinister or creepy. Does that make any sense at all?"

The sheriff rubbed a hand across his face. "Yeah, I reckon it does. I'll be frank with you, Mr. Simpson. Executions in this county—well, they ain't always been on the up-and-up like that, if you get my drift."

"I understand."

"It wasn't none of my doing, but my predecessor as sheriff, God rest his soul, well, he wan't any too concerned about, you know, legal niceties, or what they thought up in Jackson, or down in Niggertown."

"I know what you mean. That's a bad situation."

"Yes, it is. But since I took over—and the council is with me on this, y'understand, ever last one of 'em, and the preachers too—I've been doing a lot of things different, and they're going to stay different. So what you say about being above-board with all your doins, well, that sets well with me. I'm proud to hear you say it."

"I'm glad," Simpson said.

"In fact, I guess I'll go ahead and tell you what I wasn't even going to mention before, since Childress is being so assy and all. But he's been wanting to meet you, too."

Simpson grinned, an unexpected act that exposed the gaps in his teeth. "Is that a fact?"

"Been asking after you for two solid weeks, and telling us every day that he's got something to say to you when you roll in. Sounds like y'all maybe got something to talk about."

"I think so. You reckon this afternoon will be all right?"

"How about three o'clock," the sheriff said. He reached for his hat. "No, three-thirty. I got umpteen things to do, and I want to take you up there myself. I hope you'll excuse me for a while."

"Sure thing, Sheriff. I know you want it to go off without a hitch."

"Damn straight I do," the sheriff said, standing up and extending his hand. "Can I count on you, Mr. Simpson?"

"You can, Sheriff," Simpson said. They shook, and Simpson made as if to slide out of the booth.

"No, no, keep your seat. Stay in here where it's cool. I'll leave Deputy Stewart out there at the door, case anybody bothers you, but I don't expect it. You may have to sign a few autographs, I guess." He caught the triumphant glance of Doris, who leaned, arms folded, against the cash register. "Why don't you have you some more tea, or something else sweet? It's on the county. Deputy Stewart will walk you over to Miss Pearce's if you want, or back to the jail. I'll see you at three-thirty."

"I appreciate it, Sheriff. I'll see you later."

"All right, then. Doris, I'll see you."

"See you, Sheriff."

As he passed her, she whispered, "Your deputy said he didn't want none of my pie."

"He's a strong man," the sheriff said, and winked.

* * *

Doris already had the tea pitcher in hand, pleased finally to get a chance to work on her back-booth cowboy alone. The pitcher was dripping, beaded with sweat; she blotted it with her hand as she walked, then used her wet finger to draw a curl or two down across her forehead. She glanced at herself in the long mirror: yes, Joan Crawford, exactly, and like Joan Crawford not aging a bit. As she approached, her grin faltered, her step slowed. Shit on a griddle, she thought, Gary Cooper's got him a regular fan club. The tall old man approaching the cowboy's booth had been, for the past half-hour, sitting on a stool beside the cash register, sucking on a chocolate shake, and re-reading the menu as if he had never seen one before. How did he get back there so quick? She'd missed his getting up entirely. Well, he wouldn't be talking to the cowboy for long. She'd been around, Doris had, she'd kept her eyes open when she worked the bus-station lunch counter in Meridian, and she thought, forget it, Pops, he don't go that way, a gal can tell. But at that moment, the cowboy glanced up, saw the old man looming over him, and jumped as if he had been sitting in the hot seat himself.

"Mr. Ellis!" the cowboy said.

"Hello, Jimmy," Pops replied. "May I join you?"

Doris stopped in her tracks. Looking pretty damned satisfied with himself, Pops settled into the booth, his black coat bunching up around his shoulders, like a buzzard settling on dinner by the side of the road. The cowboy jerked his head around, looked over the whole cafe, then turned back to the old buzzard and started some fast damn whispering. His eyes hadn't lighted on Doris even for a half-second, any more than if she had been one of the soda machines. She whirled and stomped back toward the cash register, toward the old man's milkshake glass, empty but for a brown froth and a crimpled straw. Hell with *him,* Doris resolved. Ain't no lack of *real* men in this town. Let the faggots get their own damn tea.

* * *

As he walked alongside Mr. Ellis down Andalusia's main street, Jimmy was conscious of all his failings. The fresh cigarette burn on his wrinkled shirt front. The laborer's pants of thick, faded denim. The scars and the lumps and the schooling he'd missed. His tongue kept finding the skips in his teeth. He could shoot air through those holes as loud as a police whistle, and often he was proud of that, but not today. Mr. Ellis did not walk so much as glide, his hands clasped behind his back, his head thrust forward like the prow of a ship. And beside him was poor old Jimmy, rolling bowlegged down the street like Popeye the Goddamn Sailor Man.

"I can't tell you, Jimmy, how pleased I am finally to make your acquaintance."

"Pleasure's mutual, Mr. Ellis. I've heard a lot about you."

"And I you, Jimmy."

Passers-by stared. The children gave them a wide berth; the men occasionally nodded the silent, unsmiling Southern acknowledgment of mutual manhood, a nod without joy or welcome; the women didn't do that much. Maybe it was just that they were strangers, or that the older man's attire was so out of season, but Jimmy didn't think so.

He tried to keep his mind on the conversation. Mr. Ellis was, after all, his boss—sort of—and Jimmy felt the need to make a good impression. He stepped onto a crumbling edge of the sidewalk, and nearly fell. Swaying, he said:

"I knew I'd meet up with you sometime, and I was looking forward to it. But I don't mind telling you I never thought it would be in Mississippi. I figured I'd see you at one of the meetings, maybe New York or Chicago. Somewhere nearer Canada."

Mr. Ellis tipped his hat to a group of schoolgirls, who huddled closer together, notebooks clutched to their chests. "The meetings have become rather few and far between. I blame the telephone. Certainly guild members don't need each other any less. There will always be technical problems, pay disputes. A sympathetic ear is never out of fashion. But increasingly our business is conducted over the electric lines. Oh, I read all the reports, and I am assured that all the guild's needs are satisfied. But what about isolation? What about the loneliness of the job? How can a telephone alleviate that?"

"Oh, I haven't felt particularly lonely, Mr. Ellis. I'm doing just fine, myself."

"Good. Good." Mr. Ellis stopped to regard a Model T that had stalled in the middle of the street. Wagons and panel trucks drove around it, and a young woman with Veronica Lake hair perched on the hood, skirt way up past her knees, and waved to the drivers as they passed. Two farmers in overalls were hitching a mule team to the front of the automobile, making slow work of it and watching the girl half the time, and a man in a straw boater and a seersucker suit watched them in silence, jaw set, his furious glances directed equally at the girl, the car, the mules, the farmers, the bright red soupy ankle-deep mud, and the passers-by, including Jimmy.

"Find something else to look at, buddy," he called across the street. This diverted the farmers' attention again. They stood in the wet clay and stared, chains dangling from their hands, as Jimmy and Mr. Ellis walked on.

"She'll find her another ride soon enough, I reckon," Jimmy said.

"More machines," Mr. Ellis said. "Telephones. Motorcars. I am no lover of machines. No machine can do the work of a man, nor should any man entrust his work to a machine."

"No, sir," said Jimmy, who didn't like the turn this was taking.

"Not *entirely*, at any rate," Mr. Ellis added with a smile.

"No, *sir*," Jimmy said again. It seemed safest.

"I prefer to do guild business in person, when I can. And the most important guild business I do is meeting the new men. Making each one feel welcome and needed and cared for. It's a bit of travel, but I like travel; it broadens. As you should know better than any of us, Jimmy."

Jimmy laughed. "If travel makes a man broader, Mr. Ellis, I reckon I'll be as broad as any man in the guild, by time I retire. I'll be as broad as . . ." He faltered, then blurted: "As a barn."

"I daresay," Mr. Ellis said, rubbing his cheek. Not for the first time, Jimmy noticed the gold ring on Mr. Ellis's left hand.

Jimmy had been fidgeting with his own ring all afternoon, ever since Mr. Ellis slid into the booth. Some days Jimmy remembered to wear the ring, other days he didn't, or just decided not to. He always had avoided jewelry, even in his medicine-show days, when all his colleagues advised him that rings, pendants, necklaces, even hoop earrings, for God's sake, lent credibility to a good hypnotist act. Jimmy had left his days as Dr. Yogi (or Dr. Zogg, or Professor Stingaree) far behind, he hoped, and had not worn jewelry since, until he joined the payroll of the state of Mississippi. With the job came the guild, and with the guild came many things, including the ring that Jimmy was very glad he happened to be wearing today.

Mr. Ellis's finger was swollen on either side of his ring, as if he never took it off. Mr. Ellis reached up with his ring hand and patted Jimmy on the shoulder, startling him.

"You're a rather difficult man to catch up with," Mr. Ellis said. "I wrote to announce my visit, but I take it you didn't get the letter. I'm not sure the guild has your current address?"

"Current as it gets, Mr. Ellis. I reckon I have been living in the truck, pretty much, the last few months. Been a busy time. Twice as many jobs as they predicted when they hired me." Jimmy waited for a response, got none, and continued. "I ain't complaining, mind you, I can use the money and the experience, but I sometimes wonder if the counties ain't going out of their way to drum up business, just to see what the truck looks like."

"How many jobs have you had?"

"Nine, since I started, back in October. But one of them was a double-header."

"Beg pardon?"

"Two the same morning."

"I see."

A knot of people stood around a street-corner preacher—a very short one, evidently; his listeners hid him as completely as if they had been a wall. The preacher's voice, thin and piping, carried down the block: "When all this begins to happen, my brothers and sisters, you may be sure that the Kingdom of God is nigh. Oh, it's nigh, all right, my friends, it's nigh and near and bearing down hard!"

"Twins," Jimmy continued. "How anyone could get that mean at fifteen, I don't know." Jimmy himself had run away from home at fifteen to join the Guard, but there had been no meanness in it. When his mama sent the marshals, he hadn't even fought them. He sighed. "But it ain't my job to know, is it, Mr. Ellis?"

"Certainly not."

"So it's really ten all told, but half of 'em's been this summer, and summer ain't over yet. They keep me jumping, I tell you."

"Your reputation seems to be spreading," Mr. Ellis said. A group of old men on a bench in front of a barbershop abruptly hushed to stare, all except one white-mustached man with a hearing aid plugged into one ear, its cord coiling down his shirt front. He kept talking, loudly: "Well, that's the very man, right there! Don't shush me! If he can hear me from away over there, he's in the wrong line of work, he oughtta be in the Secret Service." As Jimmy and Mr. Ellis passed, all the old men resumed talking at once, this time with a new note of excitement, and the loud one was submerged once again in the general hubbub. "In fact, I'd say you're something of a celebrity," Mr. Ellis said. "Even a personal bodyguard. I am impressed."

"A bodyguard?" Jimmy looked around. Deputy Stewart was about a half-block behind, hands on hips, elbows out to hog the sidewalk, holsters bouncing against his thighs. Jimmy had told him, back at the cafe, just to go on about his business, he'd see him at the courthouse. He must have been following them all this while. Catching Jimmy's eye, the deputy nodded, smiled. "Oh," Jimmy said. "That's a little embarrassing, frankly." Jimmy dropped his voice to a murmur, even though the deputy was yards away along a busy street. "This sheriff down here is jumpier than a box of cats."

"Indeed?" Mr. Ellis turned and waved at the deputy, who began to wave back, then caught himself and nodded instead.

Jimmy laughed. "I'm pleased you're here, Mr. Ellis."

"Pleased to be here, Jimmy."

"That sheriff. I tell you. You should have seen him, making little notes with his pencil. He's afraid I'm gonna mess up all his fine plans. Hell, he'd do this whole thing without me, if he could."

"But he can't," Mr. Ellis said, with a note of satisfaction.

"No, sir."

Several women peered at them from the window of a clothing store, their faces tense amid the lace and crinoline.

"Do you know, Jimmy, there were members of the guild who wanted to call a meeting just this past year?"

"Is that right?"

"Yes. A matter came up that caused some of the members great concern. They felt the guild should take a public stand—and a public stand is a very rare thing for the guild, a very rare thing indeed."

"Yes, sir."

"But we on the board decided that the wiser course of action would be to monitor the situation. Do you know why I tell you about this?"

"No, sir, I don't."

"The issue that so concerned the guild, Jimmy, was you."

Jimmy stopped dead, while Mr. Ellis walked on. "Me!"

The older man looked around, smiled. "I'm sorry. I misspoke. The concern was not with you, specifically. Your name was not even known to us at the time." He waited for Jimmy to catch up. "No, Jimmy, the guild's concern was with your job."

"I don't understand."

"The guild's officers subscribe to an excellent clipping service. It is the one your Mr. Mencken uses. When the Mississippi legislature debated the purchasing of a mobile electric chair, and the hiring of a traveling executioner to maintain and operate it, we followed the accounts with the greatest interest. The public debate was paralleled by a private one, among the members of the guild. Not about the chair per se; that debate was settled more than forty years ago. But a *mobile* chair, being driven from town to town, well. There were those who considered your job a giant step backward, a return to the days of executions as public spectacles. Whoever took the job would be in a spotlight that no guild member had suffered in fifty years, and would find himself, wittingly or not, made a symbol, a spokesman for our entire unique profession. Do you understand our concerns, Jimmy?"

"Yes, sir, I suppose I do. But you said y'all decided not to get involved."

They had reached the northwest corner of the courthouse square. Twenty or more townspeople, mostly older men but a few children as well, sauntered around the tarpaulin-draped truck, chatting with the two deputies on guard. One deputy sat on the front bumper, fanned himself with his hat. The courthouse lawn was dotted with women who sat on the grass, tending toddlers and infants. Several young men in rolled-up shirtsleeves lounged against the Confederate monument, smoking. Jimmy watched Mr. Ellis take all this in. After a few moments, the older man sighed.

"Better to risk one celebrity, the board reasoned, than to drag the entire guild into the newspapers." He cast Jimmy a sorrowful glance. "The newspapers have seldom been respectful of our membership."

Jimmy nodded. That was true enough. At least his mama hadn't seen the articles in the Jackson paper, and the one in the *American Mercury,* the one that said Jimmy had to be "helped from one barroom to another" after a job. Shit. Smartass Yankee reporter hadn't even picked up the tab.

"When my predecessor, God rest him, died by his own hand," Mr. Ellis continued, "the newspapers in Canada treated the affair shamefully, Jimmy. Shamefully."

Jimmy had heard something about this. "He cut his own throat, didn't he?"

Mr. Ellis nodded, tight-lipped. It was less a nod than a sudden jerk of the head. "In life, Mr. Ellis was such a private man, yet in death his entire biography, his every foible and human fault, was placed on public exhibit, scrutinized as one would scrutinize the wrinkles of a madman's brain. After decades of devoted public service, this was his reward. Ah, well." Mr. Ellis gazed at the truck.

"Mr. Ellis?" Jimmy asked, confused.

"Eh?"

"You called him Mr. Ellis," Jimmy said, gently.

"Oh. Yes," he said, looking at Jimmy, blinking his way back to the present, and smiling. "The name goes with the job. Less a name than, well, a sort of title. His predecessor was Mr. Ellis before him. And so on and so forth. It is the custom in Canada, you see."

"I see," Jimmy repeated, though he wasn't sure he did. He tried to imagine the man with his job fifty years down the road, still answering to the name Jimmy Simpson. He couldn't see it. He could see the truck, though. Cheap-ass state would keep the same truck that long, at least.

"Ah, well. History. Where was I? Your case, of course. The board voted for caution, for public silence, and for continued monitoring of the situation."

From the courthouse came a *bang*. When everyone looked up, the sheriff was already past the steps and striding down the walk, the brass front door slowly swinging to behind him. His face was grim. The townsmen began to back away from the truck. The deputy on the bumper stood up quick and jammed his hat back on.

"Y'all get away from that truck," the sheriff barked. "No, not you two, for God's sake. Go on, now, people."

Jimmy turned back to the older man and quietly asked: "And how did you vote, Mr. Ellis?"

Mr. Ellis's silence seemed longer than it was. Jimmy heard the sheriff and the deputies scolding the younguns: "Y'all stop messing with that tarp, now. They ain't nothing to see." When Mr. Ellis finally looked around, shoulders back, somehow taller than he had been, his thick lenses caught the sun so that his eyes were hidden.

"I cast the deciding vote, Jimmy. In the past thirty-five years, I have hanged three hundred and eighty-seven people, ranging in age from twelve to seventy-three, twenty-two of them women. More than twice as many as Mr. Ellis before me. I have hanged people in British Columbia and in Newfoundland, in log cabins and stone fortresses, on permanent scaffolds and on planks laid across railroad trestles. I have heard last words in English, French, Acadian, Inuit, and a dozen other languages and dialects, including some known only to God. Three hundred and eighty-seven, Jimmy. Within the guild, I cast many deciding votes."

The sheriff was upon them, red-faced and scowling at Mr. Ellis. "Do I know you, sir?" he asked. As he spoke, Deputy Stewart trotted up to the group; he replied to the sheriff's glance with a shrug.

Jimmy cleared his throat. "Sheriff Davis, this is Mr. Ellis. Mr. Ellis, Sheriff Davis. Mr. Ellis is a, well, he's a—" Everyone looked at Jimmy. "A colleague of mine. From Canada."

"Colleague, eh? I didn't think you needed an assistant."

"Oh, no, it ain't like that. He's here to—"

"Here simply to visit my young friend Jimmy, and to learn firsthand how things are done in other parts of the world."

The sheriff looked at him without encouragement.

"Mr. Ellis would like to join us this afternoon. I told him that was OK with me—if it's OK with you, of course."

"My interest, Sheriff, is purely a professional one, and you may rely upon my rectitude and my decorum."

"Lord God," the sheriff said. "Mr. Ellis, I take it you have some experience in these matters."

"Oh, yes," Mr. Ellis said, managing to sound both proud and regretful.

The sheriff sucked at his back teeth. "Well, I can use all the experience I can get. All right, Mr. Ellis, you can go on up with us, and welcome."

"I thank you, sir."

"Assuming you still want to meet with the prisoner, Mr. Simpson."

"Sure thing, Sheriff."

"All right, then. Stewart, you keep to the square, and don't miss anything."

"I won't, Sheriff."

"And don't waste time talking to no gals."

"I won't, Sheriff," Stewart said, less happily.

"Follow me, gentlemen." The sheriff headed for the courthouse door. As they fell in behind, the sheriff asked, without looking around, "You get enough to eat awhile ago, Mr. Simpson?"

"I'm full as a tick, Sheriff."

"That's good. We *will* feed you in this town, if we can't do nothing else." He held the door open. The lobby was marginally cooler than the outdoors, and much darker, with strange acoustics; their shoes clattered on the marble floor like hooves. "Mrs. Pearce will do you up right, you'll see. Where you staying, Mr. Ellis?"

Mr. Ellis only stared at him, and Jimmy, feeling uncomfortably like the man's translator, scratched the side of his face and murmured, "Sheriff, uh, Mr. Ellis don't like people to know where he stays."

"I see," the sheriff said, regarding Mr. Ellis anew. The old man's dark clothes practically melted into the shadows, leaving his pale, sagging face looking alone and abandoned. "Well, I'm proud to meet a private man. Here's the stairs. They're right steep, I'm afraid, Mr. Ellis. We're due to have an Otis put in next fiscal year."

Mr. Ellis smiled in reply and gestured grandly. "After you, gentlemen."

On the way up, the sheriff stooped to snatch a Nabs wrapper from the floor of the landing. As he climbed he folded the crinkling paper into a tiny square. "Look at this mess," he muttered. "Old Hugh ain't been in to clean today, I don't guess. Can't say as I blame him." Hearing no footsteps behind, Jimmy glanced around, but there was Mr. Ellis's pale face bobbing up the darkened stairwell. It smiled at Jimmy, and winked.

* * *

The preceding Mr. Ellis turned to his apprentice, on the young man's first night of work, and said to him:

"Keep your face expressionless, no matter what happens. Speak only when you have to. Keep your eyes open, so that you don't miss anything important. Do everything as quickly and efficiently as possible. And don't think about it. Not beforehand, and not while it's happening, and not after. Our job is necessary, son, but it can't stand too much thinking."

Thinking nothing, missing nothing, Mr. Ellis walked down the second-floor corridor that was the only cell block in Andalusia County, Mississippi. All his senses were engaged; these men would be surprised to know how many. Jimmy, the sheriff, and the deputy all had their backs to him. Before they reached the dead end, Mr. Ellis slid from his overcoat pocket a cherry jawbreaker and popped it into his mouth. It bloomed on his tongue as he looked through the bars at the diminutive, sour-faced Negro within. *Don't give me lip you little bastard Help me with this wagon boy Ferris is more a man than you'll ever be.* A few seconds' concentration, and Childress's memories were gone, rebuffed. Or, perhaps, suppressed; the effect was the same. The tang in Mr. Ellis's mouth helped him block, for some reason. He'd figured that out himself. The previous Mr. Ellis had smoked. Jimmy would resort to his own device, eventually.

These particular jawbreakers were hard to find in Canada. He'd have to stock up.

"Here's the man you been wanting to see, Childress."

Jimmy stuck his arm through the bars and offered his hand. "Brother, my name is Jimmy Simpson. I'm the man who'll be in charge tomorrow."

Childress looked wary, but after a few seconds he shook Jimmy's hand.

"Brother, they tell me you had the choice of the rope or the chair, and you picked the chair. Is that right?"

After another pause, Childress nodded. Wrong, Mr. Ellis thought.

"Well, I appreciate that, Brother, I surely do. Let me tell you that you made the right choice, because I'm a professional and I know what I'm doing. I'm going to do a nice clean job, as quick and trouble-free as any man could do. You don't have to worry about nothing on my end. No mistakes, no delays. And I swear to God, Brother, you won't feel a thing. So you can stop worrying about my end of it, Brother, and focus on what's important, on Jesus and His mercy and on the better place you'll be in by this time tomorrow. I guess that's all I got to say, Brother, except to repeat that you're in good hands with me. I'm gonna give you the most trouble-free, easeful passing a man could ask for. You've put your confidence in me, and I appreciate it. I'm here to tell you I ain't gonna let you down."

After a long pause, Childress ticked his eyes over toward the sheriff.

"You're kidding," Childress said.

"No, sir," Jimmy said. "No jokes here. I'm telling you straight up, the way I tell all the men I work with."

Childress's eyes had ticked back to Jimmy when he started speaking. Now, after a beat, they ticked over to Mr. Ellis. "Who you, then?" he asked. "The undertaker?"

"Not at all," Mr. Ellis said, removing his hat. Like so many sweet-toothed people, he could talk fluently with all manner of candy in his mouth. "My name is Mr. Ellis. I will be assisting Mr. Simpson. And you may expect the highest degree of professionalism from me as well."

Childress stopped looking at anybody. His eyes were focused inward. The corners of his mouth twitched, held, and the beginnings of a smile crept across his face. As the grin widened, Jimmy turned to the sheriff and whispered: "A kind word does wonders, as my mama says. Look at that. Does my heart good, it does." Now Childress was laughing faintly, mostly in the form of air sliding through his teeth, *sss sss sss*. "I'm always pleased to be able to calm some poor soul's last hours," Jimmy said, sounding unsure. Childress laughed louder and louder. His shoulders shook, he bobbed his head, he gripped his knees. His eyes were wide.

"Ha ha ha HAAAAA," Childress wheezed. He was out of breath. "Oh, Lord. Oh, Lord have mercy, I can't stop laughing. Ha ha ha! Oh, you poor old cracker. You poor old stupid motherfucker."

"Shut up, Childress," the sheriff said, raking his club across the bars.

"Poor old cut-up snaggle-tooth bowlegged peckerwood. Oh, Lord, that's funny."

"What you mean, funny?"

"Don't listen to him, Mr. Simpson. Let's go."

"No, I want to know. What's so funny? What's so funny about what I said?"

Childress shut off the laughter like water from a new tap. "I'll tell you what's funny, you dumbass cracker shit. I'll tell you what I been wanting to tell you all these weeks. The sheriff here ain't got dick big enough to drag me off in the woods and cut me up and throw me on the pile with the other niggers—"

"Be quiet!" the sheriff roared, flailing on the bars with his club.

"—so he goes and hires a poor old dumbass white boy to do his lynching for him. And the dumbass don't even know it!"

Mr. Ellis stood very still. His predecessor's face had betrayed nothing, right up until the end. He was a good model, and Mr. Ellis was a worthy successor.

"*I'll* shut his face," the deputy snarled, jamming the key into the lock. The sheriff shoved him in the chest so hard he fell back across the narrow corridor, arms flailing. "Shit!" he cried, gasping. The sheriff pointed his club at the deputy's mouth.

"Stay over there," he said.

"Where's your white hood and white robe, white boy?" Childress asked. "In the truck with your bucket of nigger balls?"

When the supervisor is incapacitated, the apprentice must act. Mr. Ellis was surprised at how naturally he fell back into the subordinate role. He tugged Jimmy's sleeve. "No more to be done here, Jimmy. Please. *Please,* Jimmy."

Jimmy stared at Childress. "You talking to the wrong man," he whispered.

"I'm talking to the man what's come to kill me. You see anyone else here that wants to do it?"

"But I don't—" Mr. Ellis grabbed Jimmy's arm and yanked so hard that Jimmy stumbled sideways. The sheriff took Jimmy's other arm, and the two big men hustled him down the corridor.

"Wait," Jimmy said. "Wait, please, fellas, I want to talk to him. I want to explain to him."

"Hooper, you better be right behind us!" the sheriff yelled.

"You bet I am," the deputy muttered.

The four men burst into the sheriff's office, where two other deputies were just coming in from the stairs, demanding to know what the commotion was.

"Nat, Archie, get that corridor door locked and keep it locked. The next person gets in to see Childress is me taking him downstairs in the morning. You understand? I'm tired of this shit."

"Who'd come visit Childress anyway?" one of the deputies asked, slamming and locking the door to the cells. "Some nigger preacher, maybe?"

"I don't care if Jesus comes a-knocking," the sheriff said, slumping back onto his desk, hairs plastered to his forehead. Papers cascaded onto the floor. "Mr. Simpson, you all right?"

Jimmy nodded. He had fallen back onto a swaybacked sofa, hands pressed against his forehead, eyes screwed shut.

"Mr. Ellis," the sheriff said, "I thank you for your help in there."

Mr. Ellis nodded. His chest hurt. He had swallowed his jawbreaker.

The sheriff turned to the deputy he had punched, who stood in the corner, arms crossed, glaring. "Hooper, I'm sorry."

The deputy pursed his lips. "No problem, sir. I think I'll take me a walk." He slammed through the door. His footsteps tumbled downstairs.

"How many more hours, Lord?" the sheriff said. He hunched himself backward to sit on the desk, dislodging more papers and a coffee can of pencils that he caught at and missed. As deputies dived for the rolling pencils, the sheriff rested his feet on a swivel chair. "If it weren't for those crowds out there I swear I think I'd do it this afternoon and be done."

Jimmy spoke, sounding shaken but steady, like a man who no longer has the urge to cry. "Ain't got set up yet." He opened his eyes, braced himself on the sofa with his hands, leaned forward and sighed. "Takes time, Sheriff. Can't be rushed."

"The chair," the sheriff repeated. "Oh, the chair. Sure, sure."

He looked at Mr. Ellis, whose callused fingers itched. The sheriff had a pleading look, a look Mr. Ellis had seen before. Mr. Ellis would not think about that today. Instead he smiled, patted Jimmy on the shoulder. What a debacle. "No harm done," he said.

"Who's Ferris?" Jimmy asked.

Mr. Ellis froze.

The sheriff frowned. "Ferris? That's the man Childress killed. Buddy Ferris. Why? Who said anything about Ferris?"

"Didn't someone—" Jimmy stopped, shook his head. "Oh, never mind."

So Jimmy was starting early. "Never mind, indeed," Mr. Ellis said, quickly. "Random invective, nothing more." He patted Jimmy's shoulder again. Jimmy was young, strong. He would adjust. "Sticks and stones," Mr. Ellis said. He'd have to. A pencil had rolled to a stop against Mr. Ellis's foot. The eraser was missing, and someone had gnawed off the paint.

* * *

At first glance, as four groaning deputies wrestled it off the back of the truck at midnight, the chair seemed enormous, the throne of a giant-king. Arms, legs, and back were thick oaken blocks, more suited for ceiling beams than furniture. Later, in the floodlighted courthouse basement, Mr. Ellis realized the chair's seat was surprisingly narrow. The average department-store Father Christmas would find it a tight fit.

The chair's platform was carried in separately, by a single little bowlegged deputy who shrugged off assistance, obviously glad to have nothing to do with the chair. The platform, a square five feet to a side, was made of sawmill-yellow two-by-fours covered by a stapled-down rubber mat ribbed like the mat inside a bathtub.

As the deputies maneuvered the chair, the ceiling lights played inside the metal headpiece, a shallow bowl cocked back on a coiled metal stand that reared above the entire contraption like a cobra. After bolting the chair down, Jimmy's next move was to untangle and plug in the fat black electrical cords that fed the machine. One snaked from the helmet to the portable generator, which Jimmy had insisted on carrying in himself. ("That chair ain't gone break even if you drop it, but this generator, why it'll go queer on you if you look at it hard.") A second cord connected the helmet to the base of the chair; a third led from the left leg of the chair to the wall socket. Finding this socket caused a few bad moments, until someone thought to look behind the Christmas decorations. Fortunately, only the baby Jesus box had to be shoved out of the way. Roaches scattered. Jimmy blew dust from the socket before shoving in the plug.

The deputies who had carried the chair were trying not to breathe too visibly. "Why do you need the wall socket at all?" asked the slowest to recover, red-faced, hands on knees. "I mean, you got the generator."

"The socket ain't for current going *in,*" Jimmy said. "The socket's for current going *out*. It's gotta go somewhere. Less'n you want it," he added, yanking the plug from the wall and holding it out to the deputy with a grin.

They all laughed.

Mr. Ellis sensed the edge beneath the jape. All these bystanders, their jobs done, were making Jimmy nervous.

He cleared his throat—startling a couple of men who apparently had forgotten his presence—and said: "Mr. Simpson, is there any further assistance these gentlemen can render at this time?"

"I don't reckon so, Mr. Ellis," Jimmy said. "But I do appreciate all the help, fellows. I'll commend you all to the sheriff, I surely will."

With a slight bow, Mr. Ellis began herding them toward the stairs. "If you'll excuse us, gentlemen. Making ready the . . . *instrument* is a delicate matter, one that requires concentration and solitude." He very nearly had said *gallows*, from force of habit. "I'm sure you all understand."

They grumbled, but they went. The last one looked back and called to Jimmy. "Two of us will be at the top of the stairs. You need anything, just holler."

"I appreciate it," Jimmy said, not looking around.

Mr. Ellis smiled and shut the door on the deputies. Through the metal he could hear one of them mutter, "Who's he think he is, Arthur Treacher?" He waited, expecting to hear a padlock clank into place, but heard only footsteps ascending.

"You're good at that," Jimmy said, fussing with the generator.

"Practice," Mr. Ellis said. "How may I help you?" He placed his hands in the small of his back, and awaited instructions.

Jimmy looked up, a fleck of grease of his nose. "Just your being here is a help, Mr. Ellis. But you reckon you can fetch me a bucket of water?"

While Jimmy unloaded his carpetbag, Mr. Ellis cleaned out the junk in the corner sink sufficiently to wedge a bucket beneath the spigot. He was careful not to slop any on his return trip. He found Jimmy kneeling amid sponges, straps, and tools. Next Mr. Ellis soaked the sponges and wrung them out, handing them to Jimmy to affix to the chair. At first he used too much water, but Jimmy showed him the sponges needed to be merely damp, not dripping, and after that the work went better.

That done, Jimmy rolled up his sleeves and said: "Take off your coat, and have a seat."

The chair's angles had looked severe, but Mr. Ellis found himself actually reclining a bit. The padded headrest gave pleasantly. Two shallow depressions in the wooden seat contoured themselves to his buttocks, and the small metal drain beneath his coccyx wasn't noticeable. He felt something cold in the small of his back, so he sat forward and looked around. The damp circle on his shirt corresponded to the glistening metal disk in the base of the back of the chair. The disk was the size of a saucer in a child's tea set.

"The body electrode," Jimmy said. "That's the first sponge you did. Probably still a little wetter than it needs to be."

"Is that a problem?"

"Oh, no," Jimmy said. "Not less it's uncomfortable for you."

"Not at all." He sighed and sat back, ignoring the spreading dampness behind. He rested his elbows on the chair's broad arms. Mr. Ellis had a longstanding grudge against most chairs, especially hotel-room chairs, because the arms often seemed too high, but these were just right.

Jimmy had been watching with a smile on his creased face. "What do you think?"

"It's quite comfortable," Mr. Ellis replied. "Frankly, I'm surprised."

"Oh, yeah, it's a good-sitting chair. Nobody believes me, at first. You'd be surprised how many folks I meet want to sit in it. Women, especially."

Mr. Ellis had snagged his right coat sleeve on the bolt that held the wrist strap. "Ah, indeed?" he asked as he worked the fabric loose.

"Oh, yeah. Pretty young gals, they always want to sit in it." He winked. "I let 'em, too."

Mr. Ellis chose to say nothing.

"The original design had a footrest on it," Jimmy said, disappearing behind the chair to the right, "but it never got added for some reason. Budget cuts, I reckon. Hold still, now, please sir." He walked back into view holding the free end of a foot-wide leather strap. He moved quickly around the chair from right to left and disappeared, pulling the strap tight against Mr. Ellis's chest. "That ain't too tight, is it?"

Mr. Ellis breathed, watching the heave of his breastbone, and replied, "No, it's fine." He tried leaning forward, and couldn't. He thought he could move a little from side to side, though, and was succeeding in the experiment when Jimmy reappeared, walking this time from left to right and carrying the free end of a second foot-wide strap. "Uh-uh," Jimmy said, grinning. "None of that, now." As the second strap pulled tight around his middle, Mr. Ellis involuntarily sucked in his stomach and was vexed to find that he couldn't push it out again. He sighed, tried to inch sideways, and failed. "Still comfortable?" Jimmy asked, stepping back into view.

"Not as much, no, but tolerable."

"You want the straps tight, believe me," Jimmy said. "I mean, if this wasn't a rehearsal. If this was the real show."

Wincing at the word *show,* Mr. Ellis again chose to say nothing.

Jimmy then fastened the straps across Mr. Ellis's upper arms, wrists, and ankles. He tugged on each strap, working deftly and quickly, asking each time whether the fit was OK. Then Jimmy knelt and said, "Now let me roll up your pants legs just a little."

"Are you this solicitous with all your clients?"

"I don't talk to 'em, no, but I try to make 'em as comfortable as I can. There, now." Mr. Ellis felt the padding clamp his left shin, the metal disc cold and damp against his flesh. "That too tight? Good. The right leg, now. No need making this any worse than it has to be, right?"

"Exactly right," Mr. Ellis said, pleased. "That is the essence of our creed, Jimmy. The guild has taught you well."

Jimmy looked up with a grin, but his face fell. "What's wrong, Mr. Ellis? Oh, hell, this right one's too tight, ain't it? No problem. A lot of men have one leg thicker'n t'other. It's one of those everyday deformities. Hold on a sec."

"No, the fit is fine," Mr. Ellis said. "I just was wondering . . ."

"Yes, sir?" He remained on his knees, his face almost boyishly earnest.

"During the actual preparations," Mr. Ellis asked, "wouldn't the client be blindfolded?"

Jimmy hung his head. "Well, yes, sir, sure he would. I mean, he'd have on the black mask. But I hated to do that to you, since it ain't necessary tonight, and all."

Mr. Ellis felt a flash of anger. "Jimmy," he said, firmly, and the younger man looked up again. "If you are to test this apparatus, and this procedure, you need to do so fully. Otherwise I am no help to you."

"Yes, *sir,*" Jimmy said, duckwalking over to his carpetbag and pulling out a folded square of fabric. Its buckle clinked against the concrete as Jimmy unfastened it. "You're right, yes, sir."

Mr. Ellis swallowed and took the deepest breath he could manage. "I am no tourist, Jimmy. I am no 'pretty young gal' to be coddled and impressed." Jimmy lifted his eyeglasses off his face. "I am a fellow member of the guild, here to help you ensure that this operation is carried out—" He inclined his head slightly as Jimmy tugged the black hood over his eyes. "—with one hundred percent efficiency."

"You're absolutely right, sir," said Jimmy's muffled voice as it moved behind the chair. "I swear, usually I put on the mask right after the chest strap, second thing. Wouldn't do for the client to be able to watch all my rigmarole, now would it?" The strap at the base of the hood pulled tight across Mr. Ellis's chin, forcing his jaw backward. Startled, he lifted his chin so that the strap fell against his neck. It continued to tighten as Mr. Ellis reared his head as far back into the rubber cushion as possible. Just as he thought *He's going to strangle me* the strap loosened a bit. He heard Jimmy buckle it into place. He sighed and felt his hot reflected breath. The mask was porous enough, but it sucked in when he inhaled. He wished he could tilt his head forward, but the neck strap wouldn't allow that. He managed to tease a bit of lint off his lower lip with the tip of his tongue. A hiss, and it was gone.

"Time for the helmet now, sir." Mr. Ellis flinched as he felt Jimmy's fingertips beneath his chin. "Chin up for me just a little? There you go." Mr. Ellis tried to refocus as Jimmy bustled about. He heard water being dipped. "The helmet has a sponge in it, too, sir, so don't be surprised."

"I won't be," Mr. Ellis said. Something soft, cold, and wet pressed down on the top of his head, and he flinched again. "Sorry."

"No problem," Jimmy said. "Most folks jump more'n that. Got this one a little wet myself, I'm afraid." Cold water trickled down Mr. Ellis's right cheek to the corner of his mouth. Salty. A second runnel flowed down the back of his neck, beneath his collar, and seeped into his shirt between his shoulder blades. Mr. Ellis shivered without moving his body, a disagreeable sensation. Jimmy straightened the mask with both hands while the sponge continued to press down atop Mr. Ellis's head, as if held by a third hand. "It's the damnedest part of the business, sometimes, getting the water just right," Jimmy muttered. "Oh, well. Better too much water than not enough, believe me. How's the helmet feel? Too tight?"

"Not at all," Mr. Ellis replied. He shivered again, and hoped he wouldn't catch cold. Being able only to hear Jimmy as he moved about, his voice swooping, made Mr. Ellis uneasy. "What are you doing now?" he asked.

"Just double-checking the straps, electrodes, connections. You can't be too careful, you know."

"Yes, I know."

Jimmy's voice was farther away. "Voltmeter's at two thousand. All right, then. Ready?"

Mr. Ellis wasn't sure how to respond. "Ready for what?" he asked.

"The switch. It's kinda loud."

Mr. Ellis considered. "Yes," he said. "Yes, I'm—" He was interrupted by a metallic clash, like the coupling of railroad cars. As the echoes died, Mr. Ellis relaxed and found that he somehow had lifted himself an inch or so off the chair.

"I oil that switch and oil it," Jimmy said, his voice coming closer, "and I can't make it no quieter. At least it don't creak like it used to. Used to sound like the goddamn Inner Sanctum." The sponge lifted from Mr. Ellis's head. The neck strap loosened with a clink. Just as Mr. Ellis drew a breath, the cloth rustled past his face. Jimmy held the blank black hood aloft.

"Pee-pye," Jimmy said. "That's what Mama used to say when I was little. Other younguns always said peek-a-boo, but I've said pee-pye ever since. Your glasses, sir."

They had been riding in Jimmy's shirt pocket. When Mr. Ellis put them on, they sat crooked.

"Here, lemme get those straps undone. I sure do appreciate your helping me out, Mr. Ellis. I still got to run some tests on the generator, but I feel a lot better knowing the chair's ready to go. This'll make things a heap faster in the morning."

"How long does the preparation normally take?" Mr. Ellis asked, flexing his stomach as the strap peeled away.

"Shouldn't be more'n one flat minute from the time the client walks through that door to the throwing of the switch. With you I took a lot longer, to explain things and to check everything two and three times. I figured you wouldn't mind."

"Of course not." He stood and stretched.

Jimmy squatted beside the carpetbag, made a show of rummaging, and said, without looking up: "Mr. Ellis."

"Yes, Jimmy."

"What do you think of all that this afternoon?"

Hands on hips, Mr. Ellis took a deep breath. "Mr. Childress is an angry man, Jimmy."

"Huh!"

"And he has reason for anger, in his own eyes. The sheriff does not. Nor do the deputies. Nor do you."

Jimmy looked up. "What do you mean?"

Mr. Ellis sighed. "I was there, Jimmy. I saw your reaction. You held it in check, to your credit, but you felt it nonetheless."

Looking at the floor, Jimmy said, "I wanted to kill him."

Mr. Ellis felt his shoulders sag, his knees spasm. He sat down in the chair. He started to lean back, then remembered the clammy sponge and leaned forward, elbows on knees, his fingers lightly interlaced. "Yes," he said. "Yes, that is the danger, isn't it?" He sorted words. "There is always danger in meeting the client beforehand. Always."

"They warned me against it," Jimmy mumbled. "From the first."

"Yes. We . . . *traditionalists* avoid it, at all costs. It causes confusion. The client's emotions are so forceful as to be, shall we say, contagious. One either wants to spare the client, or otherwise . . . loses perspective."

"I couldn't help it!" Jimmy cried out. Moving more quickly than Mr. Ellis could have imagined, he snatched up a pair of pliers and cast them backhanded into the corner. They crashed against the faucet and clattered into the sink. "It was like he was inside my head," Jimmy said, balance regained in squatting position. Fingertips touched the floor to left and right. Muscles roped his arms, corded his neck. "But he don't belong there. He don't." He stared at Mr. Ellis. "He don't know me at all."

"Of course not," said Mr. Ellis, motionless.

In a quieter voice, Jimmy said, "I ain't a lyncher."

"Of course not," said Mr. Ellis.

"I ain't had a privileged life," Jimmy said. "I reckon you can tell that by how I talk, how I act. And I ain't always been the most law-abiding citizen. Hell, I'm from Thompson County, from the piney woods. That says it right there. You probably heard about Thompson County clear up your way, even."

Mr. Ellis smiled. "We have our own such places."

"You know what I mean, then. Drank myself blind. Busted heads. Shot a man in the belly for talking nasty to my mama. He crawled into the ditch like a crab. I went squalling to the doctor. Man was so grateful he lied and said he'd shot himself. Last I heard he was in Memphis, waiting tables at the Peabody Hotel. Ain't that something? Making big tips. I was fourteen."

"You learned your lesson," Mr. Ellis said.

"That truck job, I was so drunk, I don't know what I was thinking. But Governor Hugh White pardoned me in 1939. I got the letter in the glove compartment to read now and then. Spelled my name wrong, but meant well. He recommended me for this job. He's a fine Christian man."

"I'm sure he is," Mr. Ellis said.

"But I never been part of the things Childress is talking about." He added, in a whisper: "*Thinking* about." He shuddered. "No, Childress don't know me."

"Childress," Mr. Ellis said, "is a layman." He pointed to himself and Jimmy. "We are professionals. We know the truth of what we do. Don't we?" A pause. *"Don't we?"*

Perhaps it was too stern, too quick. Mr. Ellis held his breath. Jimmy sighed and slid backward on his haunches to sit on the floor. "Yes, sir," he said, massaging his arms. Calluses and scars slid together with the sound of sandpaper.

Mr. Ellis allowed himself to relax. Some days he felt he had outlived his usefulness. Some days, not. In a gentler voice, he said, "You will not get any less sensitive to the client's emotions, Jimmy. As the years pass, as you gain . . . experience, you become even more attuned. You must always fight it, Jimmy. You must maintain your self-control. Hence the creed. Have you forgotten your creed, Jimmy?"

Startled: "No, sir!"

"I'm glad. Begin."

Jimmy glanced around. "Here?"

Mr. Ellis slapped the armrest twice. "Yes, here, exactly. Please. Begin."

Jimmy cleared his throat, rubbed his neck with both hands, took a deep breath, and recited:

"I am neither judge nor jury.

"I am their instrument,

"Their right hand,

"Their Will given life—"

"Good," Mr. Ellis interrupted. "Very good. There is strength in those words. *Neither judge nor jury.* Never forget that, my boy. Never forget that."

"I won't, sir. Thank you, sir."

Mr. Ellis smiled and asked, "Have you learned only the English?"

Jimmy grinned as he stood. He swatted dust from his pants. "So far, yes, sir. That other version, I don't know, it's hard to get my mouth around."

"Keep at it. You'll get it eventually. Much correspondence among the board members is transacted entirely in the ancient tongue of the guild."

"Like the Masons."

"Hardly," Mr. Ellis said, offended. "Europe needed us before it needed cathedrals."

As Jimmy removed the sponges and toweled the metal parts dry, Mr. Ellis sat, rested, enjoyed the businesslike movement around him. No wasted energy, this boy, once the fit passed. A good lad, all in all. Dedicated. Much yet to learn, of course, before he could be entrusted with the higher levels, the higher duties. How had he, Mr. Ellis, proven himself for the ultimate duty, so many years before? He'd never been sure. Certainly he had upheld the highest standards of the guild, but just as certainly, his predecessor had seen in him something more. Something like a pair of pliers slung across the room. Something quick, and feral.

"How about you?" Jimmy asked.

Mr. Ellis started. "I beg your pardon?"

Jimmy had a slight smile on his creased face. "How many times have you met a client beforehand?"

Mr. Ellis relaxed. "Ah, Jimmy. We both are too easily read for this work. Once. Only once, and that many years ago. Quite early on, really." He laughed, sat up straight on the edge of the chair, hands on his knees. "Very different circumstances."

"How different?"

Mr. Ellis hesitated, decided he had no reason to hesitate, and continued: "It was in Moose Jaw. Much like Andalusia, only louder, colder. I was much younger, much more sure of myself. The evening before the event, all was ready in the square. I received a note at the hotel, from the principal keeper at the jail, that the condemned man desired to see me. Unprecedented. I couldn't fathom what the man might want. But I had dined well, quail with fennel, and had allowed myself a glass of port after, and I had my feet at the grate and the *Times* in my lap, only two days old, quite current by Canadian standards. I was happy with my lot in life. So when the note arrived I felt both curious and generous. I donned my shoes and my coat and accompanied the messenger to the jail. The unfortunate man was sitting on his cot, sleepless of course, as Mr. Childress no doubt is, at this moment, and when we appeared he stood and walked very near the bars, regarded me intently. A squat man, Indian, Mohawk unless I miss my guess. The keeper said, 'Do you know who this fellow is? This is Mr. Ellis, whom you were asking for, and he left his warm fire to come out and have a word with you.' The prisoner nodded but said nothing. I said, 'Hello,' feeling awkward, and I smiled, and then I asked, 'What did you want to see me about?' He replied, 'I just wanted to see what you looked like.' I nodded and did a foolish thing. I stepped back and turned about for him, as if modeling my suit. Imagine the cheek. I'm ashamed to recall that, now. The port in me, I suppose. Then I asked: 'Well? Now that you've seen me, what do you think of me?' And the prisoner said, 'I think you're just what I deserve. I'm going to be hanged by the ugliest son of a bitch in Saskatchewan.'"

Jimmy laughed. "You're shitting me," he cried.

"I *never* shit," Mr. Ellis said. "In the sense you mean. Oh, it was a chastened man who returned to his fireside that night, you can well imagine!"

Mr. Ellis's face began to fall as Jimmy continued to laugh. "I'll bet you were," Jimmy said. "Oh, boy!"

"He was silent on the scaffold," Mr. Ellis said. "I was told later those were his last words."

He stood, faced the younger man, close enough to feel Jimmy's last breath before he held it.

"From his height and weight, I knew he would require a four-foot drop. Berry's formula is quite precise, you know."

He barely touched Jimmy's jaw with his fingertips.

"I placed the noose so that it fell this way," he said, tracing the line, "with the knot here, beneath the angle of the left jaw. When he dropped, his chin went back, so." He tipped Jimmy's chin up. "Breaking his spinal cord and his first three vertebrae."

Jimmy kept his chin tipped up as Mr. Ellis stepped back.

"No lacerations. No pain. Death was instantaneous. What the editorial writers and the legislators don't know, *cannot* know, is that in the proper hands, hanging is an exact science. Speedy. Certain. That Mohawk was in the right hands. I did my job well. As you will do yours, tomorrow." He patted the younger man's shoulder. "As you will do yours." He smiled, and Jimmy smiled, first tentatively, then broadly, head still tilted slightly back. They were standing that way when the stairwell door slammed open.

"I hope that damned murderer ain't getting any more sleep than I am," the sheriff said. "What y'all doing in here, anyhow? Dancing?"

* * *

Mr. Ellis's fingers were cold and wet. He could not seem to dry them no matter how many times he applied the towel. He draped the yellow daffodil print across the back of the folding chair, raised one hand to his mouth as if to cough, and flicked out his tongue. Salt. He thought he felt the granules as he rubbed his fingers together. Perhaps it was imagination. Perhaps he should stop fretting about it.

Mr. Ellis was conscious of the stares of the sheriff, the deputies, the doctor, the witnesses. The folding chairs were stenciled CRADDOCK & SONS, and they tended to squeak. Ten people sat or stood in the already cluttered basement with nothing to do but wait and watch. Jimmy allowed no one to help him but Mr. Ellis. The sheriff looked at his watch every five seconds and sucked his teeth.

"Right on schedule," Jimmy kept saying. "We're right on schedule here."

After thirty minutes of fuss with the cords, electrodes, and sponges, Mr. Ellis at his side, Jimmy produced a snarl-clotted strand of Christmas lights that snagged and jerked forth in installments from the recesses of the carpetbag. Despite the sheriff's obvious disgust, Jimmy insisted on untangling the lights, and Mr. Ellis helped with that, too, as well as he could. The tiny cords and bulbs defied his thick fingers.

He wondered why he of all people should be so nervous, as fidgety as a boy who knew nothing of death. The answer came readily: He wasn't in charge. This was a younger man's show.

One of the deputies, chasing a roach, kicked some boxes, and Jimmy jumped as if shot. All the more reason for calm, Mr. Ellis decided. He tried to sort lights with the fewest, most economical motions.

Once the lights were plugged into the chair, both men stepped back, and Jimmy threw the switch, again with that disconcerting crash. Everybody but Jimmy and Mr. Ellis jumped. There was a whine like a fury of bees, but the lights didn't respond.

"The chair's broke," someone whispered.

"Shoot," Jimmy said, yanking the switch back down. "Hang on a second." He fumbled through the lights. His shirt rode up as he squatted, and Mr. Ellis looked away. "There," Jimmy said. "Just as I thought. Loose bulb."

"Jesus God," the sheriff muttered.

This time, when Jimmy threw the switch, the lights twinkled red and green.

A deputy said, "Well, ho, ho, ho."

"Be quiet," the sheriff said.

Jimmy announced: "The lights show that two thousand volts are passing through the chair." He cleared his throat and added, in a more normal tone: "In some states the law says you got to say that. Seems sorta silly to me."

"Well, we appreciate knowing it," the sheriff said. "It's a comfort to us. Can we bring him in now, Mr. Simpson?"

As he stooped to help Jimmy dampen the sponges yet again,

Mr. Ellis slipped a jawbreaker into his mouth. A sour ball this time. Fiery hot. He heard the chains clinking down the stairs, the steady murmur of obscene patter. Childress entered surrounded by six deputies. Handcuffed, trussed, and chained, he could walk only with short, sliding steps.

"Look at me shuffle along," he was mumbling as he entered. "Just call me Sambo. Just call me Rastus. Gimme some watermelon and put me on tour with Walcott's Rabbit's Foot Minstrels. All singing all dancing all colored all the time. Don't be feeling my ass, motherfucker. I ain't one of your grab-ass deputy girlfriends."

His nonstop mumbled diatribe was his only sign of resistance as the deputies removed the fetters and held him down long enough for Jimmy to secure the straps.

The sheriff called out, "Childress, you change your mind about wanting a preacher?"

"You change your mind about being white?"

"All right, then," the sheriff said. "Mr. Simpson."

As Jimmy tugged the hood down, Childress noticed the lights. "Damn, it Christmas already? Come sit on my lap here, boys and girls. Come tell Santa what the fuck you want him to bring."

"Childress's thoughts were a thick oil coiling about Mr. Ellis's arms, slowing him. He fought free of them, and continued to work quickly. Now Jimmy looked wide-eyed and pale. Mr. Ellis glanced around. No one else was within fifteen feet of the chair. Mr. Ellis murmured:

"The creed."

Jimmy nodded. As he worked, he began to whisper the words, in English. Mr. Ellis whispered along with him, in a tongue that was old when the forward-thinking Dr. Guillotin ran his thumb along the edge of a cleaver, and mused; old when a translator in James I's employ bared down on his stile to write, "Whoso sheddeth man's blood, by man shall his blood be shed," and smiled, pleased by the rhythm; old, indeed, when the Babylonian king had a list of capital crimes chiseled onto a seven-foot pillar of basalt, to the glory of the sun god Shamash.

I am neither judge nor jury.
I am their instrument,
Their right hand,
Their Will given life.

"Santa got some chicken in his pockets for you," Childress called. "It's gone fry up real good. Come on over here and bite Santa's chicken leg one time."

I am the blade,
The rope,
The gun,
The chair.

How the membership had debated that addition!

I am methods now shunned
And methods yet unknown,
But methods only.

"Hey, these fellas be chanting and shit! You white people got some strange-ass mumbo-jumbo, you know that?"

What I do, I do without anger,
Without malice,
Without clumsiness or delay,
Without the infliction of needless suffering,
Without thought of personal gain.

The only sounds in the room were Childress ranting, Jimmy and Mr. Ellis mumbling to one another, and the sounds of their work: water being dipped, sponges being wrung out, leather sliding and buckles clicking into place.

And with awe and reverence
For the door that I open
And for the door that I close
And for the citizens whose Will
I enact,
Whom I pledge to serve
Faithfully and obediently
And heedless of self
Until this my sad duty
Shall cease to be.

"Take off this hood, motherfuckers. I said take off this hood. It's you white folks that wears the hood in this country, don't you know that? Didn't your daddy tell you nothing? I said take off this hood!"

I am neither judge nor jury.
I am their instrument,
Their right hand.

As they spoke the last line, they looked at each other:

God, too, be just.

"How many of us you gone kill?" Childress shouted. "How many of us you gone be *able* to kill, motherfuckers? How many?"

Jimmy and Mr. Ellis now stood beside the switch. The generator hummed behind them. Jimmy's hands darted about the control panel, checking relays. Then he turned, looked at the sheriff, mouthed the word: "Ready."

The sheriff nodded. Jimmy turned back toward the chair, took a deep breath, and, with one eye on the voltmeter, gripped the switch.

"Hey, Mr. Cracker," Childress said.

No one said anything. Jimmy was motionless.

"Lynch me good, Mr. Cracker. Lynch me good so all the niggers can see. Keep all the niggers *down*."

Jimmy remained motionless, but Mr. Ellis saw a nerve jump in his jaw.

Deputy Hooper yelled: "Shut up, Childress! Shut up or I'll—" He caught the sheriff's eye and faltered.

The black hood pulsed as Childress jeered. "Ha ha ha. Or you'll do what, motherfucker? What the fuck you got left to do, you dumb shit? I ain't studying bout you, motherfucker. This is tween me and Mr. Cracker and his magic fusebox, haaaa ha ha."

"Simpson," the sheriff hissed. "End this! Simpson!"

Mr. Ellis forced himself to look away from Childress. Jimmy had let go of the switch. He stared at his hands, rubbing them together as if warming them. He turned to Mr. Ellis and whispered:

"I can't."

"What's wrong, Mr. Cracker? Can't get it up today?"

In Mr. Ellis's head was a clear picture of a Negro suspended from a tree, eyes bulging, mouth filled with—

Focus, old man. Focus.

Forcing Childress's thoughts aside, Mr. Ellis asked Jimmy:

"Why not?"

"Because I want to."

Mr. Ellis blamed himself. If he had not been here, had not insinuated himself into these proceedings, Jimmy would have done his duty, however provoked. Yet here was Mr. Ellis, a relic, a meddler, a damned nuisance. The conscience of the guild, he was sometimes called. As if a conscience was what Jimmy needed. Was what anyone needed.

"Please," Jimmy whispered.

"They's a lot more where I come from, Mr. Cracker! A whole hell of a lot more!"

Enough. Mr. Ellis's duty was clear. "I understand," he said. He looked down, reached out with arthritic slowness, and gripped the switch.

The red rubber was clammy from Jimmy's sweat, and surprisingly inconsequential, compared to the ax-handle levers Mr. Ellis was used to. He feared breaking it. He found himself leaning on it, and made himself stop. He closed his eyes, took a deep breath, blanked his mind. He opened his eyes and looked at Jimmy, who, tight-lipped, nodded once. *God, too, be just.*

"Hey, Mr. Cracker—"

There was no resistance as he shoved the switch forward.

Childress lunged.

One last image flashed into Mr. Ellis's head, gone so quickly it didn't register. Consciously.

The strap yanked even tighter across Childress's chest, held him an inch or two from the back of the chair. He kept straining forward, belly bulging, arm muscles ropy. Something sizzled. Upstairs a phone began to ring. Childress had kicked with both feet at the first jolt and now his heels were about a half-inch off the floor, trembling. All the straps held. The keening of the current increased in pitch. The flesh of Childress's arms flared dark red. Beneath the hood he began to gurgle. His knees, imperceptibly at first, made as if to knock together, but even as they jerked more violently the gap never closed. The phone kept ringing. A soft Southern voice counted Mississippis. Childress's left ankle began to spark. His fingers were outstretched. Smoke wisped from the top of his head. The phone stopped in mid-ring. The gobbling rose and fell. "Five Mississippi," Jimmy said, fingertips brushing Mr. Ellis's hand. "Half power." Mr. Ellis pulled back, and Childress's limbs relaxed. The sparks and smoke ceased. His arms darkened to normal. At thirty Mississippi, Jimmy tapped Mr. Ellis's hand, murmured, "Full power." Childress jerked forward, straining anew. There were three more cycles of Childress rising and falling. Then Jimmy placed his hand atop Mr. Ellis's, and together they inched the switch down to a thousand, to five hundred, to one twenty-five, Jimmy's hand forcing Mr. Ellis's to slow down, to twenty-five, to zero. Childress sat motionless. The smell was of hot tires and sewage and beef.

"Is it over?" someone asked.

"That's for the doctor to say." Jimmy let go of Mr. Ellis's hand to look at his wristwatch. "A little more'n two minutes. That ought to've done it."

The sheriff voiced Mr. Ellis's thoughts. "What the hell was that phone call? Who went to get it? Was it Nat? What the *hell* was that phone call?"

"Doc, you better hold on a second," Jimmy said. "Wait up."

Stethoscope in hand, the doctor stopped a few feet from the chair. "Why wait?" he asked, frowning. "Why prolong the poor nigger's miseries?"

"That poor nigger's miseries ended more'n two minutes ago," Jimmy said, "and right now the body he left behind is running about a hundred and thirty-eight degrees. I wouldn't be in a rush to touch him right yet."

The stairwell door crashed open and Deputy Nat stepped through, scratching his ear. He seemed in no hurry to speak. He looked surprised to see everyone staring at him.

"What's that smell?" he asked.

"For God's sake, Nat," the sheriff said. "Who was it on the phone?"

"Oh, the phone," Nat said, and laughed. "You'll love this one, Sheriff. It was old Miss Curry, Miss Adele Curry. Wanting to know when the execution was gonna be."

Mr. Ellis expelled his breath. Voices started up all around. The sheriff mopped his face with a handkerchief.

"I told her I was sorry ma'am but I couldn't give out that information and she said she only wanted to know because she thought the power might cut off when it happened—"

"Nat," said the sheriff.

"—and she was planning to bake her a funeral cake and she didn't want it to fall, and I told her there wouldn't be no loss of power and she wanted to know how come that was because whenever the McClellands next door turned on their radio her parlor lights got dim—"

"Your family's gone be eating that funeral cake," said the sheriff, "if you don't hush up."

"Yes, *sir.*"

One of the witnesses, a shiny-headed bald man who was pale around his black mustache, asked: "What was that gurgling sound? Oh, Jesus. That was plumb awful."

"Air in the lungs," Jimmy said. "No way to avoid it, really." He passed his hands over Childress, a few inches from his body, as if molding him from the air. "Oh, you could try and watch the rise and fall of the chest, I reckon, to time the current just right, but what's the point? That wasn't Mr. Childress talking, anyway. He was dead before you ever heard that sound."

The man did not look reassured.

Jimmy stepped back. "Ought to be OK now, Doc. Go on ahead."

"Phew, what a stink," the doctor said. "Hadn't the boy taken a dump this week?" He held the stethoscope just above Childress's chest and reached with his other hand for the shirt buttons. He jumped back with a cry. His stethoscope bounced off the rubber mat to clatter onto the concrete.

The sheriff was beside him. "What's wrong?"

"He shocked me!"

"He *what?*"

The doctor rubbed his hands, eyes wide. "Like in the wintertime, when you go to touch a radio knob and a spark jumps out at you. Whoo! Lordy."

"Are you hurt?"

"No, no. Scared me, though." With a grunt, he stooped and picked up the stethoscope.

With an index finger, Jimmy poked Childress on the shoulder, then jumped back. "Damn! It's true. Never had *that* happen before."

The deputies had not come within yards of the chair since carrying it in the night before, but now they crowded around. "Let me touch him." "Me, too." "Ow! I'll be damned. Feel of him, Earl." "Me next."

Jimmy tried to push them away. "Hey, now, boys, step back, please, step back and let the doc do what he's got to do. Come on, now. He ain't *officially* dead yet. Come on, now."

"Sparks jumping out like he's got a battery in his britches. Ow! Ain't that something? Ow!" Now the witnesses were joining the crowd.

The sheriff had been frozen, mouth open, face red and swollen. Now he bellowed: "God damn it, what's got into y'all? Come away from there! A bunch a younguns would have better sense than you men got."

The doctor squirmed his way through the melee, feinting with his stethoscope. The sheriff cursed and roared, grabbing men by their shoulders and pushing them away. Jimmy, angry now, was in Deputy Hooper's face: "You think I don't know my own job? Huh? Is that what you think?" The deputy squared his shoulders, rolled something from cheek to cheek.

Mr. Ellis stood alone, his hand still gripping the switch.

He looked down at it.

For a moment he pictured Childress lunging forward one more time, scattering the crowd, showering sparks. His hand tightened on the switch.

Then the doctor called out: "Gentlemen, I hereby pronounce William Childress dead."

Mr. Ellis let go of the switch, closed his eyes. Childress hung below him, pendulous, weighty, dignified. Hands reached up to steady him, to receive him. As Mr. Ellis sawed, the rope blossomed, strand by strand. Childress dropped away. Thus lightened, the scaffold rose and floated free.

* * *

On Friday night the deputies had unloaded the truck in a silence broken only by grunts and muttered oaths. On Saturday morning they talked and joked constantly as they hauled and lifted. A few townsfolk stood and watched, but nothing like the insistent crowds of the day before.

The tarp was a struggle. An overnight break in the weather made for a nice day, with temperatures in the low 80s and a gusty breeze that beat the Mississippi flag overhead like a rug during spring cleaning, but the same breeze kept seizing the tarp and threatening to yank it and its handlers clear to Perdition, as Jimmy put it. By the time Jimmy tied the last rope, it was nearly noon. Jimmy and Mr. Ellis shook hands with the sheriff and with a few of the more gregarious deputies.

"Boys," the sheriff said to the deputies, "thank you for all your hard work and dedication. I hereby declare you all off duty." The deputies whooped and laughed and started walking off, in twos and threes. Several unhooked their badges and put them in their shirt pockets.

One deputy told another, "Darla don't like no metal rubbing against her bosoms."

To Jimmy and Mr. Ellis, the sheriff said: "Gentlemen, I thank you. Is there anything else we can do for you here in Andalusia?"

Mr. Ellis was glad to see that Jimmy, too, could take a hint. "No, sir," Jimmy said, sliding the fat envelope into his pocket. "I appreciate it."

"Thank you for the hospitality," Mr. Ellis said.

"Thank *you*. Safe travels to you both. Mr. Simpson, we'll see you next time."

They watched the sheriff walk back to the courthouse door. He had an oddly prissy gait, short-stepped and hurried. Rather than cut across the grass, he went first to the left and then diagonally, as the sidewalk dictated. The click of his heels was audible all the way. He entered the courthouse without turning or waving again.

"He's glad to be rid of us, ain't he?" Jimmy said.

"Oh, he'll be glad enough to see you again. Eventually."

Jimmy put one foot on the running board of the truck, pulled a handkerchief from his pocket, wiped his hands. "Mr. Ellis, I ain't had the nerve to talk to you about what happened in there this morning."

"The equipment performed flawlessly," Mr. Ellis said. "You said so yourself."

"You know what I mean," Jimmy said. "He was in my head again, Mr. Ellis. Nearbouts the whole time. I saw things—things I don't ever want to see again. And I hated him for it. That's why I did what I done. I mean, what I didn't do. Oh, hell."

Mr. Ellis nodded. He had pondered for some time, as he watched the deputies wrestle the chair into the truck, what his parting words to Jimmy would be. He had made his decision. The board might disagree, but this was a field emergency, and in field emergencies, as far as Mr. Ellis was concerned, he *was* the board.

"I know what you didn't do, Jimmy," Mr. Ellis said. "You didn't pull the switch. You didn't hide your feelings. You didn't *lie*. You easily could have, but you didn't. In handing me that switch, you upheld the highest principle of the guild. And now I want you to do something else for the guild."

Jimmy stuffed his handkerchief into his pocket, squinted at the sun. "Quit, I reckon."

"No!" Mr. Ellis seized Jimmy's arm. "No, Jimmy. You misunderstand. The guild needs men like yourself, brave and principled men. What if this business were left to others, to men who weren't so brave and principled?" He let go, stepped back. Jimmy rubbed his forearm. "What then? Well. We need to know the next generation is in good hands. *I* need to know that. That's what you can do for the guild. Go on with your work, with your principles. Reassure us."

Jimmy squinted into the sun. "I didn't think you exactly saw eye to eye with the way I did things, Mr. Ellis."

Mr. Ellis shrugged. "I am a man of my time, and my place. You have your equipment, I have mine." He rapped the fender with his knuckles. "Do your work, Jimmy, with the equipment you know best. You have the guild's support, and mine."

He extended his hand. Jimmy shook it.

"Thank you, Mr. Ellis."

"I'm pleased to have met you, Jimmy."

"Likewise, Mr. Ellis." Jimmy swung up into the cab, slammed the door. The impact made the side windowpane rattle and fall askew in the frame. "Damn it all," Jimmy said. He shoved the pane down and leaned out. "Good thing the chair's in better shape than the truck. Give you a lift someplace? Oh, right. Sorry. Well, I hope to see you soon, sir. Maybe we can work together again."

Mr. Ellis smiled and

Eyes wide the preceding Mr. Ellis said Please for the last time leaned his head back and looked up

said: "Perhaps so, Jimmy. I would have every confidence in you."

Jimmy nodded, smiled, and cranked the truck. After a five-second tubercular rattle, the engine coughed to life. Jimmy revved it. The exhaust pipe vibrated and spat like a tommy gun. Gas fumes filled the square. Jimmy put the truck into gear and lifted his hand in a wave that turned into a salute as he drove away. Mr. Ellis lifted his hand, too, in a wave that turned into a futile attempt to ward the truck's flatulence away from his face. Some of the people on the street waved at the truck as it passed, but most went along their business without even a glance, as if it were no more interesting than the chicken truck that roared into the square a few seconds later, scattering feathers. In moments the gutters were white and soft with down.

Mr. Ellis picked up his valise. At the curb he waited for a Ford and a mule-drawn buggy to pass and then crossed the street, tipping his hat to a well-upholstered lady in white lace and to a thin colored girl in gingham who walked behind her holding out a parasol. On the opposite sidewalk Mr. Ellis first turned to the right, then changed his mind and went left, parting in two a surge of children who rushed past him so fast and noisy and dirty their age and sex and race were indistinguishable. He climbed the three steps to the porch of Blackburn's General Store, where an old colored man and a grey-flecked hound both studied him.

"Good morning," Mr. Ellis said.

"Morning," the old man replied. "Say."

Mr. Ellis paused, hand on the knob. "Yes?"

The old man leaned forward, overalls bunching at the waist. He had one clouded eye. "You that English feller, ain't you?" he asked in an ancient, trembling voice. "The one that came to watch —to watch old Childress go home. Ain't you?"

A small town indeed. "That's right," he said.

The old man glanced about, whispered: "How was he at the end? Won't nobody say. Was he peaceful-like? Did he go easy? Did he make his peace with the Lord?" Mr. Ellis said nothing, and the old man's face spasmed. "Oh, now, please sir, don't lie to a old feller what ain't done you no wrong. Tell me the truth. Did he put aside his hateful ways at the end?"

What harm would it do? Mr. Ellis nodded and murmured: "Yes, he did. He repented, and asked forgiveness, and went in peace."

The old man studied Mr. Ellis's face for a long time, then began to smile. He sat back, crossed his legs, and pulled a pipe from his pocket. "Did he, now?" he asked, striking a match on his shoe and lighting the bowl. "Did he, now? Old Willie Childress?" He nodded and puffed, began to cackle with laughter, still looking at Mr. Ellis, his good eye dancing. He no longer sounded old. "Yes, *that's* likely, ain't it?" he chortled. "Ain't *that* a good 'un, to tell the old nigger? And you tells it so well, too! Tells it like you was born here!"

He was still cackling as Mr. Ellis entered the store, his footsteps changing from hollow thumps to solid thuds as he crossed the threshold. At first he could see little in the relative dimness, but after he blinked and strained for a few seconds, the sausages and clothes and pots hanging from the ceiling and the crates and cans and sacks piled in the floor began to resolve themselves. He glanced toward the coiled shapes on the hardware wall, disregarded them, and focused instead on the shaving mugs and brushes cluttering one of the glass countertops. As he walked toward them, someone said:

"Morning."

Startled, Mr. Ellis replied automatically: "Good morning." It was the little headache man, who was no longer lying on the hardware counter but on the household-goods counter, quite near the shaving implements. As Mr. Ellis leaned over to peer through the glass, he could smell the mud and leather of the little man's shoes.

"I'm not in your way, am I?" asked the little man.

"Not at all," said Mr. Ellis.

"Cause if I am I'll move."

Arrayed beneath the countertop, nestled among an artful snarl of leather straps and carrying cases, were a half-dozen fully extended straight razors.

"Hey, I talked to you yesterday, didn't I, mister?"

"Yes, you did," said Mr. Ellis, without looking at him. "How is your headache today? Better, I trust?"

"Head's a good bit better, thank you kindly for remembering. But don't even ask about my sciatica. I got such a throb in my sciatica, I can't even tell you. That counter over yonder's better for my head but this one's better for my sciatica, don't ask me why. I don't question the Lord's ways His wonders to perform."

The longest blade, at nine inches, looked as if it could mow crops. To get a better look, Mr. Ellis slid aside a shaving mug that depicted a straw-hatted Negro boy holding up a fish on a line.

"But I done took me a Goody's, and that'll be kicking in rectly. Goody's don't advertise it's good for sciatica but it is. Goody's good for everything."

"I'll have to remember that," Mr. Ellis said. "May I buy you a Coke today?"

In the burnished steel Mr. Ellis could see his dulled outline and the sweeping blades of the ceiling fan.

"No thank you, sir, I just did open me one. Ain't hardly stopped fizzing good. I preciate it, though."

Once, the preceding Mr. Ellis, in an expansive mood, had taken his young assistant to dinner at a French restaurant in Montreal, where the reflected pulse of the ceiling fan in the overly polished silverware proved so distracting that the assistant laid his napkin over them. Groping for conversation, the young man studied the menu and finally said: "The snapper sounds good. What do you recommend, Mr. Ellis?" The older man gasped and knocked over his water glass. Pale and wide-eyed, he glanced about, then leaned across the darkening tablecloth to whisper: "For God's sake, man, no names in public. Do you want a riot on your hands? Think of my position, please."

Please Eyes wide Mr. Ellis said Please for the last time leaned his head back and looked up at his successor who lifted the razor and drew it once across to the right and intended to draw it once again across to the left but found that wasn't necessary and jumped back as the old man's head lolled leaving the younger man alone in the shabby farmhouse kitchen to hear a cow past milking low across the highway and hear the flood on the linoleum become a patter and then a drip in counterpoint to the faucet and while hearing these things the younger man mumbled Without anger Without malice Without clumsiness or delay Mumbled at first and then spoke aloud and then spoke loudly the creed taught him by the older man who had trained him well and then when he was ready passed on to him the duty so that Mr. Ellis who taught Mr. Ellis also became first client of Mr. Ellis and Mr. Ellis left Mr. Ellis and his darkening tablecloth and turned up his coat collar as he stood atop Mr. Ellis's back porch steps blew into hands smelling of Mr. Ellis's soap and shivered in the cold that came early to Mr. Ellis that fall and never fully left God, too, be just.

Someone with a deep voice cleared his throat, and Mr. Ellis looked up to see the two store owners standing behind the counter, gazing at him not with hostility but not with friendliness either. The man had his hands clasped behind him and a spatter of gristle on his apron. The woman was screwing on the head of a porcelain doll, a foot-high bride. As the fit at the neck tightened, the painted eyes slowed, then grated to a stop, and they, too, gazed at him.

The man with the apron asked, not unkindly, "Can we help you with anything, sir?"

Mr. Ellis cast one final glance at the longest razor. What workmanship. What efficiency. He looked up, smiled. "No, thank you," he said. "Not today."

The Premature Burials

LOOKING UP, MATTHEW SAW PICTURES IN THE ripples and dimples of satin as if they were layers of clouds over Munson's Hill. There, in the far corner: That drape looked like one of Mr. Venable's cantankerous swans. And just overhead was the familiar lumpy profile of Mr. Krohn the wheelwright, mouth yawning wide.

Matthew grinned at the thought of fat Mr. Krohn wedged into this narrow space. He slowly, noiselessly slid his arms and legs outward until they met the soft, adamant walls to left and right. Then gradually, in torturous, tense increments, he raised trembling hands and feet until knuckles and bare toes were buried in the satin of the ceiling and could rise no farther.

Not much room even for Matthew, eight years old last Tuesday, but for Mr. Krohn? No standard-sized box for him. Maybe they'd just knock the wheels off one of Mr. Krohn's own wagons, take down his barn door, and saw him a lid to fit.

Matthew came perilously close to giggling, in this space too small for both a medium-sized boy and a good-sized laugh. He froze, lips pursed and bulging, as murmuring voices approached his sanctuary from the world beyond the lid.

Matthew had noticed, long before his eyes adjusted to the dark, the dust-thin creases of light that outlined the lid on three sides. Matthew, a butcher's son, had speculated wildly on the effects of this unexpected ventilation. Now shadows crawled the length of the longest seam, filling it. Matthew heard a woman snuffling, and then the deep and placid voice of Mr. Marsh, whose words sounded recited, like Scripture.

"And this is, of course, one of our simpler models, but nonetheless popular, for reasons I'm sure you can discern for yourselves. Simple yet elegant, qualities for which your aunt herself was, if I may say so, quite well known in life."

A whimper of ladylike assent emerged from the snuffles before being choked off, and another man's voice said: "Indeed. Might this model, like the mahogany, be fitted with a bell?"

"Yes, of course," Mr. Marsh said, "or the equally effective speaking tube, which as I have said is a less cumbersome and more frugal option. In either case, your aunt would be guaranteed able to summon assistance in the event of—the unspeakable." He rushed the last two words in an awestruck mumble.

"Well, that's a mercy, anyway," the other man said, just as Matthew gave voice to the unspeakable, and sneezed.

All sounds from without ceased. For a thrilling few moments of darkness and silence, Matthew himself froze—the easiest course of action, really, in a space that so limited a boy's options. His heart raced. He felt a strange exultation he'd never felt before. He snapped shut his eyes and folded both hands over his chest just as Mr. Marsh seized the lid and lifted.

The sunshine streaming through the front window was hot on Matthew's cheeks. He opened his eyes to see three faces looking down: the right-side-up face (Mr. Marsh) swollen and agog like a frog forbidden to croak; the first sideways face (the other man) pale and aghast, a deacon's face; the second sideways face (the woman!) mostly black lace and crepe above red lips and perfect teeth, one row parted from the other in surprise. It was at her lovely half-face that Matthew smiled, and to her that he directed his greeting.

"Hullo. Mr. Marsh is quite right. This is a very comfortable model indeed."

Matthew sprang over the side of the coffin before the adults quite registered that he even had sat up. He hit the polished floor running. He skidded around a marble angel and set a candelabrum ominously rocking as he dashed for the door. Behind him the two men called for him to stop and denounced him as an ill-bred urchin, a vagabond, a ragamuffin. The woman's laughter rang out over their futility as clear and as strong as any of Mr. Marsh's old coffin bells.

Matthew ran out of the shop and into the muddy street and slid unscathed directly across the path of a rearing carriage horse. Heedless beneath flashing hooves, exultant between toe-shaped gushes of mud, Matthew began his lifelong vivid recollection of the veiled woman's naked astonishment. This private image, tinted and embellished like an illustrated weekly's engraving of Christ, would be especially dominant a few years later, when Matthew began to take a naturally keener interest in the corseted half of humanity.

* * *

"I must confess to you, Mr. Preble," Miss Charity Gorce told Matthew, "that you are not the first man to ask for my hand in marriage."

"Of that, Miss Gorce, I have no doubt."

"I must tell you, as well, that when your predecessors heard my conditions of marriage, they rescinded their offers, quit this house with more haste than decorum, and never returned—severed all relations with me. In short, Mr. Preble, they fled."

"I could not imagine having the slightest desire to flee your presence, Miss Gorce. I find it most congenial."

"Yes," she said, without inflection. "Well, you're young yet, Mr. Preble—somewhat younger than I am, if I may be so forward, though we need not speak in numeric terms. Perhaps you will be older by the time you leave here. Allow me to examine the evidence for your suit. Oh, you may sit, by the way. I'm sure your knee would be glad of the rest."

Matthew bowed his head graciously and rose from his position at Miss Gorce's feet. Three backward steps brought him to the edge of the cushioned window seat, where he reverently settled himself.

Miss Gorce adjusted her pince-nez and leafed silently through Matthew's papers. Matthew admired the contours of her arms, rather daringly revealed by her stylishly tight sleeves. He admired her face as well. Her high forehead and patrician nose were shared by all the grim ancestors whose surrounding portraits conspired to darken the room. Yet her mouth was comically wide, her eyebrows a single dark swath, her hair asymmetrically askew. Nature had marred her inherited good looks just enough to make her beautiful.

For seemingly the fiftieth time that afternoon, Matthew had a fleeting image of Miss Gorce splayed beneath him, her corset undone, waiting with an open, smiling mouth to serve as a willing receptacle for his lust. He willed away this wicked and lamentably unlikely picture.

"I remember your father's butcher shop, Mr. Preble," Miss Gorce finally said, "for my mother traded there. I confess I have no recollection of you being anywhere near the place, at least during hours in which work might be done. Since leaving Rochester, however, you seem to have been uncharacteristically industrious. Surveying team in the Aroostook Valley . . . Commendations from two governments for your role in settling that border dispute . . . Further surveying, exploring, speculating . . . These are strange times, Mr. Preble, when a man can make a fortune in land transactions without acquiring any land himself. I presume this is where I, and my family's holdings, come in? No need to protest, Mr. Preble, I'm only joking. Partially. Cultural activities seem in order . . . Founding sponsor of the New York Philharmonic . . . Et cetera, et cetera. Well."

She plucked off her spectacles and sat back in her chair, layers of fabrics and petticoats crackling and rustling. With her shoulders back, her bosom was especially prominent. "Let us set aside these papers for a moment."

"Let's," said Matthew, quivering.

"I admit that the months we have spent strolling and taking tea and visiting the infirm on Sundays have been pleasant for me, Mr. Preble."

"For me, as well, Miss Gorce."

"As long as I am being blunt, I should add that you are, in your own unique and disheveled way, quite a well-turned-out young man." As she said this, she averted her eyes downward so that she no longer met his gaze. "And so," she said, finally looking up. She was flushed. She cleared her throat and took a deep breath. "I am inclined to accept your proposition, and grant you my hand in marriage."

In the next instant, Matthew was on his knees at her feet once more, seizing her hands in his. "Marvelous! You will not regret this, Miss Gorce. I will be yours until death!"

"And beyond?" she asked, smiling down at him.

"Beyond?"

Her smile faded. She sat forward, pallid and drawn, eyes swimming with ghosts, and clutched his hands until his knuckles grated. "I have but one fear, Mr. Preble," she whispered. "My inheritance has spared me privation and want; my talents and industry have spared me the unreliable mercies of men. But nothing will spare me the chill of the tomb. My one fear, Mr. Preble, is that I will suffer the fate suffered by all my ancestors on the walls around us—that despite my money, and status, and wit, I will die and be buried alone. I have lived alone for years, and thrive upon it; but to lie in my casket alone—Oh! The dread possibility has me choking and gasping in my bed each night, unable to sleep, unable to breathe, unable to bear the thought of the blanketing, solitary doom that awaits. Do you understand now my conditions of marriage, Mr. Preble?"

Matthew opened his mouth, considered, then snapped it shut and rapidly shook his head.

"Should I die first," Miss Gorce said, "my husband must be buried with me. Immediately. Before another sunset. He must willingly lie, before his time, in an adjoining casket in our mutual plot in the Gorce family cemetery, and sail alongside me into that sea of worms."

"He must be buried alive?" Matthew croaked.

"Alive or dead, the choice is his. Buried, yes; that is my choice. My choice, my desire, my condition of marriage." She smiled faintly. "Shall I have Mr. Sterne bring your hat?"

"And if I die before you?"

She smiled more broadly. "Then I will do you the same favor, Mr. Preble. I will not remain above the soil one day more than you do. That very night, I will lie beside you in the adjacent grave."

Matthew stood, walked to the window, and looked toward fields and sheds that he did not see. He closed his eyes and summoned, as he had countless times before, an elegant mouth beneath black lace and crepe, leaning over a coffin. This time the mouth was Miss Gorce's. Then, in his vision, he was standing above the coffin looking in, as Miss Gorce's lips repeatedly formed the word "Yes."

Surging with tides he could neither name nor deny, he swung round and returned to Miss Gorce's side, where he fervently and repeatedly kissed her hand.

"May I take this as an acceptance?" Miss Gorce asked, a bit breathlessly.

Matthew made no verbal reply.

Her eyes glistening, her broad forehead cleared of furrows, Miss Gorce groped with her free hand for the bell pull, seized it, and yanked it repeatedly. She left it dancing and reached for Matthew's hair, tugging absently but fondly at the upswept curls that spilled over his collar in back.

"For if he loves me with all his heart," she murmured, "of what use will life be to him afterwards?"

The papers had lain for years in a downstairs safe. On many occasions, Miss Gorce's butler, Sterne, had transferred the papers to a silver salver and sat impassively in the pantry, watching the bell, waiting for a signal that never came. Each time, he had needed no further instructions; without troubling his mistress more, he had returned the papers to their felt-lined vault before the suitor's horse had galloped past the willow tree on the corner.

On this day, the jangling resurrection of the so-long-dormant bell caused Sterne no visible surprise. After a pause of only a few seconds, he stood, picked up the salver, and strode from the pantry before the bell had finished tinkling.

Sterne walked silently through a series of ever more ornate doorways, through a series of increasingly well-lighted rooms, and ascended a flight of stairs wide enough for a pedestrian race. At the top, he tapped at the door of Miss Gorce's office.

"Come," she murmured.

Silently, Sterne watched as Matthew and Miss Gorce signed the documents. Then Sterne signed his own name, added the date, and stamped each of the three copies with the embossed seal of the State of New York.

"So convenient," Miss Gorce breathed into Mr. Preble's ear, "having a notary on the premises."

* * *

The Prebles were as content in marriage as any couple can be in this fallen world. An early crisis on the question of brunch was defused by the decision to have it each day, only at different times, some days as late as midnight. Over brunch, tea, elevenses, and all other meals (for they were a ravenous pair), they read aloud to each other (and to Sterne, as he shimmered in and out) from *Godey's Lady's Book*, the *Southern Literary Messenger, Scientific American* and all other periodicals, including, most thrillingly, the *Workingman's Advocate*. They imported a saxophone from Belgium, a harmonium from France, and practiced fruitlessly before an audience of each other, for Sterne scheduled his errands judiciously.

They also devoted many more successful hours to perfecting

their marital arts, displaying impromptu skills that astonished and gratified in equal measure. Perhaps sensing that the new marrieds were more than normally preoccupied with matters normally left to a procreative God, the mothers of Rochester began propelling their children past the gates of the Gorce mansion at double speed. The Prebles observed this, as they observed everything else, and were happy. Then Mrs. Preble died.

* * *

Matthew lay in the dark coffin and sobbed. His cries and moans were close about him. Disgorged from his chest and mouth, they sank into the fabric lining the box and rebounded to nestle, moist, against him. Again and again he choked out his dear wife's name, careless of the squandered air. What use was air, with Charity in the grave?

Through his spasms of grief, Matthew was dimly aware that he now had far less room to maneuver than he had at age eight, inside Mr. Marsh's display model. Unable to flail his arms and legs as he wailed, he twisted and rolled from side to side, bruising his shoulders against the coffin lid. He groaned and cursed like an armless flagellant, and his tormented words crowded the box on all sides. He was awash in nightmare jibberings. The clouds of satin over his head shaped a riot of crawling, leaping, writhing things, the pandemonium of a dozen faiths.

And there, in the cloths to the left—was that lump of fabric not the placid death-mask of his poor dead Charity, his wife of barely a twelvemonth, who had looked so rosy and fair even on her bier that she scarce seemed a fit candidate for the grave? No doubt, her sure foreknowledge that her husband was willing to lie beside her even in death had eased her soul's dark dread, made her dead cheeks and brow bloom in relief.

But where was Matthew's solace now, as he churned in misery many feet below the heaped earth of the family plot?

The heavy air around him was cotton in a pill-box, holding him fixed and suffocating in the center of his prison. He rolled through this cloying ether of misery as a crated carcass in a ship's hold rolls stupidly through lard. Had Charity, blessedly insensible, been spared this ordeal? Ah, Charity! Ah, Matthew! Ah, God!

Such were Matthew's thoughts as he fell, exhausted, into the deepest, most blissful, most untroubled sleep of his life.

Matthew was awakened by a ripping, splintering, grating wail only inches from his face.

More jolts, and something heavy raking along the length of the box.

Twin thumps.

Coughs and murmurs.

A sawing rasp.

A screech.

Then Matthew's skin prickled as the trapped and clammy air released its grip and rushed upward, a dank gasp exhaled into a rectangle of star-flecked sky. Its escape fluttered the coattails and stirred the mutton chops of a black-clad, lantern-haloed figure who straddled the coffin and looked dourly down into earth, one hand supporting the casket lid.

Matthew lay still and looked up, blinking, uncomprehending. "Oh, it's you," he said.

"Who else?" Sterne asked, extending a hand.

Matthew allowed himself to be hauled from the hole and propped against the fresh mound of earth. He choked on the brandy that Sterne slopped into his mouth.

"Please, sir," Sterne kept saying. "Please, you must drink."

"Sterne," Matthew rasped. "Sterne. What is happening?"

Sterne fumbled in his waistcoat-pocket, drawing forth a sheaf of papers. "If I may explain, sir. I have spent some time studying the agreement that you and my mistress signed before the wedding. I also consulted my cousin, a solicitor in Philadelphia—in strictest confidence, I assure you, sir. He confirmed my interpretation. The document clearly mandates your interment in the event of your wife's death, but makes no provision for the *duration* of said interment." He waved the paper in front of Matthew, jabbing a gloved finger at the pertinent clause.

"You have exhumed me," Matthew said, ignoring the paper.

"I took that liberty, sir," Sterne said, dropping his eyes.

"Then my wife . . . lies there still?"

"She does, sir."

Matthew groaned, flung his forearm across his face, and would have expressed his desire to return to the earth, rather than face the sunlight alone, had all his senses not been galvanized by the faint jingling of a tiny bell, such as a gentlewoman might use to summon a lady-in-waiting.

Matthew sat up, his nose nearly meeting Sterne's. The men stared at each other. As one, they turned and regarded the adjacent grave. The bell continued to jingle.

"My wife's coffin—" Matthew began.

"The latest safety features—" Sterne began.

Matthew already was clawing doglike at the dirt with one hand and using the other to yank free squares of freshly laid sod. He flung them over his shoulder, where they puffed into dust on his own yawning casket. A tossed spade thumped into the dirt beside him. As he seized it, he saw Sterne gouge the blade of his own shovel deep into the mound, one grimy spat glimmering white in the glow of the lantern.

Silently, master and servant worked side by side, pelting the landscape with shovelfuls of dirt. As his arms and shoulders pumped like automatons, Matthew's mind ransacked a lifetime's lore concerning those strange diseases that seemed to rebuke the advances of modern medicine. Certain maladies mocked the symptoms of death, caused the temporary cessation of all vital functions except, apparently, the fluttering soul, which later awakened in the most dreadful predicament known to suffering humanity. Merciful God! Still the bell kept ringing—ringing—ringing!—until Matthew's blade jabbed into the casket lid and splintered its tiny belfry at the base. As he and Sterne scrabbled away the remaining layer of earth, the slender, severed bell-pull slithered back into its trap and vanished inside the coffin, as if tugged one last time by an unseen hand falling limp in exhaustion.

"My wife!" cried Matthew, wrenching open the lid.

"My husband!" cried Charity, reaching up to him.

Sterne's lantern then illumined a tender scene. Husband laved wife with muddy kisses as, with his last strength, he bore her out of the grave and laid her gently upon the mound where Sterne had laid him not an hour before. The two collapsed together like the walls of a tent, and in a heap they cradled each other, murmuring endearments.

Sterne, coughing discreetly, dispensed brandy, then retreated to the wagon for some rope. "No need to waste the caskets," he muttered as he went.

"I thought the most terrible moment of my life," Matthew finally said, "was when I entered your bedchamber to find you in the very shape and lineaments of death. But it was nothing compared to the terror I felt here, in this cemetery, when Sterne and I heard your cry for help ring out practically beneath our feet."

Charity tensed alongside him like a rope pulling taut. She moved back a few inches. Matthew did not care for her gaze; she seemed to see him coolly and see him whole.

"Beneath your feet, my angel?" Charity asked. "How could that be, my dove?"

Charity then turned and regarded the open pit of her husband's grave. She craned forward and looked down upon the empty coffin. Then she faced her own grave, studied her own empty casket. She silently looked from one pit to another, her appraising glance that of a vaguely interested customer presented with equally uninviting alternatives.

"My dear—" Matthew said.

"How strange," Charity said, almost to herself, "that Sterne's initial response, upon hearing my call for help, was to go next door and dig *you* up. Was your help so necessary? I always fancied Sterne more self-sufficient than that."

"My love—" Matthew said.

"If he loves me with all his heart," she said, fully to herself by now, "of what use will life be to him afterwards? What use, indeed?" She picked up a clod of clay and fisted it, raining sediment upon her shoe.

"My heart—" Matthew said.

"I think I would like to go back home, now, Mr. Preble," Charity said, in the voice she lately had reserved for tradesmen, shopkeepers, and clergy. "I would like to return to *my* house, to *my* bedchamber, to *my* life, which has been so rudely interrupted, and attempt to forget that *all* this recent unpleasantness ever happened."

As she spat out the word "unpleasantness," she looked him squarely in the face, as she was not to do again for a very long time.

* * *

Many months later, Matthew retreated to the casket.

This time, he did not open his eyes to see what portraits and playlets the satin curtains would unveil. This time, he repaired to the grave only to sleep. He lay still, eyes closed, tried to wedge himself into the sweet, sunny coffin of childhood memory, and willed sweet nepenthe to embrace him.

Night after fitful night, in his new, cold, lonely bedchamber in the servant's wing of the Gorce mansion, he had sought oblivion with insomniac singlemindedness, and had failed utterly. Partially to blame was the bed—a creaking, swaybacked ruin that had been a malevolent secret of the Gorce family for decades, the lot of generations of unwelcome cousins, unwanted drummers, and unnecessary circuit preachers. Its arthritic joints were trussed with baling wire, and its list to starboard would have been even more noticeable but for the prosthetic use of an overturned chamber pot.

At Matthew's direction, Sterne and his tool chest did the malformed bed further injury, lowering the canopy to mere inches from the occupant's nose. Still it did little more than mock the exquisite sleep Matthew had enjoyed in the grave.

Finally, with great reluctance, Sterne heeded his master's pleas. Sterne helped him wrestle the familiar casket into the patient pit (which Mrs. Preble demanded be left open, as evidence of her husband's duplicity). Sterne lowered the lid, then raised it seconds later, as an apparent afterthought, and said—

"Eight hours. No more."

—then closed it again.

At first, Matthew merely fussed and fidgeted. Why had he not brought a decent pillow, rather than rely upon this inadequate felt-covered fist that Mr. Marsh provided all his clients at no extra charge? Furthermore, the intrusive speaking tube that protruded from the lid forced him to hold his head at an unnatural angle, and the cold air that coursed down it all but guaranteed a chill. But Matthew eventually became accustomed to his circumstances, and began to doze. In his half-waking state, he fancied that a beautiful woman reached into his coffin, grasped him by his proudest member, and tugged repeatedly, as if to lift him with one hand alone—succeeding only in producing the most delightful friction, one that sent him smiling into . . . blissful, easeful, soul-repairing sleep!

"Sir.

"Sir, please wake up.

"Your wife, sir—she has need of you."

The sunshine was hot on Matthew's cheeks. But this sun was too close above his face. The lantern illumined Sterne's features from below, doing them no credit; they flickered and danced obscenely.

"What?" Matthew blinked and sat up, slowly. "It's still night. What time is it?" He groped for his watch.

"Three hours till dawn," Sterne said. "I am ahead of my time, sir, but my mistress—your wife—demanded that I wake you."

"My wife?" Matthew was not yet alert enough to envision any scenario in which his wife might desire his presence. "Why, is something wrong? Where is she?"

"She is here, sir," Sterne said. "Alongside you."

Even beyond the lantern light, Sterne's forehead and neck twitched, suggesting a fit of nerves, or an unprecedented display of emotion barely kept in check. He wordlessly helped Matthew clamber out of the pit, then pointed into the adjacent grave.

A closed casket rested there, lightly covered by a shallow layer of earth. Sterne handed Matthew a shovel.

"She wishes for you to dig her up," Sterne said. He walked away, hunching his shoulders against the breeze, vanishing three paces into the gloom.

Dazed, Matthew moved the lantern to the brink of the grave and vaulted into the hole. After a couple of experimental thrusts, he cast away the shovel, for the earth was only a few inches deep. With his hands, he raked away the clods indifferently spread across the mahogany surface in token burial.

He opened the lid.

Charity, wearing only her shift, looked up at him, smiling, twinkling, cheeks flushed. "Hello, husband," she said.

He blinked. "Hullo."

"Mr. Sterne told me what you were up to, you rogue. Embarrassing the poor man like that."

"Beg pardon?"

She reached up with both hands and twined her long fingers into the frills on the front of his shirt. She tried to imitate Sterne's familiar rumble. "He's out there in the cemetery, ma'am. Really and truly in it, I mean. Says life has no meaning for him anymore, and he won't emerge—begging your pardon, ma'am—until you come out there and save him." Her laugh was like the sweet jingle of a coffin bell, as she raised one bare foot, sidling it along the folds of his trousers. "Matthew, my love, what an enchanting—no, exciting—place to consummate your apology!"

"My dear—"

"Matthew," Charity said, "come wake me. Come wake the dead." Tightening her fingers, she hauled violently, throwing him off balance. Matthew fell atop her, and the casket lid thumped down upon his buttocks.

Untended, the lantern burned until nearly dawn.

* * *

Caskets were henceforth an important feature of the Prebles' domestic life. Funeral parlors welcomed their lingering visits. Porters and doormen cursed and marveled at the weight of their luggage. Sterne quietly purchased enough digging equipment to exhaust a vein of coal, while the children of Rochester, delighted by rumors, paid each other to run past the Prebles' house. By spring 1849, when both Mr. and Mrs. Preble set sail on that doomed Hudson steamer, its boiler ticking down the hours until explosion, the faithful Sterne had lost count of how many times he had buried the both of them.

* * *

For weeks after the double funeral, though the other mourners (mostly out-of-towners) had long departed and resumed their lives, Sterne lingered. Frequent travelers on the turnpike that spring became accustomed to seeing the buggy tethered to the gates of the Gorce family cemetery, the dappled horse cropping wild asparagus in the shadow of the arching wrought-iron legend:

IT IS A HOLY AND WHOLESOME THOUGHT, TO PRAY FOR THE DEAD.

No one looked inside the buggy to remark on the ropes, the brandy, the shovels.

Sterne took most of his noontime meals in that bee-haunted acre, straddling the sandstone wall within hailing distance of the two fresh, bare graves.

The widow Redfield, observing Sterne's schedule, began visiting her late husband (whose mother was a Gorce) somewhat more frequently than had been her custom. Her appearances became so frequent, in fact, that Sterne no longer could dismiss them as coincidence. In a stoic air of experimentation, he began loading double provisions into his picnic basket each day, and he was not disappointed.

No matter how scintillating the widow Redfield's company, however, he conversed in a polite but abstracted manner, always with one ear cocked, listening for the chimes, the knocks, the muffled halloos that never came.

On the last day of his vigil, while calmly buttering a roll, he said aloud: "I suppose all amusements must come to an end."

"Oh, Mr. Sterne," the widow Redfield said, suddenly pale.

"Eh?" Trained to react to far subtler inflections, he looked up, butter knife poised. "Oh, I don't mean our visits, Mrs. Redfield. You misunderstand me. I was thinking aloud . . . about a private joke, of long standing, between my mistress and master, and me." He nodded in their direction.

The widow Redfield dimpled anew, smacked a droning yellowjacket with one of Mr. Marsh's advertising fans, and asked: "Why, Mr. Sterne. Are you a man who appreciates amusements, then?" She threw her shoulders back, emphasizing her already considerable bosom.

"Increasingly so, Mrs. Redfield," he replied, and popped the entire golden roll into his mouth.

Fenneman's Mouth

"TWENTY-THREE CHILDREN?" ASKED GROUCHO Marx, eyebrows arched. As he reared back in his swivel chair, the swivel-chair-like squeak was just audible above the audience's gasps and murmurs. A nice touch, that, and my idea.

"Yes, sir," said the beaming Mrs. Crocetti, who giggled and made the slightest suggestion of a curtsy, her fingers laced together with—nervousness? No, decorum. Angelina Marconi Crocetti (as I had named her) was used to this reaction, surely, the titters and whispers of Eisenhower-era sophisticates, but that made her all the prouder. Somewhere in that boxy purse, no doubt, were photos of every last bambino, at all ages. We had spent more time on Groucho, of course, for obvious reasons, but I was proudest so far of Mrs. Crocetti—her broad forehead, her long teeth, her appropriately wide hips beneath her simple checked frock. The very image of fresh-faced, Old World innocence, she dimpled and awaited the mangy old roue's next question. Which was directed, as longtime viewers might have predicted, to his straight man.

"Fenneman?"

The studio audience laughed loudly, as it always did when Groucho turned, in mock desperation or annoyance, to his long-suffering, hopelessly square announcer. Groucho's voice slightly increased in pitch whenever he said Fenneman's name, as if he were just at the edge of losing his celebrated cool. This half-squawk had been funny in the stateroom scene of *A Night at the Opera* ("Steward! Steward!"), and it was still funny on *You Bet Your Life* twenty-five years later. He was a pro, Groucho was, and I did right by him; I modulated that pitch myself.

"Did you hear that, Fenneman?"

"I certainly did, Groucho," the announcer dutifully replied.

Groucho waggled his cigar and asked, "Did you have something to do with this, Fenneman?" A roar of laughter this time. Fenneman, his spreading blush evident even in grainy black and white, tried good-naturedly to answer, but Groucho interrupted: "With bringing this woman on the show, I mean, Fenneman." Each time the laughing Fenneman—his grin now slightly forced—tried to reply, Groucho interrupted again, and the audience laughed all the louder.

Seated beside me, Pamela mouthed Groucho's words along with him—a new habit. Lea once had done the same, when we were both new at this, together. Where *was* Lea, anyway? We weren't done yet—not by a long shot.

"Please, Fenneman. . . . I'm not asking about your personal life, here. . . . Let's keep this on a professional level, shall we?"

I found myself chuckling. No matter how many times you look at these old clips, they're still funny, right? We had been looking at this one for—what?—nearly thirteen hours, and still it made me laugh. Oh, sure, this wasn't technically an "old" clip; we were, after all, the first people ever to see it—I mean, *really* to see it, as opposed to just *claiming* to have seen it, *imagining* having seen it. But by the time we were done, it would be as good as anyone's memory of it. Better. I mean, it still made *me* laugh, didn't it?

Groucho had turned back to Mrs. Crocetti. "Twenty-three children, well, that's remarkable." So far, so good, but something nagged me. I made a note: *Fenneman's mouth.* "That's quite an achievement."

"Thank you."

"Even remembering their names, that must be an achievement."

There was Lea, pacing the darkness on the other side of the Plexiglas, long legs striding—when did she find time to work out?—cell phone clamped to her ear. At moments her chiseled face shone blue, bathed in television, but I couldn't see the screen. I didn't have to.

"So tell us, Mrs. Crocetti, why did you decide to have so many children?"

With a jerk of my head, I was back to business.

Pam whispered, "A half-second longer, right?" Reverence for the moment—I liked that.

"Yeah," I whispered, eyes on the screen. It was less a word than a breath.

With the aplomb of a veteran front-stoop philosopher, the authentically slightly blurred image of Mrs. Crocetti shrugged her broad shoulders and replied, "I love my husband."

Cut to Groucho's look of disbelief, which froze as Pam clicked Extend. The audience laughter flattened out—*ha haaaaaaaaah*—we'd putty over that easily. "*Wait for it,*" I said, feeling quite the old vaudevillian. I should join the Friars. "Now!" Pam clicked Resume. The laughter surged. Groucho's eyebrows rode up.

"Well, I love my cigar, too," Groucho said, "but I take it out once in a while."

"Yesssss!" we said in unison, springing up and high-fiving. "Perfect!" I said. As I yanked my headset, the pandemonium in the *You Bet Your Life* studio abruptly receded, giving way to the background hum and hiss of the late-night control room, and the murmur of Lea's voice beyond the window. My elation ebbed just as fast.

". . . It's phenomenal, Alex, it's just phenomenal, what you're doing, I am *so* proud of you, you know that? . . ."

The sweeps-week episode of *America's Funniest TV Fuck-Ups* had been my idea—a "classics" episode, full of all your baby-boomer favorites and mine: The "in the butt, Bob" episode of *The Newlywed Game,* the fumbly Julia Child snatching the chicken off the floor and slapping it back in the pan, Soupy Sales' "firetruck" joke, the *Tonight Show* when Raquel Welch asked Johnny, "Would you like to pet my pussy?" None of these actually had happened, of course, no one had seen them, but they were classics nonetheless, cherished TV memories of millions of Americans, indistinguishable from reality. I got the idea from those "blooper" LPs I had loved as a kid. Kermit Schafer was the producer's name, he made a mint off those things, and when he couldn't find, for example, an actual tape of the beloved Uncle Don calling all the tots in Radioland "little bastards"—another cherished fuck-up that never happened—why, he just hired a voice actor to "re-enact" it! So I said, hey, we've got technology Kermit Schafer never dreamed of, we're all tired of footage of The Nanny blowing her lines to hell, let's finally put these TV classics *on the air*, give the people what they want.

As for what I wanted—well, that was somewhat harder, wasn't it?

"Zell? Earth to Zell." Pam poked me in the side, her nail surprisingly sharp and deep. I had *not* found time, lately, for the gym. "What do you think, Zell? Putty over that audience hole and it's a wrap, what do you say?"

"Not so fast," I said, more harshly than I had intended, and I snatched up my legal pad to avoid seeing Pam's hurt expression, and Lea's cellular love-fest. There was one item not crossed off. "In that reaction, uh, reaction shot, while Groucho is needling him, uh? There's still something wrong with Fenneman's mouth."

"Oh, the hell there is."

"Yes, it's true, queue it up, OK? Let's take a look, I'll, I'll show you." Lea had pocketed the phone. Now she perched one-hipped on the edge of the conference table, skirt riding up, face upturned, lips slightly parted, reflections flickering across her Bryn Mawr cheekbones as she looked up at the screen, awash no doubt in the afterglow of the latest senatorial-campaign success of Alex Fucking Chiang, spin doctor to the stars.

"Zell, come on, do you know what time it is?"

"It's time to get this thing done *right* or not at all, Pam, that's what time it is. This isn't Birmingham." I slapped down the legal pad. My half-full Styrofoam coffee cup hopped off the counter and doused my slacks on the way down. I jerked backward, a split-second's expectation of heat replaced by a plastering clamminess. "Shit," I elaborated, already feeling like an ass. "Queue it up, OK? I'm going to the can." Turning my back on Pam, who deserved better—she had been hired a rookie hotshot straight from Fox's Birmingham affiliate, sure, but two years ago—I stalked off toward the can, which took me of course, O happy day, into the conference room. Lea blinked, startled, as I entered and stood there, the door to Control hissing shut behind me. She hadn't been watching Alex's stuff at all. She had been watching mine.

On the screen above, a grinning Bozo the Clown clapped his big puffy white gloves together and said, "C'mon, Billy. You can do it. One more basket, and you've won all the prizes!"

Lea gestured with the remote, and with her chin. Her mouth, when she smiled, was always a little too wide for comfort. "I hadn't watched them all straight through before. Great work, Zell. You've done it this time."

"*We've* done it," I said.

"Shh. Here it comes."

Chubby little Billy's five-year-old face was red and clenched in concentration, the tip of his tongue visible at the corner of his mouth. As he rose from his crouch, his shirt rode up, exposing his navel. He grunted as he heaved the Bozo ball into the air in a child's version of a layup.

Cut to the Bozo ball hitting the rim, bouncing, hitting the rim a second time—and bouncing out. The pipsqueak cheers of the small-fry studio audience turned to groans. Cut to Bozo, his big goofy hand patting little Billy's shoulder. Little Billy's round face, still focused on the out-of-shot basketball goal, was (as I had insisted) unreadable.

"Awwwww, that's too bad, Billy, but listen, we have your very own Bozo ball for you to take home, to say thank you for playing with us today."

Lea stepped on Bozo's next line, and I winced with annoyance, then felt ashamed. "That little shrug of Billy's, here—I love that."

"And remember—it's not whether you win or lose, but how you play the game, right boys and girls?"

Little Billy shrugged off Bozo's hand and said, "Get screwed."

The audience gasped. One little girl's voice was distinct: "Ah *woo-woo!*" Bozo suddenly looked, beneath his makeup, naked and old.

Lea never laughed out loud—just a soft clucking noise in the back of her throat, as she rocked back and forth. She did that now, her curls bouncing. If she were digitized we could dub her—a throaty chuckle, maybe, or a Dyan Cannon bray.

"Billy!" Bozo managed to say. "That's a no-no, Billy—a Bo-Zo No-No." Somewhat recovered, he shook a white puffy finger of admonishment in Billy's direction. Billy responded with a gesture of his own. Total excitement. The screen went dark.

"Oh, God." Still beaming, Lea set down the remote, hopped off the table, and stretched, her diamond-studded navel flashing like little Billy's. A gift from Alex, no doubt. "That's my favorite one, Zell. I mean, I love Groucho, too, but little Billy, you just can't beat it. And the funny thing is?" Her back was to me as she closed her briefcase, and I took the opportunity, hating myself, to stare. "I remember *seeing* that on TV, back when I was younger than Billy, even. I know that's ridiculous, but there it is." She raked one hand through her hair, shook her head as if to wake herself up. "I guess I've told you that before, huh?"

"The closest to being true is Groucho," I said. "He actually made the cigar joke, but on radio, and it was cut before broadcast —so no one outside the studio audience ever saw it or heard it. But as for little Billy, no, Lea, I'm sorry, I guess he was one of your imaginary friends." I was reciting rather than talking, but hey, it passed for conversation as she put on her jacket, delayed her going out the door. "Going somewhere?" I asked.

"Hum?" she asked, absently, picking up the remote again. "Aren't we done?" She switched from closed-circuit to broadcast, to CNN-4. A tape of Senator Whitley's celebrated press conference, for the umpteenth time. Yes, I thought, we're done. Only one of us is slow to catch on.

"Not quite," I said. "Still some touching up to do, here and there."

"But you guys don't need *me* any more, surely. Alex is waiting, I mean, I thought I'd go down to Whitley headquarters on the way home, you know? See what the latest is. I thought those poll results would be *somewhere*."

She surfed the news channels, mainly shuffling images of Senator Whitley, amid a babel of sound bites: "Controversial remark . . . Official denial . . . Senator's own recording contradicts . . ."

"Actually," I said, while telling myself *No don't say it Don't say it*, "I thought maybe you and I could clear out of here together, go have a drink, sort of . . . celebrate." Her profile expressionless, she metronomically clicked the remote. "The show being done, I mean. And your Amazing Elastic Candidate bouncing back yet again, or so it seems."

"You know that wouldn't be a good idea," Lea said. "Wait, hush, here it is."

"—of ten thousand Californians surveyed by phone and Net just 30 minutes ago reveals that forty-five percent accept the Senator's explanation of her remark, to thirty percent belief for the ABC tape, with twenty-five percent undecided. To recap, we are told that within the hour, the Senator's campaign will release a portion of a videotape made by a disinterested bystander, a high-school newspaper editor, which according to the Senator's spokesman will demonstrate that her statement was NOT in fact—"

Lea's phone purred. She muted the TV. "Jesus. Yeah?" Her pinched look vanished as she grinned, held the instrument slightly away from her ear. I heard tinny revelry. "All right, already! I'm coming! Pour me a glass before it's gone, will you? OK. Hey, Alex

—high-school newspaper editor, huh? Nice touch. Bye. Me, too."

It was the "Me, too" that tore it, that and the dreamy way she pocketed the phone, as if she couldn't remember where it went, while smiling in the general direction of the John Wayne Coors ad on the muted screen. "You'd think you worked for Senator Whitley," I said, "and not for me."

I wanted a fight, I guess. Instead, I got a darted glance of round-mouthed astonishment, and then a floorward look of thin-lipped guilt.

"Oh," I said.

She lifted her briefcase, set it down, sighed, attempted a shrug. "I wasn't going to mention it until after we were done with the show—really done, I mean. First thing Monday, I was going to tell you. Or *ask* you, really, because I haven't made up my mind, Alex *says* there's a job for me not only during the campaign but after, but who's to say she'll even be re-elected, and then where would I be?" I was sitting down by now, elbows on knees, looking at the carpet. Didn't anyone ever vacuum in here? Her feet stepped into view. On her ankle was a new tattoo, a second rose. "Then again, she's done so much for the state, for the country, and if she can survive this, this stupid *thing*, this half-audible off-the-cuff crack about the Pope, and if I can use my skills, the skills *you* taught me, to help, well, then, why shouldn't—Zell? Zell. Talk to me, Zell." She squatted, knees sharp in my face. "You know I still value your advice, Zell," she said. "I always did."

"Tell me," I said. "Do you always have to work for the people you're screwing? Or is it the other way around? Oh, Jesus. Lea. I didn't mean that. Lea. Wait!"

"Get. Out. Of my way," she said. She pushed me back, her briefcase between us like a shield.

"Lea, listen, I'm sorry, I'm so sorry, but I'm *confused* here, OK, just a month ago, that last night we worked late, remember? You said—"

"Don't you dare put words in my mouth, Zell, ever again. You always did that, it was always *your* version—"

"—Wait, Lea, you did, don't you remember? You said that given some time, you and me, we might have a chance—"

"I did not say that, I did *not*, stop it! Get out of my—my head, my *past!* Please!"

She swept past me into the corridor—was that a snort? A sob? I slumped against the paneling, looked for something to look at as her high heels stuttered across the tile. My eyes like a wino's in a bus station tracked to the TV screen. Audrey Hepburn this time, hawking Ramada Inns. The stairwell door crashed open. Lea echoed all the way down as the door creaked. Slowly. Shut. I pushed myself upright, shuffled into the corridor. Tried and failed as I passed the stairs to hear more echoes, ascending. In the gleaming brightness of the lavender-smelling can I splashed my face, left the tap running for company, had a seat, stared at the tile, rubbed my wet palms together till they were dry, listened to the hair-trigger automatic urinals, ever-malfunctioning, amuse one another: a beep here, a beep there, a flush.

I did my best to think about nothing, but I couldn't help wondering, fleetingly, how Alex, my brilliant ex-intern Alex, who was using *his* video skills not to hawk cars and cheap laughs and beer but to make the world a Better Place, and win Lea away in the process, had fixed that Pope business. Not a simple dub, certainly, no quick edit. Something more creative, more convincing. I'd find out soon enough. Not that I cared, really. Just professional curiosity.

Beep, flush, beep.

It had been a sob, there in the doorway. Definitely a sob.

When I got back to Control, Pam was sitting in lotus position on the sofa in the back of the room, her gym bag in her lap, watching the Groucho clip. She didn't look at me, mercifully, as I dropped into the prickly, coffee-smelling cushions beside her. She must have seen and heard everything through the Plexiglas. Oh, well. There are no secrets in television.

"Fixed Fenneman," she murmured.

"Yeah, I see, good job." I said it without really seeing, or caring, having already decided to bless her efforts and call it a night. Then I focused on the screen and sat forward, intent.

"Please, Fenneman. . . . I'm not asking about your personal life, here."

It really *was* a good job, an excellent job. Pam had outdone herself. In the face of Groucho's sidekick I now read not just mingled embarrassment and amusement, not just game acceptance with a hint of weariness, but something downright wise and tragic as well—Fenneman as Eternal Footman, always looking on, always providing straight lines, but seeing and understanding as the glib Groucho never could. Or maybe it was late, and I was drained, and I had looked at the damn clip too long. No matter. This Fenneman was an improved Fenneman, and the minute adjustments Pam had made, invisible though they may have been to the lay viewer, made all the difference to me.

"Pam," I said, "painters used to tell an old joke. They said, you know what a portrait is? A portrait is a painted likeness of a person with a little something wrong about the mouth. Two hours ago, Pam, what we had here was a portrait of Fenneman, but now I feel I'm in the presence of the true Fenneman, the accurate, the living, the quintessential Fenneman. I applaud you."

Had I ever seen her smile so? "Thank you," she finally said, and poked me in the ribs again. Her finger stayed there only a second too long. "Now can we go get something to eat?"

I looked at her. I was strung-out and exhausted, but I still could process, given time. When had she pierced her nose? It suited her. Before I could reply, she added: "You said, earlier, that when we were done, we'd get a bite. Or something."

"I did, didn't I?" I said. I had no recollection of it at all.

We clumped downstairs in silence, Pam waiting at each landing for me to catch up, smiling as if to say, You're almost there. At the garage level she held the door for me, and didn't quite step aside, so that I had to brush past. Her shoulder was softer than I expected. As we walked toward the guard's cubicle, our footsteps echoing, she said, "When I first came to work here, I thought you were a real jerk."

"And now you know it for sure," I said.

"You probably don't even remember that party," she said. "You were pretty wasted."

"I was not. I haven't been drunk since college." It was true.

"Oh, so you had no excuse, then. Leering. Directing all your comments down my blouse." She sounded amused.

"Hey, now, I don't remember it like that. I remember a tipsy gal from Alabama who talked too loud and sloshed me with her Heineken."

"Vodka tonic."

As I swept my card through the reader, we studied each other. "OK," I said. "A vodka tonic. And allow me to apologize, however belatedly, for my drunken behavior." I made a small bow. "It was inexcusable. Most unlike me."

"Apology accepted."

"Hiya, Mr. Elizondo, Ms. Cary," said the guard, whom my card had summoned to the TV monitor. His miked voice crackled; his face bulged on the screen, as if he were pushing it too close to the camera.

"Hiya, Morty," we said, automatically. The nightly wait for all the locks to release was interminable, made more so by Morty's wheezy good humor.

"You guys still working on that old-timer's show?"

"Just about done, Morty," I said, loudly. As the locks whirred and clanked, I murmured to Pam, too low for Morty to hear: "You left. With the bartender."

"I *never.*"

"You did."

She considered, smiled. "You mean . . . Raoul?"

I shook my head. "Herman."

As she mouthed the name Herman, Morty's voice broke in: "Hey, guys, I got one for you, oughtta be on your show. You remember that one when Arnold Palmer's wife tells Carson that before every tournament, for luck, she kisses Arnie's balls—can you believe it?—and Carson, oh my God, he says to her—"

"Yeah," I cried, "that's a great one, huh, Morty?"

His jowls shook with laughter as he reared back, Groucho-like, in his swivel chair. I never did industrial work myself, but I had to admire the craftsmanship. This upgrade was the most convincing Morty yet—only the split-second's lag time before the insertion of each employee's name gave it away. To the professional eye, that is. "Every time I see that one, gosh," Morty continued, slapping his authentically beefy thigh, "I just about pee my pants—uh, pardon my French, Miss Cary."

"See you, Morty," she said, for the door finally was trundling open.

"See you guys. Ah, me. Classic stuff, you can't go wrong."

The trapped-exhaust stink of the garage was, for a second, overpowering. "I'm over here," Pam said, jingling keys. "I'll drive. Herman. Yeah. Sure. Hadn't thought about him in a while."

"Big, muscular guy."

"Not really," she said. "Tall, yeah, but slim. With a mustache. You had one, too. Didn't you?"

"If you say so," I told her, and smiled.

Lincoln in Frogmore

From the Federal Writers' Project interview with Shad Alston at his home on St. Helena Island, South Carolina, September 21, 1936. Interviewer: Miss Jordan Matthews.

YOUNGUNS THESE DAYS, THEY DON'T WANT TO hear bout no slavery, they don't want to hear bout Mr. Lincoln. And he was just down the road a piece here, in that swamp yonder. I saw him with my own eyes, and they were good eyes then. You'd think it'd all happened to a bunch of strange niggers up in Philly-Me-York, stead of to their own blood kin, their own folks.

I start telling bout Mr. Lincoln coming down here, and what do I get? "You lying like the crossties, Mr. Shad. You lying up a nation." "Shame on you, Mr. Shad. You done quit lying and gone to flying." Huh!

Anybody ain't got sense enough to know what slavery was, won't be able to see it coming back, will they? Be slaves again and not even know it.

Now I'm gone tell you a true thing. I'll tell you bout Mr. Lincoln, just the way it happened, and you can put it in your book. That's how true it is, now: True enough for a book.

"Once upon a time was a good old time,
"Bit by a gator he'd spit turpentine."

That's how we'd start a tale when I was a youngun. I don't rightly know how old I was when it happened, but I was bout *that* high up against the doorframe, and all longleggedy like a granddaddy spider, and fast! I could outrun a coach whip. And you better believe I sure hit it a lick that evening when Maum Hannah called me from the house.

"Shad! You, Shad! You better give it the book back on here to this yard, boy, or I'll be all over you like gravy over rice."

When I heard that, I was in the edge of the woods, holding up a bright green gopher turtle in the air real still-like, to see would it think it was back on the ground, and poke its head outen its shell. But my arm had gone numb on me, and I reckon that gopher woulda outlast me even if Maum Hannah hadn't gone to fussing. I put the gopher back down in the bresh where I got him and beat it on back. Maum Hannah didn't move so quick, you see, and her voice took some working before it got loud enough to carry, so I knew if she was already on the porch and yelling loud enough for me to hear in the woods, she'd done been calling for ten minutes and was hot as a pine knot. Man! Believe me, I hauled the fast mail.

"You, Shad! I swear I'll put the water in your eyes, boy. I'll whip your sorry head to the red."

When I got to the yard she was on the porch, a-sitting on the far end of the joggling-board cause she was too heavy for the middle, she'd hit the planks and couldn't get up. She had her pipe in one hand and her walking stick in the other and blue smoke all around. She had her head down to her knees, like she'd wore herself out, but was just opening her mouth to tune up again when I cried, "Here I am, Maum Hannah, I come just as quick as I could."

"Child," she said, "where you been?" She stuck the pipe back in her mouth and sucked on it loud. I was bout to tell her when she went on, "I *know* you ain't been fooling with crawling varmints down in them tick-filled woods that I told you to stay outen."

"No, ma'am, I ain't," I said, sitting down real careful on the far end of the joggling-board, past the reach of her stick. I hadn't figured on her blocking off the truth like that, and leaving me to think up a lie with no notice at all hardly.

"Well, thank the wonder-working God for that," she said, all cast-down and quiet again. Maum Hannah was a big old gal when she was hollering, but when she was done she'd fold back down like all her air was gone, and look small. Lately she was looking smaller and smaller when she was quiet, but maybe I was just getting biggedy. Anyways, I knew she wasn't gone take a lick at me now. I eased on down the board toward the middle, started joggling up and down. Maum Hannah closed her eyes like the joggles was making her tired, but I ask you, what's the good of a joggling-board if you ain't joggling? Might's well have a rocking chair without a rock, a swing with no swang.

"I got to go on a errand this evening," Maum Hannah said, joggling there on the end of the board, her eyes closed, her knobby hands working the end of her stick. "May be I won't get back till dark, may be black dark. You stay here in the house, child, you got me? Not in the yard, *in* the *house*." She thumped the porch with her stick, and our fice dog run out from underneath, carrying something in its mouth, into the bresh. "The roads and the woods are too dangerous these nights, you hear me?"

"Yes, Maum Hannah," I said, straining to see what it was the fice had got.

She was right, too—those were dangerous days, for white or colored, slave or free. Me and Maum Hannah, now, praise Jesus, were free, like a lot of colored folks around the island and in Frogmore town. But that didn't help the poor folks none on Mr. Ravenel's plantation, or all the other plantations up and down the sea islands, or all the folks who were owned in the cities and the towns. But it wouldn't be slave times for long, no Lord, even the field niggers knew that. Mr. Lincoln's Navy was just off the coast, a thousand ships in a line from New Orleans to Norfolk, each one in sight of two others, and not even a piragua could sail any supplies through without getting blown to kindling wood. Mr. Lincoln's Navy was just sitting there, but his Army, it was getting the *job* done. They done took Savannah just before Christmas-time, and here it was January, and everybody figured Charleston was next, and there was me and Maum Hannah and all of St. Helena Island a-sitting right in the middle.

I guess that's why everybody was on the move that month. It didn't matter how many of Mr. Ravenel's niggers got whipped or hung, every day more and more of 'em just turned up gone, headed toward Savannah hoping to hook up with the bluecoats, or heading into the woods hoping to hide out till it was all over. The bravest, we'd heard tell, were rafting or swimming out into the Sound, hoping Mr. Lincoln's ships would take 'em aboard and give 'em a medal, I reckon, or leastways a job putting flint to the fuse. And paterollers were combing the country looking to string up or cut to pieces any coloreds they could find, whether they were the ones who'd run off or not—and gator-black wild niggers were living half-starved and crazy in the marsh—and Sesesh deserters, in twos and threes, were trying to get to Charleston by the back roads, or through the woods and swamps—and some said a boatload of drunk bluecoats come ashore some nights, in the fog, bored with sitting in the water and playing coon-can for nickels, and hot for some devilment. Blue can hide in the woods at night as easy as gray, and kill you just as dead.

So it was a wild time, but did I care? I was a youngun and a longleggedy jackrabbit, as I said, and my daddy was sold before I was born and my mama went away when I was little in Master Ravenel's own buckboard, wearing a pink silk dress fit for a white woman, and Maum Hannah was old and moving slow—so I ask you, who was gone stop me? I was in them woods, and in them swamps, ever chance I got, hoping I'd have me an adventure, and see for myself some of the big things a-doing in the world.

"I done fixed your supper," Maum Hannah said, her eyes open now. "It's on the stove for when you want it. Rabbit stew and beaten biscuits and black-eyed peas and gumbo and a crock of bluejohn to wet it with, and don't you push it all down that worthless dog out yonder neither. You need it more'n he does."

"Yes, Maum Hannah," I said, figuring the fice wasn't gone need no supper, the way he was working at something out there in the bresh. "You gone eat when you get back?"

"I done fixed me a bucket," she said. "I'll eat when I'm ready, I figure." She waved for me to come help her stand up. She managed it, leaning on me with one hand and her stick with the other. Didn't seem to me she needed to be going noplace.

"Where'd you say you was bound for, again?" I asked her, thinking I was being clever-like.

"I didn't," she said, "and I ain't gone to.

"Don't you like it, don't you take it,

"Here's my collar, come and shake it."

She swatted my rump. "Hand me my bucket, yonder beside the churn. I got to get on. The day's waning." She teeter-tottered at the top of the steps, fussed with the bonnet knot neath her chin, looked into the sun a-setting. "Yes, Lord," she said. "The long day is waning, and Your great work is nigh on done. Thank you, child," she said. The bucket was covered by a oilcloth, but couldn't a been much in it—it didn't weigh far from empty. She set it on top of her head, said, "Umph, umph, umph," and went off down the steps, blowing pipe smoke ever which way. "I want to hear you slam that front door behind me and lock it before I get outen the yard, you hear me?"

"Yes, Maum Hannah," I said.

This was big doins for *sure* enough sure. She hadn't in the longest time had me lock the front door. Excited now, I turned my back on her and ran to where the big old key hung on a nail above the fireplace. I slid a chair under it, climbed up there, passed the key on the way up, and stood there feeling like a mullet head. I had grown since last time we used that key; I didn't need that chair at all, now. I jumped off, reached up and snagged the key off the nail, done! Maum Hannah had reached the edge of the yard, but she didn't look around as I slammed the front door and locked it, just like I promised I'd do—cept I was outside the door, on the porch, when I done it. Now Maum Hannah was just outen sight, past the first stand of trees, just a little blue streak curling back to show she'd been there. I was set on slipping around behind her, seeing where she was going. But first I was gone see what the fice had hold of.

I tipped across the yard, trying not to mess up the sand I'd just raked that day, and not to make noise that would call Maum Hannah back down on me. "You, dog," I whispered. "What you got there, huh?" It growled at me and shinnied backward in the bresh, but switched its raggedy tail, too, like it wanted to play. "Gone get it," I whispered, on my all fours now. "Yessir. Gone get it. Gone get it. Gone *get*—!" I snatched at the near end of it and the fice jumped all feet up in the air and backwards and held on to the far end as it stretched out between us—a tore-off rag of black cloth, thin so you could see through it, and as long as my arm, or longer, cause it was mighty stretchy. I set to worrying it away from the fice. "Let go, you thin-brainded thing," I said, and he said *rrrr r rrrr*, like a fice does. I stuck a stick between his teeth and he let the rag go to gnaw on that. I held the rag up close and pulled on it and looked through it and rubbed my hands together with it in the middle—man, it was *smooth*. Pretty, too, even raggedy and dirty and full of trash from who knows what all it had been dragged through.

I figured it musta come off somebody's clothes—a shirt or a dress or a pair of britches, maybe—but whoever it was musta been one rich buckra. All the colored folks I knew, and most of the white folks, were poor as owl harkey, and my own shirt and britches felt like croker sacks next to this. The field hands' clothes didn't get soft like this even on washday till they were next to rotten and no good no more. I rubbed the black scrap against my cheek. Betcha my mama is wearing a dress this fine, I thought. Then I stuffed it in the back of my britches so it hung out a little, like a rag I'd blow my nose on, and knelt down to talk to the fice, which was wagging his whole butt end. I didn't need him yapping behind me and bringing Maum Hannah down on us like Moses.

"You, dog, stay put, now," I whispered. "Take care of the place, you hear? No, *stay.*" I chunked another stick a far ways neath the house, and when the fice went after it, I set off down the lane.

Didn't take long to catch Maum Hannah in sight again, and after that I kept to the edge of the woods, picking along and scaring up critters, just in case she looked back around at the road. But what was behind her didn't concern her none, no ma'am. She was focused on the great blue in-front-of, was Maum Hannah that evening as the shadows got long, and she was stepping along right smart, too—for her. There were other people on the road, too. Ahead of her were three younger women, and when they saw Maum Hannah coming they stopped to wait on her to catch up. But she didn't stop in the road to do no bookooing, no, they all set off together, and I was way too far back to hear what they said. Between the trees it was near black dark now, though the sun would still be low on the Sound, and the bird Maum Hannah called the *kambaboli* would be calling in the tide—*Whoot! Whoot!* And the darker it got, the more people seemed to be on the road—way up ahead, and stepping out from the trees all around, like shadows grown legs and gone to walking. And finally I stepped out there in the road, too, cause no way Maum Hannah was gone spot me now, in the dark, and I walked long with everybody else, more and more of 'em all the time.

Some woman nearby said, "We ain't gone be late, is we?"

A man said, "Naw, we be there in good time."

Musta been some shindig indeedy come to pass, get all these colored folks out in the road like this with the paterollers no telling where. Course, we'd be able to hear the paterollers up the road a ways off—*clumpety clumpety clump,* and their shackles and chains all a-jingle.

As I walked along, not studying bout the people just ahead of me or just behind, I kept yanking at the shoulders of my shirt, cause they chafed me. Oh, man, go in the creek, I thought. Quit that. Ain't nothing wrong with your clothes. I knew what Maum

Hannah would say. *Always making the big-eye bout what rich people's got. Ain't your shirt clean and fresh patched and don't it fit you good? Them rich people's mouths is cut crossways just like yourn, ain't they? Lord, for truth, you is a backslid and head-pecked child. You ain't thankful for all the things God sent you down, God gone snatch you up. Gone go in your bed and take you out.* I studied on it some, and I decided it was that soft black rag I got hold of, was making my shirt feel bad on me. I didn't think nothing bad bout my shirt before I found that. "Who needs this damn buckra cracker rag anyhow?" I said out loud. "Dog damn it." I yanked it outen my britches, made like to throw it away, then put it back where it was. "Double dog damn it," I said.

Somebody next to me said, "You mighty little to be talking such a way."

He was big and stunk like dispensary liquor, and I didn't want nothing to do with him. But he got right up longside me and said, "Ain't you is Maum Hannah's Shad?" And then I knew him, too, cause everyone on St. Helena knew old Fuss-X Quall. We called him Fuss-X cause that was the cheapest liquor there was. Even the crackers wouldn't drink nothing cheaper than Two-X, and that only if some straw boss wouldn't buy 'em Three. He grabbed my shoulder and leaned on me while he was walking—like on a crab boat in bumpty water. "You, Shad. You know old Fuss-X, don't you?"

"Yessir, I do," I said, cause Maum Hannah said God wants children to make their manners to their elders, even if that there respectular elder ain't good for nothing but drawing lightning and murdering groceries.

"You don't mind, do you, Shad, if old Fuss-X walks along with you a ways? Old Fuss-X don't want you getting lost in the dark, now, and missing out on these big doins."

"Nossir, I don't mind it, I guess," I said. I wanted to ask him what the big doins was, but I was ashamed to say I didn't know. My stomach went *rrrr r rrrr* like the fice, and I thought bout those good vittles back at the house on the stove, waiting on me. If I had me a bucket now, I could surely make that biscuit *moan.* Too late now. I done aimed high and had to follow it through.

Hold it high, sweep the sky.
Hold it level, kill the devil.

"Yessir, big old doins," Fuss-X said, like to himself. "Bout the biggest doins ever round Frogmore town, I'd say. Wouldn't you say so, Shad?"

"I reckon so, yessir." I wished he'd nail it shut, cause ever time he said something he squeezed my shoulder like he was gone pinch it off, and his breath stank like asafetida root.

"Almighty big doins," Fuss-X said. Then he got down in my ear and whispered:

"You wouldn't lie to old Fuss-X, now, would you, boy?"

"Nossir."

"To poor old Fuss-X, who's had such a hard shake of it, and who ain't so many these days, who can't walk hardly since the paterollers bout killed him alive, who goes to his knees ever night to pray, and who didn't never do you no harm, nor do any harm to any other of Aunt Hagar's children—no, nor the white folks either, no harm to any man, woman or child in this sin-sick world?"

Somewheres in there his question got away from him and he started crying, the way a stambling old drunk will do, till he couldn't talk no more and blew his nose on his sleeve. I was beginning to think he'd run out of Fuss-X and done filled up instead of home-brewed coon dick, which meant any time now he'd be fighting whatever come near, thinking he was crawling with monkies. I tried to speed up and get away from him even as I said, sorta desperate-like:

"I wouldn't lie to you, nossir, Mr. Fuss-X, I swear I wouldn't."

"Well, tell me now for the truth, then, Shad boy," he whispered in my ear again. "When we all's get to where it is that we's going this evening . . . Uh, where, exactly, is that gone be?"

I stopped in the road so sudden he walked on past me a step or two and nearbouts fell turning around. "Why, Mr. Fuss-X, you mean to tell me *you* don't know where we going, either?"

"I'll tell you *both* where you going," said a big old bald man who come up bout that time, and grabbed hold of me in one hand and Fuss-X in the other. "You both going into one of these trees with your heads knocked together if you can't stay quiet."

The little squawky woman with him said, "You two fools want to bring the paterollers down on us?"

Fuss-X started getting all wet-eyed again and crying bout how he hadn't mean nobody no harm, but I spoke up quick and pitiful: "No, ma'am, but I done mislaid my folks, and I'm scared. Would you mind if I was to walk along with y'all till we get there?" I sidled around, hanging on her skirts, till she was between me and Fuss-X. "I'll be quiet and good, I swear I will."

So she got all sweet and so nice and said I was the sweetest thing, I was just a doll baby, and how dare you take hold of that child, Cephas, what's got into you?

And she kept on a-petting me and making nice to me as our crowd massed up in the road like there was something in the way. There were a lot of hellos and how-you-beens going on, quiet-like. And then I saw our crowd had run head-smack into an even bigger crowd, a-coming down the road from Frogmore way. And all of us were turning off the road and heading into the cypress swamp down a little narrow track, between a lightning-burnt stump and a honeysuckle thicket.

I knew this way well. It was the track to the praying ground, where the colored folks on that part of St. Helena met to have their Christian worship, far from white men and their devilments. What there is bout a colored church service that so riles up the white trash, I didn't know then and I don't know now, cept maybe they hate to see us going straight to the true Master, you know, and skipping the middleman. Now I'd heard tell that some who worshipped the older ways, the African ways, met at that there praying ground, too, but I don't know bout that. All I know is, there were a powerful lot more people making their way through the swamp that night than I ever saw at Christian service before, and didn't no one seem to be missing a step, either. They's all kind of secrets between neighbors, I guess, even on a tee-ninchy island like this.

When you walk on a track through the swamp like that, the black mud sucks at your feet like it wants to keep you around, squinch squinch squinch, and every step fills with a little water like a spring welling up. Musta been a goodly number of people gone on before, like I said, cause that track was a pure loblolly by now, like a hog wallow. And there wasn't nothing to listen to but the bullfrogs and the zingers in the weeds and the squinch of our feet, cause once we got in the swamp good and proper, didn't no one do any talking. I'd lost track of Maum Hannah and Fuss-X and everybody else. There was just that squawky woman's narrow butt ahead of me, and her man Cephas a-breathing heavy just behind. Fuss-X had had some company at the dispensary that day. We hurried on, one right behind the other, cause it was too narrow a passage to walk otherwise. But when we went over the little plank bridge that meant the praying ground was nigh, I heard somebody up ahead a-talking low. Her voice got louder, meaning she was staying put while we went ahead. It was a high-yaller gal, right pretty, and she was wearing a tight little shake-baby dress, like you don't expect to see at no praying ground—though I now know a man might pray for it, yes indeedy, pardon me, ma'am. She was standing on a cypress knee to get taller, and waving us on ahead, all the while peering back the way we'd come, with a glance now and then into the trees and bogs to each side.

"Take foot in hand, people," she said. "He gone start without you. You think he ain't got business elsewhere? He's a busy man, and no mistake. Come on, now, big man." She put her hand on my shoulder to push me along, and I felt all warm where she'd touched me, but was too young, you know, to know why just yet.

"Don't you be studying bout her," said Mr. Cephas into my ear.

"Don't *you,*" his woman said, looking around. "Step it up, now. We most there."

Just then the path went between two big cypresses, and the woods fell away, and the earth firmed up and started to rise a little, and that was the praying ground. Some said it was where the Indians had scraped up enough dry earth to bury their dead folks, away back centuries before any other color man had lived on this island. Two or three pine-knot torches here and there gave all the light there was, but I could tell there was a mess of people ringing the little hill, a hundred or more of 'em, all shuffling and muttering together, men and women and old folks and a few younguns, too. All of 'em colored people. I wondered how many were free and how many of 'em slave—ain't no way to tell, just by looking, is there? No, not to this day. But some were so ragged and dirty and wild-haired that I figured they weren't just in the swamp for a visit. I stopped studying bout the crowd when I saw that on the little hill that was the middle of the praying ground was a little rickety table holding an oil lamp, and sitting on a chair behind the table, talking to an old woman standing there, was the strangest-looking white man in Christendom.

He musta been nearbouts seven feet tall, from the way his knees was drawn up a-sitting there, and his arms a-waving around looked each as long as that, with hands on the ends the size of hams. He was as shackly-built as the table, as skinny as an old swinge cat. His ears stuck out like the fice's, and the hair of his head and beard was as bristly as a hog's, and his eyes was sunk way back in his head like snake holes, and he had the widest mouth I ever saw. He laughed at something said to him, with his head rared back and his pointy knees up against his chest and his arms wrapped around 'em, and I thought the corners of his mouth gone meet in back and send the top of his head a-rolling into the marsh. You ever seen a chicken get up and run around when its head is gone? Well, I felt like this fella coulda done the same. It was like he wasn't put together solid, like regular folks—they was just stuff stuck on here and there, a beaky nose, a gangly arm, and if any of it was to come unstuck, well, it wouldn't be no crisis, he'd put the pieces in his carpetbag to sort out later. He was dressed all fancy in a black swaller-tail coat like he was ready for the cooling board, and as big as he was, the man he'd got the suit from musta been two sizes bigger. While I stared at him, he stood up—and up, and up—till the Spanish moss tickled his beard, and as he hugged that old woman like a bosom-friend, I saw his left shoulder was higher than the right one, and as he stepped around the table he lurched bout as crazy as old Fuss-X did. A slapped-together mess of a man, he was, and then the old woman turned to step back into the crowd, and Lord God! It was Maum Hannah, a-talking with the man himself like they were old relations. Cause I knew who he was, all right. When his splintery face passed above the oil lamp, I knew him from the illustrateds we put over the walls in winter. Besides, I knew there wasn't but one white man who could draw half of St. Helena to him through the dark bare-handed and alone.

He looked toward the spot where we come in, and so I looked too, and I saw that shake-baby gal step into the torchlight a ways, and nod her head. And then I looked back to the mound to see him looking straight at me, and it was to me that he began to talk—yes! Looking straight at me the whole time. That's how come I remember what he said so clear. And *could* he talk, Lord! I believe his tongue was hung in the middle so it flapped both ways. And I didn't stir, nor no one else in the praying ground, nor no creeping flying thing in the swamp, nor nothing in the heavens and the earth, while that man said what he had come to say, in a voice that was like the voice in my head when I talk to myself, just that still and true.

"My friends, I thank you for coming out tonight, to harken to a tired old man who ain't got much time. I'll be as quick as I can, cause I know we ain't the only folks abroad this night.

"Now, I'll be frank with you folks, they's some in Washington a little surprised, a little disappointed, too, that once I made my Proclamation, and freed the slaves, that you all didn't take off and go, and tell Mr. Ravenel to pick his own cotton, wash his own clothes, cook his own victuals, and nurse his own babies, and put everything in a grip-sack and swarm up North as thick as cowpeas, throwing off the paterollers like flies off a bull, and leaving the Sesesh with nothing to fight for but taxes and Mr. Calhoun's weevily wig and some turnips a-rotting in the ground. Cause what has slavery give you? Piggin to eat and oyster shell, that's what it give you—you know that better'n me.

"And I admit, I sorta felt this way for a while myself. But Mr. Douglass, he talked some sense into me. He said, first of all, they's some colored folks down here what ain't slaves, whole islands of 'em, sometimes, working and scraping for the money to buy their family free, cause free ain't free and it ain't cheap neither. And next of all, he said that free or slave, this is you all's home, same as Mr. Ravenel's, and who's to say you got to leave it, any, some, or none, just so's you all can be free? And Mr. Douglass asked me, how they gone buy a train ticket, or hire a room to sleep in, if they ain't got nothing but chicken-change? Counting railroad ties ain't a living. And Mr. Douglass also said, it ain't like Mr. Ravenel gone kiss you all goodbye and suit up his best buckboard and curry his best horse and feed you a dinner of chicken-bosom and hang a Joe Moore around your neck and say, Y'all take good care now, and make sure'n send me a pretty postcard when you get to Philly-Me-York!

"And finally Mr. Douglass said to me, even a fly on a bull spills some blood. Whose blood you willing to spill? Yourn? Your mama's? Your baby's?

"And the last thing that Mr. Douglass said to me was, Huh!

"And so I saw that Mr. Douglass was right, that just cause y'all *are* free don't mean you all can *act* free, not yet. Shoot, God thought you were free all along, and that didn't sway Mr. Ravenel none. What's Mr. Lincoln next to God?

"And so I studied it and studied it, and thought it was a pretty bad fix, and I took me a bottle of Five-X over to General Grant's tent—you didn't know the grades went up to Five, did you? Up North they do—and he sipped that good Five-X and sucked on his big cigar and he studied and studied and then he said, Well, Mr. President. If those poor colored folks can't come to freedom, I reckon freedom's just gone have to come to them.

"And so I'm here to tell you, friends, that freedom has *come* to Chattanooga, and freedom has *come* to Atlanta, and freedom has *rolled* down to the batteaus a-bumping the salty docks of Savannah, and freedom gone come *rolling* through St. Helena Island any day now, and that sound you been hearing off to the west ain't no gunshoot, friends, it's the angels of Bethlehem a-shouting hallelujah."

Now through all this, folks been busting out with an Amen here and a Yes, Lord there and a Praise Jesus yonder, and as they give him back that Hallelujah ten times over we all heard a rumbling toward Savannah, like thunder, and everybody went *ooo-o-o-oh,* sorta low.

Now at about that place in his sermon he started to look sorta swimmy to me, and I saw it was cause my eyes were tearing up, and burning. I sneezed a couple times, and wiped my eyes on my sleeve—cause that rag in my pocket seemed too good to use any such a way—and then I noticed the blue smoke a-curling all around my head. Then a hard old clawy hand snatched my shoulder up tight, the fingers wrapping around my long bone like it was a clothes iron, and in my ear Maum Hannah said: "Young coon for running, but old coon for cunning. Boy, you are mine."

"Now, Maum Hannah, now listen, I'll tell you what happened, I—"

"Umph, umph, umph," she said. "I'm gone shake you like a gourd, boy. I'm gone whup you till Shiloh come."

"Shhhh!" someone said, and she hushed, but didn't let up on my poor shoulder none. I was stuck like a pig on a spit, and my only comfort in the world at that moment seemed to be Mr. Lincoln's hard-timey gentle face.

"Now, y'all probably know by now that I have some differences of opinion with Mr. Jefferson Davis. I think Mr. Davis is an American, same as me, same as you all, no worse than any of us and better'n some. But the plain fact of the tragedy is, he just don't accept that honor; if it's Americans that's invited to the party, he says, nossir, I better sit outside in the dirt with my lip poked out, and be all suscautious, cause that party ain't for me. And that's how come me sitting down with Mr. Davis and jabbering with him and breaking out the Four-X ain't gone do any good to get this war over and done with. Mr. Davis was a Senator, you know, before he become a professional Southerner, and a Senator can out-talk any man—can make you think a horse-chesnut is a chestnut horse. And Mr. Davis's egg bag ain't gone rest easy till I'm willing to tell him, all right, Mr. Davis, you win, you ain't an American no more, and now that I think bout it, Mr. Davis, why, I don't rightly know who *is,* if not being an American is as easy as that, as easy as changing your flannels in springtime. And I ain't a-going to tell him that, because friends, I don't believe it. But Mr. Davis don't pay no rabbit-foot to what I believe.

"So Mr. Davis and all those Sesesh that agree with him, they gone have to be made to listen. Y'all ever try to get the attention of a mule? It ain't easy to get, is it? And once you get it, you got to keep on getting it. And that's what General Grant and General Thomas and General Sherman are helping me to do. They're helping me get Mr. Sesesh's attention the only way they is to get it—to fret him and fret him, and chew him and choke him, and shoot him when shooting will do any good."

Maum Hannah was one of those who said Amen at this, and she give me a little shake besides, like this was gone be my lot too.

"We got a lot of work yet to do," Mr. Lincoln went on, "yes Lord and no mistake. They's places in this country so parched up the people got nothing left to cry with. Following around ahead of this army, I seen hell, I seen heaven, I seen all kinds of things I never expected to see on this earth. But God never made two mountains without putting a valley in between. And I'm counting on all the good people of Frogmore, every God one, to stand reformed and ready. And General Sherman is counting on you, and General Grant is counting on you, and what's more, your generations here are counting on you, too. So that when you tell your babies, Honey, you were born a *slave,* and you lived through a *civil war,* they'll look up at you and say, Mama, what's that mean? And all your suffering will seem to 'em like some made-up story, from a country far away. I'm finished and through.

"The saddle and bridle is on the shelf,
"If you want any more you can get it yourself.

"Mr. Cephas, will you lead us in song?"

"Yessir, Mr. President," said the big bald man I had walked to the praying ground with, and he commenced to singing, low but strong:

"Go down, Moses, way down in Egypt land,
"Tell old Pharaoh, let my people go!"

And others picked it up and sang along, a-swaying a little, mamas holding their babies, and men holding their women, and Mr. Lincoln not singing but walking around the circle shaking hands with people and hugging 'em and even kissing some of 'em. I never seen white and colored kiss before. I seen even old Fuss-X Quall stand up straight to shake Mr. Lincoln's hand, with his other hand a-resting on the ragged lapel of his old tore-up jacket, looking so proper you'd think he was the mayor of Charleston.

"Mr. President, sir," I heard Fuss-X say, "I been drunk since you was elected the *first* time."

Mr. Lincoln laughed and patted Fuss-X on the shoulder and said: "You're an honest man, sir. But you'll need to be a sober man, too, if you're going to be any help to me."

"Yes, sir," Fuss-X said. "For *you*, sir, I'll be that sober man, yes indeedy. Bless you, sir."

"Mr. Sherman burned Atlanta town,
"Let my people go!
"The pillar of fire again come down,
"Let my people go!"

When Mr. Lincoln got around to us, he patted Maum Hannah on the shoulder and looked down at me right kindly and said, "Why, Maum Hannah, who is this here fine young strapping man?"

"Don't you get too close to this one, Mr. Abe. He ain't no bigger'n kindling, but he sparks like the Devil himself. I *told* Shad and *told* him to stay at the home place, but for all the good it done I mights well brought the word of Jesus to a hog. I got to light his shucks a few times fore he's fit to talk to decent folks."

"Oh, now, Maum Hannah, I'm sure he's not as fearsome as all that." Not minding his fine britches, he knelt down closer to where I was, one knee mashing into the soggy grass. He still was a lot taller than me, but he'd evened it up some. He reached out and shook my hand with both hisn—big hairy monkey hands, to look at, but so gentle they held my hand like they was cradling a chick. "I'm sure this boy is here for a reason, same as the rest of us," Mr. Lincoln said.

"Long years to come before the dawn,
"Let my people go!
"Too soon our leader will be gone,
"Let my people go!"

Lots of folks were still singing, but I was starting to think I misremembered the words. I didn't much like the way they were going, neither. But Mr. Lincoln didn't pay the song no mind. "Always obey your elders, Shad," he said. "I always obeyed mine—till I was old enough to stop." He winked and let go my hand. I wanted to say something back, but I just stood there rooted and dumb as a yambo, as he stood and hugged Maum Hannah again, whispering something I couldn't hear. She finally let go my poor achy shoulder. Man! Old Sherman was a caution, but he didn't have nothing on Maum Hannah.

"Old Pharaoh robbed us of our youth,
"Let my people go!
"But the worst robber is old John—"

And right there Cephas stopped singing—stopped, and stood still, eyes staring at nothing, like he was harking to something a ways off. And cause he was leading the song, everybody else noticed, and the singing trailed off, and then all the folks was quiet, and listening. I strained and strained, but couldn't hear nothing but the pine knots sputtering, and a little breeze that swayed the moss overhead and made the shadows move funny in the praying ground. I saw that Mr. Lincoln heard it, too, though, whatever it was. His face was a study, like nothing I can line out for you in words. It was the face of a man who sees his death coming, and is ready for it.

Then I heard, away off in the swamp, something like a bridle jingling.

"Paterollers," Cephas said, and not loud neither, but in the next second the pine knots and the oil lamp snuffed out and everybody was in the dark and on the *move.* I could hear the branches cracking and bushes thrashing and reeds snapping and mud plopping as that praying ground emptied out, as fast and as quiet as people could go, in all directions, path or no path, and me and Maum Hannah and Mr. Lincoln in the middle standing stock-still, like the man in a hurricane who hears the water coming and knows there's noplace to run. The coal-tip of Maum Hannah's pipe was the only light left that wasn't the moon and the stars. Even the skeeters and the bullfrogs had hushed, so the only sound in the pitch-black praying ground was the picking-up breeze and the jingle, jingle, jingling of bridles, of coffles, of chains.

"Lord have mercy," Maum Hannah said.

"It's me they want," Mr. Lincoln said. "I'm sure of it. They're between us and the Sound, too. You and this child skedaddle, Maum Hannah. Get as far into the swamp as you can, and lie low. I'll make sure they can find me."

"No!" I cried. It was the first thing I had managed to say for the longest time, and it blew out of me like the cork from a jug. Then I was pulling on Mr. Lincoln's sleeve, on his swaller-tails, on his britches leg, on anything I could grab hold of, trying to haul him away from the path we come in on. "Come on, Mr. Lincoln, please sir, you can't let them get you, you just *can't,* I'll show you the way, you and Maum Hannah both, I'm in the swamps all the time, Maum Hannah licks me for it but I go there anyways, I know all sorts of paths to the Sound, to Frogmore, anyplace you wants to go, why, I'll lead you to Washington town, but please, Mr. Lincoln! Tell him, Maum Hannah. Don't let the paterollers—or *whoever that is a-coming*—don't let 'em get you! Mr. Lincoln, Maum Hannah, *please!*"

The grownups looked at each other.

"The boy's talking sense," Maum Hannah said. "He knows these swamps, for sure. He's half snake, half possum, half *bobobo* bird. You keep up with him, you might make it to the Sound, sure enough."

"But this child—" Mr. Lincoln started to say.

"Don't talk back to me like I was Congress. You done enough talking for tonight. You said we had to help, now we gone help, and you stuck with it. Now get on, both of you."

"What about you, Maum Hannah?" I asked.

She sucked on her pipe, and the coal flared up a funny color, sorta purple-red, so's I could see a little of her broad, set face, flickering like it was lit from inside, like a gourd at Christmas-time. "I got my own ways home," she said. "Old slow ways. Don't study bout me." She took hold of her pipe and stuck her thumb into the bowl and *hist,* the light went out, and out of the dark her voice said: "Get on, now, both of you." And then she just wasn't there no more—it was so pure dark, she coulda been a foot away, and me not known it. But I don't think to this day that she was. Maybe Maum Hannah could tamp herself down the same as the pipe, and wink out like a coal.

"Come on, sir," I said, half-crying but trying not to sound it.

"Wait!" Mr. Lincoln said, and for a second I thought he was gone, too. Next thing I knew a match was struck, and the oil lamp on that rickety table come back alive. He trotted back with something long and pipe-shaped in his hand. "That light'll give 'em something to aim for that ain't us," he said. "Besides, I'd be purely lost for sure, Shad or no Shad, without my hat." He breshed it with his sleeve and settled it on his head as delicate as if he was on the front porch of the big house. I couldn't see the hat too good in that light, but I could see it made him stand up a good deal straighter. He looked bout eight feet tall, and half comical, but only half, and if he got comfort from that hat, well, I got comfort, somehow, from looking at him. "What you waiting on," he asked, "Judgment?" He snapped his fingers. "*Wake up, Jacob, day's a-breaking.*"

I grinned and finished it: "*Get your hoecake baking and your shirt tail shaking!* Yes, *sir.*" I turned and ran across the praying ground, past the persimmon tree at the far end, and into the swamp, Mr. Lincoln right behind me. He made more noise than me a-going through the bresh, but less than I expected—as much as a buck deer, I guess, when it's running flat out. And ma'am, let me tell you, any deer on St. Helena woulda had a time outrunning us that night.

We splashed through creeks and crawled through brambly places and teeter-walked over logs and scrambled up one side and slid butt-first down the other of mounds plenty larger than the one at the praying ground—and plenty older, too, I reckon—and jumped half-rotted fences and wallowed through bogs and scared the life out of six or seven muskrats, two gators, and a squinch owl, though that old owl bout took it out of us, too, hollering any such a way. We were mosquito-bit, briar-scratched, mud-plastered, and salt-crackly with dried swamp water by time the water rose up and left us to jump from cypress knee to cypress knee. Then—whoa!—we run out of knees, and there we were, hassling like dogs and draped across a low branch and looking out across the Sound, breathing that sweet rank mud-marsh smell, the tidewater lapping at the knees neath us and something we'd awaked, a moccasin probably, a-plopping into the shallows behind. Do you know that stovepipe hat was still on Mr. Lincoln's head—how, I don't know. The pace we set through that wild country, I was surprised we still had our britches.

"What you reckon we do now?" I asked. I didn't have no idea myself, but I figured, shoot, he's the President, he must be smart. "You got soldiers waiting on you?"

"Not *with* me," he said, and I wasn't sure what that meant. He went on: "My boat's somewheres on this shore. I tied it up under a rotted pier. Beside a grove of palmetto."

"I know that place. Come on." So we thrashed on down the water's edge to the palmetto grove—it wasn't more'n a half-mile south, but felt longer, the way so overgrowed and us so wore-out. There was the skiff, just like he'd said, though if you didn't know to look for it you'd a thought it was just another old plank a-floating there. He clambered around the rotted pilings and eased the skiff on out into the water, and undid the rope and settled down in the stern. Plumb filled the boat up, with his knees nearbouts in his face. The moon come out from behind a cloud then, and I saw for the first time that his hat was bent at a sorry angle, with a long raggedy strip hanging down.

"Your hat's bout done its last do," I said, not wanting to say goodbye but not knowing what else to say neither.

"I know it," he said. "It's a shame." He took it off and looked it over. "I had to lie low in a thicket just after sunset, waiting on a patrol to pass by, and I left a big strip of my hat behind there."

I realized something. I felt around behind, and sure enough, there was that strip of cloth, the one I had wrestled from the fice, still stuck into my pants. I pulled it out and handed it to Mr. Lincoln. "You mean a strip like this right here?"

"Why, that's it exactly. Where'd you find it?"

"In the yard. The dog brought it up. I figured it wasn't none of this island."

"Well, I'll tell you what," he said, handing it back. "You can keep it, and the hat too, with my thanks." He stood, removed the stovepipe all solemn, and handed it over with a little bow, like he was offering me a crown. Nearbouts swamped the boat. "Whoa," he said, settling down again. "Shad, I thank you again most kindly. I got to get back out to my ship, before the sun catches me. Will you be able to get back home all right?"

"Yessir, it ain't far," I said. What I wanted to say was Take me with you, but I didn't say it, and he didn't offer.

"Well, thanks again, and goodbye," Mr. Lincoln said, and commenced to pull on the oars.

I don't know why I asked it. I guess I was just trying to keep him there awhile longer. What I asked, standing straddle-legged on two old pier pilings, was: "Do you like being the President?"

That stopped him, and he laid down the oars in his lap and thought bout it, the skiff drifting sideways, already caught by the current and heading out to sea. When he finally made his answer, his voice got louder as he got farther away. "Shad, I'll tell you like this. There once was a man who'd got powerful unpopular, so unpopular that all his neighbors grabbed him and tarred him and feathered him and run him out of town on a rail. And in the middle of it all, one of the neighbors that tormented him so, asked him, Well sir, how do you like it? And the man said back, Frankly, sir, I'd just as soon walk, if not for the honor of the thing. Goodbye, Shad."

"Goodbye, sir," I said, but he was way out in the Sound by then, a-pulling on the oars, and probably didn't even hear me. Just before he was out of sight, there was a flickering in the sky, and a rumble of thunder, and I heard him say: "God, how I love a storm." And then he was just one more dark patch against the far shore, and then he was gone. Least I never saw him again. So I turned around and dragged myself on back home, got there just as the sun was coming up, and Maum Hannah was a-sitting there—

No. I ain't gone tell it that way. I told you from the start, true enough for a book. I'm gone tell you the part of the story that I don't tell the young folks, and you can spice it or shuck it, same as all else.

I stood there a while, feeling the smart cloth of that poor ragged hat between my fingers, watching and listening—for what, I didn't know. I tried putting on the hat, but it was too big, I couldn't see nothing that way. So I held it in my hands as I turned and stepped off that old pier and onto the muddy ground, and I hadn't gone two paces before I saw a row of little stars about five feet off the ground, twinkling in the air between me and the trees. I stood there and blinked until the shapes around 'em firmed up some and I saw it was a row of soldiers standing in front of me, the moonlight shining off their buttons and hat-brims and rifle barrels.

I dropped the hat and made a sound like, "Ah," and wet my britches like a baby—the last time *that* ever happened, let me tell you, on that end of my life. But they weren't studying bout me. They were peering off across the water, over my head, looking toward where Mr. Lincoln went. They weren't Sesesh. Their uniforms were too new, their boots too shiny, their voices not Southern but sharp and squawky like chickens.

"Lost him again, God damn him to hell."

"They'll pick him up when he tries to board."

"Stanton will court-martial the lot of us."

"The hell with old fuzz-face Stanton. Secretary of War, my ass. What outfit did *he* ever soldier for, huh?"

They quarreled on like that, I couldn't understand the half of it. I started stepping real slow and careful off to the right, a-walking around 'em. Maybe they hadn't seen me at all, or maybe didn't care. I was just bout to the edge of the old weed-choked road that led off from the pier through the woods, when one of 'em said, all unconcerned-like: "What about the little pickaninny?"

I froze up and nearbouts lost my water again.

"Reckon he'll tell what he saw?"

"I don't reckon he could help it."

"Looks like he stole himself a hat."

"A Southern thief in wartime. And thieving from the Gorilla in Chief, at that. Our duty is clear, gentlemen."

"Hey, pickaninny. Cuffee. Hey, Hercules. How fast can you run, d'you suppose?"

"Faster than a Federal can shoot?"

Then I heard a *snick-snick* sound. And then another one. And then another one.

I'm ashamed to say now that I was too scared to pray even, but if I had prayed for anything, it wouldn't a been for what happened next. I couldn't have imagined such a thing. What happened was a voice from the trees, a new voice but sorta familiar, and praise Jesus a Southern one, too:

"Excuse me just a moment, please, sirs. Hello, sirs? Yankee soldier gentlemen? A moment of your time, if you please."

All the soldiers whirled around away from me and toward poor old Fuss-X Quall, who came strolling out of those black and midnight woods as natural and casual-like as at noon on the main street of Frogmore, one hand fanning skeeters with his hat. The last time I ever saw the man was the only time I'd seen him walk a straight line. Straight toward the rifle barrels a-pointing at him.

"Just one moment," said old Fuss-X—no, *not* old Fuss-X, neither. The man's name was Quall. Just in time, I caught that he was really talking to me. "One moment, sir, is all that I need. A single moment's *opportunity*."

I made use of that moment Mr. Quall gave me. I took off running, straight down that dark road. Behind me the rifles fired. Again. Again. Bullets went *zing* past my head, kicked up dust to my left, splinters to my right. *Zing. Zing.* I ran and cried and ran. Farther and farther behind, the soldiers hollered like dogs. After a while I couldn't cry no more, but I still could run, so I kept on a-doing that. The *zing* in my ears now were skeeters, I reckon, but I ran just the same. I outran any skeeter. I ran out of those woods tiddy umpty, ran home straight as a martin to his gourd.

When I dragged on into the yard just before sunrise, I saw Maum Hannah a-sitting on the joggling board, a-talking to herself, her pipe glowing like a third eye. I tried to call to her, but didn't have no breath. Closer up, I heard who she was talking to.

"When little Shad come down to die, I want you, Master, to be to the head and be to the foot for the last morning. When you see Shad done knock from side to side on Helena, I ask you, Jesus, to be his mother and his father for the last new day. Oh, God! Stand to him as his hair to his head. Take charge of him one more time—on the road, in the field, up to the fireside, oh, God! to the well."

By that time I was at the foot of the steps, and so wore-out that when I tried to climb I just fell a-sprawling in the sand. And then the fice run out from neath the porch to lick my face, and Maum Hannah was plumb all over me, mashing me into her sweat-smelling bosom so I couldn't breathe and hollering—

"Thank you Jesus! Mama! Master! Thank you Jesus! Mama! Master!"

—till the sun come up on St. Helena that day.

I reckon I'm the only one left that heard Mr. Lincoln's talk at the praying ground that night. I was the youngest one there, and now I'm the oldest one here, and the others all done died in between.

Now, hold up there, ma'am, hold up there—don't be starting in on me, pulling out your history-book learning and all such mess as that. I done heard it all. These younguns around here, they take the ferry into Beaufort, they get some free schooling and come back telling me I don't know shit from Shinola bout Lincoln or nothing else. And the Yankee schoolteachers who come out here to take pictures and write everything down, I get it from them, too. Oh, I get it from all sides. People say Lincoln didn't come no further south during the war than Hampton Roads. People say Lincoln wasn't really all that hot to free the slaves nohow, that it was all just politicking for votes and soldiers. People say we coloreds were better off before the war, when the likes of Mr. Ravenel were taking care of us. People say the mockingbirds all fly to hell on Fridays, toting grains of sand to squinch the flames. You ever hear that one? Yes, Lord, people will say just bout anything. That don't mean I have to believe it. What I see with my own eyes, that I believe. And these eyes when they were good saw Lincoln, a lot better than they seeing you now. Maybe they see him again, before too long. Maybe we be needing him again. Yes, ma'am, that's the end of that tale. You know how to end a tale, don't you?

"I stepped on a pin, the pin bent,
"And that's the way the story went."

—For Sam Doyle (1906–1985) of St. Helena, who painted the speech of Lincoln at Frogmore

The Map to the Homes of the Stars

LAST NIGHT, I HEARD IT AGAIN. ABOUT ELEVEN, I stood at the kitchen counter, slathered peanut butter onto a stale, cool slice of refrigerated raisin bread, and scanned months-old letters to the editor in an A section pulled at random from the overflow around the recycling bin. "Reader decries tobacco evils." "Economy sound, says N.C. banker." The little headlines give the otherwise routine letters such urgency, like telegraphed messages from some war-torn front where issues are being decided, where news is happening. "Arts funding called necessary." As I chewed my sandwich, I turned one-handed to the movie listings, just to reassure myself that everything I had skipped in the spring wasn't worth the trouble anyway, and then I heard a slowly approaching car.

We don't get much traffic on my street, a residential loop in a quiet neighborhood, and so even we single guys who don't have kids in the yard unconsciously register the sounds of each passing vehicle. But this was the fifth night in a row, and so I set down my sandwich and listened.

* * *

Tom used to identify each passing car, just for practice.

"Fairlane."

"Crown Victoria."

"Super Beetle."

This was back home, when we were as bored as two 17-year-olds could be.

"Even *I* can tell a Super Beetle," I said. I slugged my Mountain Dew and lowered the bottle to look with admiration at the neon-green foam.

Tom frowned, picked up his feet, and rotated on the bench of the picnic table so that his back was to Highway 1.

Without thinking, I said, "Mind, you'll get splinters." I heard my mother speaking, and winced.

Now Tom looked straight ahead at the middle-school basketball court, where Cathy and her friends, but mostly Cathy (who barely knew us, but whose house was fourth on our daily route), were playing a pick-up game, laughing and sweating and raking their long hair back from their foreheads. As each car passed behind him, he continued the litany.

"Jeep."

"Ford pickup."

"Charger."

I didn't know enough to catch him in an error, of course, but I have no doubt that he was right on the money, every time. I never learned cars; I learned other things, that year and the next fifteen years, to my surprise and exhilaration and shame, but I never learned cars, and so I am ill-equipped to stand in my kitchen and identify a car driving slowly past at eleven o'clock at night.

Not even when, about five minutes later, it gives me another chance, drives past again in the other direction, as if it had gotten as far as the next cul-de-sac, and turned around.

It passes so slowly that I am sure it is about to turn into someone's driveway, someone's, mine, but it hasn't, for five nights now it hasn't. I couldn't tell you if I had to precisely what make of car it is.

I could guess, though.

Maybe tonight, if, when, it passes by, I'll go to the front door and pull back the narrow dusty curtain that never gets pulled back except for Jehovah's Witnesses, and see for myself what make of car it is. See if I recognize it. But all I did last night, and the four nights before, was stand at my kitchen counter, fingertips black with old news, jaws Peter-Panned shut (for I am a creature of habit), stare unseeing at the piled-up sink, and trace in my head every long-gone stop on the map to the homes of the stars.

* * *

Even when all we had were bicycles, Tom and I spent most of our time together riding around town. We rode from convenience store to convenience store, Slim Jims in our pockets and folded comic books stuffed into the waistbands of our jeans. We never rode side by side or single file but in loopy serpentine patterns, roughly parallel, that weaved among trees and parked cars and water sprinklers. We had earnest and serious conversations that lasted for hours and were entirely shouted from bike to bike, never less than ten feet. Our paths intersected with hair-raising frequency, but we never ran into each other. At suppertime, we never actually said goodbye, but veered off in different directions, continuing to holler at each other, one more joke that had to be told, one more snappy comeback to make, until the other voice had faded in the distance, and we realized we were riding alone, and talking to ourselves. I remember nothing of what we said to each other all those long afternoons, but I remember the rush of the wind past my ears, and the shirttail of my red jersey snapping behind me like a hound, and the slab of sidewalk that a big tree root thrust up beneath me in the last block before home, so that I could steer around it at the last second and feel terribly skillful, or use it as a launching ramp and stand up on the pedals and hang there, suspended, invincible, until the pavement caught up with my tires again.

Then we were sixteen and got our licenses. Tom's bicycle went into the corner of his room, festooned with clothes that weren't quite ready to wash yet; mine was hung on nails inside the garage, in a place of honor beside my older sister's red wagon and my late Uncle Clyde's homemade bamboo fishing poles. Tom had been studying *Consumer Reports* and *Car and Driver* and prowling dealerships for months, and with his father's help, he bought a used '78 Firebird, bright red exterior, black leather upholstery, cassette stereo, and a host of tire and engine features that Tom could rattle off like an auctioneer but that I never quite could remember afterward. Being a fan of old gangster movies, Tom called it his "getaway car." Tom and his dad got a great deal, because the getaway car had a dent in the side and its headlights were slightly cockeyed. "Makes it unique," Tom said. "We'll get those fixed right up," his dad said, and, of course, they never did. I inherited the car my father had driven on his mail route for years, a beige '72 Volkswagen Beetle that was missing its front passenger seat. My father had removed it so that he'd have an open place to put his mail. Now, like so many of my family's other theoretical belongings, the seat was "out there in the garage," a phrase to which my father invariably would add, "somewhere."

We always took Tom's car; Tom always drove.

We went to a lot of movies in Columbia and sometimes went on real trips, following the church van to Lake Junaluska or to Six Flags and enjoying a freedom of movement unique in the Methodist Youth Fellowship. But mostly we rode around town, looking—and *only* looking—at girls. We found out where they lived, and drove past their houses every day, hoping they might be outside, hoping to get a glimpse of them, but paying tribute in any case to all they had added to what we fancied as our dried-up and wasted and miserable lives.

"We need music," Tom said. "Take the wheel, will you, Jack?"

I reached across and steered while he turned and rummaged among the tapes in the back seat. I knew it was the closest I ever would come to driving Tom's car.

"In Hollywood," I said, "people on street corners sell maps to the stars' homes. Tourists buy the maps and drive around, hoping to see Clint Eastwood mowing his lawn, or something." I had never been to Hollywood, but I had learned about these maps the night before on *PM Magazine*.

"What do you want? You want Stones? You want Beatles? You want Aerosmith? What?"

"Mostly they just see high walls," I said, "and locked gates." I was proud to have detected this irony alone.

"We should go there," Tom said. "Just take off driving one day and *go*."

"Intersection coming up."

"Red light?"

"Green."

Tom continued to rummage. "Our map," he said, "exists only in our heads."

"That's where the girls exist, too," I said.

"Oh, no," Tom said, turning back around and taking the wheel just in time to drive through the intersection. "They're out there. Maybe not in this dink-ass town, but somewhere. They're real. We'll just never know them. That's all."

I had nothing to add to that, but I fully agreed with him. I had concluded, way back at thirteen, that I was doomed to a monastic life, and I rather wished I were Catholic so that I could take full advantage of it. Monastic Methodists had nowhere to go; they just got gray and pudgy, and lived with their mothers. Tom pushed a tape into the deck; it snapped shut like a trap, and the speakers began to throb.

* * *

Lisa lived in a huge Tudor house of gray stone across the street from the fifteenth fairway. To our knowledge she did not play golf, but she was a runner, and on a fortunate evening we could meet her three or four times on the slow easy curves of Country Club Drive. She had a long stride and a steady rhythm and never looked winded, though she did maintain a look of thoughtful concentration and always seemed focused on the patch of asphalt just a few feet ahead, as if it were pacing her. At intersections, she jogged in place, looking around at the world in surprise, and was likely to smile and throw up a hand if we made so bold as to wave.

Tom especially admired Lisa because she took such good care of her car, a plum-colored late-model Corvette that she washed and waxed in her driveway every Saturday afternoon, beginning about one o'clock. For hours, she catered to her car's needs, stroking and rubbing it with hand towels and soft brushes, soaping and then rinsing, so that successive gentle tides foamed down the hood. Eventually, Lisa seemed to be lying face to face with herself across the gleaming purple hood, her palm pressed to the other Lisa's palm, hands moving together in lazy circles like the half-hearted sparring of lovers in August.

Crystal's house was low and brick, with a patio that stretched its whole length. From March through October, for hours each day, Crystal lay on this patio, working on her tan—"laying out," she would have called it. She must have tanned successive interior layers of her skin, because even in winter she was a dusky Amazonian bronze, a hue that matched her auburn hair, but made her white teeth a constant surprise. Frequent debates as we passed Crystal's house: Which bikini was best, the white or the yellow? Which position was best, face up or face down? What about the bottles and jars that crowded the dainty wrought-iron table at her elbow? Did those hold mere store-bought lotions, or were they brimful of Crystal's private skin-care recipes, gathered from donors willing and unwilling by the dark of the moon? Tom swore that once, when we drove past, he clearly saw amid the Coppertone jumble a half-stick of butter and a bottle of Wesson oil.

Gabrielle lived out on the edge of town, technically within the city limits but really in the country, in a big old crossroads farmhouse with a deep porch mostly hidden by lattices of honeysuckle and wisteria. She lived with her grandparents, who couldn't get around so good anymore, and so usually it was Gabrielle who climbed the tall ladder and raked out the gutters, cleared the pecan limbs off the roof of the porch, scraped the shutters, and then painted them. She had long black hair that stretched nearly to the ragged hem of her denim shorts. She didn't tie her hair back when she worked, no matter how hot the day, and she was tall even without the ladder.

Natalie lived in a three-story wooden house with cardboard in two windows and with thickets of metal roosters and lightning rods up top. At school, she wore ancient black ankle-length dresses in all weathers, walked with her head down, and spoke to no one, not even when called upon in class, so that the teachers finally gave up. Her hair was an impenetrable mop that covered her face almost entirely. But she always smiled a tiny secret smile, and her chin beneath was sharp and delicate, and when she scampered down the hall, hugging the lockers, her skirts whispered generations of old chants and endearments. Natalie never came outside at all.

* * *

Cynthia's was the first house on the tour. Only two blocks from Tom's, it sat on the brink of a small and suspect pond, one that was about fifty feet across at its widest. No visible stream fed this pond or emptied it, and birds, swimmers, and fishes all shunned it. The pond was a failure as a pond, but a marginal success as an investment, an "extra" that made a half-dozen nondescript brick ranch houses cost a bit more than their landlocked neighbors. Cynthia's house was distinguished by a big swingset that sat in the middle of the treeless yard. It was a swaybacked metal A-frame scavenged from the primary school. In all weathers, day and night, since her family moved to town when she was six, Cynthia could be found out there, swinging. The older she got, the higher she swung, the more reckless and joyful her sparkle and grin. When she was sixteen, tanned legs pumping in the afternoon sun, she regularly swung so high the chains went slack for a half-second at the top of the arc before she dropped. "Zero gee," Tom said as we drove slowly past. Tom and I didn't swing anymore, ourselves; it made us nauseated.

Once a year Cynthia actually came out to the car to say hi. Each Christmas the people who lived on the pond, flush with their wise investment, expressed their communal pride with a brilliant lighting display. For weeks everyone in town drove slowly, dutifully, and repeatedly around the pond and over its single bridge to see the thousands of white firefly lights that the people of the pond draped along porches and bushes and balustrades, and stretched across wire frames to approximate Grinches and Magi. The reflection on the water was striking, undisturbed as it was by current or life. For hours each night, a single line of cars crept bumper-to-bumper across the bridge, past Santa-clad residents who handed out candy canes and filled a wicker basket with donations for the needy and for the electric company. Painted on a weatherbeaten sandwich board at the foot of the bridge was a bright red cursive dismissal: "Thank You / Merry Christmas / Speed Limit 25."

At least once a night, Tom and I drove through this display, hoping to catch Cynthia on Santa duty. At least once a year, we got lucky.

"Hey there, little boys, want some candy?" She dropped a shimmering fistful into Tom's lap. "No, listen, take them, Dad said when I gave them all out I could come inside. I'm freezing my ass off out here. Oh, hi, Jack. So, where you guys headed?"

"No place," we said together.

She walked alongside Tom's Firebird, tugging down her beard to scratch her cheek. "Damn thing must be made of fiberglass. Hey, check out the Thompsons' house. Doesn't that second reindeer look just like he's humping Rudolf? I don't know *what* they were *thinking*. No? Well, it's clear as day from my room. Maybe I've just looked at it too long. When is Christmas, anyway? You guys don't know what it's like, all these goddamn lights, you can see them with your eyes closed. I've been sleeping over at Cheryl's where it's dark. Well, I reckon if I go past the end of the bridge, the trolls will get me. Yeah, right, big laugh there. See you later." Then, ducking her head in again: "You, too, Jack."

With the smoothness of practice, Tom and I snicked our mirrors into place (his the driver's side, mine the overhead) so that we could watch Cynthia's freezing ass walk away. Her Santa pants were baggy and sexless, but we watched until the four-wheel drive behind us honked and flashed its deer lights. By the time we drove down to the traffic circle and made the loop and got back in line again, Cynthia's place had been taken by her neighbor, Mr. Thompson.

"Merry Christmas, Tom, Jack," he said. "Y'all's names came up at choir practice the other day. We'd love to have you young fellas join us in the handbells. It's fun and you don't have to sing and it's a real ministry, too." He apologized for having run out of candy canes, and instead gave us a couple of three-by-five comic books about Hell.

* * *

Tina's house always made us feel especially sophisticated, especially daring.

"Can you imagine?" Tom asked. "Can you imagine, just for a moment, what our parents would do?"

"No," I said, shaking my head. "No, I can't imagine."

"I think you should try. I think we both should try to envision this. That way we'll be prepared for anything in life, anything at all."

I cranked down the windowpane until it balked. "I don't even want to think about it," I said. I pressed the pane outward until it was back on track, then I lowered it the rest of the way.

"Oh, but you've *been* thinking about it, haven't you? You're the one that found out where she lived. You're the one that kept wanting me to drive past her house."

"It's the quickest route between Laura's and Kathleen's, that's all," I said. "But if it's such a terrible hardship, then you can go around the world instead, for all I care. You're the driver, I'm just sitting here."

He fidgeted, legs wide, left hand drumming the windowsill, fingertips of his right hand barely nudging the steering wheel. "Don't get me wrong, I think she's a babe. But this neighborhood, I don't know, it makes me nervous. I feel like everybody we pass is looking at us."

"Do what you like. I'm just sitting here," I said. I craned to see Tina's house as we drove around the corner.

Tina lived in what our parents and our friends and every other white person we knew, when they were feeling especially liberal, broad-minded and genteel, called the "colored" part of town. Tina's yard was colored all right: bright yellows, reds, oranges, and purples, bursting from a dozen flowerbeds. As so often when she wasn't at cheerleading practice, Tina knelt in the garden, a huge old beribboned hat—her grandmother's, maybe?—shading her striking, angular face. Her shoulders tightened, loosened, tightened again as she pressed something into place. Without moving her hands, she looked up at us as we passed. She smiled widely, and her lips mouthed the word "Hey."

Once we were around the corner, Tom gunned the engine.

"Uh-uh, no sir, hang it *up*," Tom said. "Not in my family, not in this town. Thousands of miles away, maybe. That might work. Oh, but then they'd want *photos*, wouldn't they? Damn. The other week, all my aunts were sitting around the kitchen table, complaining about their daughters-in-law. My son's wife is snotty, my son's wife is lazy, they aren't good mothers, they aren't treating our boys right, and so on and so on. Just giving 'em down the country, you know?"

"Uh-huh. I hear you."

"And I finally spoke up and said, 'Well, I know I'm never going to introduce y'all to any wife of *mine*, 'cause y'all sure won't like *her*, either."

"What'd they say to that?"

"They all laughed, and Aunt Leda said, 'Tom, don't you worry, 'cause you're the only boy in the family that's got any sense. We know we'll like *any* girl you pick out.' And then Aunt Emily added, 'Long as she isn't a black 'un!' And they all nodded—I mean, they were serious!"

After a long pause, he added, half to himself, "It's not as if I'm bringing *anybody* home, anyway—black or white or lavender."

"You bring me home with you sometimes," I said.

"Yeah, and they don't like *you* either," he said, and immediately cut me a wide-eyed look of mock horror that made me laugh out loud. "I'm kidding. You know they like you."

"Families always like me," I said. "Mamas especially. It's the daughters themselves that aren't real interested. And a mama's approval is the kiss of death. At this moment, I bet you, mamas all over town are saying, 'What about that nice boy *Jack?* He's so respectful, he goes to church, he makes such good grades,' and don't you know that makes those gals so hot they can't stand it."

Tom laughed and laughed.

"Oh, Jack!" I gasped. "Oh, Jack, your SAT score is so—so *big!*"

"Maybe you should forget the girls and date the *mamas*," Tom said. "You know, eliminate the middleman. Go right to the source."

"Eewww, that's crude." I clawed at the door as if trying to get out. "Help! Help! I'm in the clutches of a crude man!"

"Suppose Kathleen's home from Florida yet?"

"I dunno. Let's go see."

"Now you aren't starting to boss me around, are you?"

"I'm just sitting here."

He poked me repeatedly with his finger, making me giggle and twist around on the seat. "'Cause I'll just put you out by the side of the road, you start bossing me."

"I'm not!" I gasped. "Quit! Uncle! Uncle! I'm not!"

"Well, all right, then."

* * *

On September 17, 1981, we turned the corner at the library and headed toward the high school, past the tennis courts. The setting sun made everything golden. Over the engine, we heard doubled and redoubled the muted grunts and soft swats and scuffs of impact: ball on racket, shoe on clay. The various players on the adjoining courts moved with such choreography that I felt a pang to join them.

"Is tennis anything like badminton?" I asked. "I used to be okay at badminton. My father and I would play it over the back fence, and the dogs would go wild."

"It's more expensive," Tom said. "Look, there she is. Right on time."

Anna, her back to us, was up ahead, walking slowly toward the parking lot on the sidewalk nearest me. Her racket was on one shoulder, a towel around her neck. Her skirt swayed as if she were walking much faster.

As we passed, I heard a strange sound: a single Road Runner beep. In the side mirror, tiny retreating Anna raised her free hand and waved. I turned to stare at Tom, who looked straight ahead.

"The *horn?*" I asked. "You honked the horn?"

"Well, you waved," he said. "I saw you."

I yanked my arm inside. The windblown hairs on my forearm tingled. "I wasn't waving. I was holding up my hand to feel the breeze."

"She waved at *you.*"

"Well, I didn't wave at *her,*" I said. "She waved because *you* honked."

"Okay," he said, turning into the parking lot. "She waved at both of us, then."

"She waved at *you.* I don't care, it doesn't matter. But she definitely waved at you."

"Are we fighting?" he asked. He re-entered the street, turned back the way we had come. Anna was near, walking toward us.

"Course we're not fighting. Are you going to honk at her again?"

"Are you going to wave at her again?"

Anna looked behind her for traffic, stepped off the sidewalk, and darted across the street, into our lane, racket lifted like an Olympic torch.

"Look out!"

"What the hell?"

Tom hit the brakes. The passenger seat slid forward on its track, and my knees slammed the dash. Dozens of cassettes on the back seat cascaded into the floor. Only a foot or two in front of the stopped car stood Anna, arms folded, one hip thrust out. She regarded us without expression, blew a large pink bubble that reached her nose and then collapsed back into her mouth.

"Hi, guys," she said.

Tom opened his door and stood, one foot on the pavement. "For crying out loud, Anna, are you okay? We could've killed you!"

"I was trying to flag you down," she said.

"What? Why?" Tom asked. "What for? Something wrong with the car?" I saw him swivel, and I knew that, out of sight, he was glancing toward the tires, the hood, the tailpipe.

"Nothing's wrong with the car, Tom," she said, chewing with half her mouth, arms still folded. "It's a really neat car. Whenever I see it I think, 'Damn, Tom must take mighty good care of that car.' I get a *lot* of chances to think that, Tom, 'cause every day you guys drive by my house at least twice, and whenever I leave tennis practice, you drive past me, and turn around in the lot, and drive past me *again*, and every time you do that I think, 'He takes mighty damn good care of that goddamn car just to drive past me all the fucking time.' "

Someone behind us honked and pulled around. A pickup truck driver, who threw us a bird.

"Do you ever *stop?* No. Say hi at school? Either of you? No. *Call* me? Shit." She shifted her weight to the other hip, unfolded her arms, whipped the towel from around her neck and swatted the hood with it. "So all I want to know is, just what's the *deal?* Tom? Jack? I see you in there, Jack, you can't hide. What's up, Jack? You tell me. Your chauffeur's catching flies out here."

Looking up at Anna, even though I half expected at any moment to be arrested for perversion or struck from behind by a truck or beaten to death with a tennis racket, purple waffle patterns scarring my corpse, I realized I had never felt such crazed exhilaration, not even that night on Bates Hill, when Tom passed a hundred and twenty. My knees didn't even hurt any more. The moment I realized this, naturally the feeling of exhilaration began to ebb, and so before I lost my resolve I slowly stuck my head out the window, smiled what I hoped was a smile, and called out: "Can we give you a lift, Anna?"

A station wagon swung past us with a honk. Anna looked at me, at Tom, at me again. She plucked her gum from her mouth, tossed it, looked down at the pavement and then up and then down again, much younger and almost shy. In a small voice, she said: "Yeah." She cleared her throat. "Yeah. Yes. That's . . . that's nice of you. Thank you."

I let her have my seat, of course. I got in the back, atop a shifting pile of cassettes and books and plastic boxes of lug nuts, but right behind her, close enough to smell her: not sweat, exactly, but salt and earth, like the smell of the beach before the tide comes in.

"Where to?" Tom asked.

"California," she said, and laughed, hands across her face. "Damn, Anna," she asked, "where did *that* come from? Oh, I don't know. Where are y'all going? I mean, wherever. Whenever. Let's just *go*, okay? Let's just . . . go."

* * *

We talked: School. Movies. Bands. Homework. Everything. Nothing. What else? Drove around. For hours.

Her ponytail was short but full, a single blond twist that she gathered up in one hand and lifted as she tilted her head forward. I thought she was looking at something on the floor, and I wondered for a second whether I had tracked something in.

"Jack?" she asked, head still forward. No one outside my family had made my name a question before. "Would you be a sweetie and rub my neck?"

The hum of tires, the zing of crickets, the shrill stream of air flowing through the crack that the passenger window never quite closed.

"Ma'am?"

"My neck. It's all stove up and tight from tennis. Would you rub the kinks out for me?"

"Sure," I said, too loudly and too quickly. My hands moved as slowly as in a nightmare. Twice I thought I had them nearly to her neck when I realized I was merely rehearsing the action in my head, so that I had it all to do over again. Tom shifted gears, slowed into a turn, sped up, shifted gears again, and I still hadn't touched her. My forearms were lifted; my hands were outstretched, palms down; my fingers were trembling. I must have looked like a mesmerist. You are sleepy, very sleepy. Which movie was it where the person in the front seat knew nothing about the clutching hands in the back? I could picture the driver's face as the hands crept closer: Christopher Lee, maybe? No: Donald Pleasence?

"Jack," she said. "Are you still awake back there?"

The car went into another turn, and I heard a soft murmur of complaint from the tires. Tom was speeding up.

My fingertips brushed the back of her neck. I yanked them back, then moved them forward again. This time I held them there, barely touching. Her neck so smooth, so hot, slightly—damp? And what's *this?* Little hairs! Hairs as soft as a baby's head! No one ever had told me there would be hairs . . .

"You'll have to rub harder than *that,* Jack." Still holding her hair aloft with her right hand, she reached up with her left and pressed my fingers into her neck. "Like that. Right—*there.* And there. Feel how tight that is?" She rotated her hand over mine, and trapped between her damp palm and her searing neck I did feel something both supple and taut. "Oooh, yeah, like that." She pulled her hand away, and I kept up the motions. "Oh, that feels good . . ."

The sun was truly down by now, and lighted houses scudded past. Those distinctive dormer windows—wasn't that Lisa's house? And, in the next block, wasn't that Kim's driveway?

We were following the route. We were passing all the homes of the stars.

Tom said nothing, but drove faster and faster. I kept rubbing, pressing, kneading, not having the faintest idea what I was doing but following the lead of Anna's sighs and murmurs. "Yeah, my shoulder there . . . Oh, this is wonderful. You'll have to stop this in about three hours, you know."

After about five minutes or ten or twenty, without looking up, she raised her left index finger and stabbed the dashboard. A tape came on. I don't remember which tape it was. I do remember that it played through both sides, and started over.

Tom was speeding. Each screeching turn threw us off balance. Where were the cops? Where was all the other traffic? We passed Jane's house, Tina's house. Streetlights strobed the car like an electrical storm. We passed Cynthia's house—hadn't we already? Beneath my hands, Anna's shoulders braced and rolled and braced again. I held on. My arms ached. Past the corner of my eye flashed a stop sign. My fingers kept working. Tom wrenched up the volume on the stereo. The bass line throbbed into my neck and shoulder blades, as if the car were reciprocating.

Gravel churned beneath us. "Damn," Tom muttered, and

yanked the wheel, fighting to stay on the road. Anna snapped her head up, looked at him. I saw her profile against the radio dial.

"I want to drive," she said.

Tom put on the brakes, too swiftly. Atop a surging flood of gravel, the car jolted and shuddered to a standstill off the side of the road. The doors flew open, and both Tom and Anna leaped out. My exhilaration long gone, my arms aching, I felt trapped, suffocating. I snatched up the seat latch, levered forward the passenger seat, and stepped humpbacked and out of balance into the surprisingly cool night air. Over there was the Episcopal church, over there the Amoco station. We were only a few blocks from my house. My right hand stung; I had torn a nail on the seat latch. I slung it back and forth as Tom stepped around the car. Anna was already in the driver's seat.

"You want to sit in front?" Tom sounded hoarse.

"No," I said. "No, thanks. Listen, I think I'll, uh, I think I'll just call it a night. I'm nearly home anyway. I can, uh, I can walk from here. Y'know? It's not far. I can walk from here." I called out to Anna, leaning down and looking in: "I can walk from here." Her face was unreadable, but her eyes gleamed.

"Huh?" Tom said. It was like a grunt. He cleared his throat. "What do you mean, *walk?* It's early yet."

The car was still running. The exhaust blew over me in a cloud, made me dizzy. "No, really, you guys go on. I'm serious. I'll be fine. Go on, really. I'll see you later on."

"We could drop you off," Tom said. He spoke politely but awkwardly, as if we had never met. "Let's do that. We'll drop you off in your yard."

Anna revved the motor. It was too dark to see Tom's expression as he looked at her. Her fingers moved across the lighted instrument panel, pulled out the switch that started the emergency flashers, *ka-chink ka-chink ka-chink,* pushed it back again. "Cool," she said.

"I'll see you later," I said. "OK? See you, Anna. Call me tomorrow," I said to Tom.

"OK," he said. "I'll call you tomorrow."

"OK," I said, not looking back. I waved a ridiculous cavalier wave, and stuck my hands in my pockets, trying to look nonchalant as I stumbled along the crumbling asphalt shoulder in the dark.

Behind me two doors slammed. I heard the car lurching back onto the highway, gravel spewing, and I heard it make a U-turn, away from town and toward the west, toward the lake, toward the woods. As the engine gunned, my shoulders twitched and I ducked my head, because I expected the screech of gears, but all I heard was steady and swift acceleration, first into second into third, as the Firebird sped away, into fourth, and then it was just me, walking.

* * *

They never came back.

Tom's parents got a couple of letters, a few postcards. California. They shared them with Anna's parents but no one else. "Tom wants everyone to know they're doing fine," that's all his mom and dad would say. But they didn't look reassured. Miss Sara down at the paper, who always professed to know a lot more than she wrote up in her column, told my father that she hadn't seen the mail herself, mind you, but she had *heard* from people who should *know* that the letters were strange, rambling things, not one *bit* like Tom, and the cards had postmarks that were simply, somehow, *wrong*. But who could predict, Miss Sara added, *when* postcards might arrive, or in *what* order. Why, sometimes they sit in the post office for *years*, and sometimes they never show up at *all*. Criminal, Miss Sara mourned, criminal.

Anna's parents got no mail at all.

I never did, either, except maybe one thing. I don't know that you could call it *mail*. No stamps, no postmark, no handwriting. It wasn't even in the mailbox. But it felt like mail to me.

It was lying on my front porch one morning—this was years later, not long after I got my own place, thought I was settled. At first I thought it was the paper, but no, as usual the paper was spiked down deep in the hedge. This was lying faceup and foursquare on the welcome mat. It was one of those Hollywood maps, showing where the stars can be found.

I spread it across the kitchen table and anchored it with the sugar bowl and a couple of iron owl-shaped trivets, because it was stiff and new and didn't want to lie flat. You know how maps are. It was bright white paper and mighty thick, too. I didn't know they made maps so thick anymore. I ran my index finger over sharp paper ridges and down straight paper canyons and looked for anyone I knew. No, Clint Eastwood wasn't there. Nor was anyone else whose movies I ever had seen at the mall. A lot of the names I just didn't recognize, but some I knew from cable, from the nostalgia channels.

I was pretty sure most of them were dead.

I searched the index for Tom's name, for Anna's. I didn't see them. I felt relieved. Sort of.

"California," I said aloud. Once it had been four jaunty syllables, up and down and up and down, a kid on a bicycle, going no place. California. Now it was a series of low and urgent blasts, someone leaning on the horn, saying, come on, saying, hurry up, saying, you're not too late, not yet, not *yet*. California.

* * *

It's nearly eleven. I stand in the cool rush of the refrigerator door, forgetting what I came for, and strain to hear. The train is passing, a bit late, over behind the campus. My windows are open, so the air conditioning is pouring out into the yard and fat bugs are smacking themselves against the screen, but this way I can hear everything clearly. The rattle as my neighbor hauls down the garage door, secures everything for the night. On the other side, another neighbor trundles a trash can out to the curb, then plods back. I am standing at the kitchen counter now. Behind me the refrigerator door is swinging shut, or close enough. I hear a car coming.

The same car.

I move to the living room, to the front door. I part the curtain. The car is coming closer, but even more slowly than before. Nearly stopping. It must be in first gear by now. There was always that slight rattle, just within the threshold of hearing, when you put it in first gear. Yes. And the slightly cockeyed headlights, yes, and the dent in the side. I can't clearly see the interior even under the streetlight but it looks like two people in the front.

Two people? Or just one?

And then it's on the other side of the neighbor's hedge, and gone, but I still can hear the engine, and I know that it's going to turn, and come back.

My hand is on the doorknob. The map is in my pocket. The night air is surprisingly cool. I flip on the porch light as I step out, and I stand illuminated in a cloud of tiny beating wings, waiting for them to come back, come back and see me standing here, waiting, waiting, oh my God how long I've been waiting, I want to walk out there and stand in front of the car and make it stop, really I do, but I can't, I can't move, I'm trapped here, trapped in this place, trapped in this time, don't drive past again, I'm here, I'm ready, I wasn't then but now I am, really I am, please, please stop. Present or past, alive or dead, what does it matter, what did it ever matter? Please. Stop.

Please.

From Alfano's Reliquary

IN YOUR TIME THE CHURCH IS UNIMPORTANT, and popes die of old age, but I am speaking of my time. In the years after Charlemagne, I served no fewer than nineteen of Christ's apostles on Earth, all scrofulous old Romans who perched on the edge of the throne of St. Peter for a season or two, pissing their vestments whenever the tapestries rustled. Such men attracted the clumsiest of assassins. Emetics were used as poisons. Frayed garrotes, unable to withstand the throes, snapped. Feebly struggling pontiffs were dropped repeatedly from low balconies. Cheaply made bread knives, shoved gracelessly into breastbones, splintered. One subtle fellow hacked away at the side of the chest opposite the victim's heart, causing needless delay and unpleasantness. It was not an age of efficiency. Yet because these murderers were seldom rushed, and tended to bring, as secondary instruments, rocks and hammers, the night's work eventually would be accomplished, and yet another prelate would be sent mewling to hell.

Of all the popes I served, only Stephen VI moved boldly against his enemy, but, of course, only Stephen VI was mad. Always awake, always anxious, he scampered along the corridors throughout the night, causing restless sleepers to dream of rats. Some nights, unobserved, I stood at intersections, a shadowed column among other columns, and watched him pass. He was a fat man with spindly legs and tiny feet. Even by day he never quite stood still, but teetered, like a balancing turnip. During mundane audiences, for no discernible reason, his sagging, ruined face would bubble with rage, and he would scuttle about the room until the mood was past, kicking dogs, bishops, furniture, with his absurd feet. He never kicked me.

These fits were not serious. Stephen feared no one in the chamber. He perceived no real enemies in his covetous entourage, in the fearful and filthy peasantry of Rome, in the restive occupation army of recently godless Franks. Certainly he perceived no threat in me, his mute counselor, at least not initially. No, the sloping garret of his skull had room for only one enemy, and that single enemy was already dead.

Many men derive comfort from their enemies—I have relished mine through the centuries—but Stephen chewed his like bitter cud. His hated predecessor, Pope Formosus, lay at rest within the Aurelian Walls, his head soothed by cool marble, yet as far beyond Stephen's grasp as the harem-couch of the Moslem caliph. Between the two popes yawned the unspanned gulf of the grave.

For months after buying the papacy, Stephen brooded about his thousand imagined injuries. He and Arnulf, the fitfully holy, never Roman emperor, carried on an interminable secret conversation, employing a corps of exhausted messengers who struggled back and forth across the mountains. Some of Stephen's most telling points went over precipices and had to be repeated.

Then, after a night of unusually resolute galloping about the palace, Stephen summoned me.

* * *

When the guard announced my arrival in his sleeping chamber, Stephen was creeping about beneath the tapestries, an obscene bulge among the unicorns. His attempts to plug the ratholes were unceasing. I knelt as he thrashed free of the decorations, then, blessed, rose to loom over him, as I loomed over everyone in the papal court. I gazed coolly down on the pope.

"My bastard predecessor has fouled his plot of sanctified earth long enough," Stephen said. "Bring me Formosus. Rouse him from his undeserved rest, that he may stand accused before God and His Holy Church." He chuckled and added, "You are accustomed to such damp work, eh, Alfano?"

I inclined my head modestly. Stephen knew I first served the

Church by stocking reliquaries—transmuting unused bits of rotting paupers into the toes and teeth of saints. I had, in fact, procured one of the heads of John the Baptist so popular among pilgrims in those days. Stephen knew I was uniquely suited to this work: A childhood of labor in the steaming dye-works of Amalfi robbed me of my sense of smell. Stephen also knew that in my years of papal service, I had not so much as touched a shovel. But I merely nodded in answer to his baiting. I was mute and wise; I had outlived six popes.

Stephen's bloated fingers toyed with the wattles beneath his chin. "It will be another Resurrection," Stephen said, "but one not born of love."

I took care to kiss his ring with my usual fervor—no more, no less—on my way out, as I hurried to put into motion the abomination.

* * *

Within the hour, I was striding along a narrow corridor that spiraled downward beneath the floor of Formosus's favorite Roman church. Somewhere above was a noisy, crowded altar; somewhere below were the peaceful, crowded vaults. I kept my head bowed in reverence to the low, uneven ceiling. A half-dozen guards and workmen shuffled behind me, clanking and panting in the clammy dark.

Beside me was my invaluable servant Torriti, whose mumblings offered an unobstructed view into the thoughts of the ignorant. With his left hand he held aloft a guttering torch; with his right he crossed himself repeatedly.

"To judge the dead!" Torriti whispered. "Is this not God's task and God's alone? What will the townspeople think? And the pilgrims? And the Franks? And the many friends of Formosus? What of them? Ah! It is an ill omen."

At a sign from me, Torriti lapsed into silence, but his right hand continued to sketch the outlines of his fear and doubt. His shaven head gleamed in the play of the torchlight upon the walls of the crypt.

At the end of the corridor, as the workmen wrestled the bundle from its tomb, I gathered my cloak about me for warmth. I recalled that Formosus blessed me one day, not long before his death, with unusual gravity, saying: "God our Father has blessed me, and with this right hand I bless you in turn. Now you, in turn, will bless another, and he, in turn, another, and at each step something of the power of God's blessing is lost. Each downward rung has less of God and more of man." Then this chamber is the holiest in Christendom, I thought, for it contains the two men who are closest to God. I would have laughed, but my yawping bark grated my ears, and I seldom indulged. Safer, too, to keep laughter inside, with the uncounted other blasphemies.

Do not be misled. Formosus did not count me among his intimates. Yet I was valuable to him, as I was valuable for decades to the Lord and His Apostle of the moment. Because I could not speak, I was in great demand as an audience. When pontiffs tired of confiding and confessing to an unresponsive God, they confided and confessed to me. I shone with the outward and visible signs they craved. Oh, the litany of gestures, subtle facial expressions, head movements! I was summoned at all hours of the day and night, and I always earned my blessing.

I served the popes in another way as well. Many ambitious men unfamiliar with my unique position foolishly thought me a trained ape, a gangling half-wit, deaf or stupid as well as mute. They indiscreetly confessed their sins in my presence—and so they received their reward on Earth and not in Heaven.

For these offices I enjoyed dank and verminous accommodations that were among the finest in Rome; a modest treasury sufficient to buy most of the citizens, as needed; many ornate titles, garments and privileges; and a place in all processionals—though cheers, I noted, tended to falter as I passed. I retired each night to my lumpy couch with a guiltless soul and, better still, a full belly. I was most proud of that, for I survived my youth only by huddling with other miserable beggars each day in the portico of the Lateran for a portion of meat, bread and wine, the fruits of the *domas cultae*. Ah, those sanctified fields and vineyards, always heard of but never seen! Surely there, we thought, the starving could pluck and eat in peace, free of the pious prattle that we choked down with our meals in Rome.

In this we were correct. As I rose higher in the Church, the meals grew more substantial and the piety less burdensome. I saw the lame and the dying leaping like frogs around a finger bone that had been fondling a milkmaid not two weeks before.

I saw some of them healed.

Torriti cleared his throat. Before me yawned the open tomb. Behind me, at the bend in the corridor, waited Torriti, the guards, and the workmen bearing Formosus on a litter. The torchlight surrounding them was distant and feeble. I stood alone in the flow of darkness from the tomb.

"Is there more?" Torriti asked.

I brusquely shook my head, my reverie over, and hastened up the slope toward the light.

* * *

As a witness to Pope Stephen's infamous cadaver synod, I recall most vividly that the decaying corpse of Pope Formosus made a stubborn and unruly defendant. Perhaps it merely sagged beneath the weight of the charges: perjury, coveting the papacy, arcane violations of bureaucratic procedure; new items were added daily. At any rate, attendants had to be watchful, for whenever propped upright on the papal throne, the corpse began slowly, almost imperceptibly, to lean forward, like an arthritic reaching for his shoes.

I thought it imprudent for Sergius, a toadying bishop who was one of Stephen's chief spokesmen, to stand close enough to the defendant for his spittle to fleck Formosus's face as he railed. This dramatic effect was for Stephen's benefit, no doubt, but a more dramatic effect ensued when Formosus lurched over onto Sergius, and accuser and defendant fell together to the floor. The corpse seemed to clutch at Sergius's robes and hiss the breath of the grave into his face. Sergius, gibbering blasphemies, scuttled backward to be rid of Formosus's lolling head, of his unwholesome purple vestments spilling across the flagstones like a dark and seductive pool.

Stephen began to howl. "Villain! Wretched, scraping, puking villain!" He charged across the chamber, and the hapless Sergius quailed beneath his fouled robes, not realizing the pope was addressing Formosus until Stephen kicked the dead man in the stomach. As the pope wrenched his foot free, Sergius choked and turned away—displaying a squeamishness he would not display years later, after he himself acquired the papacy.

Thereafter, stout ropes bound the defendant to the throne during trial. Even then, welling bubbles of noxious gases kept Formosus's robes astir. Their gentle, flirtatious undulations seemed to mock the the sweat and labor of the many strutting accusers.

Each night I sat with the prisoner in his cell to hear and transcribe any statements or confessions he might wish to make, and also to frustrate his escape. This was a redundant precaution given the thickness of the door, the stoutness of the lock, the presence, in the corridor outside, of a turnkey. That worthy man cared not for his duty, and gagged on his rations, but I was comfortable enough with my cheese and my biscuit, my seared nostrils, and my rich and varied thoughts. I asked Formosus how his trial was proceeding thus far.

Less and less of God, and more and more of man.

It is of God, as well, I replied. It is mad, and pointless, and inefficient. It is godlike.

As are you.

One night Stephen demanded that the prisoner and I dine with him in his apartments. Course after course was set before the moldering guest, then cleared away untouched. Stephen gobbled his fowl and fruits as always. Only I, who knew starvation, truly appreciated the textures of the meal. Stephen downed much wine and spouted opinions in unusually high spirits. Alone with his deceased predecessor and his mute factotum, his conversational brilliance was unrivaled. He spoke at length about Regino's generally excellent *De harmonica institutione,* in which he nevertheless spied some errors of interest to the trained musician. He spoke about the well-chewed topic of the millennium—did the worthy Formosus and the good Alfano believe, as did some in the Church, that the tenth century would be the final act of history? Some histories will end even sooner, I thought, and I fancied a responsive twinkle in the sockets to my left.

* * *

On the darkest night of the year, as Formosus and I traded silences, I heard the clanking of the lock and the screeching of the hinges. The door swung open to admit Stephen, who cast me from the cell with the briefest glance and a backward wave of his hand. As I bowed low in passing, he crossed to Formosus's bunk on the far wall; he was as brisk and placid as a man striding into a corner to piss. Through the grille in the door I saw him stoop over Formosus, muttering inaudibly, and lift the corpse's right hand, the hand with which Formosus blessed. Stephen pawed at the hand's middle three fingers, clutched them and violently tugged them, stripping the bones. With an oath, he cast aside a wad of flesh. Do you squirm at this? Your day has seen worse.

Stephen lifted one of his dainty feet, his bulk swaying precariously, and stomped once, twice, upon Formosus's hand. Then he produced a knife and sawed into the fingers until they broke loose with a crack. I watched Stephen pocket the fingers, then murmur into the better of Formosus's crumpled ears, then press his own ear against the corpse's lips, then murmur again. Twice he straightened, with poisonous glances toward the door.

When he emerged, after an hour of these whispered confidences, he glared coldly at me and stated, evenly, "He has much to say of *you,* Alfano." Without speaking further, he trotted away, his heels resounding off the stone like tiny hooves.

I entered the cell.

He thinks I am his enemy, I said. What have you told him?

He has heard nothing but the chittering in his mind.

He thinks I am his enemy, I repeated. He has made me his enemy.

You have made yourself what you are.

Why not? I asked. I have touched the shrouds of harlots and turned them into martyrs. I have touched the bones of plowmen and made them into saints.

I stood over Formosus's corpse, held my hand just above his body, not quite touching it, and laughed until I winced.

* * *

When closeted with a corpse, one has little to do but plot, so I soon had various plans at my disposal. I pridefully chose the most complex.

Days passed. Formosus was found guilty, as this was the only possible verdict, and was deemed unfit for Christian burial, as this was the only possible punishment. A hired mob paraded his corpse through the streets and flung it into the Tiber. Several of the most vocal and physically imposing members of the mob were doubly salaried, in the employ both of Stephen and of my good assistant Torriti. Torriti's minions managed to exert considerable influence over the mob's route and its final riverbank destination, so that the body was flung into the water past sunset and at a spot directly upstream from where Torriti and I waited.

Dressed in the coarse robes of fishermen, we crouched in darkness on the slimy planks of a floating mill. Its grist wheel ground mindlessly, helpless to stop the current, as we raked our barge poles through the scum.

"We have become fishers of men," Torriti whispered. I watched him carefully for other signs of wit, and was relieved to see none.

Recovering Formosus's body was not strictly necessary—rumors and visions already were darting through the crowds, thanks to the calculated loose talk of my emissaries and to native Roman credulity—but I was nevertheless relieved when, after several minutes, Torriti yelped at the sight of Formosus's gaping jaw at the end of his hook.

When we spread the sack of bones across the planks, we saw

that the Tiber had claimed parts of the late pontiff, but that the mauled right hand was still joined at the wrist. "Thank you, my Lord, for your divine assistance," Torriti whispered, as I swung down the cleaver.

We stripped the corpse of its tattered surplice, dumped it into a wagon, pitched over it a concealing layer of hay, and trundled it for safekeeping to an ambitious hermit who lived in the shadows of the Colosseum. I considered merely returning Formosus to the fishes, but as a former procurer of relics, I knew the value of thrift.

Those members of the mob with the most spiritual fervor had smeared the surplice with excrement, presumably their own, but we dared not risk laundering lest the ruined cloth shred altogether. Also, the pitifully soiled garment would add a note of pathos.

With the distinctive surplice over my shoulders, and the mauled right hand protruding from my right sleeve, I made a convincing vision indeed in my three brief appearances. Each time I was illuminated in a window, gazing in upon a member of a pro-Formosus faction noted for zealous and sometimes violent piety: first, a Frankish lieutenant; second, the elder son of a city aristocrat; third, a leading conniver of the papal court. All saw precisely what the roiling streets without and the prayerful anguish within had prepared them to see, a sight a good deal more convincing and terrifying than I actually could have been.

The lieutenant leaped from his supper table, drew his sword, slammed it blade-first into the floorboards, and began to weep in astonishing Frankish profusion, beads of tears and soup alternating in his beard.

The elder son thrashed and twisted and cocooned himself in fabrics—sheets, cushions, even the canopy of his bed—leaving only his twitching face naked and suggestive of the sensuous inheritances he had dreamt of moments before.

The papal functionary merely fainted, a pile of robes on a marble floor. But as with the Frank and the noble, I made sure to move the clawlike right hand in a way that aped the spastic movements of a blessing.

The effect was immediate and gratifying. Within hours, the members of Stephen's guard were being eviscerated in the streets, and every altar was thronged with keening flagellants begging forgiveness for the city's sin. Several people claimed to have been healed of lameness, blindness and, I believe, suppurating wounds by the triumphant shade of the desecrated Formosus—people who, Torriti assured me, were not on our payroll. Similarly, the earthquake that collapsed the Lateran basilica, widely viewed at the time as divine judgment, was, if not divine, certainly beyond my powers to engineer. Suffice to say that after weeks of chaos, Stephen was dragged shrieking from his chambers and cast into jail, where he was found strangled soon afterward, apparently by an unusually resilient garrote.

* * *

My own death, many years later, proved uninteresting, even commonplace. Among the broken columns of the *disabitato,* that pagan city of ruins, were swamps and stagnant pools that bred black toads. In summers a dark mist sprawled from these evil bogs and breathed fever into the town. One year I inhaled unwisely and, weakened by advanced age, died.

No portion of my carcass ever was enshrined and offered to the pilgrim trade. Neither venerated nor desecrated, I was allowed to decay at my leisure. Many in torment long for less. Yet I ask you: What altarpiece saint with upturned face and outspread hands and the painted eyes of a cow could take a cadaver's claw and a shit-stained surplice and endow them with even a taint of the miraculous?

Liza and the Crazy Water Man

SHE WAS LONG DONE SINGING, BUT THE SCHOOL-house was still full of her voice. It flowed into the corners. It washed along the ceiling and the floorboards. It surged against the backs of the farmers and mill workers as they shuffled out the door. It claimed all the space they had occupied. It crowded them, ready to pour out, into the cool night, and roll freely across the face of the mountain.

The woman who owned the voice sat on the edge of the little stage and shook out her hair of silver and gold, raked her fingers through it once, twice, as she sweated in the lamp's kerosene glow. I stood there in the dimness, sweltering and damp, my tie undone. The people leaving whooped and laughed, but I feared to say a mumbling word. No room was left in that place for my voice.

So, wordlessly, I stepped into the circle of light, and held out my business card. It was all the offering I had.

Alvin Pleasants, Charlotte office
CRAZY WATER CRYSTALS COMPANY
Of Mineral Wells, Texas
"Making weak men strong since 1880"
Sponsor of "CRAZY BARN DANCE"
Saturday nights on WBT

She read the card gravely and thoroughly, as if it were bad news from far away. Then she handed it back and smiled. "Thank you," she said, "but Aunt Kate and I have no need of laxatives. Thank you again, and good night."

"It's not a laxative," I said. "It's an all-purpose tonic."

"Is it, now? That sounds much more interesting. If you'll excuse me?" She picked up her guitar case, hoisted it onto one hip to get a better hold, then swung it between us and headed for the door. I followed and matched her stride, for she was as tall as I. I had not driven halfway up the mountain called Yandro just to go back to Charlotte empty-handed, however pleasant the drive in springtime.

All my other leads had come to nothing: a mandolin player in Blowing Rock, a gospel quartet in North Wilkesboro, two fiddling brothers in Boone. None wanted to be broadcast all over the Carolinas on a 50,000 watt station in between advertisements for Crazy Water Crystals. None wanted to pick up and move to Charlotte and become famous, like the Monroe Brothers and the Delmore Brothers and Fiddlin' Arthur Smith. None even wanted a steady radio salary. The year was 1936, and I apparently no longer could get 1931 mileage out of the phrase "ten dollars a week."

I kept right alongside as she swept through a knot of people on the porch. "Good night, fellas," she said. "I'll see y'all in church."

"Evening, Liza."

"Good night, Liza."

"Take care, Liza."

They stared at me as I kept pace, nearly at a trot, down the steps and into the parking area. She walked right through the middle of a terrible snarl of wagons and shying mules and Model T's that churned around in circles slinging gravel. She looked neither to left nor right, as if charmed. I had seen this in mountain women before, this grim set of the jaw, this purposeful, loping gait, as if all slopes were steep. But I soon stopped comparing other mountain women to Liza Candler.

I tried my usually surefire sales pitch: I told the truth. "You have a voice like the voice of the mountain," I said, panting. "I want to put that voice on the radio. I don't want to sell you anything. I just want people to hear your voice."

"They hear me now," she said.

"Not many, though. How often do you play a dance like this? Once a week? I doubt it. Once a month, more like? And always for the home folks. The same people, month after month, year after year."

"Don't you like the same people, month after month, year after year? Do you change the people you like every month, like shifts at the furniture plant? And do you aim to run alongside me all the way home like a haint?"

I stopped and watched her stalk on down the road. "No, I thought you'd stop and talk to me, so I could offer you a ride."

"I ain't stopping," she said, her checked dress indistinct in the dark, "but if you drive up alongside me and open the door I might get in."

I ran back for the Packard.

"And then," she called after me, "we can see what Aunt Kate has to say."

* * *

All the way up the road, I worked on her.

"You could come to Charlotte, stay for a week, visit the studio, get to know people, do a Crazy Water show on Saturday night, see how you like it. See how much mail comes in. Heck, I know people at RCA Victor. I could set up a recording session for you while you're in town. Do you know that Mainer's Mountaineers made eighteen thousand dollars last year for a half-hour's work in Charlotte? Just for 'Maple on the Hill'? They earned a half-cent in royalties off every record sold. How about that?"

Liza had her eyes shut and her head out the window, so that her hair streamed out behind. She had a profile like a cameo brooch. "A lot of people must have no music of their own," she said, "if they'll pay good money to try to hang on to somebody else's."

* * *

In the front parlor of the Candler place sat an ancient woman in a rocking chair, her feet propped on the grate of a cold iron stove. We walked in as she pushed a pinch of snuff into her mouth with one hand and snapped shut a small pouch with her other. She wore a tattered sweater, a gingham bonnet, and square eyeglasses as thick and grimy as windshields. Behind her, a gleaming shotgun leaned against the wall.

"Hello, Aunt Kate!" Liza cried, so loudly that I jumped. "This is Mr. Alvin Pleasants, from down in Charlotte."

Aunt Kate tucked the pouch into an apron pocket, pulled her

eyeglasses down to the tip of her nose, and tilted her head back to look at me. Then she grunted and leaned sideways, slowly reached out behind, groped the air in the vicinity of the shotgun.

"No, Aunt Kate!" Liza yelled. "He ain't a fella! He wants to put me on the radio! He works for WBT!"

"Actually, I work for the Crazy Water Crystals Company, but I do have an office at WBT. And I know the Monroe Brothers personally." I sat on the edge of a horsehair davenport, which pricked me something awful, and handed Aunt Kate a brochure. "Here's a copy of WBT's Official Radiologue, the seasonal programming schedule, compliments of Crazy Water Crystals." Aunt Kate bent over the brochure and scanned it with the tip of her nose. Liza looked at me meaningfully. Her eyes were gray. "Oh, I'm sorry," I said, and I began to yell, too. "It's a copy of the station's schedule! A gift for you!"

Aunt Kate slowly looked up at me and asked, very quietly, "Who in the world raised you to holler inside the house any such a way?"

I glared toward where Liza had been. I heard her bustle around the next room, humming. "I'm sorry, ma'am. Your niece gave me the impression that you were deaf."

Aunt Kate swatted the air. "Shoot. Ain't no telling what that gal will come up with. But if you know so much about radios, how 'bout turn on that one over there?" She pointed at a cathedral set across the room. "It's time for my story."

I turned the knob, heard a familiar click, then felt the vibration as the tubes started to warm up. As Liza walked in, tying back her hair, the radio started that slide-whistle sound that said the station would arrive in just a few seconds.

"Aunt Kate," Liza asked, at a normal volume, "haven't you wanted to visit Aunt Oese in the TB sanitarium in Charlotte?"

"You know I have, honey," Aunt Kate said. "Just been waiting on you to take a notion to come with me."

"Then I reckon I might as well come do your program," Liza told me. "Just for one show, of course."

The station faded in on a commercial: "If you care for your loved ones' laundry, banish tattletale gray with Fels Naptha! Yes, banish tattletale gray with Fels Naptha!"

"Good night, Aunt Kate," Liza said, and kissed the old woman on the cheek. "Mr. Pleasants said he'd be happy to keep you company while you listen to your story."

"I did?"

"Good night, Mr. Pleasants," Liza said, standing in the doorway. "I hope that laxative company pays you well to drive around the countryside and bother people."

I enunciated carefully. "It's an all-purpose tonic."

"Is that so? Good night to you once again. I do hope you enjoy the program." She watched me through the narrowing crack, and I watched her, until the door thunked shut between us.

"And now—*The Romance of Helen Trent!* The real-life drama of Helen Trent, who, when life mocks her, breaks her hopes, dashes her against the rocks of despair, fights back bravely, successfully, to prove what so many women long to prove in their own lives: that because a woman is thirty-five—or more—romance in life need not be over. That romance can begin at thirty-five!"

As the organ music trilled, Aunt Kate leaned forward and puckered, sucked in her cheeks, squeezed a big dark drop from between her lips, and let it plop into a half-full Kiwi shoe-polish tin at her feet. She daubed her lips with a corner of her apron and sat back. The rocker and a floorboard creaked in harmony. The horsehair in the davenport worked its way a little further into me, as if to seize and haul me down into the brocade, fix me in that parlor forever.

* * *

Two months later, on the afternoon I met Liza and her aunt at the train station, my boss was pan-fried drunk. Had I known that, I might not have been so eager to drop Aunt Kate at the boarding house and whisk Liza immediately up to the station, hell-bent to show her the glories of radio. As I threw open the door to Mr. Ledford's office, I realized my error.

"Oh, dear," I said.

Empty bottles of Crazy Water's chief competitor, Peruna, formed three rows of pickets that guarded three sides of his desktop from all comers. Despite the mutter and jerk of the electric fan atop the file cabinet, the office was sweltering, and Ledford's ever-present homburg sagged over his ears like a deflated pudding. He gazed sightlessly forward, his expression placid, mournful, and expectant of all bad things. I timidly introduced Liza, and in reply his bullfrog voice rasped even more than usual.

"Good afternoon, Miss Candler," Ledford said. "Please forgive me, but I am drunker than Cooter John."

"There is no need to apologize," Liza said, "but who, pray tell, is Cooter John?"

"Cooter John does not exist," Ledford said. "He is a mythic figure, a wraith with a legendary capacity for drink."

"Thank you," Liza said.

I cleared my throat. "Probably we should come back later," I said. "Mr. Ledford sometimes likes to sample the competitors' products, just to, uh, investigate the market."

"I no longer wonder that Peruna sells so well," Ledford said. "It virtually sells itself, in all its smoothness and guile." He lurched sideways, rummaged in his trash can, and came up with a clutch of empty Peruna boxes. "If you will excuse me," he said, "I have box tops to redeem."

"You can talk to Miss Candler later," I said, hastily. "Maybe I could show her around downtown? Come back here just before 'Briarhopper Time,' so she can watch the broadcast?"

Ledford flapped a hand at us, and we fled.

Out on the sidewalk, we walked into a hot breeze of exhaust fumes. We had to raise our voices to be heard over the rattles and growls of the Model T's and Model A's and the clangs of the streetcars that slid along the tracks in the middle of the traffic. Many of the Ford drivers seemed to keep one hand on the wheel and one on the horn, judging from all those honks and bleats. Drivers clawed at their collars, mopped their faces with handkerchiefs, wriggled out of suit jackets as their mindless automobiles rolled forward. Businessmen with briefcases, farmers in overalls, packs of dirty-faced children jaywalked at will, trotted from sidewalk to sidewalk, dodged the three streams of vehicles. Kids skipped merrily in front of the streetcars as the cowcatchers jabbed their shins.

"I am so sorry," I said for about the fifteenth time.

"I quite understand," Liza said.

"I handle all the talent—the singers, musicians, specialty acts. I don't have anything to do with the business side. But Mr. Ledford spends all his time dealing with the head office in Texas, and all he hears from them is sell, sell, sell. He gets discouraged. Me, I just listen to a lot of music. Good afternoon, Mr. Jennings!" I waved at the portly, gray-haired man at the rolltop desk in the lobby of the Union National Bank. He just glared back.

"Not very friendly," Liza said.

"He can't afford to be. He's the president of the bank. After the Crash, when so many other banks closed their doors, he moved his desk into the lobby and started handling all withdrawals personally. That's what kept him in business, probably—bullying people into not withdrawing their money."

On the next corner, a skinny young man with an open valise at his feet held swatches of cloth draped across his forearms. Around his neck dangled a ribbon of measuring tape. "Made-to-measure suits!" he cried. "A complete suit for a five-dollar deposit! Sir, that's a fine suit you have—couldn't you use another just like it? Have a good day, sir. Made-to-measure suits! Hi, Alvin, how's the boy?"

"Can't complain, Cecil, can't complain. Wife and kids all right?"

"Just fine, Alvin. That job lead I had last week went south, but hey, something will turn up. No, no need to linger, Alvin—you bought three suits off me last month, and I know you haven't worn through the pants yet. Beg your pardon, ma'am."

"Come by the station sometime, Cecil. We'll go downstairs and get a bite to eat. The family, too, if you like."

"I appreciate it, Alvin. I'll see you. Made-to-measure suits! Just like mine, only twenty-three fifty! Nice cool seersucker, only eight ninety-five!"

We crossed the street in silence. I felt that if I looked around at Liza, she simultaneously would turn to look at me, and the thought made me flush as if it had happened. Instead, I waved at Mr. Tate, who draped a towel across a customer's face as we passed his shop—five white men in tilted chairs, five Negro men in a row behind. Mr. Tate grinned and ran his hand through his non-existent hair, a visual reminder that I should come in for a trim.

Finally Liza asked, "If you own so many suits, Mr. Pleasants, why have I seen you in only one?"

I jammed my hands into my pockets. "Maybe some people need new suits more than I do," I said. I watched the cracks in the pavement go past.

To my surprise, Liza cut in front of me and walked backwards for a few paces, so that we faced each other. She studied my face the way a fiddler studies the bow, the way a mill worker studies the thump of the shuttle and loom. Then she whirled and dropped back alongside me.

"Mr. Pleasants," Liza said, "I'd be honored if you were to buy me a cup of coffee."

* * *

The Star Lunch had only a couple of other patrons—wrong time of day—and so Ari Kokenes gave Liza the royal treatment. He poured her coffee and fussed over her. Up front, I leaned over the display case and peered at the pastries, but my reflection got in the way. I rubbed my chin. I thought I had shaved myself raw that morning, but now my face felt and looked like an empty burlap sack.

"How about some of the baklava, Illona?" I asked. "And two forks, maybe?" I looked up. Ari's daughter shrank from the counter, dark eyes wide as she looked past me. I turned just as Earl Gillespie seized my shoulder and breathed Sen-Sen into my face.

"Cheer up, Alvin, you'll curdle the cream." He slapped my back and barked a laugh. "Just a joke, pal, just a joke. Hi, Illona, how's my ready steady?"

Illona silently busied herself with the baklava and a small square of wax paper. She wrapped and unwrapped and wrapped it again, her eyes downcast. She moved her body as little as possible. If Earl watched her long enough, she'd dwindle down to nothing.

"Wait up for me, willya, Alvin?" Earl asked. "I need your help, OK? Great." Earl blew a kiss at Illona, winked at me, and barrelled onward past Ari, who stood at attention at the end of the counter. "Use your phone, Ari? Great," Earl said, without a glance at the man.

"Sure, Mr. Gillespie, whatever you say," Ari said without enthusiasm. He slapped the countertop with the end of his towel and looked at me fast and blank, as if I had been replaced by a stranger.

I paid Illona and smiled at her until she flashed one in return. As I turned away, she had a hurried conversation with her father in Greek, maybe one sentence apiece, and then dashed into the back. The beaded curtain danced behind her.

As Earl watched my progress across the room, he rocked on his toes, jingled change in his pockets, and shouted into the telephone's mouthpiece as if the nearly empty Star Lunch were Grand Central at noon. "Get me WBT, please." I shoved my chair around between him and Liza, with my back to the phone. As he blew a long wolf whistle, I tipped my hat up and tried to square my shoulders to make them wider.

"Who's that," Liza stated.

"The announcer who says, once a week, 'For fifty-six years, Crazy Water has come to the aid of the weak and ailing, and it has made of them men and women ready to face life's hardships.'"

"He does have that look about him," Liza said.

"Damn these people!" Earl cried. "Can't anyone answer a phone anymore? Can't anybody do an honest day's work? Has the whole world gone union?"

"Who's he calling that's so important?"

"Himself," I said.

Adelaide must have picked up, finally, because Earl dropped his normal deep radio voice and went into an exaggerated nasal twang. "Yes, please, is Mr. Gillespie in? Mr. Earl Gillespie? No? Could you please ask him to call Monica at Metro-Goldwyn-Mayer as soon as possible?" I pictured Adelaide at the other end as she rolled her eyes and drew shaded triangles on her blotter. "I'll be on the lot until three, West Coast time. Tell him I'm at the bungalow. Yes, he has the number. Thank you so much." He hung the earpiece back on its cradle and walked over, showing Liza all his teeth and slicking back his hair with one hand.

"You aren't fooling anybody, Earl," I said. "One day while you're busy chasing shopgirls at the five and dime, you're gonna get a real phone call, and Adelaide will just think it's you and laugh and hang up."

He didn't look at me. "You forget your manners, Earl. Aren't you going to introduce me to your friend?"

I sighed. "Earl Gillespie, Liza Candler." Liza nodded just enough to acknowledge her name. "Liza Candler, Earl Gillespie." Earl bowed with an Errol Flynn flourish. "What do you need, Earl? We got to go."

"Now where in the world did Alvin Pleasants, of all people, find a pretty gal like you?" Earl turned a chair around and straddled it, his arms crossed over the back, and fished in the little jar on the table for a toothpick. "I've seen him drink coffee with street peddlers and hillbilly bands and nigger barbers, but never with anyone as high-class as you."

"I reckon you don't know him too well, then."

Her gaze would have frozen a smarter man, but Earl, like any mule, sometimes needed an ax handle. He just looked her over and shoved a toothpick into his mouth and chewed it with slow relish. "Yes, indeed. Alvin's outdone himself this time. Let's see now. You surely aren't a nigger barber. I don't see you carrying anything on your person to sell. So I'd say you must be a singer. And if you sing as pretty as you eat that pastry, why then I bet they've already put you on a record or two, am I right? I sure would like to hear one. Oh, yeah, that's it, I was right. See her blushing, Alvin, you see that?"

I saw it, and I was surprised. “Miss Candler? Are you all right?”

“I *tried* recording before,” Liza blurted. “It didn’t work out, that’s all.”

“What do you mean it didn’t work out?” I asked. “They didn’t *like* you?”

She stabbed me a look. “I’ll have you know Mr. Peer said I could sing the clouds across the sky.” Right then, her voice was almost as flat as Aunt Kate’s. Almost.

Earl grinned as he watched us go back and forth.

“Peer?” I repeated. “Ralph Peer? You recorded for the top field producer in the country?”

“Oh, I was just a youngun,” Liza said, laughing a little. “It must have been five years gone.” She stabbed a stray pistachio with her fork, glanced at me, sighed and went on. “I was visiting some cousins down here in the flats, and we saw the ad in the paper, and we just went over there and sang and that was it. Just some giggly mountain gals out having fun, clomping around in our brogans, tracking in mud. Mr. Peer was just being nice to us ’cause it was the end of the day. They were glad to get rid of us, I bet.” She smiled real quick at me and then at Earl and then at me, and then she let it go and turned to look at something on a shelf that had all of a sudden become plumb fascinating.

Earl cleared his throat. “You ever met a real-life radio star before, Liza honey? Why don’t you come up to the studio while we do the Briarhopper show this afternoon? Just tell ’em you’re there to see me, they’ll let you right in.”

“C’mon, Earl,” I said, “save it for the bungalow. And if you’ve got a favor to ask me, ask it.”

“Oh, it’s not big, Alvin,” Earl said, swiveling his head around at me like a turtle. “Not worth interrupting a nice conversation. You need to slow down and enjoy yourself more. But since you asked, I’m working on next month’s banquet for the Alf Landon campaign at the Hotel Charlotte. I thought it’d be nice to have some local musicians perform before all the speeches. Might help people’s dinners set better. You suppose some of your hillbilly friends would be interested in that? I figured I’d ask you before I asked anyone else, just as a favor.”

“I seriously doubt it, Earl. How much you gonna pay?”

“Now, Alvin. Remember, this is a benefit. Everyone’s donating their time and energy. I am, and Colonel Macon, and Mrs. Steere, and everyone else. It’d be a little unfair if the musicians wouldn’t donate their time, too.”

"They make little enough money working for Colonel Macon and Mrs. Steere in the mills all day long," I said. "Now you want 'em to work for those same people at night, and do it for free? Forget it, Earl. Besides, I don't know any hillbillies, myself included, who would donate to the Landon campaign so much as a—a cold cup of coffee."

That said, I drank the rest of mine, flustered again. Both Earl and Liza looked at me. So did Ari, in a sense, even with his back turned. He stayed scrupulously within earshot and rearranged bottles of olive oil with great industry.

"Why, Alvin," Earl said. "I'm surprised at you. Saying such anti-American things in front of this impressionable young woman. You don't want her to think you've bet on a losing horse, do you?"

It was like batter turning golden in a pan. Liza suddenly beamed at Earl as if his mask had dropped off and revealed Clark Gable. "A losing horse, Mr. Gillespie?" She reached across the table and touched Earl's forearm, just long enough to rivet his attention.

"There's no doubt about it, young missy," he said. "All the papers say it's over, it's Landon over Roosevelt two to one." He proceeded to tell us how much better off the mill workers would be without government meddlers and Communist labor agitators, and how the Democrats in Washington kept finding new ways to pick an honest man's pockets. "Do you know they plan to assign a number to every worker in America, and fingerprint everybody, and issue dog tags? It'll be just like prison. Just like Russia."

"That sure is scary, Mr. Gillespie," Liza said. "In fact, I'd say you're the scariest man I've met in Charlotte. I believe we've got to be going, isn't that right, Mr. Pleasants? But I wish you and Governor Landon luck, Mr. Gillespie."

"Thank you, thank you, Miss Candler," Earl said, and rose with us. "Hey, Alvin. Alvin! About that banquet—"

"I already told you to forget it, Earl."

"Did I forget to mention," Earl said, as he examined the frayed end of his toothpick, "that the performers would be welcome to help themselves to the buffet? Prime rib? Shrimp cocktail? Peach melba? All the trimmings?"

I stood there, my hat halfway to my head. Ari waited, holding open the door.

"Can they take home leftovers?" I asked. I looked not at Earl but at the tiles beneath my feet.

"I don't see why not," Earl said. "No sense in it going to waste."

"I'll ask around," I said. "I'll see what I can do."

Outside, the three smallest Kokenes kids jumped rope on the sidewalk. Patent-leather shoes smacked the pavement to the rhythm of a singsong chant:

"Roosevelt's in the White House, waiting to be elected, Landon's in the garbage, waiting to be collected, Alf Alf Alf Alf Arf Arf Arf Arf, Roosevelt's in the White House . . ."

Earl glared at Ari, who shrugged broadly and smiled. One gold tooth sparkled in the sun. "Who knows where kids hear such things?" he said, and lifted his hands in resignation.

Earl grunted, tipped his hat to Liza, and strode away. He gave the jump rope a wide berth.

"We'll see you later, Ari," I said. I walked off in the opposite direction from Earl, even though he was bound for the station like us.

Halfway down the block, I said, "I'm sorry about that, too," assuming Liza was beside me. She was. I added: "I guess I'm sorry about everything today. Earl sure pushes my buttons, though. He knows my weaknesses."

"I'd call them strengths," Liza said. As she walked, she traced the brick wall alongside with her finger.

* * *

Briarhopper Time aired live each weekday afternoon right before *The Lone Ranger.* Although their sponsor was Crazy Water's chief competitor, I had to admit that the Briarhoppers were one of the most popular bands at WBT, among the staff as well as among the public. When Liza and I got back to the station that evening, just as the show began, we joined about a dozen people gathered in the corridor outside the studio to watch the show through the soundproof plate glass.

From the loudspeaker above our heads came the familiar opening—"Do y'all know what 'hit is? 'Hit's Briarhopper Time!"—and then the first licks of "Hop Along Peter." Eventually, Earl Gillespie, on the other side of the glass, stepped up to the microphone, and Liza watched him attentively.

"Have a nice walk?" asked Ledford, who gnawed the tip of a new cigar beside me. He looked considerably more focused.

"Mr. Ledford," Liza asked, "could I please borrow your lighter?"

"But of course," Ledford said, and handed it over.

"I didn't know you smoked, Miss Candler," I said.

"I don't," she said, and walked away with the lighter.

"Hey," Ledford said. She disappeared around the corner. He looked at me like he expected me to sprint after her.

In the studio, Earl had launched into a commercial. His lips moved on the other side of the plate glass; his dulcet voice crackled through the loudspeaker. "And now a word from the Consolidated Drug Trade Products Company of Chicago, Illinois, home of the wondrous laboratories that gave the world Radio Girl perfume, Kolorbak hair dye, and Zymole Trokeys cough drops."

The studio door in the far wall opened, and Liza sashayed through, ushered by a smiling security guard who held the door and waved to get Earl's attention. Liza high-stepped over microphone cords as she approached Earl, the hem of her dress swinging.

Ledford's cigar drooped in his mouth.

Earl beamed at Liza and glanced up from his script at every other word to mug and preen. She smiled and waved, wiggling her fingers like a little girl.

"Friends, does your medicine chest include a bottle of Peruna? Yes, I said Peruna—That's P-E-R-U-N-A, the all-purpose wonder tonic that so many of your friends and neighbors rely upon when they feel under the weather."

Liza stood directly in front of him, still smiling. Earl winked at her, oblivious as she slowly raised the lighter.

"I'm sure all you Briarhopper fans out there don't need a reminder that for each Peruna box top you send in, you get a photograph of everyone's favorite hillbilly band—the Briarhoppers!—absolutely free and suitable for framing."

Liza flicked the lighter aflame, and apparently jammed an important cog in Earl's mind.

"But right now I want to address the, the medicinal benefits of—of Peruna, which is safe and effective for adults as well—I mean, for children as well as adults."

Liza set the top of Gillespie's script on fire and walked away, smiling and waving at me. What else? I waved back. The paper rushed into flame like it was soaked in Peruna, and Gillespie desperately tried to speed up his last few lines.

"Mothers and fathers, when your little ones wake up with a stomach ache or a chill you'll want a bottle of Peruna on hand won't you?" He held a torch by his fingertips. "Of course you will! Sleep better tomorrow night because you have Peruna in your medicine chest that's P-E-R-U-N-A just-ask-for-it-by-name-and-now-we-return-to-the-Briarhopper-show! Shoot!" he hissed, and dashed his flaming script to the floor as the band solemnly stepped forward and began "More Pretty Gals Than One." A technician ran over and tried to kick apart the ashes quietly, like a soft-shoe dancer in a medicine show.

"What a pro," Ledford said. "Note how he said shoot and not shit, and turned away from the microphone just in case? Read all the copy before it burned up, too. He does have talent, the son of a bitch. Thank you, ma'am," he told Liza, and accepted his lighter with a little bow.

"I just set your announcer on fire," Liza said. "Aren't you mad?"

"No, ma'am," Ledford said. "He's our announcer only on Saturday nights. On weekdays he works for the competition, and I happily consign him to the flames."

I watched through the glass as Gillespie bolted. "On the other hand," I said, "this might be a good time to go out and get a sandwich." I hustled Liza toward the elevators as Gillespie charged into view around the corner, holding his hand and cursing.

"Hold the car!" I cried.

As the door on the cage slid shut, I heard Ledford say: "You hush that bad talk, Earl. No one buys tonic off a cussing man."

Half a floor down, I asked Liza, "That damn fool stunt was for me, wasn't it?"

"You can have it if you like," she said with a grin.

I laughed. "OK, I'll take it, then."

"Done."

"Done." We shook hands violently, as if pumping water, and then hollered laughing like younguns. The operator gripped the handle and shook his head.

* * *

I showed her around town, what town there was. The old U.S. Mint had been moved out to Eastover and reopened as an art museum, of all things, the first in the state, so I took her there out of civic duty. I showed her that the eye of the eagle above the door was really the taillight off a Ford, and she agreed that was the best part of the museum. We watched airplanes land and take off at Douglas Field, and I told her how Mayor Douglas made a big speech at the dedication about the brilliant future of air travel and then, when invited to go up in one of the things, replied, "Thank you, no." We went to the kiddie matinee at the State Theater, the

New York Grand before talkies, because Johnny Mack Brown was signing autographs in between episodes of *Rustlers of Red Dog.* Those younguns were screaming wild, and if their popguns had been loaded, why I wouldn't have given you a nickel for the life of Johnny Mack Brown. Then we ate fifteen-cent hamburgers and five-cent Cokes at the Canary Cottage, the cheapest good place in town, and from there went over to the Hotel Charlotte. We couldn't afford to do anything there but sit on the plush furniture in the massive, marbled lobby, watch people go by, and enjoy the curious breeze that constantly stirred the palms no matter the weather outside. We sat on facing sofas, sprawled our arms along the backs, and took up as much free space as we could.

"If anybody tries to run us off," I said, "tell them we answer only to J. Edgar Hoover."

After a while, I ran out of jokes and other things I felt comfortable saying, and so I just sat with my chin on my fist, listened to Liza talk, and watched her finish a cup of cider that she had bought at a sidewalk stand down the street.

She jiggled the straw up and down in the ice. "Just what are you smiling about, Mr. Pleasants?"

"About a song, actually."

She laughed and looked at her cup. "Oh, I bet I know what it is." Then she sang the first few lines:

The prettiest girl
That ever I saw
Was sipping cider
Through a straw.

And just that snippet of a silly little ditty nearly filled that lobby, her voice was so clean and full and true. The whole place got a little quiet to make way for that voice, and heads turned and looked our way, through ferns and around fluted columns.

"Is there any song you can't make beautiful?" I asked. "We sang that song a thousand times, and yet I'd never heard it before now."

"Who's 'we'?" she asked.

I fidgeted and checked my nails. "Oh, a band I used to be in. Years ago. We toured around. That was our most requested song, believe it or not. Grove Keener—it was his band, Grove's band—he used to call it our 'signature tune,' can you believe it? Like we were Les Brown's big band at Duke. We'd do that song three times, some nights, before the audience would let us go."

"Tell me," Liza said. She curled her legs up beneath her on the sofa, her gray eyes for a second turning wide and somehow reproachful, as if what I said hurt. Then her crooked, dimpled smile crept out again. “Tell me what it was like.”

“Being in a band?”

“Yes.”

“OK.” I took a deep breath, and then I told her.

* * *

Back before Roosevelt, but after the Crash, I worked at the Gastonia mill five days a week and spent the other two days on the road with the Carolina Cavaliers. Seems like they were the same two days, over and over and over again. Each Friday evening we piled into Ira Cannon’s Model A, all six of us and our instruments, and jolted along a hundred miles of dirt roads and mud tracks to get to some crossroads in the middle of nowhere with a thrown-away schoolhouse.

A couple of farm boys would carry the desks outside and stack them against the wall to clear a dance floor. The sun would sink behind the mountain long before showtime, so the boys also lighted kerosene lamps and situated them someplace in the school so that they wouldn’t get knocked over and burn the place down like in Tobaccoville in ’29.

If the show was announced on the radio the week before, maybe some neighbor called the station and invited us to supper, but if not, we stopped on the way at a general store. The man at the store, because we were musicians, stared at each bill, front and back, and tugged at its corners before folding it into his cash drawer.

Later, outside the schoolhouse, we sat on the running board of the car and ate Nabs, sardines, sweet rolls, Co-Colas, whatever we’d bought. Usually I bought a few inches of baloney, say, and Ira bought some crackers, and so on, and then we portioned it out. We didn’t look at each other or actually ask for anything, just nodded and said, “Much obliged.”

Later we sat on the car or in the grass, smoked and listened to the crickets. With about twenty minutes till showtime and no customers in sight, we started making light of ourselves.

“Well, fellas, I wonder what tunes these cows would like to hear?”

“I just remembered, Greta Garbo’s doing a fan dance tonight at the barbershop down in Valmead. No wonder we got no crowd. Bad timing, boys.”

But with about five minutes to go, we saw lanterns flash like lightning bugs on the slopes all around, and heard faint talk and laughter in the pasture on one side and the woods on the other, and then a long string of cars hauled up the grade, and ten minutes after that, people packed that schoolhouse so thick, you'd think the attraction was indeed Garbo instead of a bunch of worn-out mill hands singing songs everyone knew already.

When it all ended, a couple of hours later, we divvied up the till. Fifty cents apiece on a good night, with maybe a dime extra for Grove 'cause it was his band and a dime extra for Ira 'cause it was his car. Then we all climbed into the Ford and rattled back to Charlotte, just in time to go on the air live on WBT's 6 A.M. farm show. That Saturday evening, if we were lucky and had the work, we were on the road again. Sometimes I put on my dress shoes Friday afternoon and didn't get the chance to take them off again until late Sunday night. Then back to the mill on Monday, of course.

In my dreams I'd try to play a tune on a spindle, feed into a loom a pearl-inlay guitar.

* * *

"Did you record?" Liza asked. She looked at her cider, now mostly water, and set the cup on the coffee table with strange deliberation, as if where she set it mattered.

"No," I said. "The band has, though, since I left 'em. In fact, they're scheduled to cut some sides tomorrow morning. In fact—" I gnawed my thumbnail.

"In fact, what?"

"In fact, I talked to the RCA Victor people just today. They had a cancellation in tomorrow's schedule, right after the Carolina Cavaliers. They said that based on my glowing recommendation, they would—"

"Oh," she said.

"—pencil you in, if I called them back by five. And then I wondered whether I should call Grove, to see if he and the boys could record a second session, as your backup band. And to lend you, you know, moral support."

We sat there and looked at each other.

"I appreciate your eventually getting around to telling me this," Liza said.

"You're welcome."

She took a deep breath. "Call them."

"I did," I said. "That's why I waited so long to tell you."

* * *

The RCA Victor studio, at the Southern Radio Corporation offices on Tryon Street, was a big cleared-out storage room. Crates of Victrolas and radio sets were stacked along the walls of the nearest corridor. Liza and I sat on the floor in this narrowed passage, surrounded by dozens of men and women who talked, smoked, and tuned. They cradled guitars, fiddles, mandolins, banjos, washboards, jugs. A string-bass player stood with his arm around the waist of his ungainly instrument. They looked like an awkward couple waiting for a dance to start.

All the musicians wore their stage clothes: embroidered Western shirts, white cowboy hats, neckerchiefs. The members of the Woodlawn String Band stood out in their stiff new overalls and bow ties. Everyone's outfits looked crisp and clean, except for a few mud-spattered pants cuffs. Not everyone could afford the streetcar.

"I don't know why we get so dressed up to record," a banjo player once told me. "No matter how good we sound, won't no one be able to see us. Maybe we dress up out of respect for the folks who sang the songs before we did."

Liza asked me, a little too loudly: "How come everyone looks like Gene Autry? I didn't know there were so many cowboys in North Carolina."

"There aren't any," I said, "but the new Gene Autry picture has a Charlotte band in it, and everybody here has seen it about a dozen times. To these folks, *Ride Ranger Ride* is not a Gene Autry picture but a Tennessee Ramblers picture that has Gene Autry in it. Now everybody tries to look like the Tennessee Ramblers."

Liza asked, "If they're a Charlotte band, how come they call themselves the Tennessee Ramblers? Are they from Tennessee?"

"No. Crazy Water Crystals brought them down from, uh, Rochester, New York, I believe."

"Well, where'd they get Tennessee from?"

I sighed. "I swear I don't know, Miss Candler. It's all show business, and I just don't have time to explain show business to you on this day and in this place."

Liza laughed. "Well, I'll be sure and quiz you later about all this Hollywood business, Mr. Laxative Man."

"I'll thank you not to call me Mr. Laxative Man. I'm a talent scout. I do not fool with laxatives. Besides, it's an all-purpose tonic. Ah, hell. I would like to know whether you pester the life out of your Aunt Kate like this. Is that why her face has closed up like a fist?"

"You can just hush about Aunt Kate, and what's wrong with you this morning anyway? You've been too sour to live." She squinted at me like the sun was in her eyes. "I swear I believe you're more nervous than I am."

"Yes, I'm nervous," I said. "You're about to step into that room and try to lay across a sheet of wax a voice that's the most beautiful sound in God's world. If these people like it, they'll roll it up like a sausage and run it through a press and stack copies of it in trucks like pulpwood and sell them for a few cents apiece, and you don't even know these people. To be honest with you, Miss Candler, I don't know whether they deserve to hang on to a voice like yours, or even to sully it with their fingers as it passes."

We looked at each other steadily.

"I believe I judge people pretty well, Mr. Pleasants," Liza whispered. "I don't think you need to worry at all."

I heard a pair of brogans scrape along, and Aunt Kate stood over us, blocking out the light, looking even more grim than usual. It is a thousand wonders she didn't empty that sanitarium.

"I just saw a streetcar run over a dog and keep on going," she said. "This place you live in is a bad place, Mr. Pleasants. This place you live in is the last place God made."

A bald man in a sweat-blotted shirt banged through a door a few yards down the hall. "Candler!" he read off his clipboard. "Liza Candler? We're ready for you, Miss Candler."

Liza didn't budge. She still looked at me. She didn't look scared, exactly; that would have been all right, that I would have understood. She looked at me as if I had forgotten the words in the middle of a duet.

"You'd best get up, ma'am," a fiddle player told her. "Get it over with."

I reached out a hand to help her up. She looked at it a moment, then grabbed it.

"Are you Miss Candler? I'm Frye Gooding, with RCA Victor. Pleased to meet you. Hello there, Alvin. Good to see you again."

"Yeah, nice to see, uh . . ." But Gooding already had swept her away, talking in her ear as if he were telling loud secrets: He had fallen behind schedule because some people kept blowing take after take, and he really wished more entertainers would learn at least the rudiments of the recording process, but now time was of the essence, he was sure she'd understand; and all the while he tap, tap, tapped her in the small of her back with his clipboard as he herded her toward the studio door. I followed them, waggling my fingers. Quite a grip that woman had. Thought for a second she wasn't going to let go.

I looked up just before I bumped into them. Aunt Kate had blocked all of us with a broomstick arm thrust across the doorway. Her eyes were shut and her face balled up like she smelled something awful.

"Dear Lord," she called, "smile upon Liza, your daughter, who pleases You so each Sunday with 'The Great Speckled Bird' and other hymns in Your name, and be with her as she sings for these strange New York men in their dark room full of machines. Amen."

"Amen," Liza muttered, and ducked beneath Aunt Kate's arm.

Bolts of black monk's cloth covered the walls and the ceiling. A lone microphone, the size and shape of a billy club, hung at eye level from the ceiling in the middle of the room. A technician cinched it up a bit on its cord, and when he let go, it swung slowly like a pendulum, not enough to stir the stifling air. The musicians stood around it, instruments at the ready: two fiddles, banjo, mandolin, guitar, upright bass. I stepped forward and shook the guitarist's slick, damp hand.

"Good to see you, Alvin," Grove Keener said.

I shook hands all around. "Morning, boys. How's everyone?"

"You shoulda brought your guitar, Alvin," Ira Cannon said. "A band can't never have too many guitars."

"I brought something better than that worn-out old guitar," I said. "Fellas, if you can't say anything else good about me when I'm gone, at least tell people that I'm the man who introduced you to Liza Candler."

After the introductions, Liza and Grove and the others huddled for a few minutes to run down the songs she had selected. As I expected, the Cavaliers knew all of them. I made myself scarce, perched on a stool behind the sound engineers' equipment, which looked like a dismantled tractor motor spread across a series of tables. Then Gooding gave the performers their final instructions. This was old hat to the Cavaliers, and they fidgeted and joked around, but Liza solemnly listened to every word.

"First you'll hear one buzz. Sid, let them try on that buzz for size. . . . Got that? OK, then we'll have a wait—of a few seconds or a few years, depending on that damned equipment, ha ha, right Sid?—and then you'll hear two buzzes right together. Like this. . . . After those buzzes, count to two—one Mississippi two Mississippi—then go ahead, 'cause I'll be pointing at you, and we'll be recording by then. Any questions?"

"Mississippi's been sorta bad luck for us," Grove said.

"Yeah," Ira said. "The last time we played in Mississippi, the audience left in the middle of the show 'cause someone's cow had got out."

Grove asked, "Would you mind if we counted 'One Jimmie Rodgers two Jimmie Rodgers' instead?"

"Hell, you can count 'One Liza Candler two Liza Candler' if you want to. Just count to two before you sing. OK? All set? Here we go. . . ."

The wait between buzzes was about a year and a half. I held my breath. Then the fiddlers, poised with their elbows up, drew their bows across their strings and pulled the rest of the band along. I watched the music, the way you can see it happen if you pay attention to the fingers and the strings and the flash of the picks, until Liza started singing, when the whole dark, close, choking box of a studio was replaced by other sights.

Let us pause in life's pleasures
And count her many tears
Oh we all share in sorrow with the poor.

I saw Mr. Jennings braced for the worst at his rolltop desk, and I saw padlocked front doors all over Charlotte, at bank after bank—the Merchants and Farmers, the Independence National, even the First National in its brand-new twenty-one-story skyscraper. Against its titanic brass doors, a small boy listlessly bounced a ball.

It's a song that'll linger
Forever in our ears
Oh hard times come again no more

I saw a tall but neat stack of furniture on a sidewalk. A man and a woman sat upright at opposite ends of the sofa, their children between them. All stared straight ahead at nothing. On the porch, a deputy nailed up a sign with a series of hammer blows.

It's a song this side of the weary
Hard times, hard times,
Come again no more

I saw hundreds of people in a slow single file around the Salvation Army building. Sawhorses funnelled them into the side entrance, where women in uniforms handed them each a bowl and a spoon. Two blocks down the street, a newcomer with a valise hurried to get in on the end of the line. It was Cecil, measuring tape flapping around his neck.

Many days you have lingered
Too long around my door
Oh hard times come again no more

And it went on like that, for the rest of that song and for the next three songs, too. When the session ended I felt a hand clamp my shoulder. I jerked like a hare and suddenly rushed back into my body. My foot had fallen asleep, and my rear end hurt from the stool.

"Some people come in and do take after take, use up nearly all the wax," Gooding said. "But I never saw such a flawless session as this."

"It ain't natural," an engineer said, rapt in the roll of the wax cylinder.

"New York won't believe it," Gooding said. "This woman could be bigger than the Carter Family. Where in the world did you find her, Alvin?"

"A lot of people have asked me that," I said. Liza and the band and the technicians talked excitedly and slapped each other on the back and hugged each other. I do believe Ira cried, there beneath that suspended microphone. I glanced around and saw Aunt Kate, posted with folded arms beside the door. She looked like she wanted to show pride but was too sad to do it, as if Liza had just sung a solo at a funeral.

* * *

Charlotte wasn't a big town, then or now, and word got around. I talked Liza up a bit myself. That Saturday night, a good half-hour before the *Crazy Barn Dance* went on the air, the corridor outside the studio filled not only with the usual Monroe Brothers fans but also with Grove Keener and his boys, a bunch of other musicians, numerous members of the Kokenes family, and several of the reporters from the *Charlotte News.* The reporters, as a group, hailed Mr. Tate when he arrived, fresh from the barbershop.

"Why so many damn newspapermen?" Ledford growled as he stared through the control-room window. "Burke Davis, and Shipp, and Cash—and there's Hargrove, too. What is this, a press conference? Since when did any of those eggheads get interested in hillbilly music?"

"What?" I said. "Oh. Well, I showed Liza around the *News* office yesterday, and they got more interested than usual. Especially in the threat of a party afterward. What time's it?"

"Quit asking," Ledford said. "And sit down, willya? I see enough marching in the newsreels."

I couldn't sit down. I roamed the control room, picked my way over electrical cables and boxes of equipment, got into people's way, bumbled and fumbled and tried not to stare at Liza. She sat smiling in a folding chair across the studio, where she chatted with the Monroes and with George Crutchfield, the guest announcer. I was too anxious even to enjoy the news that Earl Gillespie had called in sick at the last minute. "Probably burnt up with fever," Ledford said. "*Please,* Alvin, sit down."

"Have a spoonful of Peruna," Aunt Kate said, her back to us. She stood in front of the window like a fence post in gingham, and said nothing else before the show began.

The red light flashed once, twice, then burned hellish and steady. The Monroe Brothers sang "What Would You Give in Exchange for Your Soul?" George Crutchfield talked about the wondrous virtues of Crazy Water Crystals. Then I had to sit down.

"This is a song for my Aunt Kate," Liza said, with a smile into the iron bloom of the microphone. She turned aside a little and coughed, so that I died for a second or two. Then she returned the smiles of Charlie Monroe on her left, Bill Monroe on her right. They nodded at each other over her head, and commenced the simple, familiar tune, Charlie on guitar and Bill on mandolin. Liza smiled at me, and at Aunt Kate, and at me again, through the plate glass and began to sing the hymn as no one on the airwaves had sung it before.

What a beautiful thought I am thinking
Concerning a great speckled bird.
Remember her name is recorded
On the pages of God's holy word.

When the song ended, I continued to listen to it. The Monroe Brothers swapped banter with Crutchfield. Liza stood to one side, tightened her guitar strings, and waited for her next song cue. I still listened to the song that had ended.

Ledford interrupted. "I mightily wish we had a clear-channel station," he said. "Fifty thousand watts blankets the Southeast, but some places still won't be able to tune in to Miss Candler tonight."

"Mr. Pleasants?" One of the technicians held out the earpiece of the wall phone. "Call for you, Mr. Pleasants."

"Huh? Me?"

"It's Mr. Gooding. From RCA Victor."

Aunt Kate turned to watch me as I made my way over. "Hello?" I cupped a hand over my other ear. "Hello, Frye?"

No preamble, no pleasantries. "Alvin, I just got off the phone with New York. I sent 'em the rolls immediately, special courier."

"Oh, really? That was fast. So tell me, tell me, what did they think?"

His voice quavered. "They don't know what to think, Alvin. And frankly, I don't know what to think either."

"What's wrong? Didn't they like the record?"

"They liked it fine. What they could hear of it."

"I don't follow. Did something go wrong?"

"I'll say it went wrong. Not a word of Liza's singing got recorded. Not a word, Alvin! It's the damnedest thing—"

"Oh, for—Jesus, Frye, what the hell kind of operation are you running, anyway?" The others looked at me quizzically. "I mean, I expected better from Victor, for God's sake. This is awful. She will be so, so disappointed. Well, you'll just have to give her another chance on another date, with some equipment that actually works—"

"Alvin, you don't get me. Listen to what I'm saying. There was nothing wrong with the equipment. It picked up everything. Everything except the girl."

"You've lost me," I lied, much more quietly.

"It picked up every sound in that studio—the coughing and shifting around between numbers, the cues I gave the technicians, the buzzers, every note the Cavaliers played. Whenever they joined in at the choruses, that came through loud and clear, too. But there's no female voice on the record *anywhere.* I tell you, Alvin, it's as if she wasn't in the room."

"But of course she was in the room. I mean, we were there, we saw her. Frye, this is crazy."

"You think I don't know that, Alvin? You think I can't tell that for myself? I listened to her on the earphones the whole time the wax rolled. You should see me here, whiskey all down my tie because I can't hold my hand still long enough to take a shot. You should come over here and stumble around in the dark with the rest of us, among thousands of dollars of equipment dismantled and flung all over the floor of the studio, and no problems anywhere that we can see. You should see some of the top sound engineers in the country cross themselves and mumble about haints and witchcraft—Witchcraft, Alvin! The evil eye! In the year of our Lord nineteen hundred and thirty-six!"

"Frye. Calm down."

He cut his voice to nearly a whisper. "I asked you before, and I'll ask you again—Where did you find that woman? But this time, Alvin, I don't want to know the answer."

Then he hung up.

In the studio, Crutchfield made another pitch for Crazy Water Crystals. I waved my hands wildly, like a controller at Douglas Field, until I got Liza's attention. Then I pointed toward the door to the corridor.

"Alvin. What's up?"

"Call Adelaide," I told Ledford as I headed out. "Call anybody with their radio on. Hell, call Earl. Ask 'em what they just heard broadcast. Ask 'em if it sounded all right."

"Alvin—"

"Boss, please, do it! Aunt Kate can explain." I vaulted the rail and landed beside the steps in the middle of the corridor, just as Liza shoved open the steel, red-lighted studio door.

"What in the world?" she said. "I have to be back in there in about two minutes—"

"RCA Victor called."

She froze.

"This happened five years ago, didn't it? This is why your session with Peer just 'didn't work out,' isn't it? Liza, what does this mean? *Why can't your voice be recorded?*"

"We don't know," Aunt Kate said. She stood in the control-room doorway and stared down at us.

"I can speak for myself!" Liza cried, then closed her eyes and took a deep breath and said, more calmly: "I have heard tell that in the old stories, the women and the men with powers wouldn't show up in mirrors, wouldn't be reflected if they looked into a pool. Maybe this is the same thing, only they didn't have all this fancy equipment back when those stories got told. . . . I don't know. . . ."

"An angel won't never show up in no photograph," Aunt Kate said.

"I'm not an angel!" Liza said. "And I'm not a witch either! I want to sing to people, Alvin. I want to perform, and record, and travel all around. *I want what you had, what you gave up.* For the past five years, I've been scared even to leave Yandro—knowing what I knew about myself—but when you came for me—I thought it might be—a sign—"

I nodded, eyes wide. "It was. That's exactly right. It was as much a sign as either of us ever will get in our lives. You did right to come."

Ledford poked his head out of the door, behind Aunt Kate's shoulder. "Alvin, Adelaide says it's coming through loud and clear, no problems at all. Now what in the world did you—Miss Candler, you best get back into that studio this very *instant!*"

She whirled and dashed for the studio door. When she reached it, she looked back around, her eyes like stars, her hair astream around her face, and she told me: "Yes. I was right to come." She slammed back through the door, and I stood in the corridor as those words whipsawed into me just the same as if she had sung them.

I don't remember how I got to the street, elevator or stairs or window or wings, but I remember the screech of tires and the horns and the shouts as I ran from one sidewalk to the other, back and forth, into diners and cigar stores and newsstands, and reached across people to wrench radio knobs until I heard what I needed so desperately, and so on all the way down the block, leaving a wake of shouts and jeers and laughter and a street filled with Liza's song.

* * *

I am proud to say that Liza sang in my presence just about every day for more than forty years of marriage, and in all those days I never heard her hit a note that wasn't true and good and fine. She did some radio, and she played a right many shows all around. I still get a few letters from people in the Carolinas and Virginia and Tennessee, folks who heard her in person years ago in Asheville or Greensboro or Union Grove or especially the Merle Watson Festival, that big mess of a crowd in North Wilkesboro she sang to in the last year of her life. Before she went on, she stood in the wings, in front of a big upright fan that made her hair float like a gray cloud, and I came back from the edge of the stage and reported at least one whole county out there on the hillside, and she smiled and said, "Well, Mr. Laxative Man, I reckon I'll just do like always, and pretend I'm singing to you."

It's a hard job to write these people back and say that Liza's gone, but I take the opportunity to reassure them that she ever existed at all, that their memories have not played tricks on her voice, and that's what everybody really wants anyway.

Liza traveled with me all over the mountains after I quit Crazy Water Crystals and got on with the Smithsonian. We must have lugged my equipment into every hollow in the Appalachians, every schoolhouse dance and fiddlers' convention, trying to record and transcribe everything we could before it all vanished, before it all headed to Nashville and turned into Crazy Water and Martha White Flour and Purina Dog Chow and whatever else needs selling today. People that want to hear about all that would be just as well served to go to the fourth floor of Wilson Library in Chapel Hill. All my tapes are in their Southern Folklife Collection, along with thirty-seven thousand other recordings. Gospel choirs, washboard and Jew's-harp pickers, fiddlers, bluesmen, string bands, medicine-show pitchmen. So much music otherwise gone from the world.

I'm up there in the library about once a week myself. Takes me about near forever just to walk across Franklin Street these days, and I feel like a spectacle with my walking stick and my gray suit and hat, while skateboarders and tattooed women parade around me. But the young folks on the fourth floor know me and bring me whatever tapes I want to hear, and then they leave me alone as best they can. But I can tell they're nervous. They're afraid I'll just up and die with my headphones on, there in my favorite booth, the one with the framed receipt on the wall. I've got the numbers memorized: For song royalties in the last quarter of 1928, Pop Stoneman received $161.31, including $1.53 for 340 copies of "Prisoner's Lament." I wonder whether Pop Stoneman ever knew, even for a second, how lucky he was to make even a nickel off a lament.

I sit in that booth and listen to Mainer's Mountaineers and Fisher Hendley's Carolina Tar Heels and the Crazy Bucklebusters and Dorsey and Howard, the Dixon Brothers. I listen to "Wreck on the Highway" and "Let Me Be Your Salty Dog" and "Cocaine Blues" and "Let the Church Roll On" and "What Would You Give in Exchange for Your Soul?" So many others. I know them all by heart, but I need to hear them just the same.

And no matter what else I listen to beforehand, I always end up with one of the Liza tapes. I made dozens of them, with every new technology that came along, over the course of forty years. When I finally handed them over, all carefully dated and labeled just like the others, the librarians thought there was some mistake. They wondered why in the world I would record the zing of crickets, the bark of a distant hound, the scrape of a chair, and sometimes a cough.

That's all I heard on the tapes as well, to begin with. But as the years pass, my ears get better. Nowadays I hardly strain at all to hear "Hard Times" and "The Great Speckled Bird" and even

The prettiest girl
That ever I saw
Was sipping cider
Through a straw.

When I'm slumped in that booth, and the librarians creep past me thinking I've died or at least nodded off, I'm really just listening to a voice that never falters or fades, a voice that fills the library and the campus and the world and the mountain and the schoolhouse and yet finds room for me, calls me out of the dark and to the edge of the stage, to Liza in a kerosene glow.

Fortitude

MY LIFE STARTED OVER ON MAY 14, 1916, IN A hut in the foothills of the Sierra Madre, between Rubio and San Geronimo, about 300 miles south of El Paso.

Pershing had put me in command of a party of twelve, sent to town in three automobiles to buy maize for the horses. That accomplished, we devoted most of the day to my own project: We went looking for Villa's lieutenant, Cardenas. That's what brought us, eventually, to the hut, where we found, not Cardenas, but—I was informed—his uncle.

"*Por favor, Senor, por favor!*"

In the thirty minutes since Private Adams had unsheathed his knife, we had learned a number of things from this fat uncle: that he did not know any Cardenas; that we were filthy American pigs; that he had not seen Cardenas in months; that the merciful Jesus would save him; that the Americans should be crushed underfoot like lizards; that he had seen Cardenas a week ago, but not since; that our fathers were bastards and our mothers, whores; and, again, that the merciful Jesus would save him. All this in Spanish, though these bandits could speak English as least as well as I could. Spanish seemed to be a point of honor with them. I respected that.

"*Santa Maria!*"

The man heaved and strained against his bonds, trying to avoid the knife. His sweaty shirt pulled taut over his belly, and one button popped off to fall onto the dirt floor. I picked it up, rubbed it between my fingers. Brass.

"Madre de Dios!"

At that moment, with a sudden, sickening exhilaration, I realized something. I knew I had held this man's button in my fingers before. I'd heard these squeals and bleats, seen my men's sunburned, darting scowls, suffered the fried-bean-and-motor-oil stink of this miserable hut.

Since my youth I had been accustomed to sudden, vivid memories of lives in other places, other bodies, other times—memories that lingered, became part of my present self. I still could taste the urine I was forced to drink from my helmet when I was dying of thirst for the glory of Carthage; it was brackish and sweet in the back of my throat, and as real as my mother's orange punch, gulped at the end of a day's sailing off Catalina. That son of a bitch helmet—it leaked like a sieve. But what I relived in that Mexican hut was not a life centuries removed. No, I relived a previous May 14, 1916, when I stood in the same hut, among the same men, holding the same button, and was the same person, likewise named George Smith Patton, Jr.

This was a first, a past life as myself. The initial disorientation passed, replaced by a giddy surge of confidence. I savored the moment. Would the feeling last longer than a second or two? It did. In fact, the memories became more complete, rushing into my head and filling it the way one's youth rushes back because of a piano tune, a whiff of gunpowder, a slant of light.

Some intellectual pissant would call this déjà vu. Any soldier would call it intelligence, and act.

"That's enough," I said. I flicked away the button. "Let's go."

"What about this rat right here, Lieutenant?"

I leaned over him, lifted his bloody chin. "You're a good man," I said into his face, in Spanish. "You have been very unhelpful. Carry on." I saluted him, and walked out.

As we waded into the broiling sun, wincing at the glare off the hoods of the Dodges, I said, "Son of a bitch should get a medal. Too bad he's not in a real army. Saddle up, boys." The auto sagged sideways as I clambered aboard. Waller spat on his hands and went to work on the crank.

"Where to, Lieutenant?"

I could remember everything. Everything. I died at age sixty in a German hospital room, with tongs in my temples and fish-hooks in my cheeks to keep my head from moving and crushing what was left of my spine—

No time for that.

"San Miguelito," I said.

"But Lieutenant," Adams said, "that ranch has already been checked out. Cardenas ain't there."

"He's there now. Take my word for it, soldier. He's there." The Dodge farted and shivered and started to chug, and Waller jumped behind the wheel, shirt plastered to his back. I reached for my cigars as we lurched forward, tires spinning in the dirt. I knew the fat uncle would stagger to the door, rubbing his wrists and staring at us as we drove away, and when he did I waved and tossed him a cigar. Same as he had before, he just let it fall to the dirt. Lay there like a turd. Don't know when they've got it good, these Mexicans.

As we drove I remembered the gunfight that awaited us. I told the men exactly what to expect. They looked at me like I was crazy, but they listened. Hell, they were good soldiers. They didn't care whether I was crazy, they just wanted someone capable to tell them what to do.

Before, there had been some question about who actually killed Cardenas—not in the papers, which gave me all the credit, of course, but in the ranks, since there was such a volley it was hard to tell whose .45 had done the job. We hadn't even identified Cardenas until after it was all over. I'd wasted most of my bullets on some damn horse-rustling nobody. Not this time. If I had to live the next thirty years knowing I was doomed to a worse death than Hitler, then goddamn it, I was going to make use of my other knowledge, too. Shouting to the other cars as we drove along, I described Cardenas and his horse, and made it clear: He's mine.

San Miguelito was just the same. Mostly. Same sun like a hot rough hand squeezing your temples. Same four bowlegged hombres outside the gate skinning a cow, hide coming off in jerks and pops. They didn't even look up when the shooting started, when the three riders burst out of the gate and tried to outrun the Dodges.

That silver saddle made a damned impressive display. Hard to miss. I fired two shots, and he hit the ground like one of Caesar's winesacks. "BANDIT KILLER," the headlines had said, and they'd say it again.

As we searched the hacienda, Cardenas's wife and mother

stood in the hallway beside a new Victrola and its crate, stared at us. The missus, about Beatrice's age, rocked a baby in her arms. As I passed, the granny spat on me. I shot the lock off the chapel door and kicked it in to find three old ladies praying in the corner, holding up their hands to God. No surprises . . . although: Hadn't the baby been awake before? Now its bundled silence made me suspicious. "Excuse me, senorita," I whispered, as I gently pulled back the blanket. It was, indeed, a baby: little wrinkled face, thick black hair plastered over its forehead, sound asleep. I teared up. I always had a soft spot for babies. "Congratulations," I told its mama, and the baby's granny spat on me again. More guts than some American boys, sad to say. More guts than that yellow bastard in Sicily would have, so many years in the future.

There was one more difference at San Miguelito, a big one. Before, I had climbed onto the roof to make sure no one was waiting up there to ambush us as we left. No one was, but I stepped on a rotten place and fell through up to my armpits—not a prime fighting position! Damned embarrassing, too. This time I walked a different route, gave the rotten place a wide berth, and kept an eye out for similar dark patches.

I was so intent on not falling through that I let a gap-toothed *Villista* get the drop on me. He darted around a corner, pistol in hand, and Adams shot him almost before I could look up.

As Adams searched the bandit's pockets, I stood there like a fool, dumbfounded for the first and last time in the Mexican campaign. "He wasn't supposed to be there," I said.

"Rats're liable to pop out from anywhere," Adams said. He flipped a gold piece into the air, caught it. "Good weight. Don't let it rattle you, Lieutenant," he added, and I resolved to give him a week's latrine duty for that. In addition to his commendation, of course. Fair's fair.

The rest went pretty much as before. As we drove off, about fifty *Villistas* came galloping up the ravine, and we fired a shot or two, but they didn't chase us far. Wasn't much of a race. God, the speed of the motored units to come! What Jackson could have done with them in the Shenandoah, I thought as dust billowed around me—or Napoleon on the steppes! I rubbed my shoulder, remembered my last backward look at the torches and spires of Moscow, felt again the Russian numbness that always lurked somewhere in my bones, even as my cheeks began to blister in this damnable Mexican sun. I tugged my goggles out a few inches and poked my face. Beneath my eyes was a sore borderline I could trace with my gloved finger. I let the goggles snap back into place. "Soldiers never fight where it's comfortable," I told Adams and Waller. "Think of all those Marines sweating it out in Haiti, or in Panama. Why, if they sent us to the French Riviera, it'd be a hellhole soon enough. How fast will this thing go, anyway?"

All the camp business faltered and got quiet as our little procession drove in. We took it slow, giving everybody plenty of time to look, and many fell in with us, walking alongside. Cardenas's lolling head on the hood seemed to return the soldiers' stares. By the time we hauled up the brakes and let the engines die in front of the command tent, dozens of doughboys were standing around, whistling and muttering *the Old Man did it* and nothing else I could hear. Two or three had potatoes and paring knives in hand. Never again, I thought, no more of that for me. Then Black Jack stepped out, standing ramrod straight as usual, a mustache for a mouth. The men and I stood in the autos and saluted, and then I stepped down and stood at attention and said, "We've brought in Cardenas, sir."

Pershing nodded. "So you say, Lieutenant. Which?"

I grabbed Cardenas by the hair and lifted. His eyes were black with blood, and his face was a little burnt from the hood.

Pershing acted as if he didn't know what to do with his hands, finally put them behind his back and said, "Yes. That's him."

I let the head down gently so as not to dent the auto. Pershing looked at the other two bodies strapped across the other two hoods. He stepped a few paces toward the back of the automobiles and nodded when he saw the sacks of grain.

"General, there's a fourth bandit, but he's stowed in the back. No room, you see. He's the one who would have shot me, if Corporal Adams hadn't got him first."

Adams smiled and nodded, then looked mortified, as if he feared smiling and nodding were uncalled-for.

"Good job, Corporal, good job, Lieutenant, good job, all of you," Pershing said, turning back toward his tent. "I'm sure commendations will be in order—and if the Army gave medals for dramatics," he murmured as he passed me, close enough for me to smell the jalapenos on his breath, "then you'd certainly have a chestful of those, wouldn't you, Patton? Report after you bury them. And Patton—you're lucky you remembered the maize."

How could a letter-perfect salute look so perfunctory?

I stood at attention and held my salute as he stalked away. I had been thinking in the Dodge about the strange opportunity afforded me, and now I wondered again, as I watched my idol stride back into the command tent, why I had been given another chance. Did Pershing have anything to do with it? Did Villa? I thought not. Even in childhood I had been convinced that my destiny was to lead a great army in a great battle in a great war, perhaps even the greatest war in the history of the world. That had proven true once, and I believed it would prove true again. No, I knew my destiny would not be achieved on some dusty road in Mexico, chasing the minions of a murdering border bandit. My destiny lay where it always had lain, in Europe, against the Nazis. But how much could I change along the way, and could I change it for the better?

Pershing vanished into the shadowy triangle, and the flap snapped down. Behind me a Dodge backfired, and my head jerked as if struck: Mannheim, December 9, 1945. Hap Gay said, "Sit tight." At ten miles an hour, the loudest sound I ever heard. Silence. My head! Oh Jesus my back! The Cadillac's glass partition was spiderwebbed with gore. I sagged sideways, blood in my eyes, tried to wipe it away. *Will* it away. My arms wouldn't move. I couldn't sit up. My head lolled on Hap's shoulder. "Hell," I moaned. Drool on my chin. "Oh, hell."

The wind kicked up, blowing that acrid needling Mexican dust into my nose and throat. Coughing, I forced myself back to the present, back to Mexico, 1916, thinking: Even if I can't live a better life, I damn well can die a better death.

I dropped my salute, whirled, and bellowed for the ditch-diggers. Before, they had been found asleep in the back of the mess tent after a half-hour search. This time I had them front and center in five minutes flat, and they shouldered their shovels with wary glances, wondering how in the hell I knew.

That night, alone in my tent, I sat, knees wide apart, hunched over the upended trunk that served as a makeshift desk. I opened one of the tablets I'd been carrying since West Point: class notes, battle scenarios, quotes from Clausewitz, snatches of poetry, pledges to myself. "I hope I have got enough sence to be kiled in a great victory and be born between the ranks in a military funeral and morned by friend and foe alike," how old was I when I wrote that? Nineteen? Jesus God. I turned to a fresh page, creased the spine so that it would lie flat, daubed my pen in ink, and wrote a list.

Writing never had come easy for me, but I wrote without pause for a long time. I'd had all day to think about what I would do, what I would change. The list almost filled the page. When I couldn't think of anything else, when I could avoid it no longer, I sighed and wrote at the top:

DECEMBER 9, 1945

KAFERTAL. OUTSIDE MANNHEIM

Then I circled it. I stopped, pen suspended. What could I add to that? "Look out for the truck!" or something equally inane? Just avoid the damn intersection altogether, Georgie. Hell, don't take a trip at all that day. The ink on the pen nib beaded, bulged. I dared it to fall. Ten goddamn miles per hour. Not a soldier's death at all. I moved the pen to the right just before the drop let go. I heard it dot the trunk. Perfectly easy to avoid, really. Maybe the easiest thing on the list.

I heard something behind me: a faint scrambling, tiny claws on canvas. I set down my pen and reached for my knife. At night the desert creatures sought warmth and shelter. There, at the edge of the lamplight, a tail. Well, well, another Gila monster wanted to bed down with old Georgie. As I aimed, the tail stopped moving, as if the lizard knew what was coming. Tail looked to be about three inches—that meant the head would be just about—*there*. I threw the knife and the tail spasmed, lay still. I carried over the lantern, lifted the little bastard by the hilt of the knife (how its scales shine in the light, it's almost pretty), carried it to the tent flap, and flicked it outside with the others. Setting the knife aside to clean later, but not too far out of reach, I sat again on the rickety cot, picked up the pen. Hmm. Must be something else to list. Must be. But it was a damn good life the first go-round, wasn't it, Georgie? Hell of a good time. Look at that knife, would you. Not proper blood at all. More like some sort of oil, clotted with sand. Damned scuttling nuisances. Five since Tuesday, all out front in a little ant-teeming pile. They were only lizards, but you'd think they would learn.

* * *

I miss that Mexican campaign. Hell, I miss all the campaigns. So many battles worth fighting again.

"Isn't that right, Willie? Willie."

Damn dog can't sit still two minutes without sleeping, even in the damp and miserable Limey outdoors. Didn't they teach him any discipline in the R.A.F., before his owner got shot out of the sky?

"Willie!"

I tap him with my crop. He looks up and yawns.

"Look alive, Willie. God knows we need some signs of life around here."

I tug the leash and he flops to his feet, raises one leg and waters the tread of a tank. The balsa wood darkens and streaks. "Good dog, Willie."

So many great battles, great campaigns.

Enemy scouts rustled in the hillside firs as I splashed my face and head with the cold foam of the rushing Rhine and stood up grinning, slinging droplets to left and right, daring some filthy goatherd to draw his bow against me, against Caesar, against Rome . . .

The pipes wailed like our women and the mud gripped my toes as the clans marched across the sodden moor, pacing off the minutes until we could lift our swords and shed our blood for the one true king of Scotland . . .

My granduncle put his callused hand in mine as we charged side by side and whooping across the northernmost ground claimed by the Seventh Virginia, hearing nothing but our blended gasping voices and the rush of tall grass against our legs before we leapt as one over that last stone wall—

God, that death was good!

But this is not Gaul, not Culloden, not Gettysburg. It's the first thing I wrote down, back in my tent in Mexico, the chief thing—besides the obvious—that I wanted to avoid: FORTITUDE.

But here I am. Stuck here in England once again, a puppet commander of a paper army, mounting a phantom invasion out of canvas and paint.

Willie depleted, he and I step into the road, lined for a hundred yards in both directions with facing rows of dummy tanks. Shermans, mostly. We stand there, all alone, blinking at the sunset. This has been one of those endless Limey midsummer days, when everybody but me looks up at the sun and pretends the day is over and retires for drinks and *din*-nah, with teatime still lead in their guts. What a place. Even the nights are fake.

Over my head is one of the 75-millimeter-sized "guns." I grab it with both hands and squeeze. It's Ike's neck, and Hitler's too. The tin buckles with a *plank*. When I let go, the barrel is crooked. Those few inches off true would be enough to send a shell a dozen yards wide of the enemy. If there were a shell. If there were an enemy.

"Dammit, Georgie, of course there's an enemy," I say aloud.

Willie snorts and wags his tail and nuzzles my jodhpurs. "Want to kill some Nazis, boy?" I scratch rough between his ears. "Want to kill some krauts?"

He lolls on his side and twitches one hind leg as I rub his belly.

"Well, first we've got to sit here awhile. We've got to play pretend. Yes we do we do we do. We're just having a good time, a good good time, aren't we Willie, playing with our toys, playing war in our cold wet sandbox? Goddamn Eisenhower."

I stand and kick a splintered dent in the front of a tank. Its walls sway in and out, back and forth, like a tent in a sandstorm.

"If he thinks old Georgie is going to sit out Overlord a second time in this purple-pissing Limey Hooverville, well, then, Ike has another—"

"Be careful with the armor, please, General Patton, we've had rather a shortfall of nails."

A tall, short-haired woman stands behind me, smiling. I don't know her. She wasn't here before. No matter; that's increasingly common. No cause for alarm, no threat to my destiny. Brit, of course. Posture good. Uniform not regulation, but close: khaki shirt, khaki slacks, boots, a dark brown jacket with a military cut, a knotted scarf where a man would wear a necktie. Bare-headed, though, goddamn it. Helmet hangs from her belt, along with a host of tools and implements, none regulation. She laughs.

"Please don't be embarrassed, General. In the cinema we *all* talk to ourselves. It's the best rehearsal." She sticks out her hand. "I'm Madeleine Thomson—Maddy, on the set. I'm pleased to meet you."

I don't take her hand. I don't smile or speak. I square my shoulders. I look her in the face, glance down at her helmet, glance at the top of her head, and look her in the face again. I make a low throat-clearing noise, and Willie growls.

After a pause, the woman blinks, sighs, detaches the helmet and sets it on her head, practically covering her eyes. A size too big, at least; slackness in the quartermaster's office again. Then she salutes, and I salute in return. Hers is pretty sloppy—head bobs sideways to meet the hand, forearm is at a definite angle, and she drops it a good second before I drop mine—but I'm willing to make allowances, in the name of Anglo-American relations. Hell, I won't even bawl her out for the helmet. I'm a regular Cordell Goddamn Hull.

"At ease, Miss Thomson," I tell her. "You may say hello to Willie, if you like."

The little bastard is snuffling up to her feet and whining and wagging his whole behind. She gives me a dirty look and squats to rub the dog's neck, the tools on her belt rattling and jingling.

"My mum has a bull terrier. Ugly little buggers, aren't they? This one's friendly, though. A British dog, General?"

"Willie's an inheritance," I say. "His owner was a pilot."

She keeps looking at the dog, though her chin moves as if she almost glanced up. "Didn't make it, eh? Well, I'm sorry for you, Willie." He wallows, ecstatic, as she scratches his belly with increasing violence. "But you've found someone else. That's the important thing." She pats his flank, stands, yanks a hammer from her belt, and begins to pound the tank gun back into place, words coming out through clenched teeth as she flails away. "That's what a lot of us will have to do before this war's over, Willie—find someone else."

I clear my throat. "Believe it or not, Miss Thomson, that helmet could save your life one day. Bombs could start falling on this base any time. Real bombs," I add, glancing at the slapped-together monstrosities all around. Before, there had been no bombs, but it wouldn't do to let Thomson know that. Bad for discipline.

"Things have been remarkably quiet thus far, General. I've had closer calls in Birmingham repertory."

"That could change in moments, Miss—I'm sorry, Miss Thomson, I don't know what to call you. I don't know your rank."

"My title at Shepperton Studios," she says, delivering one last hammer blow, "is second-unit production coordinator." She steps back to study her handiwork. The gun is now visibly battered, but unbowed.

I wave my crop. "But you're in charge of all the Shepperton people on this site?"

She returns the hammer to her belt, hitching at her pants as she secures it. "All the carpenters, designers, painters, seamstresses—yes, General, to the extent they can be commanded at all, I have that singular honor. And may I add, General—" She folds her arms and glares. "—that despite the extraordinarily short notice, the dreary accommodations, the dearth of materials, the miserable weather, the inadequate blueprints, and the constant meddling memos from headquarters and from Intelligence, my people have done a bloody good job, for which they've received no official recognition whatsoever except the heel of your boot and the lifted leg of your, your, familiar, but I, for one, am quite proud of this—what's the phrase, General?—purple-pissing Limey Hooverville."

Now this *is* new. Before, my Shepperton liaison during the

winter of '43 and '44 was a hangdog little Cockney fellow with less backbone than a Cornish pasty. I feel a ridiculous stab of optimism, a joy almost painful, like a bullet. I make myself scowl anyway. I slap my boot, once, with my riding crop. The woman stands a little straighter, slightly widens her eyes, but doesn't look away, and keeps glaring. I'll be damned. Maybe I can turn this sorry-ass assignment around.

But then I feel a wave of weariness (even as I put my fists on my hips and hunch my shoulders and brace my legs, my prime chewing-out stance), and I think, you're no longer that young man in Mexico, Georgie. The changes, my God, they get harder and harder. Sicily was the last time I even bothered to try, and look how that turned out. So tired. So old.

But still the boss of this goddamn outfit.

"I'm not accustomed to being spoken to that way, Miss Thomson, by any American below the rank of colonel, or by any Brit below the rank of prime minister."

Jaw a little tighter, she holds her ground. Damn. Lucky thing I'm not cheating on Beatrice anymore.

After a pause, I add, "So I suppose I'll have to call you Colonel, at least. At ease, Colonel Thomson."

I turn and kick another hole in the tank. The whole contraption shudders, but stays intact.

"So far so good," I say, turning back to her and smiling for the first time. "I do commend you and your crew, Colonel, for making a damned good start on this thing. But we have a lot left to do, a *hell* of a lot. When's the tour?"

She blinks. "The tour."

"You are no doubt aware, Colonel, that I am here for a guided inspection tour of Fortitude headquarters."

She looks at her watch. "And *you* are no doubt aware, General, that you were not expected until nine o'clock—" She catches my glance. "—Ah, bloody hell—oh nine hundred hours tomorrow morning."

"I'm impatient. But I *am* here, and I *am* at your disposal, Colonel, so please show me this magnificent deception of yours."

She sighs, grins, shakes her head, plucks a large flashlight from that amazing belt—could that be a holster? Must make a note of how that thing is put together. Tank crews could use something like that. "Well," she says, "I suppose Agatha Christie won't solve the case while I'm away. Do you care for murder mysteries, general? Or do you get enough of killing on the job? This way. Down the column."

Willie scampers ahead, sniffing at the painted treads. The tanks loom on either side, their bulks somehow more realistic in the darkness. I almost could convince myself—no, no I couldn't, it's gone. Not now. The gravel beneath our boots is a good sound, a soldier's sound. Set a smart pace on gravel, and you sound like you're really going somewhere. Thomson sets a smart pace.

"So," I say, "what do you think of the boys at headquarters?"

Crunch, crunch.

"Let me put it this way, General. On a film set, I wouldn't entrust them with a clapper board. The injuries could be frightful."

"I don't allow officers to mince words with me, Colonel. You must speak freely and frankly."

"General, they are ignoramuses."

"I believe the phrase you're groping for, Colonel, is *goddamn worthless* ignoramuses, but you're definitely on the right track. Listen, Colonel—I'm not sure what you've been told or not told, but if I'm going to be even the figurehead in charge of this fake invasion, then that makes you one of my people, and I don't like for my people to be in the dark about their duties. Do you have any questions for me that the lords of St. James have not satisfied?"

"I do, General." She stops and switches off the flashlight. All around us, in the absolute darkness, the base strains toward battle. In the pregnant silence I hear a crewman, his final inspection complete, shinnying out of a hatch and dropping to the ground—or is it just a garter snake?

"We are told that so far, the Germans seem to be taking the bait. They genuinely believe that East Anglia is a staging area for a great cross-Channel invasion, aimed at Calais and led by you. Is that true, General? Have my people helped convince the Nazis this absurd story is real?"

Absurd—let that pass. "You have, Colonel, you have." I hope she can't tell that my eyes are closed. The breeze carries the smell of cordite, boot polish, sweat. "You have indeed convinced the krauts. But now you have a harder job. Now you have to convince *me*."

* * *

The tanks weren't moving, and so I had no choice but to find out why.

"Goddamn it, what's the holdup back here?"

Despairing that I ever would be heard over the artillery and the machine guns and the engines, I half-strode, half-slid down the pulverized sod of the hillside and regained my balance on the edge of the trench where the whole ragged tank column, Renaults and Schneiders alike, had come to a halt. As I stood there weaving, pistol in one hand and walking stick in the other, I heard my batman, Private Angelo, reach my side, gasping; a strong lad, but I could outrun him any day.

Beneath me, several dozen infantrymen huddled in the ditch, arms over their heads. Their shovels lay every which way, like scattered kindling.

As I stood there, aghast, a shell blew several feet from me, spewing a gout of mud that spattered down on us all. I didn't flinch. I had expected it.

It was 10 A.M. on September 26, 1918, at the start of the Meuse-Argonne offensive. We were about 625 yards south of the village of Cheppy. If I acted as I had before, in about forty-five minutes I would take a bullet in my left upper thigh, a life-threatening wound, and would lie suffering in a shell hole for two hours before being rescued; and so my Great War would end, and I'd be sent home to Beatrice for many years to come.

I knew all this. And all morning, all week, all month, I had pondered what I might do differently to avoid this calamity. Giving up my tank command was out of the question; it would leave a greater scar on my career than any bullet. Ignoring this holdup in the column, too, was impossible; our men needed relief, and fast. No, I knew that I had played a crucial role at this location, at this time. How could I be elsewhere? I was an officer. I had to do my duty.

Mouth dry at the thought of that oncoming bullet, I shook my head, raised my walking stick, and drummed on the steel plates of the nearest Schneider. "Let's get this column moving," I bellowed. "These tanks are needed up there in the field, not sitting in a goddamn ditch."

The hatch flung open, and out leaned a greasy-faced soldier with a big chew inflating his cheek. "Colonel, if somebody don't dig us a path through this trench, we ain't going nowhere." Bullets stitched the side of the tank in a diagonal. "Jesus!" the tank man cried, and ducked inside.

"We tried to dig 'em out, Colonel," one of the men in the trench called up, "but then the krauts got us pinned down."

"Pinned down, shit. You don't see them shooting me, do you? Where are your officers?"

"Dead, Colonel."

"You've got a new one, then. Come on, boys," I yelled. I holstered my pistol and picked up a shovel, held it out. "The sooner we dig a path for these tanks, the sooner we all can get out of here."

Slowly, the man who had spoken reached up and took the shovel from my hand, holding it as if it might explode.

"Come on, goddamn it," I cried again, holding out another shovel. "Let's get a move on. You don't have to dig the Panama Canal." Just as a soldier reached for the shovel, a bullet hit the blade, knocking it out of my hand. The soldier drew back with a cry. "Never mind that," I said, grabbing another shovel from Angelo, who was stacking his arms with them. "A lucky shot, that's all. No Buffalo Bills over there. They haven't got our range yet."

"Tell that to Phillips," the soldier said, snatching the new shovel from my hand. A dead man lay a few feet away, his eyes and mouth open, his arms still wrapped around his shovel. The soldier who had spoken glared at me and fell to, digging like a madman. Good. Bravery works, and honor, but so do spite, and hatred.

"You'll all die like Phillips if we don't get this column moving," I said. By now Angelo was distributing shovels at a frantic pace; as I expected, the men were glad to have something to do, something other than panic. I stepped over to Phillips, tugged free his shovel, and offered it to a man beneath me, the last man to huddle against the trench wall, eyes wide.

"Come on, son. Take the shovel. Finish what Phillips started."

No reaction.

"Take the shovel, goddamn it!"

He gave his head two sideways jerks—shaking it, I presume.

"Take the shovel, you miserable son of a bitch, or by God I'll kill you *myself*," I cried, as I swung the shovel sideways, like a baseball bat, and slammed the side of his helmet. He howled and fell over, arms over his face. I raised the shovel high over my head, and he held out his hands and gibbered:

"I'll do it! I'll do it! Just hand me the shovel, Colonel, I'll do it! I swear."

"Good man," I said, and dropped the shovel into the dirt at his feet. I turned away, faced the reassuring geometries of the tank column, watched the bullets ricocheting off their iron flanks. Rotten coward. Would I have killed him? Didn't matter; the decision hadn't been necessary. He had done his duty. But what of *my* duty?

"Get these wagons ready to move!" I shouted, rapping on the side of each tank as I strode past. I rapped harder and harder as I went, shouted louder and louder, tried to clear my mind so that, when necessary, I could act without thinking, act like a soldier.

When the column started moving again, Private Angelo and I had an awful time ordering the infantrymen to march alongside. They knew the tanks would draw all sorts of enemy fire, including artillery.

"Sitting ducks, hell! That's what you'll be if you stay *here*. Not only are these tanks going to clean out those kraut nests that are picking you off, but these tanks are, furthermore, your only real cover, and as you can see—" I waved my stick at the Renault rumbling past. "—that cover is *on the move*. So let's get going, and I mean now! Fall in! Follow me!"

So many back-of-the-line command-post generals never realize that on the battlefield, the most effective order is "Follow me!" Those ashen-faced troops put their heads down, shouldered their shovels, and trudged along behind me, hoping against hope I knew what I was doing.

Before, that hope had been sorely misplaced. We had been marching to the *left* of the column, and had been cut to pieces by machine-gun fire. But staying in that damn trench, in the middle of hostile territory, was just not an option. So this time I led the men to the *right* of the column, and hoped that even if I weren't spared, this time at least most of them would be.

As soon as we set off, I felt a new anxiety clutching me, not fear, exactly—no, that had been with me for weeks, and was still there, and growing, and I hated it—but a sort of fresh overlay of nausea, of uneasiness, a feeling not that something bad was going to happen but that everything was *already* bad, and I just didn't realize it, though at any moment I might, and then choke on the newfound ugliness of the world. I was attempting to change the day's outcome, of course. But I hadn't felt this way in Mexico, or in the months since, despite occasional . . . adjustments. What was different? I picked my way more carefully through the sucking soil of the battlefield. There was an ache in my joints, a seemingly sourceless pang like the one in the jaw that steals up on you, gradually pulses the news that while asleep you've been grinding your teeth.

We walked. How much time had elapsed? Two minutes? Three? How much time did I have left? Up ahead, one of the Schneiders met a 150-millimeter shell and blew up with a sound like a rifle-shot pumpkin. Flaming shards twinkled down on us, and the heat seared my face. But we kept walking, and the column kept rolling forward, detouring around the flaming wreck—that tight turning radius was serving us well today—rumbling ahead, guns firing, bullets pinging off the sides and whining past.

Each time I glanced around, Private Angelo and the others were still in line, though each time the line was a man or two fewer; and so I soon stopped glancing around. I tried to refocus my thoughts enough to be proud of those tank boys. I remembered my final orders to them:

Remember that you are the first American tanks. You must establish the fact that AMERICAN TANKS DO NOT SURRENDER. *As long as one tank is able to move it must go forward. Its presence will save the lives of hundreds of infantry and kill many Germans.*

Surely I should have been shot by now. Had I changed my destiny? Merely by walking on the right rather than the left? Was war that meaningless? I refused to accept it. Suddenly I knew: I was going to be shot, no matter what I did. But when?

"Strange clouds, Colonel," Private Angelo said. I looked up into that roiling brown sea of dust, smoke, and gas that for days had been our sky and saw ranks upon ranks of soldiers, their shapes outlined like those of men standing a distance away in fog, their faces indistinct and unreadable. Yet I knew who they were. They were my ancestors. They were my grandfather, my granduncle, and all the soldiers in our line, and all the soldiers who, at one time, I had enjoyed the honor of being.

They had looked down on me that other Sept. 26, moments before I was shot, and they had given me a feeling of great satisfaction, a certainty that I was doing as they would have done, and that whatever happened, I was a true soldier, a man, a Patton. But now, looking up at those ghostly ranks, I felt only a tautness in my gut, a parched mouth, and shame.

"Angelo," I barked.

"Sir?"

"Maintain the march." Without looking behind, I darted between two of the tanks, emerged on the left side of the column. Head down and pistols drawn, I sprinted alongside, outrunning the tanks, teeth bared, looking only at the soupy, pockmarked, bone-and-metal-glinting mud beneath my feet, refusing to look into the sky again until—and then came the bullet like a fist to my left leg, and though I staggered on another forty feet I knew I was down. I managed to holster both pistols before my wounded leg planted itself in the mud like a post and jerked me to a stop, forcing me to pivot and topple in a slow spiral until I was face down in the flesh-smelling sludge. No pain, not yet, not in the leg. I heaved myself onto my back, spat dirt, and glared at the empty khaki sky.

"Hatred works, too," I said, and blacked out.

I came to just as a long white bone, a femur I think, moved past my eyes, followed by a canteen, several rocks, a mound of something rotten, and a brick-colored puddle that was rushing to refill itself, having just been disturbed by something, perhaps a foot. I couldn't breathe. I was upside down, bent double. Someone was carrying me on his shoulder. Then I remembered.

"Angelo," I said.

"Almost there, Colonel," he said. Still no pain, though I could feel nothing, move nothing, could barely lift my head. Now I was looking into a big shell hole, maybe ten feet across and five feet deep, and the bottom of it was rising to meet me. Then I saw the damnable sky again, and Angelo was laying me down at the foot of the hole, trying to straighten me as best he could, which wasn't very straight. When he quit fussing, I was half sitting up like a sultan taking his ease, the back of my head pillowed by a tuft of needle grass.

"The tanks," I said.

"Still moving," he said.

I coughed. "The men."

He looked away. "Sit tight, Colonel," he said. "Once the tanks have shut off those machine guns, they'll be back for us."

He meant, they're all dead. "Not back," I said. "Forward." Then I blacked out again.

When next I awoke, the first person I saw, standing atop the thrown-up dirt at the lip of the hole, wearing his awful plaid weekend jacket over his slate-colored courthouse uniform of vest and baggy trousers, was my father, who was transparent but aglow within, like a reconnaissance balloon. Papa was looking into the hole with a slight frown, vexed, as if he'd mislaid his glasses again. He loomed over Private Angelo, who lay on his belly and sighted along his rifle into the smoke.

I expected Papa to start patting his pockets. Instead he saw me, smiled, and punched the air with his walking stick by way of greeting. "Tell me something, Georgie," he called. As he headed my way, he stepped on Private Angelo's back; his foot just seeped in, then reappeared, whole. As Papa stepped into the pit he darkened considerably, and I saw his inward glow had merely been a flare guttering down the sky, briefly visible through his chest. "I'm curious. And think it over carefully before you answer." Having reached the bottom, he sat on nothing and leaned back with his fingers together, as he always did at his desk in the study at Lake Vineyard. "Do you ever—how shall I put it? I want to speak precisely, now. See people who aren't there? Images from the past, or of the future?" He leaned over to where his desk drawer would be, pulled on it, made familiar motions with his empty hands. "Drink, Georgie? No, of course not. Ah." He smacked his pale lips. "There's profit in grapes, but more character in grain. Visions, Georgie. There, I said it. Fine Episcopalian I am, eh, to be talking about visions. Do you believe in visions, Georgie?"

"Paralyzed" isn't the term; rather, I felt as if I had nothing left to move. I sensed, rather than felt, my life ebbing away through my wound, somewhere out of sight but vital, as a child senses his parents' despair. Yet I seriously considered Papa's question, even as I watched through his vest a rat that clawed out of the dirt, looked around, then scrambled back out of sight, long tail whipping about beneath Papa's watch fob. I felt I had been given a trick question, the kind that tormented me at West Point. Papa kept rocking back and forth, but without the comforting squeal of his chair. I missed it. I missed *him.* Sixteen months since I had waved to him on the dock from the Governor's Island ferry. Finally I said: "I believe in *you,* Papa."

He chuckled, nodded. A mortar exploded nearby. "Jesus!" cried Angelo, and clods rained down as Papa said: "Good answer, Georgie. But do you know, I never had visions myself. Never. Not even as a child, after the war, when I almost died with the typhoid. All I could envision then was the pitcher of water across the room, and that was certainly real, because I crawled across the floor and pulled it over on top of myself, didn't I?" He chuckled and rubbed the palms of his hands along his thighs, patted his knees.

Private Angelo slid down the crumbling slope on top of Papa, then crawled through him and leaned over me, examining my eyes and face.

"Now, other people in the family have seen them," Papa said. "You know that, don't you?"

"Yes, Papa," I said.

"Sorry, Colonel," Angelo said. "Can't understand a word you're saying. Follow my finger with your eyes, Colonel. OK? Please, Colonel."

"Why, Georgie, your step-grandfather, Colonel Smith, told me that once as he was walking through a hotel lobby in Sacramento, he heard a dance in progress behind a closed door, and was drawn to open the door and look in—curiously drawn, he said, because he was not a prying man, as you know, Georgie. He was the very figure of a Virginia gentleman, was your step-grandfather."

"Shit," Angelo said, wiped his mouth, and scrambled back up the slope, kicking through Papa's head as he went.

"And he found that ballroom filled, Georgie, with officers in Confederate uniform, and their women and servants, all in the dress of a generation before." Papa again made familiar motions, drank the air. "Excuse me," he said, covering his mouth and puffing his cheeks. "And the Colonel found himself in the middle of the room, and everyone had fallen silent, even the musicians, and one of the violinists—the Colonel would never forget this—was scratching his nose with a bow. What a thing for him to notice, Georgie, in the circumstances!" A splatter of guns and some not-so-distant shouts briefly drowned his voice as he examined his string tie. "—stood there as each of the officers in the room passed before him in silence, single file, to bow and shake his hand and look him in the face, and he recognized each man in turn as a man who had served under him in the Shenandoah, and died there. *Died* there, Georgie."

"Hail Mary, full of grace," said Angelo, from the edge of the pit.

"But he wasn't afraid, Georgie. And when he came to himself, why, he was out in the lobby again, leaning against a wall and staring into a spittoon. A colored man asked him if the Colonel was all right. 'All right?' he replied. 'Why, this is the most honored day of my life.' " Papa chuckled and hitched up his trouser legs as he rocked backward and rubbed the side of his face, no doubt because the sun was high and hot through the study window that looked out onto the vineyards. No doubt Papa soon would reach up and pull the shade. "Now, you don't have to tell me a thing, Georgie, you never did," he continued, "but I've seen a certain look on your face many a time. Do you remember how Polvo used to jump up from the rug and look at something that wasn't there, and growl? That's the look I mean, Georgie, only you don't growl."

Private Angelo suddenly was at my side again, this time muttering and fussing with my leg, I suppose, though I saw only the top of his helmet and his mud-encrusted shoulders moving. I could look only at Papa. Angelo straightened, ripping a long strip of white fabric from a roll, then ducked again, muttering.

"Jesus God. Hold on, Colonel. This'll be over in a sec."

"Just look at me, Papa." I tried to laugh. Angelo reached up to my face and daubed at my lips with a handkerchief. "Look at me. Lying helpless in the goddamn mud."

Papa stiffened, brought his invisible chair back down to all fours with a *thunk* I could almost hear. "No public man uses coarse speech, Georgie."

I flushed—the first sensation I had felt since the shot, hot and full in the face. "No, sir."

"Helpless," Papa said, and looked away from me. Crawling through him, Private Angelo knelt at what might have been the corner of the study, tugged at his pants, and began to piss, spattering the dirt and himself.

"Papa, I couldn't even walk to the foxhole! The private here had to carry—" Papa looked back at me, stern. "Had to drag me," I finished.

Angelo moved well away from his muddy pissoir and sat in the dirt, arms clasping his knees, chin resting on arms, staring at me.

"Hold on, Colonel," Private Angelo whispered.

"Papa," I said. "Papa, I've been here before."

His eyes narrowed, and he leaned forward. "What's that, Georgie?"

"Here, in this shell hole. Years before. I'm doing it all over again, Papa, everything. I don't know whether it's my will or God's will or fate, but—I've got another chance, Papa."

"Another chance," Papa said, rubbing his chin and looking up, toward the east. His face flickered with reflected gunfire.

Private Angelo rubbed his face and muttered, "Christ Almighty, I bet they're ice fishing at home."

"You know, I was almost a soldier once, Georgie . . . more than thirty years ago."

"You *were* a soldier, Papa. You commanded 'A' Company at VMI. You led the cadets in Philadelphia, at the centennial parade."

Now Papa and Angelo talked at once, only not quite. They paused between sentences, and overlapped their speeches only slightly, so that the effect was of two impatient, self-centered people having a conversation, or of one person speaking and the next person, translating. Papa was a trained public speaker, and was telling a story long familiar to both of us, but Angelo was halting, less sure, speaking mostly to himself.

"Parades. That's not soldiering, son. Before you were born,

before I met your mother, I signed up to join the Hicks Expedition, to fight in the Sudan against the Mahdi."

"You know what everybody in the unit says about you, Colonel? I'll tell you. We think you're the all-time eternal brass-plated bastard from hell."

"I read in the papers they were recruiting in Los Angeles, and during a recess in yet another interminable civil case I told my second to resume without me if I was delayed, and I trotted downstairs and ran down the street, coattails flying, to the hotel listed in the ad."

"But you know what else we say about you, Colonel? We tell all the other guys that you're *our* bastard, and furthermore we all think you're a damn good soldier."

"The recruiters had a suite with a potted date palm in the middle of the floor. 'Didn't know the dashed things grew here naturally,' the sergeant said. He had one leg, and a chipped front tooth. 'Might have saved some money on the passage, what, if we'd left that bastard in Cairo.' I laughed and shook everyone's hand. They called me *pasha* Patton, which is a title of great respect in Egypt, you know."

"You ain't gonna die this way, Colonel. Not if we can help it. Not if I can help it."

"Oh, I signed my name to everything, I did. When I came home that evening the family met me at the door, saying Mama had fallen again, and before I hung up my hat and cane I knew that I would never go."

"I ain't leaving you, Colonel. I'll wait on our boys, or the Germans, whichever comes first."

"At Kashgil, that November, Hicks was ambushed, and the expedition was wiped out very nearly to the last man. I read the news on the streetcar, headed for yet another victory dinner for President Cleveland."

I coughed. "That was good luck, wasn't it, Papa?"

"Don't try to talk, Colonel. Want some water?"

"Yes, they were lucky, son. They died like your grandfather, and your granduncle. They died like men."

"Here you go, Colonel. Have a drink. That's right."

I spluttered. "No, Papa. I mean, it was good luck for *me*. Papa—what if you had died?"

"Hm? Oh, of course, Georgie, of course you're right. I have no regrets. I've been blessed with a wonderful family, Georgie, and a wonderful son. A son who's making the *most* of *his* big chance."

He leaned forward and patted my leg, and I felt pain such as I had never known. I screamed.

"Christ! Colonel, shut up, sir," Private Angelo said, lunging toward me.

My father was getting up, patting his pockets, preparing to leave. "Papa!" I cried. "Papa!"

"Geez, he wants his old man now. Listen, Colonel," Private Angelo whispered into my ear, "you've gotta hold out just a while longer, and lay low and be quiet, you got me? We ain't got a hell of a lot of friends in this neighborhood, you know?"

"Papa," I said, my leg throbbing, my forehead sizzling. Papa was making his way over the lip of the hole, rubbing the small of his back. He looked back at me as Angelo upended his canteen over my face, blurring the slope-shouldered outline of the only Patton I had ever known.

I heard Papa's voice: "Another chance. Imagine that. Well, Georgie, maybe that's true for you. I hope it is. I hope it is true for one of us . . ." His last words were swallowed by the spitting rumbling grind of tank engines, and by the shouts of what sounded like a thousand men.

"We're done for, Colonel," Private Angelo said, still swabbing my face.

Up on the crest behind him, where Papa had stood a moment before, was a tall, gangling, sunken-cheeked soldier through whom I could see nothing.

He turned, cupped his mouth, and called, "Criminy, Sarge! There's someone alive down here!"

I later found out he was one of a hundred troops of the 138th Regiment of the 35th Division, who had arrived on the scene a good ninety minutes faster than I had expected. The German resistance just seemed to melt away, they said. Good thing, too: My wound turned out to be even more serious than before; I wouldn't have lasted another half hour. My father would write to tell me that very day he had been curiously restless, kept pacing his study, knew something was terribly wrong. But all I knew as I lost consciousness was Private Angelo's tearful, grimy face. The details of my deliverance came to me later; their implications, later still.

* * *

Chaos, as before. Bugles. Police whistles. A haze of gas. A rain of garbage from office windows. Rearing horses. Hundreds of people in the middle of Pennsylvania Avenue, slowing our advance—running across our path, or clutching at our reins and stirrups, or just standing there dazed. Some were Bonus, I was sure, but which? Screams and curses. A lunch pail bounced off the pavement once, twice, and tumbled away, spraying scraps. Up ahead, through the cherry trees, I could see the Capitol getting blessedly nearer. One of the trees swayed and fell, and a tank trundled into view, lurching upward as it rolled over something.

I long had dreaded my return to July 28, 1932. But now that it was here I was going to do just what I did before, by God: my duty. And, later, something more.

Ahead was a streetwide melee, as the infantry steadily pushed the front line of Bonus marchers back toward the Anacostia Bridge. It was no rout, though. These were American vets, all right; they scratched and struggled and threw punches and wrestled the whole way down Pennsylvania. I heard no shots except the thumps of the gas canisters, but I saw plenty of doughboys using the butts of their rifles. No bayonets in use, not that I could see, not yet.

A pack of a dozen Bonus boys, all in uniform, ran toward me. Somehow they had made it past the infantry. Some had bloody faces. Two were waving shovels, and one a crooked umbrella. They looked wild-eyed, crazy. I whistled to the riders on my left and right and we charged. The veterans wheeled so fast they skidded, stumbled, then ran back the way they had come, cursing us the whole way. We swept them along with the flats of our sabers. I gave one straggler a good smack in the pants, and he yelled, "I'm going, General! I'm going! Don't hit me!"

General. Promoted by a goddamned Bonus marcher. I slowed to a trot and stared down the crowd lining the sidewalk. What shocked, snarling, hateful looks, what howls and oaths—as if I were the Lindbergh kidnapper, or Scarface Al. And from Americans! Watching American troops do their duty, sweeping an organized Bolshevik occupation force out of Washington! I was glad to wield the broom—as glad the second time as the first.

A rock, I suppose, struck my helmet, knocked it sideways; I righted it immediately, and kneed my horse forward. Ahead, a stray cloud of gas made a hotel awning bulge upward. From beneath it a man in uniform stumbled into the street, holding his throat: a goddamn doorman. A horse reared; its rider yelled: "Out of the way, sir! Out of the way, please!" The doorman staggered to the sidewalk, clawing at his epaulets. Two fat men in business suits grabbed him, hauled him through a revolving door, glared back at me.

The gas was dissipating quickly in this windy canyon, yet my eyes were streaming. I touched the mask hanging from my saddle, tapped its goggles, decided against it. Some officers, I knew, had donned their masks before they were a block from Fort Myer.

Above me, looking down from the office windows, a hundred anguished faces in a row. "Shame!" cried a woman's voice. "Shame!" I selected a woman in a wide white hat, saluted her, and rode on.

Coming down a side street toward Pennsylvania was a lone tank, an old Renault. Hadn't that idiot been issued a map? A gang of boys in knickers chased the tank, hanging all over it, throwing round projectiles that splattered off the plate. Apples. Still in service after fourteen years—amazing.

Much later, after the charge across the bridge, after the clearing of the Flats, after the fire that swept "Hooverville" into ash, after it all was left to the newspapers and the politicians, I was standing, as before, talking to several of my fellow regimental officers at the picket lines, when I heard the footsteps on the sidewalk behind me: two men marching smartly, one man shuffling. Once again, without turning, I knew who he was.

In the wards, after Cheppy, I had talked to boys who were bayoneted. They described what it was like. I had begun to feel something similar whenever I thought of Private Joe Angelo.

I turned to face him. He was the same. His face and uniform were filthy, matted with grass and mud and flecked with—blood? Had he been dragged? The Distinguished Service Cross was in place, though. Crooked, but there. Runnels of sweat, or tears, had smoothed the dirt on his cheeks. I couldn't meet his gaze, God help me, not yet. Never noticed before how bowlegged he was, I'll be damned; in Virginia they'd say you could throw a hog through his legs.

"Major Patton," said the sergeant at his right elbow, "this one says he knows you, won't come quietly until he speaks with you—begging your pardon, sir," he added, misreading my expression.

Before, my shame had turned to embarrassment and anger. I had snorted:

"Sergeant, I do not know this man. Take him away, and under no circumstances permit him to return!"

And then I had turned my back on Joe Angelo, who did not speak, and who went so quietly that I heard nothing as I stood there chatting with my fellow Cavalry officers about what a sad spectacle it was, a damn good enlisted man gone to rack and ruin, hat in hand with the Bolsheviks, each word welling up like acid in my throat.

Not this time. But the hell of it was, as I stood there, looking at Joe Angelo again, knowing this was my second, perhaps last, chance, I felt those very same words roiling out; I very nearly said them. "Sergeant—I mean, I—" I had to clench my jaw, get hold of myself (discipline or death, Georgie, discipline or death), force myself instead to say the words I had practiced so bitterly, so often.

"I *do* know this man, Sergeant." Damn my throat; I was barking like Willie, Willie who wasn't even born. "This man is Joe Angelo. Fourteen years ago, Sergeant, in a hole in the ground near a pissant crossroads in France, Joe Angelo saved the life of a cowboy lieutenant colonel who let himself get shot in the ass while daydreaming." I twitched a smile, and forced myself to look at him. I hoped it was a smile. "Hello, Joe. I'm sorry we're on opposite sides today."

I sounded like a Latin-school brat quavering his way through "The boy stood on the burning deck." I could not read the expression on Angelo's face. I had to go on, quickly, before I lost the energy, before the other words took over. "And Joe, while I don't agree with your methods out here—all this agitating and public disturbance and socialism and all—I want you to know that, well, if there's anything Beatrice and I and our family can do to help you out, and your family, then Joe, you only have to say the word. I don't hold with handouts, but that, Joe, that wouldn't be a handout, that would be—I'd say that would be something like justice. And I'd be proud to do it. *We'd* be proud to do it. I hope you believe that, Joe."

The Capitol seesawed. I fought to stand upright.

Joe swallowed once, twice. Damn, he had to be scrawnier than at Cheppy, else how the hell could he have carried me even a foot? Sawed-off little bowlegged runt?

"I do believe it, Colonel." He sounded raspy, too. He cleared his throat, laughed a little. "I surely do."

I was aware of the officers behind me, staring at my back the same way the smug bastards used to stare at me at West Point, when I gave the whole parade ground holy hell while they stood behind me and disapproved, with their thin lips and their narrow eyes, but had nothing to say. To my face, disapproval is nothing, it's dust, it's lint, it's the prick of a cactus, but from behind it's a strong enemy hand pushing, pushing. The hell with West Point; the hell with *them*. But the words were harder and harder to say. I thought I was going to choke, or vomit.

"Can't call me Colonel anymore, Joe," I spat out. "I'm a major, now. Got busted down after the Armistice. Too many officers." I glanced sideways. "More than any sane army needed."

He flashed a smile that did not reach his eyes. "Yeah, peace is hard on everybody, huh, Colonel?"

"Oh sweet goddamn, that's true," I said. "Yes sweet Jesus yes."

"Uh, Major, the truck is waiting—"

"I just wanted to see you, Colonel." Joe took a deep breath. "I just wanted to have a good look at you. I wanted . . . I just wanted . . ."

He seemed to be having trouble finding words, too. I held out my hand. Would it feel clammy to him? "I'm glad you found me, Joe."

He took my hand, held it limply for a second, then let it go. "Colonel, I—"

"Please, come see us in Fort Myer, have dinner with us. Bring your family. If they're home in—New Jersey? I thought so—we'll bring them in, too, on the train."

"Colonel, I want to say—"

"Take care, Joe."

"Don't worry about me, Colonel. Shit!" He flinched from the sergeant's hand on his shoulder. "Wait a minute. Hey, Colonel. How about this? I got an idea, see. What do you think of this idea, huh?" As he kept shrugging off the increasingly insistent guards, tried to wriggle away, he did a sort of shimmy dance, keeping his gaze on me, and talking more quickly, as if energized. "When I get out of jail, because I guess I will get out, right? One day. Well, when I do, I'll go on back to New Jersey, back to my wife and my kids, no job or nothing, no pension or nothing, empty-handed, just good old Joe, good old Dad with nothing in his pockets as usual, that is if they're still there, oh Jesus," and his voice broke, "if they're still there waiting on me, waiting on fucking nothing, and then maybe we'll all get together, the Angelos and the Pattons, for a nice little *dinner*, maybe with caviar and crackers and, and, hell, what do rich people eat? Fucking finger sandwiches, but in the meantime, Colonel—let go of me, you fathead son of a bitch—in the meantime, Colonel, do you know what you can do? Huh? You can go straight to hell! How about that?"

I couldn't speak. I couldn't move. I stood there watching the two sergeants, enraged now, haul Joe Angelo away.

"That a fair deal, Colonel? Huh? That a fair goddamn deal?" He yanked a hand free, ripped off his medal, and flung it at me. It bounced off my chest, I suppose. I didn't feel it, but I heard it plink against a button, and then the pavement. "Let go of me. I said I'm going, goddamn you! For God's sake! Can't a man walk?"

Muscles taut and aching, forearm barely able to bear the weight, I saluted. I held it after the little man was invisible in the crowd, for as long as I could distinguish the sergeants' helmets bobbing. Only when they were two bubbles among hundreds did I drop my trembling hand, and then slowly.

I turned back to the officers and croaked, "If you'll excuse me, gentlemen."

They broached goodbyes as I walked away, concentrating: shoulders back, left foot, right foot, left. Alongside the walkway was a waist-high rail, flowering shrubs on the other side. Hydrangeas? I gripped the rail for support as I walked, hauling myself along left-handed. I heard murmurs behind me, something about "the Old Man." Old Man to my soldiers in Mexico at thirty, now Old Man at forty-six, and thirteen years to go—No! Mustn't think about that. Tendrils of gas seeped out from the shrubs, through the railing, curled around my ankles, made my eyes tear up. I had to say the words, I had to. My throat was on fire. I whispered, fast and desperate, mouth foamy dry. "Sergeant, I do not know this man. Take him away. Take him away, Sergeant, I do not know this man." I passed a flaming barrel. A doughboy fed it leaflets, snatched them one by one from a crumpled bundle beneath his arm.

VOTE THE BONUS
BONUSES NOW
BONUS OR A JOB

The doughboy gave me a queer look. The heat licked my face. I clasped my forehead, forced myself to suck in air. Discipline, Georgie, discipline! Focus! Some changes would be easy, others, not. I knew that. Destiny is hard. Adjusting it is harder. Harder with every passing year. I knew that. I could live with that. Fair deal, Joe, fair deal. "Take him away!" I choked, and kicked free of the clutching gas.

* * *

Leave a real Army camp at night, and you can watch it vanish in the rear-view mirror. Even under blackout conditions, there's always something to see. But when I say goodbye to Thomson, and Mims wheels the Mercedes along the gravel turnaround, and Willie scrambles, whining, into my lap, I glance up and I see nothing in the mirror but blackness. Turn your back on it, and all of Fortitude disappears, buildings and tanks and personnel and Thomson too. If only I could forget as easily.

It's a long drive back to Peover (who but the Brits would give a town a name like that?), and I don't sleep as well on the road as I used to. That's an understatement. I don't sleep well *anywhere* anymore. The closer I get to that left-turning truck in Germany . . . but no matter. As Willie snores in my lap, sides heaving beneath my crossed forearms, I open my old notebook from Mexico and look at all the items I've crossed off, just to reassure myself that this second life was worth living, that I might avoid that truck yet. My eye lights on the name

DICK JENSON

and I grin. That's one achievement, surely. On April 1, 1943, a Junker squadron dropped several bellyfuls of five hundred-pounders on the First Armored command post in the Wadi Akarit, north of Ei Hamma. I had been expecting the attack, of course, and I had taken steps to prevent the only casualty. Before, everyone made it to the foxholes OK, but one of the holes suffered a hit—the one that contained only one man, my young aide, Dick Jenson, whom I had sent out there, God help me, for some front-line experience. Not again. I made sure Dick was with me all that day, behind the lines, and so I never had to write Dick's mother that letter, and instead of someone else getting killed in Dick's place (which I had half-expected but accepted as a necessary risk), the Junkers didn't do any harm other than rearranging Colonel Benson's furniture, which I'm sure needed it anyway, and giving that nattering old woman Omar Bradley a lingering earache, which is a kind of justice, if you ask me.

Got a card from Dick just the other day. He's quite the hero back home, his wife's sulking because all the girls want to dance with him, leg brace or no. Four days after the Junker attack, Dick stepped on a mine outside Sidi-Bou-Zid—well, actually, the poor bastard to his left stepped on it. We thought that stretch of road had been swept clear, but, what the hell, can't predict everything.

Feeling a bit better, I close my notebook, settle back, and peer out the window, where a white stone wall has been twisting alongside for what seems like an awful long time.

* * *

Mount Etna was hazy in the distance Aug. 10, 1943, when we skidded to a stop along a muddy ditch outside the 93rd Evacuation Hospital. Why hadn't I just let Sergeant Mims drive past? Had I even intended to call halt, or had it just—happened? I still didn't have to go in. But the very thought of ordering Mims forward made me feel faint, abruptly feverish. I suppressed a gasp, dug the fingernails of my left hand into the palm of my right until the landscape stopped shimmering.

Changing my future had become so difficult, so painful, I had almost given it up. But today I had to do something. I had to.

It was a breezy day, and the three-star pennants fluttered nicely even when the jeep was standing still. Someone must have seen them and alerted the receiving officer, a major, who came running, white coat flapping, while I still was in the jeep dithering and taking in the view and feeling grateful that I could regain my strength sitting down.

"Yes, General, yes, delighted to have you look around, visit with the men, a great morale-booster, we're very honored . . ."

Before I followed him in, feeling better but still a little shaky, I looked back at the old volcano and thought, Mims, better you should have driven me to the edge of the crater and over the side.

"You'll have to duck your head here, I'm afraid, General. That's right. *Attention!*"

Ah, hell. If I had let Mims drive on by, I'd have been running away from a fight, wouldn't I? And who's to say I wouldn't have run into the same goddamned malingerer, ten miles down the road? No, much better to face my future, and stand up to it.

Sicily might have been cleaned free of krauts all the way to Messina, but as I walked through those canvas wards, chatting and smiling and patting boys on the shoulder, I was as tense as I had been during the invasion. As if I were braced for one of the patients to lift a pistol and shoot me where I stood. Goddamn fear! Goddamn nerves!

"How are you feeling, soldier?"

"I'm all right, General. Don't you worry about me."

"Oh, I'm not worried about you, soldier. I'll let the goddamned Huns worry about you, when you're back on your feet again with a gun in your hand. Right?"

"That's right. You tell 'em, General."

More differences. Before, there had been a soldier with staring eyes, his face badly burned, who lay on his belly in a cot and kept moving his arms and legs as if crawling. "Poor soul kept that up all night," the nurse had said. But now I didn't see the wretch anywhere.

"What happened to you, son?"

"Hell, General, I was just in the wrong place at the wrong time, that's all. The docs are fixing me up, though. I'll be back out there with you soon."

"I'm glad for that, son. You're a fine soldier, and you and I have a lot of killing left to do. You ready for that?"

"You say the word, General!"

"God bless you, soldier."

Others were where I expected them. Here was the poor bastard with his head half blown off, who couldn't talk but who reached out to shake my hand and then gave me a thumbs-up sign. Here was the nurse who gave me her pan and washcloth and let me bathe an unconscious man's fevered forehead. "When he comes to, he's never gonna believe it," she kept saying. "Never in a million billion years." Here was the big nigger comedian, bandaged head to foot, who made us all laugh when he said, "Hey General—You oughtta see the other guy."

"God, I love my army!" I said, and those who could cheered.

When I entered the last ward, by now at the head of a little jostling procession of doctors and nurses, I immediately looked to the bunk where I knew the yellow bastard would be. He wasn't there.

Could it be? Would I be spared?

"Where you from, soldier?"

"South Carolina, sir."

"South Carolina, eh? You know, I met a soldier the other day from South Carolina, and he said a Southern boy could shoot even better than he could screw. Do you agree with that, soldier?"

"I'll let you know, General. I need to do a little more shootin'."

"You do that, soldier. You do that." Laughing with the rest, I turned to the cot across the aisle.

And there he was.

Different cot, different place in the ward. Otherwise the same.

As before, he wasn't a small man. Not scrawny and weak-looking at all. Big, hearty fellow. Standing, he'd have been my height. He sat on the edge of a cot, feet on the floor. His hands clenched his knees. No bandages, no hospital dress at all. He was in full artilleryman's uniform, from helmet to boots, every inch regulation. Needed a shave, though. One dark eyebrow smeared across his forehead. His eyes were screwed shut, and his lower lip was sucked in. His body was as rigid as if sitting at the trigger, awaiting an order to fire.

I thought of all I could avoid: the Drew Pearson broadcast, the headlines, the demands in Congress for a court-martial

to curse and slap and physically attack a man in his hospital bed, my fellow Senators, is not the act of a general but the act of a coward

the endless chewings-out from Ike

a miserable coward

and I told myself, let it go this time, Georgie, let it go. Just walk past him. Don't even look at him. That's right, Georgie. Just keep on walking.

The bones in my knees and hips seemed to grind together. I bit my tongue to keep from crying out.

I stopped. I turned to him. I fought to keep my voice low, controlled, polite. Polite!

What did you do in the war, granddaddy?

Kissed all the ass in Europe, honey, Yankee ass and Limey ass, brass ass and khaki ass, just like I was told.

"What's your name, soldier? What's your unit?"

His name was Paul G. Bennett. He was 21 years old. Private, First Battalion, Seventeenth Field Artillery Regiment. Hadn't my family sent me all the clippings, for Godsake? But as before, he told me nothing. He just sat there.

I reached out—gently! gently! I pictured Beatrice's neck at sixteen, the day of the Catalina picnic with the Pattons and the Ayers, the first photograph with both of us in it. That's how gently I reached out. My fingertips rested, trembling, on Bennett's shoulder; I almost stroked it. I gave him a push so small it was little more than a mental pulse down my arm from me to him. "Hello. Soldier? Can you hear me?"

"Yes, sir," he quavered. His bottom lip, before it vanished again, was bloody.

"That's a bad lip you got there, son. Is that why you're in here? That why you're in the hospital?"

I just want to hear him admit it, I told myself. I just want to hear him say he's scared. I want the brave men around him to hear his yellow mouth. Hell, the papers said he had begged to stay with his unit, that his battery surgeon was the one who ordered him to pack it in, sent him to the medics. Why didn't he *say* that? He could if he wanted to. "Hell if I know why I'm here, sir," he could say. "Doc said I needed a checkup. I'll be back out there killing krauts before you know it, General." It'd be so damned easy.

Hadn't he been listening to the others? Didn't he know what he was supposed to say?

Bennett—no, I wouldn't think of his name, he hadn't earned it yet—the yellow soldier opened his mouth, jaw dropping like a pin had been removed. It gaped open. I leaned closer. From the back of his throat a word was welling up, a slight sound like a distant scream or a rusty hinge. I stooped there, quivering, waiting.

Beatrice wrote me once that when little Georgie was learning to talk, he'd get hung up on a word, and he'd stand there holding onto her deck chair, mouth open, trying to remember what the sound was, and she'd sit there in suspense trying to will him to say something, anything. I never knew what the hell she was talking about until that moment, trying to coax a word or two out of that yellow rat in Sicily. Different words. Even "Screw you, General" would have made me happy. Something—anything!

"It's my nerves," he said.

The same goddamn thing all over again!

"What?" I yelled. "What did you say?" Behind me a nurse gasped.

"It's my nerves, General. I just can't stand the shelling anymore. I can't." Eyes still shut, he started to cry, with a low and maddening whine like Willie at the door, wanting to be let out. A noise fit for a dog.

I knew what I

goddamned coward

wanted to say and needed to say

yellow son of a bitch

and had said before

shut up that goddamned crying

but I remembered the headlines, and the hate mail, and the packs of reporters pecking at my daughters' windows, and my orders from Ike's hatchetman to crawl

disgrace to the Army

on my belly to every last unit in the Seventh Army asking forgiveness

back to the front, my man

and then the months of doing nothing, and then finding out that my next "command"

ought to be lined up against a wall and shot

was to lead a non-existent army in a non-existent invasion—and *that* only because the last person who still believed I could do the job in combat was Hitler.

No. Not again. Shut up, Georgie.

God damn you

Just shut up.

"I can't," the miserable rat whispered.

I leaned forward farther, gently laid my hands on his shoulders, my mouth against his left ear. He flinched, the corner of his mouth jerked, but he didn't resist. His whiskers pricked my cheek. He was a smoker. The pain had returned, spasms in my back, my arms, my legs. Mother of mercy, Georgie, don't fall on the boy. Anything but that. So low that not even the man in the next cot could catch it, in a desperate rush to speak before my voice gave out, I breathed into his ear:

"You worthless, Godless, pitiful, no-dicked bastard, in another lifetime I slapped the living shit out of you, you disgraceful excuse for a soldier. And I'd like to do it again, rather than let you sit here pissing on all these good brave men around you. This time, though, I'm going to walk away from you, the way I'd walk away from a turd I left hot in a ditch, and maybe my life will be the better for it. I don't know. But whatever happens to me, you wretched stinking traitor, I hope what you get is worse."

I kissed his ear, let go of him and jerked to a standing position, wiped my mouth with the back of my hand. He sat there as before, still trembling, but not crying any more. As far as anyone else in the ward knew, I had spoken words of private encouragement—and by God, I had! Sure I had. More than he deserved. I turned to go. A few inches' movement, but so, so hard. I felt the cords in my neck pull taut, resisting. The pain wasn't the worst of it. Turning my back on that soldier was like turning my back on myself.

"I just can't," he murmured.

Where the South Carolinian had been, lying in the bed in front of me, was my granduncle, Col. Walter Tazewell Patton, a bloody bandage over most of his head but his good eye shining. His Confederate grays were spattered with red and with orange clay. Sitting beside him in a canvas chair, likewise staring at me, was my gray-clad grandfather, George Smith Patton, bandaged hand on the hilt of his saber, splinted leg sticking into the aisle so that I'd have to step over it to reach the door. Across the aisle, with tubes feeding into his arm, lay a centurion, free hand drumming a pursuit rhythm against his breastplate, eyes intent on me beneath the crest of his legion. Beside him lay a huge man in a horned helmet, beard wild and matted around his strapped-on oxygen mask, his great chest rising and falling alarmingly but his face still and sure.

All around the ward were men in chain mail, redcoats, bear-skins, tricorne hats, all writhing or gasping or clutching their wounds, all staring at me. The nurses were gone. In the doorway where the doctor had stood was my father, in his suitcoat and plaid vest, his pants a bit baggy. He wore a stethoscope and held a clipboard under his arm. His lips were pursed, his eyeglasses low on his nose. It was the expression he used when withholding judgment.

"Not again," I murmured. I closed my eyes and tried to restrain my shudder.

"General? General. Are you all right?"

I opened my eyes. The doctor was back, and the nurses, and the other wounded men of the U.S. Seventh Army. They looked less real than the phantoms had been. They had less life in them, even the ones who weren't wounded. They were frozen like a medical-school tableau, a closed-down waxwork, waiting on me to do something to get their lives, the war, history, moving again.

I felt nearer death than any of them.

Behind me the yellow bastard sobbed. Bennett. His name was Bennett.

I muttered, "Ah, the hell with it," whirled and slapped the living shit out of him.

* * *

Willie trotting at my side, I stride into the St. James Square office of the Supreme Allied Commander, who stands and returns my salute, then leans across the desk, grinning, to shake my hand. So this is going to be one of those across-the-desk things. Willie's leash goes taut as he snuffles the rug, the legs of the davenport, the bar—all these SHAEF offices are tricked out like a goddamn bordello.

"George, Christ, it's good to see you."

"You, too, Ike, you, too."

I hear a scramble beneath the desk, and a hairy muzzle pokes out, sniffing. It sweeps from left to right like a turret gun. Then it bares its teeth and growls.

Willie stops so suddenly he nearly falls. He whimpers and shinnies backward, huddling against my boots.

"Uh-oh," Ike says. He reaches beneath the desk to seize Telek by the collar. The Scottie yaps and struggles.

"Hang on, Ike. I'll put him out." I scoop the trembling Willie into my arms—Jesus! How heavy do bull terriers get, anyway? He's harder to lift all the time—and turn to the door.

"No, don't bother, George, Willie can stay. I'll put Telek out."

"No, no, Ike. Telek outranks Willie. Besides, this is Telek's home. Protocols, eh? *Mims!* Thank you. Now, Willie, don't take on so, I won't be long, go with nice Sergeant Mims, Sergeant Mims will give you a treat. You *did* bring the treats, didn't you, Mims? Good man. That Mims is a good man," I say, as I close the door, leaning on the knob for support, and turn back to Ike. He is reassuring Telek, who has disappeared beneath the desk again.

"Have a seat, George." He jerks a hand in the general direction of the hideous armchair—Are all the man's gestures awkward?—and, instead of crossing to the davenport, or to the other armchair, sits at the desk and rummages papers. Fine.

"Thank you, sir," I say. Seating myself, determined not to show my relief at sitting down, I cross my legs at the knee and fold my hands in my lap. Ike looks up and blinks his huge, bright eyes.

"Oh, come on, George, relax a little. Take your helmet off, at least. The stars are shining in my eyes. Heh."

I lift it off, set it in my lap, smooth my hair, and fold my hands atop the helmet. So tired. Good thing no one could doze off in this upholstered torture device.

"Juice? Soda water? I'm told there's real lemonade today. A convoy got through."

I glance at the ice bucket, the tumblers, the amber decanter that sparkles in the lamplight.

"No, thank you," I say, my mouth dry.

"Trip into town go all right?"

"Just fine, Ike. No complaints."

He fusses with his papers again. I need something to focus on, so I study him. If he were going to chew me out for something, he'd have started already, would hardly have let me get in the door. If he were going to go over plans, discuss Third Army's progress, update me on the war news, he'd have waved me over to the map, talked a blue streak; he loves organization, he lives for chalk talks and pointers. Hell, if he just were feeling lonely at the top again, Miss Summersby indisposed or something, he'd have sat on the sofa—or come out into the countryside to see me, not called me down to this damned fancy house.

"Do you want anything to eat, George? I could have something sent up. I can't remember what we had tonight. I think it was just bangers again—I've somehow got to get an American cook assigned here without splitting the Alliance— but hell, bangers would be better than nothing."

I haven't eaten in days. My gorge rises at the thought of chewing, swallowing. I'll avoid the question with a joke. "In America," I say, "we call them sausages, Ike."

I grin, but that was a cheap shot, and we both know it. He pulls off his spectacles—always a laborious task with Ike, who unhooks first one shank and then the other, frowns that great flat face as if his ears were coming off with them—and then looks at me without expression, tapping the spectacles on the blotter.

"I know what you call them in America, George." He winces. "What *we* call them. Shit."

I suppress another grin. "Sorry, Ike. Just a joke."

He tosses the spectacles onto the desk. "Goddamn it, George, I didn't bring you in here for you to give me another lecture about kissing British ass."

"I'm curious to hear why you did bring me in here, Ike."

"Maybe I just wanted to have a pleasant visit with my oldest friend in the Army. Maybe I just wanted to stay up all night shooting the shit like we used to do."

"That would be great," I say, "maybe. And maybe what else?"

He sighs, twists his mouth sideways, as if he had bangers in his teeth. "George, I'm worried about you."

This is new. "Worried," I say.

"Look at yourself, George. You barely can carry your medals around. Your uniform hangs on you like an empty tent. You walk like a colored man in a zombie movie, and your eyes are a snowman's buttons. How much sleep have you been getting lately? Christ, even a Sherman has to be serviced now and then." He glances at the bar, and I follow his glance, then look back to see him staring at me. "George, for God's sake, you haven't—"

It actually has been a good day, considering; I haven't felt any pain since lunchtime. Until now.

"Ike," I say.

He sighs again and folds his arms, leaning on his elbows. He studies the paper-strewn desktop. "All right, George, I'm sorry for asking. I know you swore it off. But goddamn it, George, I've known you for twenty years, and I can tell when something's the matter. Now, as your friend and your commanding officer—the only goddamn commanding officer you have between here and the Potomac—I've got a right to know what it is."

I shrug and flap my hands, make a show of gruff nonchalance, despite my growing unease. "Sure I'm tired, Ike, we're all tired. We'll all *be* tired until we've swept the Nazis out of Europe, and then we'll all have to go to the Pacific and be tired there, too. Hell, no one's any more tired than you are, Ike. The question is, whether my being tired is impairing my efficiency as commander of Third Army. Do you have any signals that it is?" A note of generous cooperation might be helpful here. "Because if you do, Ike," I continue, voice chirping as I suppress a cough, "I want to hear about it straight up, straight from you—as my friend *and* as my commanding officer."

The wall map behind Ike boasts a snarl of red arrows through France. None follows the straight, ancient roads that William the Conqueror used. The map in my own office is different.

Ike shakes his head, flips through a thick sheaf of reports, many of which bear my signature. A show of busyness; he hasn't put his spectacles back on. "No, George, no I don't. In fact, I hear nothing but glowing reports from Peover. All the equipment and personnel coming in on schedule, absolute secrecy at all levels, the training going well—hell, George, you could train Veronica Lake to be a tank commander if you had to, everybody knows that. No, those boys won't be green long. I presume you've got the usual bitching about the helmets and neckties, eh?" He looks back up, closes the folder, lets his fingertips rest on it, his hand crouched like a spider. "Any other problems in Peover that I should know about?"

I laugh, give him the million-dollar grin. "Well, Ike, the men at headquarters are having a bit of trouble pronouncing the name of their town. Instead of 'Peever,' they keep saying 'Pee-over,' and so now a lot of them are calling it 'Piss Over.' Maybe it'll catch on, and the Brits will have to change their maps." He's not laughing. "Other than that, no, Ike, I'm real proud of everyone in Third. No real killer instinct yet in many of them, but that will come, that will come. Walker in particular, he's doing a fine job with Twenty Corps."

"Yes, yes, it's in the reports. Glad to hear it." He reaches out for the spectacles, and my gut clenches. "But I see other reports, too, George." He hooks his spectacles back on, pulls from beneath a stack a lavender folder that's unfamiliar to me. He opens it and leafs through it, which doesn't take long, as it only contains a few sheets of paper, typed, single-spaced, and unsigned but stamped with an unfamiliar seal. "And those reports are a bit more . . . well, I guess perplexing is the word for what these are."

"What do you mean?" I ask. Suddenly it's stifling in here. I want to mop my forehead, but I don't dare. This is bad. This is very bad.

He scratches his head and squints. "Fortitude, George. Operation Fortitude. The fake invasion of Calais, the one we're feeding the Germans. Now, initially, George, I recall you weren't thrilled about your role in that. 'Goddamn figurehead,' those were your words, I believe."

My knees are beginning to ache again. I shift, and that lousy armchair makes farting noises. "In the heat of the moment, I may well have said something like that."

"I'm sure of the 'goddamn,' at any rate. But you seem to have become wildly enthusiastic about this fake invasion headquarters the movie studio built in East Anglia." He traces the lines of type with an index finger. "Why, in the past few weeks alone, you've been out there . . . twelve times. You were there on the 17th, the 20th, again on the 23rd and 24th—you stayed the night that visit, George . . ."

I once saw Ike sit between two chattering machine guns on a practice range while working out tactical problems with a stubby pencil. He certainly isn't going to let himself be distracted by me—but I try for heartiness anyway. "You ought to come out there with me sometime, Ike." I slap my thigh. "It's a remarkable setup, just fascinating."

"It certainly fascinates *you*, George. The 28th, the 30th . . . George, I know we asked you to be seen in that area occasionally, but two or three times would have sufficed." He clears his throat, rubs his jaw. "And then there's the matter of your behavior on the site."

Something is rubbing my boot. Telek. The Scottie sniffs around my feet, then sits up and cocks its ears, trying to be adorable. "My behavior," I say, thinking fast.

"Assigning rank to all the civilian workers. Requiring them to adhere to military codes of dress and deportment. Haggling over blueprints. Making demands that are, at the very least, strange. I mean, really, George. Unused roads must be kept in top repair. Unused airfields must be graded once a week. The hospital must be enlarged to accommodate expected . . . casualties? George, that hospital's an empty shell." He looks at me, expressionless, sucks the corner of his mouth a moment.

I reach to pat Telek, who shies away with a whimper. My hand is left groping at nothing. "It's all part of the deception, Ike. If that camp isn't convincing on the ground, it won't be convincing from the air."

"Uh-huh. Talking to yourself, George—is that another part of the deception?" Now I'm cold, but sweat is trickling into my left eye. Ike's tracing finger begins tapping the page, with an increasingly staccato rhythm. "Roaming the grounds all night, muttering to yourself, or to somebody. Addressing soldiers who aren't there. Dressing them down, giving them pep talks."

Thomson. What a fool I've been. Always stepping out from behind something, surprising me. Always wanting to tag along, show me new things. Always so attentive to everything I say and do, as if she privately admired me, as if she were storing up information to share with her friends.

"I'll be goddamned," I say aloud. "A spy."

Ike sighs and says, "Oh, come on, George, Fortitude is an Intelligence operation. They're all spies, or they wouldn't be there." He sits back, laces his fingers across his stomach, what there is of it. His chair moans softly. "At any rate, this report tells me what you've been up to during your off hours. Running the real Third Army by day and the fake First U.S. Army Group by night and running yourself into the ground in the process. My question, George, is still: Why? What the hell's going on?" He waits. "Please tell me you've got something going with the Thomson woman, and she's so good that you see visions afterward."

I make a contemptuous noise in my throat. One of the first things I wrote down, that night in Mexico, was

BEATRICE

and I've done right by her this time, by God; I've made sure of that. My conscience is clear on that score.

What I say is: "That's a bit personal, Ike."

"Shit," he says, flat and commanding, as if he had said, "Fire." Another bad sign. He continues: "When one of my top officers begins to display every sign of confusing fantasy and reality, that's gone way beyond the personal." He rocks in his creaking chair. "Talk to me, George. I'm serious. Talk to me, or I'm liable to forget I'm your friend, and remember I'm the guy in charge of seeing that Operation Overlord doesn't fall apart before we reach Paris, much less Berlin."

"Goddamn it," I say, standing up. My helmet hits the floor, rolls. Too fast; a wave of dizziness as I lean both fists on the desk. Ike sits there like a Buddha. "That's just it, Ike."

"What's it?"

"Overlord. Put me in it, Ike."

Now, for the first time, he looks tired, too. "Oh, for—"

"Monty and Bradley don't know what they're getting into, no one does, but I do, Ike, I know what needs to be done—"

He shakes his head, stares at the wall. "I don't believe this."

"—you know and I know that if the troops in Normandy get bogged down behind those hedgerows, we'll have a real risk of trench warfare on our hands. The goal shouldn't be capturing territory, it should be killing Germans." With a burst of energy that's almost painful, I bang the desk with my fists. "Sir," I add.

Ike shoves his chair back and stands, running his hands over his head as if polishing it. "No," he mutters. "No, no, no, no, no."

"Ike, I've been sending you papers, proposals. You've read them."

"Yes, George, read them and re-read them and shook my head and put them in the file of old business. *Old* business, George." He thumps the wall map with the side of his fist. "In case you hadn't noticed, our invasion plan has already been decided."

"Ike—"

He keeps thumping the map, punctuating his points. Another damned chalk talk. "I mean it, George. Overlord *is* workable, it *will* succeed, and it's the *only* one all the Allies agree on—*all*, George. Now I know you're pissed off that you have to sit here in England with Third until the beaches are held, and I sympathize, but George, that's how it's going to be. After that hospital business in Sicily, you're lucky to be in charge of *anything* and crossing the Channel at *all*, and you know it." He takes a deep breath, closes his eyes, and rubs his forehead. "My God, George," he says, more quietly. He chuckles, eyes still closed, and shakes his head. "I swear. You act sometimes like one of those tent evangelists, like Aimee Semple McPherson with a pipeline to the heavens. Like you can wave your hands and call down the angels and have them whisper in your ear exactly what we all ought to do, and exactly how this war is going to turn out."

He starts to say more, but something, a thought, a realization, stops him. He opens his eyes. We stare at each other across the desk. Ike blinks, opens his mouth, closes it again.

It is small of me, I know, but I cannot restrain a surge of pride. How many years has it been since I last saw Ike afraid?

He puts one hand to his forehead. The hand trembles. "Jesus Christ," he murmurs, still looking at me.

"Now, Ike—"

"Hang on, George. Hang on a second." He turns to the bar, wrestles the top off the ice bucket, and begins flinging cubes into a tumbler.

"Ike, listen to me." I reach up to grab his shoulders, think better of it, falter. "There's something I should have told you years ago."

I have never told anyone, not even Beatrice, not even Papa—the real Papa. Not anyone.

"I've lived all this before."

Drink in hand, his back to me, Ike straightens. The ice chuckles in the glass.

"You see, I know how things are going to turn out . . . or, at least, how they're likely to turn out . . . and so I know, better than anyone else, Ike, how risky Overlord—"

Ike turns, tumbler to lips, and holds up one index finger for silence. Usually this means the fuse is lit. I shut up and grit my teeth. He gulps his drink, then lowers it. He keeps the finger raised.

"First of all, George," Ike says, very quietly, "I don't want to hear one more word, tonight or ever, about all this psychic reincarnation mumbo-jumbo, or I swear to God your war is over."

"Ike—"

"I mean it, George. Second. No more complaints about Overlord. Not to me, not to anyone. Hear me, George?"

I swallow, hang my head, look as contrite as possible. So tired, and so much to do. "I hear you, Ike."

"Third." He swigs his empty drink, gets a mouthful of ice, talks around it. "I want you to lay off Fortitude. It's a wonderful deception, George, but that's all it is. A deception. A fake. A Quaker cannon. Don't take it seriously. It'll make you crazy. OK? OK? George?"

May the God of war and all my ancestors and all the soldiers I have been and am, be with me now, and always.

"George. Are you listening, George?"

I look up, try to grin. "Yes, Ike. Perfectly. I've been—I've been under stress, you know." I choke out the words. "Just like Sicily. But I'll get hold of myself, sure I will." I pat his shoulder, as awkward as Ike himself. "You can count on me." I clear my throat. "Anything else?"

My destiny depends on how convincing that was. It didn't sound very convincing to me.

"Yes," Ike said. He sighs and leans against the bar, his shoulders drooping. "You can have a drink with me, and we'll talk about old times, and you can try to persuade me that this lousy job won't cost me all my friends. What'll you have?"

Swallowing my exultation, I say, in a smooth, even voice: "Lemonade will be fine, Ike. Just fine."

Much later, on the way out, down marble stairs and along carpeted corridors—what a palatial warren these Limey offices are—Ike is in chummy mood, arm around my shoulders, grinning up into my face like an elf. I'm not fooled. I know he'll be watching me even more closely than usual from here on, and that means Marshall and Stimson, too. How many phone calls, how many telegrams, before I'm sent home? So little time.

As we reach the lobby, we pause in front of a vast window and watch the fires. People come and go behind us in the echoing darkness, and near the front door, illuminated by the flickerings outside, I see the shapes of Willie and Sergeant Mims, also watching. I long to get back in the Mercedes, to have a couple of hours' rest, just sitting down, but I stand as upright as possible. Wouldn't do to let Ike support me.

"George, do you remember Camp Meade?"

"I sure do."

"Hard to believe now that we once were so bored, we'd drive through the countryside armed to the teeth and hope robbers would jump us. Do you know, George, I still wish they had."

"So do I, by God, so do I."

"At least then we'd have accomplished something in that do-nothing assignment."

"But we did, Ike. Remember? We proved that if we had to, you and I could take a tank apart and put it back together again single-handed. And I bet we're the only two generals in this whole miserable war who can say that."

"That's right. By God, I had nearly forgotten! You and me in the garage the whole damn weekend. I never thought we'd be able to do it, George, but goddamn if you weren't right, as usual. Every last nut and bolt back in place."

"We were nothing but grease from head to toe, a couple of Jolsons."

"And when we were done you made a big show of being horrified and pulled that big old washer out of your pocket—said, 'Oh, shit, we forgot one!' For a second I believed you. Nearly wet our pants laughing."

"Nearly?"

"Almost got killed fooling with those tanks, George. You remember when that snapped cable went whipping past our heads, and cut down those saplings behind us?"

"Hell, yes, I do. Scared the shit out of us, didn't it?"

"George." His voice is different. His face is grim in the firelight. He nearly whispers. "When I look at you now, George, do you know what I think of? I think of that cable. Snapping."

We stare at each other for a second or two. Then from across the lobby comes a terrible burst of snarling. Sergeant Mims and a couple of MPs are dancing in a circle, waving their hands and yelling, while at their feet is a roiling, yipping mass of fur and teeth.

"Aw, shit. Telek!" Ike yells.

"Willie!"

The dogs might have killed each other already, if it not for the parquet floor. No traction. Willie a fighter! I can't believe it. Ike and I holler and curse and snatch at their collars but can't grab hold. WACs and staff officers come running from all the doorways and gather around and add to the din. The ruckus rebounds off the vaulted ceiling. Finally Sergeant Mims grabs a William Morris vase and empties it on the mutts, flowers and all. A good man, Sergeant Mims. Ike and I seize the chance to lunge, and soon both of us have an armload of wet, scrambling dog. A few damp daisies droop from Willie's ears like a garland. Ike has his hand clamped around Telek's muzzle, but I let Willie bark, and bark, and bark, the echoes sounding like an army of terriers pouring through the building, converging on the entryway from all directions.

"Sorry, George," Ike says, loudly. "I must have left the door ajar. No harm done, I hope."

"Harm done? Ike, I'd say this is Willie's finest hour." The pain hasn't entirely gone, but I feel energized again, rested, rejuvenated. I beam at everyone. "Did you see the little bastard go? Did you see him? I'd say he was getting the best of it, what do you all say?"

A general murmur of cautious assent, with wary glances toward the Supreme Commander, who grins and says, "I think you're right, George, Willie won this round. But maybe we can keep the fighting to a minimum from here on—right, George?" His grin doesn't extend to his eyes. I beam at him, too.

"Ike, if even my Willie can become a fighter, then who knows? Anything might happen. Anything at all." I kiss the sodden, yipping mutt on the top of his head. The bystanders applaud. Whew! What a smell. I kiss him again, hard.

* * *

I shuffle as fast as I can along the main road through the camp, trying not to pass out. No lights, except a couple of feeble dim rectangles in the black bulk of the main construction shed. I left my flash in the car; no need for it. I know my way well, and soon we'll have lights enough.

As I pass the shed, I hear the erratic heartbeat of a hammer. All across the camp, tents snap and thump in the ocean breeze. Behind me, gravel grinds beneath the Mercedes as Mims rolls forward, headlights off, tailing me with gravity. Otherwise, silence.

It's tempting to think that I am the only person abroad in the camp, in the British Isles, in the world. But I know I'm not. I can't take refuge in that fantasy. My senses are too acute. I hear small murmurous movements in the shadows that I know aren't hedgehogs. I begin to smell, not sawdust and turpentine, but grease and gasoline. I know a flashlight beam would pick up, all around me, the gleam of rivets and steel. I try to hang onto the sensation, firm up the silhouettes, people the darkness. It's a queer feeling, doing all my seeing with the corners of my eyes. But it's what I've been doing for weeks now, and I'm getting good at it. Tonight, God of war willing, it pays off.

I think often about September 26, 1918, the start of the Meuse-Argonne offensive, when a hundred troops of the 138th Regiment of the 35th Division appeared ninety minutes sooner than previously, and saved my life. For years, I pondered their timely appearance. Happenstance? Just one of countless small, random differences between lives? Or was I partially responsible for those men? In my pain, in my despair, in, most of all, my knowledge of what should be, had I somehow . . . summoned them?

Once I began thinking in this way, I couldn't stop. I filled notebooks. Take the unexpected sniper on that Mexican rooftop. If he had lived to croak out his story, what reason would he have given for being up there, for not riding out with the other bandits? Perhaps he wouldn't have had a reason. Maybe he just felt compelled to be there. Compelled by what, or whom?

And Thomson. Well worth thinking about, Thomson was. A real asset to Fortitude, yes. That's probably her in the shed now, burning the midnight oil. Damn glad to have her, even if she is a Limey spy. But where did Thomson come from? How did she wind up in charge out here, instead of that hapless Cockney I dealt with before?

Then there was Joe Angelo. Unlike Thomson, he was someone I knew, or thought I knew. But in Washington that bloody day he was different. The previous Joe never would have said those things. But the previous George Patton never would have said what I said, either. Was one difference the chicken, the other the egg? To what extent did I create that different Joe?

In everyone's life there are crossroads, moments of decision, however insignificant. To spot the crucial moments in his life, and act, makes a great soldier. To spot the crucial moments on a larger scale, a grand scale—that's the work of a general.

Maybe going through life a second time . . . *disturbs* things. Throws up sparks. Creates turbulence. Maybe the identical set of circumstances can't be duplicated, because it would violate, say, some universal law. So my surroundings get rearranged in new patterns, new circumstances. New people. If I couldn't remember my previous life, I'd never realize I had this power. I'd be as dumb as I was the first time through. Even with my memories for comparison, I've been damnably slow on the uptake. Only here, in England, pondering my options, watching Thomson watch me, have I begun to suspect: All this time, without even realizing it, much less using it, I've graduated from merely having visions; I've been creating people out of thin air.

It's an insane idea, yes, but hell, this is war. If insanity works, a general is duty-bound to use it.

But the closer I get to that fatal car wreck in Mannheim, the harder it becomes, physically, to change things. Even an attempted change is hard; just ask that pissant Bennett. The past few weeks have made me a sick old man. But I won't sit on this rock like a puffin for a second D-Day. I won't. I'll get myself a real invasion force, or I'll die trying.

There! Wasn't that the sound of a match being struck? A rifle barrel being broken open? A letter from home being unfolded yet again? A can opener working around a hoarded snack of potted meat? A nickel being tossed into the pot? A whisper of conversation between two soldiers who can't sleep?

Whatcha thinking about?

Nothing. Home, I guess. You?

Nah. Just my girl. She's in New York.

That's home, too, I guess.

Yeah. Smoke?

Sure.

As I pass, something thrashes in the tall grass of the ditch, skips away across the road, between the tanks. I don't look to see what it is, but surely wild creatures wouldn't venture inside an active Army camp. Must be my imagination. The wind has picked up, and now I hear whispers on all sides.

Old Man
look
it's him all right
What's up?
better follow

I don't look around as I hear the footsteps behind me, first one set and then ten and then twenty and then many more, walking nearly in unison, crunching the roadway with a quiet, harsh sound.

In the center of the camp, the main road intersects three others, and their union is a wide turnabout. Here I stop. I close my eyes and ponder what to say, as the footsteps move to surround me.

Normally, on the eve of battle, I do this in the daytime, with a battery of microphones and loudspeakers and a hillside full of troops like the Sermon on the goddamn Mount. But nothing's normal about this operation, is it?

Someone coughs, and then someone else. Enough. Time to get started, or I've lost them. If an army isn't inspired, it's nothing.

"Men," I say.

Even without amplification, my voice carries. All is silent again. As I speak, I keep my eyes shut.

"You've heard what Ike and Bradley and all the pencil pushers in London and Washington say about you. They say you're not a real army. They say you're nothing but a bunch of fakers. They say there's no fight in you. You've heard all these things, and so have I."

Utter silence. They don't know what to make of this.

"But you know, and you know, soldier, and you and you and *you* know"—eyes still closed, I "look" from one soldier to the other, a surefire technique—"just as *I* know, that all that talk is nothing whatsoever but *bull*-shit."

Some whistling, a couple of cheers, applause. The wind is picking up again.

I continue: "And we all know whose opinions really matter, don't we? Who we should pay attention to? Those son-of-a-bitching Germans, that's who."

I start to pace, slowly, crouching to emphasize a point and standing upright again, then wheeling to retrace my deliberate steps. Many hours I've spent at zoos, watching panthers and other hypnotic beasts.

"That's right. Those Germans are as clever and as practical as a nest of rats, and they don't waste time with fantasies. They see the truth. When they look at you, they don't see a lot of fakers. They don't see a laughing matter. They don't see a paper army. No, they look at you, and they look into your eyes and your guts and your souls, and they see who your commander is, and do you know what they do? Do you know what they're doing right now, in Bitburg and Frankfurt and Dusseldorf and Heidelberg?"

Tell us, General

What are they doing

You tell 'em, General

"I'll *tell* you what they're doing. They're knocking their knees together and pissing in their pants and jumping headfirst into ratholes and wailing, 'Goddamn it all to hell, it's that goddamn First U.S. Army Group and that son of a bitch Patton again!' "

Laughs, shouts, applause, rushing upward like a bonfire freshly caught.

"They know we're going to come over there and kick their asses west to east for a thousand miles and hunt them down and kill every last one of them, from the first beachfront machine-gunner in France to the goddamn Fuhrer himself, hiding beneath the seat of the last upright shithouse in Berlin."

Now they're really whooping it up.

Hot damn

He can put it down there, can't he

Tell us, General, tell us

Time to quiet them down again, sober them up. I start sneaking glances at the dark and shifting shapes all around, at cigarettes glowing bright and then dimming like fireflies, at tank guns outlined by the stars.

"I know what you men are thinking. You're wondering whether you have what it takes in battle. You're wondering whether you're going to honor yourself, or disgrace yourself. Honor your country, or disgrace your country."

Mostly silent now. I can hear the faint caress of the surf.

"Well, men, I know what's going to happen to each of you, and I'll tell you in advance so that you won't have to worry any more. Each of you is going to fight, and fight, and fight, until there's no more fighting to be done."

Hell yeah!

We'll fight, sure we will

Bring 'em on

"Because you are Americans. All Americans love to fight, and you men are no different."

Goddamn, I'm out of practice. My throat's like beef. I raise my voice to be heard over the rising tide of approval.

"It is your *duty* to fight, it is your *nature* to fight, it is your *divine destiny* to fight, and it is your *pleasure* to fight, and kill, and keep fighting and killing until every last Nazi in Europe is dead. And then it's the goddamn *Nazi* army that will be a figment of the imagination, and not you, because you will have proved yourself real with your sweat and your blood and your guts."

Now I detect smells, too—shoe polish and hair tonic and C rations and Lucky Strikes and chewing gum and axle grease and old boots and freshly laundered fatigues and the pungent sweetness of gasoline and tank exhaust. I gulp the air.

"The job ahead of you, men, is the biggest job ever undertaken by an American army, the biggest job ever undertaken by any army in any war. And you are ready for it. You may not think you are ready, but I am your commanding officer, and I am here to tell you that you are. I have absolute confidence in each and every one of you to do his job and keep on doing it no matter what."

Now I'm bellowing to be heard. My knees are weak. God, how I have needed this. I step backward a few paces, grope behind for something to lean on.

"Hell, I might even feel sorry for those poor sons of bitches we're about to kill, but they brought it on themselves. Those Nazis started all this goddamn son-of-a-bitchery, and by God, you and I as Americans *are going to finish it.*"

Pandemonium. I feel the crowd surging around me, hot and close, but I still can't distinguish faces, individuals, even though my eyes are wide open. I back into something smooth and massive: a tank. I lean against it, grateful, run my hands along its flank, prick my finger on something, take a last deep breath, and raise my hands for order.

Listen up, you bastards

Listen to the General

Ten-SHUN

The racket fades into a murmur, and as I open my mouth for a final push, I focus on my smarting finger and realize—

A splinter? From a Sherman tank?

Oh, Jesus, no. Jesus God.

I close my eyes, reach behind me again. The crowd around

me, so close, so stifling, so . . . familiar. And now I smell burning pyres, the reek of longboats, blood on armor, and a thousand Shenandoah campfires.

Goddamn it, I smell the *past.* But I don't want the *past.* I don't want it! I want—

Before I can yank my hand away in fear, my fingers brush steel: cold, riveted. I lift my fingers to my nose, smell metal and oil.

I whisper, "Another chance, Papa," and I crumple to the ground. First to my knees, then sideways, no strength left to catch myself. A general gasp around me.

You OK, General?

Still with us?

He's a good one, ain't he?

He's gonna let us have it, you watch

Look at him

Here he goes

Spitting dirt, I roll over and try to lift my head. I can't see a damn thing, just spots before my eyes.

I'd like to be there when Ike gets the news. But maybe it won't be news to him anymore, this unexpected reinforcement, this change in plans, this change in destiny. Maybe, like these men, he knows the voice of command, and forgets everything that came before. Because he, like these men, is a soldier.

Somehow I manage to shout: "Men!" Then a coughing spasm hits me, and then, with my last reserves of air, I continue:

"I tell you the truth tonight when I say that you are the best army, the most dedicated army, the most American army, that I have ever had the privilege of commanding. You, my friends, are that thing so rarely seen on the face of this sorry earth—a real army! And you will continue to make me proud, and win victories, and kick German ass, until this war is over. Remember. The shortest route home is through Berlin! So follow me, men! Let's piss in the Rhine, and then go home!"

A tremendous cheer pins me to the ground, gasping, and then I hear a series of *whunts* as the floodlights go on, and I feel the light hot on my skin like a new sun. I hear a gunning of engines, a storm of voices, a rush of cracks and snaps like wildfire, as thousands of men lift their rifles, shoulder their packs, secure their gear. Above me I see only blackness, but I hear everything. Sergeants bark orders. Convoys of vehicles snort and spit exhaust as they grind past—jeeps and supply trucks and ambulances. Platoons trot alongside. Their packs rustle in unison, and the running men huff as one, like a steam engine. A deafening roar overhead: must be a bomber, low but climbing; a second one, a third. Ours. And the tanks! Nothing else like that clanking rattling trundling growl, that single file column churning the earth in a huge turtle furrow leading straight to the sea. By God, I wish I could see it. I want to whoop, to dance, to find Willie and kiss him again, but I can't even lift my head. It lolls in the damp grass. The blades prickle my cheek. I would turn over if I could. "Mims," I whisper. Why haven't any of these goddamned nincompoops picked me up, set me upright? They wouldn't dare leave without their general, start the battle without me—would they? "Mims!"

Amid the racket—now melding, tanks and trucks and guns and men, into a single featureless roar—I hear people bustle about me. Strong hands roll me over, and brisk fingers brush the grass and dirt from my face, fingers sharp and stiff as a whisk broom. Someone pants hot, rancid breath into my face, then licks my cheek. I immediately feel better. My voice sounds unnatural, raspy, as I say: "Hi, there, Willie, did you miss me? That's the boy. That's the boy."

A Yankee murmur in the background. Mims, conversing with someone.

I continue: "Now *this,* Mims, *this* looks like a goddamn *army,* wouldn't you say?"

Willie whines and rips the grass, digging in, as someone pulls him away. Thomson's voice: "Come away from there, Willie. Come here, you cur. General? General!"

I wish I could salute. "Colonel Thomson," I say.

"Bugger that," she says.

"Now, Thomson—"

"What the devil is going on here, General?" She's close to my ear, perhaps kneeling on the ground. "I demand an explanation, do you hear me? And what *is* wrong with you, Willie? Come here, then. Don't kiss me! Oh, appalling. What do you feed him, General, damned souls and fish heads?"

The longer I lie there, surrounded by the rumble of an army on the move, listening to Thomson's small struggle in the middle of a war, the more elated I feel. Can't change everything. Just ask Hitler. So, Fortitude has changed, but Thomson is still Thomson. Must be a reason for that. Must be. Interesting to find out what the hell it is.

Thomson, on the other hand, is getting madder and madder. "Oh, grin, grin, grin away, then. You Yanks are quite the grinners, aren't you? Your bloody president is positively sharklike. No, Willie, no, you can't get down, Mims will be back in a minute with a treat. Stay still, you bastard. You needn't look so amused, General, I intend to have my answers."

I no longer can distinguish the sounds of the army. Everything that isn't Thomson is just a single glorious background noise, like a violent shore, and steadily louder. "You'll have your answers," I say. "But it'll have to be en route, Colonel. I have an urgent appointment to keep. Mims!"

Thomson, who's in better voice, begins calling as well. "Damn it all. Mims! *Mims!*"

As she calls, I hear the thunder. Willie whines anew. I hear Thomson scramble to her feet, and Willie, apparently in her arms, begins to yelp in earnest. Calling Mims, Thomson fades, as if moving away, and the thunder gets louder, like a new radio show fading in and taking the place of another. This battle's begun. I squint toward the east, trying to find the first faint glimmers of the sunrise, but even the airfield looks dark to me. I picture the first wave of naval artillery hitting the ancient waterfront of Calais, twenty-one miles across the Channel. I picture the medieval watchtower slumping into the water, the bricks of the old city raining onto the cobblestones, Rodin's statue of the unhappy burghers being pounded into slag. At the end of the great siege of Calais six hundred years before, King Edward ordered me to put those burghers to the sword, then at the last minute changed his mind, told me to sheathe—

But that is in my past. Ahead of me, for the first time in many years, is my future.

"Mims!" I shout as the concussions grow louder, mimic my heartbeat. "Willie! Thomson!"

They can't hear me. Too much racket, of course. Listen to that army! By God, we've turned this sorry-ass assignment around, haven't we, Thomson? We won't be sitting out *this* invasion, no ma'am! Follow me, men! They know who their leader is. The guns are layered in cotton, pound, pound, pound. Murdering border bandits. Damn Gila monsters. I salute the jeering galleries overhead. A rotten pear bursts against my helmet. I've done my duty, you hear me, you bastards? How many of you can say the same? You don't see me getting shot, do you? The bandit looks up from the hood and grins. Look at the yellow son of a bitch, look at the crying baby. You're going to make something of yourself this time, Georgie, yes you are. Fair deal, Joe, fair deal. I can't be still, Ike, for God's sake, don't you see? You think I can be immobilized so easily? Suspended in wires with a hose in my ass and pins in my neck and a spreading brown spot on the ceiling for entertainment? I won't do it again, Ike, I won't. This is where I belong, right here, at the head of an army. That's all I want, all I've ever wanted, and I've got it. I've done it. I've won. As long as one tank is able to move it must go forward. I won't just lie here, I won't. Follow me, men. Come on! There's nothing left for you here, nothing, I tell you, but death in a ditch, and there's no one else to lead you. No one but Georgie. Follow me, men. We're out of the trenches, and moving forward. Follow me.

Afterword

Final Grade Report: Andy Duncan

ON COLD WINTER NIGHTS, I WARM MYSELF WITH the memory that Andy Duncan was once a student of mine.

My first acquaintance with Andy came when he, as writer for the Greensboro *News and Record,* reviewed my story collection *Meeting In Infinity* (available at fine bookstores almost nowhere). He liked it. In particular, he liked a story about Dr. Faustus as Groucho Marx that I had been unable to sell to any magazine—the only unsalable story in the book. It happened to be one of my favorites. I put this down to some chance moment of lunacy by an oddball reviewer, but did not give it much thought.

I first met the man himself at a North Carolina Writers' Network annual conference some time later, and he looked relatively normal. He and the friends he was hanging out with seemed to have an interest in theater, talking about some complex production they were planning, the nature of which I never quite grasped.

A year or two after that Andy enrolled in the graduate writing program where I teach at North Carolina State University. He had quit a perfectly respectable job as a journalist, the kind of career our students are eager to land, to come back and make big bucks studying *Moby Dick.* I began to wonder if there was something seriously wrong with him.

Then in the Spring of 1994 he enrolled in my graduate writing workshop, and the stories started coming in.

Anyone who has taught writing for any length of time will tell you that the best thing that can happen to a writing teacher is to have a person who is touched by the Holy Fire show up in class. It's a gift from the gods. Every day becomes a brighter day, knowing that you may find a manuscript from him or her in your mailbox. And later that afternoon, in your cluttered office, you may have a conversation with this soul so like your own but different.

But the advent of that star writer also scares you silly. The biggest responsibility a teacher has is dealing with such a student. You have to provide all the support you can, yet tell the truth. You have to challenge the writer not to take the easy way out, but not put out the fire. Most daunting of all, you must be able to tell the difference between a mistake and a breakthrough. The two worst things you can do are either to strap the student to the procrustean bed of your accumulated wisdom, or not provide any structure at all for him to shape himself against.

Andy presented this delightful challenge from day one. The first story he turned in was about a medieval Pope who was exhumed by his successor and tried for heresy. Most of the students in the workshop did not understand that it was a comedy.

Later came a historical story about the Paris theater, the Grand Guignol, complete with details about eyeballs with "more bounce!" In this one, without any bluster, Andy pulled off the near impossible technical feat of telling a coherent story, each scene of which was presented from the perspective of a different character.

Another was about Robert Johnson in Hell. Hell was exactly like the Louisiana delta. Though full of wit, this was not a comedy.

Much later, as the last story in his master's thesis, came a long and incredibly detailed novella (unfortunately not included in this collection but, as of the time I write this, soon to be published) about the man responsible for the Soviet space program, a man whose identity was so secret that for years American intelligence officers did not even know his name. They called him "the Chief Designer." His name was Sergei Korolev. Even I could see this was a major work, heroic, sincere, and in the end profoundly moving. The only problem was that it did not fit easily into any genre, and I worried that it might never find its audience.

The problem of definition—if it is a problem—arose in Andy's work from the beginning. No two of his stories were alike. Or if they were alike, they were alike only in their odd sensibility, their quirky investigation of historical backwaters, their sidewise dissection of the corners of the human soul. Their humor, their occasional gothic excess, their humanity.

Working with Andy was one of the most rewarding experiences of my almost twenty years now as a teacher at NCSU. Mostly, what I did with Andy was rack my brain to think up questions to ask him that he hadn't already asked himself, and otherwise keep the hell out of his way. I can't tell you unequivocally that I taught him anything, but damn did the boy learn! He has had many teachers before and after me—ask him about Angela Davis-Gardner or Michael Grimwood or Michael Swanwick or Howard Waldrop—and he's not done learning yet, but I have to say I hope to take all the undeserved credit I can from the fact that he once sat in my classroom.

* * *

One of the stories I had not read until I got the manuscript for this collection is "Map to the Homes of the Stars." As a way of telling you what I like about Andy's writing, let me go on a bit about this one. I'm assuming you've read the story already, so if you haven't, maybe you'd better skip this part lest I spoil your fun.

On its simplest level, this is the story of Jack, a man who is being haunted by the ghosts of his best friend Tom and of Anna, a girl from their town, both of whom disappeared more than a decade ago. The ghosts never appear on stage, but simply cruise past Jack's house in Tom's Firebird at night, evoking terror.

It's a quietly creepy ghost story. But the ghost story works only if you feel the human story lurking beneath it. The human story is about a man who is not willing or able to take a chance. We learn what Jack was like when he and Tom were seventeen years old and used to cruise the streets of their small town in that same car, past the homes and hangouts of the various pretty girls they fancied—but never had the nerve to approach.

I love the detail with which Andy evokes these boys and their town. The description of them riding bikes and talking through the long afternoons. The conviction that Tom and Jack have (I know I had it) that life is going on out there someplace else, anyplace else but here. Life happens on television, on movie screens, in New York City, in California—especially in California, to movie stars whose lives are so much brighter and more romantic than ours. Sometimes it seems like we might have a chance to grasp that glamorous life (isn't that the American dream?—in the late 20th century that's what we mean, whether we admit it or not, when we talk about "the pursuit of happiness"). At other times it seems the dream's an ungraspable phantom, forever beyond the reach of ordinary people like ourselves. Especially ourselves at age seventeen.

For a young boy, a virgin, this dream has everything to do with sex. The girl we see walking back from the tennis court every day in her short skirt is in possession of this dream, we imagine. If we could only ask her out. But that's not possible. Not for Jack, anyway.

Why not? Other guys ask girls out all the time. But Jack is not those other guys. He can't make the first step that might liberate him. As Kafka (another lonely bachelor) says in his "Letter to His Father": "It is as if one person had to climb five low steps and another person only one step, but one that is, at least for him, as high as all the other five put together; the first person will not only manage this five, but hundreds and thousands more as well, he will have led a great and very strenuous life, but none of the steps he has climbed will have been of such importance to him as for the second person that one, first, high step, that step which it is impossible for him to climb even by exerting all his strength, that step which he cannot get up on and which he naturally cannot get past either."

Tom and Anna, when they leave town, manage to climb that first step. And they are never heard from again.

That's what Jack is afraid of. The ghosts that cruise in front of Jack's house are the ghosts of what he might have done. He might have broken the rules—sexual, social, racial—by which he has been constrained. Of course, when you break rules you put yourself at risk. You swivel around on the wooden bench, you might get splinters. You leave home and you might end up dead, like Tom and Anna. But as you get older the fact that you never tried begins to kill you all by itself, only more slowly.

The strength, subtlety and economy with which Andy realizes this idea floors me. Read the story a second time and notice the numerous sly illustrations of this town's repressions, and Jack's desperation. At Christmas, drive once around the block, and sexy Cynthia handing out candy canes is replaced by good Christian Mr. Thompson handing out comic books about Hell. It is absolutely impossible even to contemplate dating a black girl. "I'm just sitting here," Jack says. In the very first paragraph, Jack stands in his kitchen in the middle of the night eating something "stale and cool." He reads the movie ads in the newspaper "just to reassure myself that everything I had skipped in the spring wasn't worth the trouble anyway." *Yes.* This is Jack's life. And it is precisely as he has this thought, reaffirming his inertia, that he hears the car coming to take him to life, or to death. To California. Or Hell. If he can muster the nerve.

* * *

Some of my favorite moments from Andy Duncan stories:

* * *

"Are you a man who appreciates amusements, then?"—The droll wit in every line of that sexy divertissement "The Premature Burials."

* * *

"Hell's about full."—The moment in the first scene of "Beluthahatchie" where the voice of the old woman calling out for Jesus is cut off in mid-word.

* * *

"Not just game acceptance with a hint of weariness, but something downright wise and tragic as well."—In "Fenneman's Mouth," the implicit parallel between the video synthesis of events that did not happen, and people's subjective memories of their interpersonal relations—which turns a comedy into a personal statement.

* * *

"Stress? Love? Syphilis? Who can say?"—Just about everything in "Grand Guignol."

* * *

"But as the years pass by, my ears get better."—The loving, leisurely portrait of 1930's radio in "Liza and the Crazy Water Man."

* * *

"Private Angelo slid down the crumbling slope on top of Papa, then crawled through him and leaned over me, examining my eyes and face."—In "Fortitude," the overlapping actions of Angelo and Patton in the shell hole, and Patton's conversation with the ghost of his father.

* * *

"I'm talking to the man what's come to kill me. You see anyone else here that wants to do it?"—In that ambiguous epic of ordinary Americans perpetuating the age-old custom of capital punishment, "The Executioners' Guild," the fact that the phone begins ringing in the middle of the execution. And the reason for that call.

* * *

I wish I had written all of these, and am damn proud to know the man who did.

* * *

Those of you who have been lucky enough to meet him know that in person, as much as on the page, Andy Duncan has the Southerner's gift for words. When he wants to, he can crank up a South Carolina accent as broad as the Piedmont, and those Northerners who automatically assume anyone with a southern drawl lacks twenty IQ points are ripe for a plucking. Andy has a few stories to tell. If you stop by the Duncan residence for a brief word with him, don't leave your car running and a quart of ice cream on the front seat.

Had he been born in the nineteenth century, I imagine Andy might have found himself at home in some dry goods store or print shop, idling away the afternoon gossiping about the town eccentrics (of whom he would be the prime example)—if you will allow a small town rustic an anthropologist's interest in UFO cults and the life of the waitress and medieval history and the European avant garde. And in the alternate history where Andy was born in 1835 instead of 1964, if he'd managed not to get himself killed in the Civil War, I can easily imagine him striking up an acquaintance with another backwoods eccentric with an active mind, a guy named Sam Clemens from Missouri who wrote, "If I'd a knowed what a trouble it was to make a book I wouldn't a tackled it."

Here's one reader who's glad both of them did.

John Kessel
Raleigh, North Carolina
February 2000

Author Notes

"FROM ALFANO'S RELIQUARY." ONE WINTER DAY in Raleigh, North Carolina, in 1993, I dropped by my friend Elise Hooper's house and found her standing on a chair in front of a wall of crowded bookcases. "I read this the other day," she said, "and thought of you." She handed me *The Oxford Dictionary of Popes,* her index finger indicating a couple of hair-raising paragraphs on the infamous "Cadaver Synod," in which Pope Stephen had Pope Formosus's exhumed corpse placed on trial.

"Wow!" I said.

"Yeah, isn't that *cool?*" she said. "You should write a story about that."

That Christmas break, I wrote the first draft of the story during a weekend, most of it in a single sitting. I had written stories before (bad ones), but this was the first time I sat down and started writing without an outline, without any preconceived ideas whatsoever. Well, I take that back, I had *one* idea: That the narrator of the story should be the poor sap whose duty it was to guard the corpse during trial. The first paragraph I wrote was the first paragraph of the story. I sat back, read it aloud, and laughed. I asked myself, "Where did *that* come from?" Obviously, this narrator was no "poor sap"! But I continued typing in the same vein, just to see what would happen. It was a voice piece, from beginning to end, and what little plot it had, evolved from that voice.

With some trepidation, given the voice and subject matter, I brought the story to my graduate fiction workshop when it convened in January. Since it was my only new story, I couldn't very well *not* bring it in. But I had terrible jitters the day my story was slated for discussion, especially since this was my first class with a teacher whose fiction I much admired but who otherwise was an unknown quantity to me: John Kessel.

My jitters did not lessen as my classmates took their turns talking about my story, five minutes each. My story had polarized the class. A third of my classmates loved it, thought it was simultaneously horrifying and hilarious, said they had read it aloud to friends and roommates. (One of these supporters, I remember, was Cynthia Killough, who became one of my best friends that day!) Another third of the class was mystified by the story—dumbfounded by the apparently dead narrator, first of all, uncertain whether it was supposed to be funny, frustrated by the archaic tone and the many obscure words, from *reliquary* onward. (One student said: "I can't imagine any editor taking a chance on a story by an unknown writer that's this hard to read.") And the final third of the class was *outraged,* demanded to know just what I had against Catholicism, against religion, against God, etc., that I would write such a thing?

Now, these three schools of thought were not reflected in the seating arrangement, of course, so as the discussion proceeded clockwise around the table, I experienced quite a roller-coaster ride of varying opinion. A few quarrels broke out, as people interrupted one another with challenges and questions. And through all this sat John Kessel, his face unreadable, making an occasional note on his legal pad, calling time when necessary, and never *once* looking at me. By the time it was his turn to speak, I was a wreck. There was a long moment of silence as all eyes turned to Kessel, all sides awaiting his pronouncement.

Kessel made a final note, cleared his throat, and said, "I think this is a terrific story." He proceeded to echo everything positive that had been said, and added some points of his own. Then he picked up the legal pad and said, "There were a lot of objections raised, and perceived problems, that aren't really problems, and that Andy doesn't need to worry about at all. Among them—" He proceeded to dismiss *every criticism* that had been aired in the past hour, checking each one off as he went down the list.

Before that class, I had many doubts about whether I really wanted to be a fiction writer. But as I left that class, barely able to walk, I *knew* that was what I wanted to be. Whether they had liked the story or not, I had stirred those people *up!* I had affected them—and the teacher had said that was OK! Imagine.

Kessel was tougher on me in private conference, and rightly so, pointing out that the story wasn't finished yet. He asked me a chilling and unforgettable question, one I have asked myself countless times since: "So what is this story *about*, *other* than the caperings of fools?" Once we were done talking about "Alfano," Kessel started demanding to know what I was working on next, and pulling books off the shelves that I "really ought to read." Six years later, he's still demanding to know what the next project is, still telling me to read stuff, and I hope he never stops. I am forever in his debt.

I cherish "Alfano" because it was my introduction to Kessel, because it was my first story to take on a sort of willful, independent life even as I wrote it, because it was the submission story that got me accepted into the Clarion West writers' workshop in Seattle in summer 1994, and finally because it was rejected by seventeen different editors over the course of five years before Darrell Schweitzer, bless him, gave it a home in *Weird Tales*. Advice to writers: Never, never, never give up.

Besides all those named above, I thank Nancy Kress, who at Clarion West rightly pointed out that the whole story need not be an expository lecture—that there *was* room for dialogue, action, even, what the hey, a fully dramatized *scene* or two, something—*anything*—other than the intoxicating sound of my own prose. I do my best to remember this, Nancy, but it's hard!

* * *

"Beluthahatchie." This story began in one of my graduate classes at North Carolina State University: Short Story Form & Theory, taught by Angela Davis-Gardner. Each student was required to do a presentation on the technique of one short-story writer. I don't remember what writer I picked, but one of my classmates picked Zora Neale Hurston—whom I never had read—and specifically Hurston's "Story in Harlem Slang," accompanied by Hurston's own glossary. That glossary, drawing upon African-American folklore much older than 1920s Harlem, included several vividly named suburbs of Hell, the most vivid, to my mind, being Beluthahatchie. My first thought was, "I've read a lot of stories set in Hell, but never one set in Beluthahatchie."

Months passed, during which I toyed with various terrible ideas for a story set in Beluthahatchie and titled "Beluthahatchie." At one point, I decided to write the story of a boundary dispute between the sleepy suburb of Beluthahatchie and the bustling city of Hell, and wasted time looking into the intricacies of annexation law before blessedly losing interest. My salvation, if I may use that word in this context, began when I started researching African-American folklore about Hell, figuring I needed to know a lot more than a list of place names. This research led me to the folktales of the slave John and his owner, Old Massa, who forever played cruel tricks on one another, united only in rascality and in mutual terror of the Devil. My research also led me to the Lake of the Dead, a myth apparently widespread in my homeland of central South Carolina that I, growing up white, had never heard. But most crucially, my research into African-American visions of Hell led me to the songs of the late Delta blues artist Robert Johnson—and once I realized my suburb-of-Hell story also needed to be a Robert Johnson story, all the story's main elements clicked into place in my head. (I'm glad I didn't know then, as I know now, that enough fantasy stories about Robert Johnson have been written in recent years to fill an anthology; I might well have abandoned the idea, assuming it had "been done." Advice to writers: It's never been done, until *you* do it.)

I didn't attempt to write the story down until several months later, during the first week of the six-week Clarion West writers' workshop in Seattle in summer 1994. We were expected to write a story a week, and I had come prepared, with a suitcase full of notes. What made me turn to "Beluthahatchie" first was, I am ashamed to admit, spite. During the first day or two of the workshop, one of the manuscripts we discussed was a fine Devil story, set in the Louisiana bayou, by my classmate, Syne Mitchell. One of our classmates, I forget whom, announced that he/she was prejudiced against Devil stories, was in fact heartily sick of Devil stories, hoped indeed never to read another Devil story in her/his life. I thought, "Well, you'll read ONE more, like it or not."

I went back to my dorm room and started the draft of "Beluthahatchie" that very afternoon, banging away on the typewriter I had borrowed upon arrival from Eileen Gunn. (My computer hadn't arrived yet.) I found out later that my start-and-stop typing at all hours of day and night, loud enough to be heard up and down the dormitory corridor, drove many of my classmates nuts—though they were too polite, that first week, to say so. But Eileen had told me this was a Lucky Typewriter, on which she had written her first published stories, and so my hopes were high.

Flash forward to the following January, and the registration table at Chattacon '95, a science-fiction convention in Chattanooga, Tennessee. Standing in line near me was one of my Clarion West teachers, Michael Swanwick, whom I greeted happily.

"Hello," Michael said, "and congratulations."

"Congratulations on what?" I asked.

"Gardner is buying your story," Michael said.

I had submitted "Beluthahatchie" to Gardner Dozois at *Asimov's* months earlier, but had heard nothing. Sure enough, I came home from Chattanooga to find Gardner's acceptance letter waiting for me. It was my first fiction sale.

Three years later, the membership of the World Science Fiction Convention named "Beluthahatchie" a finalist for the Hugo Award for Best Short Story of the year. And now it's the title story of this, my first book. A lucky typewriter indeed, Eileen!

While I'm acknowledging people, I should note that of all the comments I received on the story at Clarion West, the most helpful were Syne Mitchell's exhortations to work in as much of the applicable legendry and folklore as possible—to make the story, in short, Mythic with a capital M. "If you don't take Syne's advice," Eric S. Nylund said at the time, "then you're a fool." Eric and Syne are married now; how could she resist?

A final note: People ask me where my idea of the Devil came from. It mostly came from the late actors Dub Taylor and Strother Martin—check out *Bonnie and Clyde* and *Cool Hand Luke,* respectively. But when I read his lines aloud, I sound a lot like Strom Thurmond, whose South Carolina hometown is about a half-hour's drive from mine. As my grandmother would say about a family likeness: I get it honest.

* * *

"Grand Guignol." I wrote the first draft of this the second week of Clarion West, by which time my computer had arrived—shipped UPS from Raleigh by my long-suffering friend Lynn Chandler, who also had packed my suitcase and poured me into the airplane. (Me? Nervous? True, very, very dreadfully nervous I had been and am; but why will you say that I am mad?)

For all its Gothic trappings, I view this story (eventually published in *Weird Tales*) as my love letter to community theater in Greensboro, North Carolina, in which I was happily involved, mostly as an actor, for several years in the late '80s and early '90s. My two big roles were the Devil in *Damn Yankees* and Pulver in

Mister Roberts. (A friend said I got "all the wandering-asshole roles.") I long had wanted to draw on that experience by writing a backstage comedy; I also long had wanted to write a story set in Paris, a city I fell in love with in 1991, while my friend Barry Johnson lived there. But it was in a secondhand bookstore in Norfolk, Virginia, that I ran across Mel Gordon's fascinating book *Grand Guignol,* a history of that weird little theater, which finally triggered the idea for the story.

The multiple-narrator structure was inspired, again, by spite; someone at Clarion West announced that whereas a novel could have several narrators, a short story could have only one, and I wrote on my legal pad: "Says who?"

For all my weeks of wandering around Paris, the only landmark that wound up in the story was Pere Lachaise, which I haunted nearly as obsessively as Andre. The lunch Andre eats in the cemetery was my own, right down to the woman in crepe.

Finally, the scene in which Charles wakes and pads through the apartment, only to have his erotic reverie shockingly interrupted, is a verbatim description of the most vivid nightmare I ever had, a nightmare that was all the more scary because I had it during the day, while I was awake—in fact, while taking a shower. Make of that what you will.

* * *

"Liza and the Crazy Water Man." I wrote the first complete draft of this story in my third and fourth weeks at Clarion West, but the idea had been with me for a while. That previous New Year's Eve, while I waited in line with friends in front of the Terrace Theater in the Friendly Shopping Center in Greensboro, North Carolina —the movie we had come to see being *Shadowlands,* based on the life of C. S. Lewis—the conversation turned to folk music in general and Appalachian music in particular, and how so much has been lost despite the best efforts of the archivists and preservationists. I don't remember whether the crucial sentence was vocalized by me or by another, but I do remember that as I bought my ticket and took my seat my conversation had become absent-minded, because I kept turning over in my head the sentence: "Not everything can be recorded." By the time I left the theater, I had the story's premise: During the first wave of field recording, in the 1930s, a singer appears in the mountains whose voice is so good that it literally can't be recorded; it will die with her. (Whether the movie, as it unfolded, affected my thinking, I don't know; I should watch it again, and look for clues.) That the singer could be a *man* never occurred to me, perhaps because most lost culture, alas, is female culture (see Alice Walker's "In Search of Our Mothers' Gardens"), but perhaps for more chauvinistic reasons as well; that a *woman* be rendered thus voiceless simply seemed more poignant to me.

My research for this story was easy, because I had a very specific time and place in mind. The North Carolina Division of Cultural Resources recently had sponsored a celebration in Charlotte of the city's nearly forgotten country-music heritage, reuniting many old-time performers for whom Charlotte had been a home base in the 1930s. I hadn't attended, but my friend Barry Johnson had, and told me all about it. I also had a copy of *The Charlotte Country Music Story,* a wonderful historical booklet, rich with text and illustrations, that Cultural Resources had published in commemoration of the event. (When you're a features writer for a daily newspaper, as I was for four years, you receive all sorts of interesting stuff in the mail; I'll be drawing ideas from that mail for years to come.) The place being obvious, I settled on 1936 for various reasons, partially because I knew I could use the presidential election, partially because I wanted a cameo appearance by the Monroe Brothers, who were the toast of Charlotte at the time; the act would break up soon thereafter, and Bill would go on to Nashville, to become the founder of bluegrass music, while Charlie would go on— well, perhaps into another story of mine, yet to be written. We'll see.

Place and date decided upon, I simply went through every illustrated book of Charlotte history that I could lay my hands on, and jotted down reams of notes. When I wrote the story, I made use, no lie, of *every single note.* This is hardly the recommended working method of any writer, much less a fiction writer—I remember the late newspaper editor Irwin Smallwood used to say, "The better the stuff left in the notebook, the better the story"—but in this case the obsessive layering of local color seems to have paid off. So while all my main characters are, of course, fictional, almost all the bit players—Mr. Tate the barber, Crutchfield the announcer, the Kokenes family at the Star Lunch, the staff of the Charlotte *News*—should be familiar names to anyone who lived in Charlotte in the 1930s. I did not make up the story about Mayor Douglas and the airplane, nor about Mr. Jennings saving his bank single-handed. Except for Grove Keener and the Carolina Cavaliers, all the bands and songs named are actual bands and songs of Charlotte, circa 1936. Johnny Mack Brown really did sign autographs at the State Theater, the Canary Cottage really was the cheapest good eats in town, and so on and so on. Various people have called this story "magic realism," and while I can't vouch for the magic, it's certainly the most realistic story I ever wrote. It's historical fiction, with a bit of propelling weirdness at the core.

Although "Beluthahatchie" was my first fiction sale, "Liza" my second, "Liza" actually was published first, in Patrick Nielsen Hayden's acclaimed anthology *Starlight 1*—which went on to win the World Fantasy Award. I couldn't have asked for better company. I'm grateful to Patrick, and to Beth Meacham, who talked me into overnighting the "Liza" manuscript to Patrick on the eve of his deadline. I often need help helping myself.

* * *

"Saved" and "The Map to the Homes of the Stars." I think of these stories as a pair because they were written back to back, submitted together, and published together. In fall 1996, I received a letter from Gardner Dozois that said he was editing a sequel to his 1995 anthology *Killing Me Softly: Erotic Tales of Unearthly Love*. His deadline was approximately yesterday, and did I have any unpublished stories on hand involving sex and ghosts? I wrote him back immediately, confessing that I had two such stories on hand and was working on the third. (Make of this what you will, but I *am* Southern.) Did Gardner want these stories submitted one at a time, or all at once? All at once, he replied; time is short! I hurriedly finished the story I was working on and mailed Gardner all three, and he bought, to my astonishment, *two* of them—with some sage rewrite advice on both, which I happily followed to the letter. And so both "Saved" and "The Map to the Homes of the Stars" appeared in *Dying for It: More Erotic Tales of Unearthly Love*. My mother hid her copy.

"The Map to the Homes of the Stars" is my most autobiographical story to date. I drew upon my teenage years in my hometown of Batesburg, South Carolina, for ten percent of it and made up the rest, so my friends from back then should recognize some of the local color. In hindsight I see that I was one of the kids like Tom and Anna, who blew town and never came back, though hardly in so dramatic a fashion. Many of the folks I went to high school with are still in Batesburg; what both stayers and goers gained and lost is endlessly poignant to contemplate. The first scene I wrote, with no idea where I was going, was the scene of the Christmas lights. In finding the story I wanted to tell, I was inspired by my favorite Stephen King story, "Mrs. Todd's Shortcut," which has the same structure—the guy who stayed behind telling the story of the guy and the girl who didn't—and which also has a car in the middle. This is my favorite story to read aloud, perhaps because the voice is so close to my own. But perhaps, too, because my reading of the climactic scene, at one of Cynthia Killough's parties in Raleigh in summer 1996, was my first experience of trying out new material on a live audience and knowing, from the opening lines, that I really *had* them—a heady feeling! Finally, as I have in the past, I dedicate this story to one of my longest-suffering friends from Batesburg, Richard O'Malley, whose Firebird it was, and who happily is still on the map.

"Saved" was a very different project, springing from two related fascinations. First of all, I'm determined, one day, to translate the peculiar, unearthly *feel* of a silent movie into prose. "Saved" represents my first attempt at this, but not my last. Secondly, thanks in part to Frank Thompson's wonderful book *Lost Films: Important Movies That Disappeared,* I'm fascinated by the movies (like *Saved from the Titanic*) that to the best of our knowledge no longer exist—I mean literally, in the sense of no copy is known to survive. All that's left are participants' recollections, contemporary reviews, stills, press kits, and so on: the stuff of scrapbooks, the stuff of folklore, the stuff of fiction. "Saved" will not be my last dip into *that* trove of material, either. The lost *Titanic* film that intrigues me is not Dorothy Gibson's but the Pathe newsreel that was filmed during the voyage and that presumably went down with the ship; "Saved" springs from my idea to conflate the two. I know next to nothing about the real Dorothy Gibson, though I admire her industry in getting her *Titanic* movie released a month to the day after the sinking; as Frank Thompson observes, she must have driven from the pier directly to the studio. For this reason, my original conception of the character Dorothy was a ruthless opportunist. As I wrote her, of course, beginning with the story's first scene, she became something else entirely.

I can't speak for the other contributors, but many people have teased me about the packaging of the *Dying for It* anthology. One of my students, for example, was much impressed by the front cover claim of "today's most seductive authors." "Did you know," she announced in class one day, "that our teacher is one of today's most seductive authors?" (No one did.) But I get the most grief about the one-line summary of "Saved" as a story about a guy who "can only get it up on a ship that's going down." As I regaled a crowd at a science-fiction convention with this deathless line, the great fiction writer Terry Bisson—who free-lances as a writer of jacket blurbs—spoke up: "Yeah, I wrote that line. Isn't it *great?*"

* * *

"The Premature Burials." This story began as an updated rewrite of "The Three Snake-Leaves," one of the more obscure fairy tales collected by the Brothers Grimm. In "The Three Snake-Leaves," as in my story, a beautiful but strange princess makes the outrageous demand of all her suitors that they be buried with her upon her death, whether they're dead or not. This demand turns all her suitors away save one brave soul, who gambles that the princess' imminent death is unlikely, but who soon finds that he chose poorly. This seemed a very 19th-century story to me, given that century's fascination with premature burials and resurrection men.

The sex, too, seems appropriate, because "The Three Snake-Leaves" is a pretty sexy story, overtly and covertly. For example, the prince is rescued by a talking snake that wriggles into his tomb and—well, never mind. The second draft of "The Premature Burials" had more sex, added so I could submit it to an erotic-horror anthology Paula Guran was editing. Guran said it didn't fit her anthology, but she'd happily take it for the electronic magazine *Gothic.Net*—if I'd cut out some of the sex. Such is the life of the free-lancer. (In fact, this book is the first print publication of this story.)

As if the Brothers Grimm weren't enough to grapple with, I also found myself, during the writing of this story, re-reading a lot of Poe—hence the title. The name "Preble" I got from James Thurber's macabre short story "Mr. Preble Gets Rid of His Wife," another comedy of collaborative domestic gravedigging. I enjoyed telling friends that I was writing an Edgar Allan Poe-James Thurber-Brothers Grimm pastiche. None seemed surprised.

The first draft of the story was a third again as long, because I somehow was determined to drag the Fox sisters into it. The Fox sisters were the supposedly spook-haunted siblings in New York state whose claims, since discredited, launched the 19th-century spiritualism craze in the United States. So I had the Prebles communicating to Sterne via the Fox sisters, and on and on, until I finally realized that the Prebles' story had ended way back in the cemetery. (This may seem obvious to most of you, but in my experience, the death of a main character seldom ends his usefulness.)

Trivia: The wrought-iron cemetery gate with the peculiar motto actually exists. It's the gate to the Wisconsin cemetery where August Derleth, founder of Arkham House publishers, is buried. Maybe this story really is a Poe-Thurber-Grimm-Derleth pastiche. I hope not.

* * *

"Fortitude." In the marvelous and harrowing future-war story "The Quaker Cannon" by Frederik Pohl and C. M. Kornbluth—which John Kessel thrust at me one day and, rightly, told me to read—there is a glancing mention of Patton's role in that triumph of World War II espionage code-named Fortitude. This massive counterintelligence campaign was designed to blind Hitler to the true D-Day site, Normandy, by convincing him that the true invasion would be a landing by Patton at Calais. The deception worked: Even hours into D-Day, Hitler remained convinced Normandy was a mere feint for the *real* invasion. As a history buff since childhood, I knew about Fortitude, but not until reading "The Quaker Cannon"—perhaps because it's a disturbing story in its own right—did I find myself disturbed by Patton's role in it: humiliated, ignored, shunted aside, exiled to the English countryside as the dummy commander of a fake army. My immediate thought was: "Boy, did they pick the wrong person for *that* duty." Patton had been (in my opinion) crazy for years, and was a dangerous man in any circumstances, but to humiliate him in the particular way that Fortitude did must have been akin to chunking a rock into a hornets' nest, or goading a bull elephant to charge.

For weeks after reading "The Quaker Cannon," I was haunted by an image: Patton standing on the seashore, gazing across the Channel, quite mad and utterly alone but for powers and principalities of the air, straining to hear, to will into audibility, not the surf, but the walls of Calais being pounded into the dust—as a sort of berserk fulfillment of his "duty." For all its length and complexity and alternate-history game-playing, "Fortitude" is ultimately my attempt to write Patton into that scene of madness.

Ironic, then, that so many people demand to know what's going on at the end of the story! (I sometimes feel like Bill Murray's avant-garde playwright in *Tootsie*: "I saw your play. What happened?") I re-wrote the ending many times, trying at each pass to get deeper and deeper into my fictional Patton's head, because by then, of course, all his universe has contracted into a single burning pinpoint of will somewhere behind and between the general's cold eyes. When I finally was so far in that I feared not being able to climb out again, I quit re-writing and called it done, and my partner, Sydney—who felt she had been living with Patton for many months—was vastly relieved. This story took a lot out of both of us.

While my Patton is a fictional character, much of what he does, sees, and thinks is inspired by the real-life Patton, whose daily world was more bizarre by far than any I could invent. During World War I, for example, Patton did claim to have seen his ancestors in the sky on the battlefield, and to have been visited by the ghost-in-life of his far-distant father. His claim of total recall of countless past lives, all militaristic, is well known. The movie *Patton* barely scratches the surface of all this; to those interested in the real Patton, as opposed to fictional ones, I highly recommend Carlo D'Este's masterful biography *Patton: A Genius for War*. (The real Patton looked like Max von Sydow, not George C. Scott, and had a squeaky voice.)

I might add that at the back of my mind throughout the writing of this story was Brian Aldiss' remark, at one of the International Conferences on the Fantastic, that he never had read a convincing fictional characterization of a general. I don't know whether this qualifies, but I tried.

Finally, I must thank Sydney, who read each very long draft of this story and offered wise counsel each time; Shawna McCarthy, who braved the wrath of the castle-horse-and-unicorn crowd by publishing this in *Realms of Fantasy*; Scott Edelman, who suggested I send it to Shawna in the first place; and the attendees of the 1997 Sycamore Hill Writers' Conference, whose suggestions, observations, and (good-natured) howls of protest helped me make the story much more coherent than it otherwise would have been.

At ease!

* * *

"The Executioners' Guild." This story also began at North Carolina State, in a Faulkner seminar taught by Mike Grimwood—which remains, incidentally, the best literature class I ever had. Among many other assignments, we were sent to the library to roam among magazines of the Depression era, researching the social context in which Faulkner wrote his most celebrated stories and novels. Fresh from the library one day, a classmate—I believe it was Mick Philp—told me, "I found something that made me think of you."

In my experience, a statement like that always portends a discussion of something really bizarre (see "From Alfano's Reliquary," above). This was no exception. What Mick had found was a Depression-era article about a professional executioner in Mississippi who hauled a portable electric chair from town to town in the back of a truck. Mick was right, of course; I was enthralled, and demanded to see the article.

"Sorry, I didn't make a copy," Mick said. "And no, I can't really remember where I saw it, either. I just stumbled across it on my way to something else, but I'm sure you can find it easily, if you look."

Well, I looked, but I didn't find it easily. I didn't find it at all. I spent months looking for solid information on this remarkable individual, without success. (All I found was mention of a 1970 movie starring Stacy Keach, *The Traveling Executioner,* which I still haven't seen.) Then I mostly gave up, but at conventions and parties for years afterward, whenever I was among writers or other connoisseurs of odd information, I asked whether anyone ever had heard of this portable electric chair.

Finally, someone had. It was in 1997, at a party during the first Slipstream Conference at LaGrange College in Georgia. When I asked my inevitable question, Kathleen Ann Goonan looked thoughtful and said, "That rings a bell. I can't remember why, but it does." A few days later, she mailed me a couple of Xeroxed pages from *Worse than Slavery: Parchman Farm and the Ordeal of Jim Crow Justice,* by David M. Oshinsky; huzzah, there was a passage about the portable chair and a footnote directing me, at long last, to the *American Mercury* article Mick had stumbled across years before. The article turned out to be a condescending but ultimately somewhat inspiring portrait of a drunken idler with a shady past who found, in this highly unusual job, not just a steady income, but a shot at redemption. So there was one of my main characters, ready-made and waiting for me.

Now, during all this time, while waiting for Kathy Goonan to come along, I had done *some* work myself, and unearthed a lot of interesting lore about executions in the first half of the 20th century. I was especially fascinated by a short 1930s profile in *Time* magazine of the mysterious and mild-mannered Mr. Ellis, the longtime official hangman of Canada, who supposedly was the latest in a long line of Mr. Ellises, the name being a sort of job title. I found out much later that the article got many facts wrong, but never mind—it set my imagination racing. And to put the old veteran hangman in the same story as the young rookie electrocutioner seemed absolutely right to me. So there were my two main characters: Now all I needed was a plot or, better yet, a theme. A conflict between the old ways and the new ways, certainly, but what else?

I found my *what else* in an astonishing book, *Agent of Death: The Memoirs of an Executioner,* by Robert G. Elliott (Dutton, 1940). Elliott had been the longtime executioner of New York state; he finished the manuscript on his deathbed. Plainly and often clumsily written, without a hint of artifice, the book is an unforgettable document, by turns hair-raising, darkly hilarious, thought-provoking, and moving. Besides all the expected stuff—"How I began," "Murderers I have known," "How the electric chair works," etc.—the book also is full of Elliott's protestations that he really is a quite normal person; to prove this point, he includes photos of his family, describes games he played with his small children, and so on. He devotes a chapter to excerpts from the thousands of letters he received through the years, which range from savage condemnations to equally savage howls of encouragement, from sadistically detailed fantasies of alternate methods of execution to prayers for his soul and offers to become his assistant—many people apparently being willing to work without pay, just for the ecstasy of pulling the switch. And most remarkably of all, Elliott explains, at considerable length, his reasons for believing that the death penalty *serves no legitimate purpose whatsoever* and should be abolished—and explains further why, believing as he did, he nevertheless continued executing people, month after month, year after year. The short answer is that the executions would have proceeded with or without him; better, Elliott reasoned, that these unfortunate wretches be dispatched by *him,* a dispassionate and humane professional, than by someone careless, or hate-filled, or sadistic. It is not an exaggeration to say that in this man's elaborate system of self-justification, executions were a form of *ministry* to the condemned. When I finally put the book down I sat in my armchair, shaken, and stared into space for an hour or more. Among my thoughts: How many other executioners felt, *feel,* this way? View the job as a sort of priestly duty? Suppose they *all* did—were *required* to feel this way, as a requirement of membership in—what? The union? The guild?

Somewhere during all this, Sydney and I took a field trip to the courthouse square of Philadelphia, Mississippi, because I knew the portable chair had visited it, and because I knew a bit of Philadelphia's history of lynchings, before and during the civil-rights era. I had that square, and its Confederate monument, in mind as I wrote, although my fictional Andalusia is really a lot of towns, alas.

After that, all that was left was to write the damn thing. But while I did, I read Stephen King's *The Green Mile,* to make sure I wasn't re-inventing the wheel, and after I was done with my story I read Faulkner's *Intruder in the Dust,* for the same reason. I already had read Harper Lee's *To Kill a Mockingbird*—hasn't everybody?

Nearly all the proper names in the story are names associated with the history of executions—Tyburn, Blackburn, Woodham, etc. I'm ridiculously proud of that.

The first, even longer draft of the story included, between chapters, quotes from the letters Mr. Ellis had received through the years. The invaluable Gardner Dozois, in helping me rewrite the story for *Asimov's,* advised me to lose those and add other things. I am thus indebted to Gardner for the cherry jawbreaker, and much else, including the longest and funniest acceptance letter of my career to date.

I finished this story on the day Karla Faye Tucker was murdered in Texas.

* * *

"Lincoln in Frogmore." In summer 1995, the North Carolina Museum of Art, five minutes' drive from my Raleigh apartment, housed a wonderful touring exhibit curated by the New Orleans Museum of Art. It was titled "Passionate Visions of the American South: Self-Taught Artists from 1940 to the Present," and I could not stay away from it. I kept going back to the museum, week after week, whenever I could spare an hour, just to sit and stare at the works of Howard Finster, Mose Tolliver, Jessie and Ronald Cooper, Jimmy Lee Sudduth, Clementine Hunter, and the dozens of other artists represented, all of whom were new to me. (If these names are new to you, too, and even if they aren't, I highly recommend the catalog of that exhibition, published by the University Press of Mississippi.) I found it as inspirational, for the writing I wanted to do, as the Clarion West workshop had been the previous summer. My head has been filled with the images, the voices of that exhibit ever since, and they have influenced my writing in a host of ways. Yet "Lincoln in Frogmore," written more than four years later, and published here for the first time, is my first story directly inspired by one of those works I first saw in Raleigh in summer 1995.

The painting "Lincoln at Frogmore" is by the late Sam Doyle (1906–1985), a native of St. Helena Island, South Carolina. For a living, he toted boxes at a wholesalers' in Beaufort, and worked in the Marine-base laundry at Parris Island, but he rightly considered his chief occupation to be painting. His canvases were large sheets of roofing tin that he propped against the outside wall of his house, and his paints were enamel or latex house paints. Once he was done with a painting he'd leave it propped up in the yard; it was a yard full of art. Doyle painted what he remembered of life on old St. Helena, he painted family and friends, he painted scenes of local folklore, and he painted his heroes—Joe Louis, Jackie Robinson, Ray Charles, Jack and Bobby Kennedy. And at age 76, on a 6-foot-by-3-foot window shade, he painted Lincoln.

"Lincoln at Frogmore" depicts a hatless, gray-faced Lincoln, dressed in a natty black suit with tails, standing beneath a tree, his arms uplifted in praise or exhortation, and preaching—yes, *preaching* is the only possible word—to a flock of black people, perhaps children, all of whom look like Pygmies beside the mighty figure of Lincoln. The deep blue sky against which Lincoln is framed is an isolated pool in an otherwise somber palette of dark greens, grays, browns, and the jet-black slash of Lincoln's suit; it's easy to miss, at first viewing, the bright red eerie glow of Lincoln's eyes.

It's a mysterious painting, made more so by Doyle's explanation of it. At the time of the Civil War, Doyle's father was a free black man, a former slave, living among other free blacks in the St. Helena Island town of Frogmore. When little Sam came along decades later, his father told him that President Lincoln himself had come to Frogmore during the war on a secret mission, an attempt to persuade Sam's father and the other free black men to enlist in the Union forces.

One wonders to what extent Sam Doyle believed this story. It spoke to him on some level, though, else he wouldn't have painted it. The final result is ambivalent: Doyle's somber, red-eyed Lincoln might be preaching hellfire as easily as salvation. The onlookers seem wary to me, and rightly so. All this is reason enough for the painting to haunt the memory, but to think that Doyle painted it on a window shade! Pull the shade, and there's Lincoln, preaching. Raise the shade, and there's a window to—what? What takes Lincoln's place?

In this painting, Doyle captured, I think, the essential creepiness of folklore, even the family folklore we grow up with, its tendency to pose disturbing questions and leave them unanswered. I hope some of that creepiness is in my story, too, and I hope Sam Doyle would have liked it.

Historical notes for the Civil War buffs (you know who you are): I set Lincoln's visit in winter 1864–65, in the weeks after the fall of Savannah, because that was a portentous time in the Low Country (as Shad correctly recalls) and because a parade of Union dignitaries, including Secretary of War Stanton, visited Savannah in the wake of Sherman's triumph, so why not Lincoln, too? Because of the timing, I based Lincoln's speech/sermon on his December 1864 message to Congress on the progress of the war. The joke my Lincoln tells Shad about the tar-and-feathering is a joke the real Lincoln loved, and told on several occasions. (Assuming, of course, that it *is* a joke.) And yes, the real Lincoln loved electrical storms. You can look it up.

* * *

"Fenneman's Mouth." This story occurred to me while I was washing dishes one Sunday. Later that afternoon, I sketched the outline on a legal pad while waiting for Sydney to meet me at Subs 'n' You in Tuscaloosa, one of the world's great sandwich places (hi, Carrie). I wrote it the next three mornings—Monday, Tuesday, Wednesday. As you may have determined by now, this is not my usual way of working—but it was fun while it lasted!

Not much left to say about this one, which is published here for the first time. I've long been fascinated by urban legends, as I suspect most fiction writers are. Besides being a trove of story ideas, urban legends are worth thinking about because they simultaneously affirm and undercut the whole fiction-writing enterprise. I highly recommend the books of folklorist Jan Harold Brunvand to those who haven't had the pleasure. The TV legends mentioned in this story are well covered on a first-rate Web site by Barbara and David P. Mikkelson, sponsored by the San Fernando Valley Folklore Society: www.snopes.com/radiotv. And yes, the legend of Johnny Carson and the cat was attributed to many different actresses through the decades, but I like Raquel Welch, and it's my story, so there!